Rachel Lee was hooked o[...] and practised her craft as s[...] all over the United States. T[...] author now resides in Flori[...] [...]joy of writing full-time.

Debra Webb is the awar[...] [...]ing *USA Today* bestselling author of more than one hundred novels, including those in reader-favourite series Faces of Evil, the Colby Agency and Shades of Death. With more than four million books sold in numerous languages and countries, Debra has a love of storytelling that goes back to her childhood on a farm in Alabama. Visit Debra at debrawebb.com

Also by Rachel Lee

Conard County: The Next Generation

Missing in Conard County
Murdered in Conard County
Conard County Justice
Conard County: Hard Proof
Conard County: Traces of Murder
Conard County: Christmas Bodyguard
Conard County: Mistaken Identity
Conard County: Christmas Crime Spree
Conard County: Code Adam
Conard County: Killer in the Storm

Also by Debra Webb

Lookout Mountain Mysteries

Disappearance in Dread Hollow
Murder at Sunset Rock
A Place to Hide
Whispering Winds Widows

A Winchester, Tennessee Thriller

The Safest Lies
Witness Protection Widow
Before He Vanished
The Bone Room

Discover more at millsandboon.co.uk

CONARD COUNTY: MURDEROUS INTENT

RACHEL LEE

PERIL IN PINEY WOODS

DEBRA WEBB

MILLS & BOON

First Published in Great Britain 2024
by Mills & Boon, an imprint of HarperCollins*Publishers* Ltd
1 London Bridge Street, London, SE1 9GF

www.harpercollins.co.uk

HarperCollins*Publishers*
Macken House, 39/40 Mayor Street Upper,
Dublin 1, D01 C9W8, Ireland

ISBN: 978-0-263-32224-8

0424

MIX
Paper | Supporting
responsible forestry
FSC™ C007454

This book contains FSC™ certified paper and other controlled sources to ensure responsible forest management.

For more information visit: www.harpercollins.co.uk/green

Printed and Bound in the UK using 100% Renewable Electricity at CPI Group (UK) Ltd, Croydon, CR0 4YY

CONARD COUNTY: MURDEROUS INTENT

RACHEL LEE

To the far-too-many veterans who struggle daily with reentering civilian life.

Prologue

Krystal Metcalfe loved to sit on the porch of her small cabin in the mornings, especially when the weather was exceptionally pleasant. With a fresh cup of coffee and its delightful aroma mixing with those of the forest around, she found internal peace and calm here.

Across a bubbling creek that ran before her porch, her morning view included the old Healey house. Abandoned about twenty years ago, it had been steadily sinking into decline. The roof sagged, wood planks had been silvered by the years and there was little left that looked safe or even useful. Krystal had always anticipated the day when the forest would reclaim it.

Then came the morning when a motor home pulled up beside the crumbling house and a large man climbed out. He spent some time investigating the old structure, inside and out. Maybe hunting for anything he could reclaim? Would that be theft at this point?

She lingered, watching with mild curiosity but little concern. At some level she had always supposed that someone would express interest in the Healey land itself. It wasn't easy anymore to find private land on the edge of US Forest, and eventually the "grandfathering" that had left the Healey family their ownership would end because of lack of occupancy. Regardless, it wasn't exactly a large piece of land, unlikely to be useful to most, and the Forest Service would let it return to nature.

Less of that house meant more of the forest devouring the eyesore. And at least the bubbling of the creek passing through the canyon swallowed most of the sounds that might be coming from that direction now that the man was there. And it sure looked like he might be helping the destruction of that eyesore.

But then came another morning when she stepped out with her coffee and saw a group of people, maybe a dozen, camped around the ramshackle house. That's when things started to become noisy despite the sound baffling provided by the creek.

A truck full of lumber managed to make its way up the remaining ruined road on that side of the creek and dumped a load that caused Krystal to gasp. Rebuilding? Building bigger?

What kind of eyesore would she have to face? Her view from this porch was her favorite. Her other windows and doors didn't include the creek. And all those people buzzing around provided an annoying level of activity that would distract her.

Then came the ultimate insult: a generator fired up and drowned any peaceful sound that remained, the wind in the trees and the creek both.

That did it. Maybe these people were squatters who could be driven away. She certainly doubted she'd be able to write at all with that roaring generator. Her cabin was far from soundproofed.

After setting her coffee mug on the railing, she headed

for the stepping stones that crossed the creek. For generations they'd been a path between two friendly families until the Healeys had departed. As Krystal crossed, she sensed people pulling back into the woods. Creepy. Maybe she ought to reconsider this trip across the creek. But her backbone stiffened. It usually did.

She walked around the house, now smelling of freshly cut wood, sure she'd have to find *someone.*

Then she found the man around the back corner. Since she was determined not to begin this encounter by yelling at the guy, she waited impatiently until he turned and saw her. He leaned over, turning the generator to a lower level, then simply looked at her.

He wore old jeans and a long-sleeved gray work shirt. A pair of safety goggles rode the top of his head. A dust mask hung around his neck. Workmanlike, which only made her uneasier.

Then she noticed more. God, he was gorgeous. Tall, large, broad-shouldered. A rugged, angular face with turquoise eyes that seemed to pierce the green shade of the trees. The forest's shadow hid the creek that still danced and sparkled in revealed sunlight behind her.

This area was a green cavern. One she quite liked.

Finally he spoke, clearly reluctant to do so. "Yes?"

"I'm Krystal Metcalfe. I live in the house across the creek."

One brief nod. His face remained like granite. Then slowly he said, "Josh Healey."

An alarm sounded in her mind. Then recognition made her heart hammer because this might be truly bad news. "This is Healey property, isn't it?" Of course it was. Not a bright question from her.

A short nod.

"Are you going to renovate this place?"

"Yes."

God, this was going to be like pulling teeth, she thought irritably. "I hope you're not planning to cut down many trees."

"No."

Stymied, as it became clear this man had no intention of beginning any conversation, even one as casual as talking about the weather, she glared. "Okay, then. Just take care of the forest."

She turned sharply on her heel without another word and made her way across the stepping stones to her own property. Maybe she should start drinking her morning coffee on the front porch of her house on the other side from the creek.

She was certainly going to have to go down to Conard City to buy a pair of ear protectors or go mad trying to do her own work when that generator once again revved up.

Gah!

JOSH HEALEY HAD watched Krystal Metcalfe coming round the corner of his new building. Trouble? She sure seemed to be looking for it.

She was cute, pretty, her blue eyes as bright as the summer sky overhead. But he didn't care about that.

What he cared about were his troops, men and women who were escaping a world that PTSD and war had ripped from them. People who needed to be left alone to find balance within themselves and with group therapy. Josh, a psychologist, had brought them here for that solitude.

Now he had that neighbor trying to poke her nose into

his business. Not good. He knew how people reacted to the mere idea of vets with PTSD, their beliefs that these people were unpredictable and violent.

But he had more than a dozen soldiers to protect and he was determined to do so. If that woman became a problem, he'd find a way to shut her down.

It was *his* land after all.

Chapter One

No.

Nearly a year later, that one word still sometimes re-sounded in Krystal Metcalfe's head. One of the few words and nearly the last word Josh Healey had spoken to her.

A simple question. Several simple questions, and the only response had been single syllables. Well, except for his name.

The man had annoyed her with his refusal to be neigh-borly, but nothing had changed in nearly a year. Well, except for the crowd over there. A bunch of invaders.

At least Josh Healey hadn't scalped the forest.

Krystal loved the quiet, the peace, the view from her private cabin at the Wyoming-based Mountain Artists' Retreat in the small community of Cash Creek Canyon. She was no temporary resident, unlike guests in the other cabins, but instead a permanent one as her mother's part-ner in this venture.

She thought of this cabin and the surrounding woods as her Zen Space, a place where she could always cen-ter herself, could always find the internal quiet that unleashed wandering ideas, some of them answers to questions her writing awoke in her.

But lately—well, for nearly a year in fact—this Zen Space of hers had been invaded. Across the creek, within view from her porch, a fallen-down house had been renovated by about a dozen people, then surrounded by a rustic stockade.

What the hell? A fence would have done if they wanted some privacy, but a stockade, looking like something from a Western movie?

Well, she told herself as she sat on her porch, maybe it wasn't as ugly as chain-link or an ordinary privacy fence might have been. It certainly fit with the age of the community that had always been called Cash Creek Canyon since a brief gold rush in the 1870s.

But still, what the hell? It sat there, blending well enough with the surrounding forest, but weird. Overkill. Unnecessary, as Krystal knew from having spent most of her life right here. Nothing to hide from, nothing to hide. Not around here.

Sighing, she put her booted feet up on her porch railing and sipped her coffee, considering her previous but brief encounters with the landowner, Josh Healey.

Talk about monosyllabic! She was quite sure that she hadn't gotten more than a word from him in all this time. At least not the few times she had crossed the creek on the old stepping stones.

The Healey house had been abandoned like so many along Cash Creek as life on the mountainside had become more difficult. For twenty years, Krystal had hoped the house's steady decay would finally collapse the structure, restoring the surrounding forest to its rightful ownership.

Except that hadn't happened and she couldn't quite help getting irritated from the day a huge motor home had moved in to be followed by trucks of lumber, a noisy generator and a dozen or so men and women who camped in tents as they restored the sagging house. A year since then and she was still troubled by the activity over there.

The biggest question was why it had happened. The next question was what had brought the last owner of the property back here with a bunch of his friends to fill up the steadily shrinking hole in the woods.

No answers. At least none from Josh Healey. None, for that matter, from the Conard County sheriff's deputies who patrolled the community of Cash Creek Canyon. They knew no more than anyone: that it was a group residence.

The privacy of that stockade was absolute. At least the damn noise had quieted at last, leaving the Mountain Artists' Retreat in the kind of peace its residents needed for their creative work.

For a while it had seemed that the retreat might die from the noise, even with the muffling woods around. That had not happened, and spring's guests had arrived pretty much as usual, some new to the community, others returning visitors.

Much as she resented the building that had invaded her Zen Space, Krystal had to acknowledge a curiosity that wouldn't go away. A curiosity about those people. About the owner, who would say nothing about why he had brought them all there.

Some kind of cult?

That question troubled her. But what troubled her more was how much she enjoyed watching Josh Healey laboring around that place. Muscled. Hardworking. And entirely too attractive when he worked with his shirt off.

Dang. On the one hand she wanted to drive the man away. On the other she wanted to have sex with him. Wanted it enough to feel a tingling throughout her body.

How foolish could she get?

ACROSS THE CREEK, Josh Healey often noticed the woman who sat on her porch in the mornings drinking coffee. He knew her name because she had crossed the creek a few times: Krystal Metcalfe, joint owner of the artists' retreat. A pretty package of a woman, but he had no time or interest in such things these days.

Nor did he have any desire to share the purpose of his compound. It had been necessary to speak briefly with a deputy who hadn't been that curious. He imagined word had gotten around some, probably with attendant rumors, but no one out there in the community of Cash Creek Canyon, or beyond it in Conard City or County, had any need to know what he hoped he was accomplishing. And from what he could tell, no one did.

Nor did anyone have a need to know the reentry problems being faced by his ex-military residents.

Least of all Krystal Metcalfe, who watched too often and had ventured over here with her questions. Questions she really had no right to ask.

So when he saw her in the mornings, he shrugged it off. She had a right to sit on her damn porch, a right to watch whatever she could see...although the stockade fencing had pretty much occluded any nosy viewing.

But sometimes he wondered, with private amusement, just how she would respond if he crossed that creek and

questioned her. Asked *her* about the hole in the woods
created by her lodge and all the little cabins she and her
mother had scattered through the forest.

Hah! She apparently felt she took care of her environment but he could see at least a dozen problems with
her viewpoint. Enough problems that his own invasion
seemed paltry by comparison.

As it was, right now he had more than a dozen vets, a
number that often grew for a while, who kept themselves
busy with maintaining the sanctuary itself, with cooking, with gardening. And a lot of time with group therapy, helping each other through a very difficult time, one
that had shredded their lives. All of them leaving behind
the booze and drugs previously used as easy crutches.

Some of his people left when they felt ready. New
ones arrived, sometimes more than he had room for but
always welcomed.

Most of the folks inside, male and female, knew about
Krystal Metcalfe, and after he explained her harmless
curiosity to them, they lost their suspicion, lost their fear
of accusations.

Because his people *had* been accused. Every last one
of them had been accused of something. It seemed society had no room for the detritus, the *problems*, their
damn war had brought home.

He sighed and shook his head and continued around
the perimeter of the large stockade. Like many of his
folks here, he couldn't relax completely.

It always niggled at the back of his mind that someone
curious or dangerous might try to get into the stockade.
Exactly the thing that he'd prevented by building it this
way in the first place.

But still the worry wouldn't quite leave him. His own remnant from a war.

He glanced at Krystal Metcalfe one last time before he rounded the corner. She appeared to be absorbed in a tablet.

Good. Her curiosity had gone far enough.

Chapter Two

The rusticity of the peaked dining room at the Mountain Artists' Retreat recalled a much earlier era. Dark wood covered the walls, wood planking covered the floor and the arched ceiling. Heavy beams bore the weight of exterior walls made of stone and glass. Two huge stone fireplaces decorated a pair of the walls. Wood tables, sofas and comfortable chairs, plus self-serve food bars, completed the room.

Even after all these years, Krystal entered it with both a sense of awe and a sense of home. She'd grown up here, she'd watched and then helped with the restoration as she grew older, and this room was as much a part of her life as the woods of the forest outside.

Once this had been a hunting lodge for those with plenty of money. Then there had been a brief stint as a ski lodge. Finally Joan Metcalfe had taken the reins and turned it into a popular retreat for artists.

Mason Cambridge, the retreat's star writer—at least according to him—showed up for lunch in the lodge's dining room along with a group of other writers. Krystal smothered a sigh the instant she saw him, then glanced at her mother, Joan. Joan offered an almost imperceptible shrug.

Well, hell, Krystal thought as she kept an eye on the steam table and salad bar, making sure the trays remained full. Mason, a leonine man with wild gray hair, had already gathered a small coterie of admirers around his favorite table. It sat beside one of the tall windows beyond which leafy branches tossed about in a strong breeze.

Krystal had always held the sneaking suspicion that Mason's physical appearance was as much a matter of public relations as personal preference. Regardless, as Joan occasionally reminded her, Mason's frequent visits to the retreat were about the best publicity they could hope for. Bestselling authors drew young, less successful types like bees to flowers.

Oddly, Mason's followers mostly seemed to be women. Smothering a smirk, Krystal replaced a tray of sliced roast beef with a fresh one. Maybe, given Mason, it shouldn't be a surprise at all that women were drawn to him.

The other big draw at the retreat was Davis Daniels, a successful digital artist with a collection of comics to his name as well as some advertising work. A movie poster of his resided proudly in the Smithsonian art collection, no small achievement.

There was nothing oversize about Davis, however. A quiet, slender man, he was always polite when approached, always willing to offer advice and help when other artists asked.

Krystal was glad to head his way with a roast beef sandwich just the way he liked it. She had grown fond of him over the last few visits, and when she saw he had not yet made his lunch, she decided to look after him. Time had taught her that he was pretty much an introvert.

As always, he offered her a gentle smile and a sincere thank-you for her kindness in making his lunch, which didn't come as part of the retreat package. For an extra fee, dinners would be served by waitpersons, but only for the extra fee. Most residents chose the buffet. Well, except for Mason. Mason was an exception to every rule, even right now as he sent one of his admiring followers to get his lunch for him.

Waste of flesh, Krystal sometimes thought of him.

Forgetting about the food service for now, Krystal sat in a chair at Davis's table and rested her chin in her hand. "How's it going, Davis?"

He made a so-so gesture with his hand. "Nothing ever goes right the first time. I'm sure you know that."

"What are you working on this time?"

That cracked his face into a smile. "I'm loving it. Comic art with an impressionistic twist. Just wish I had more training with impressionism."

"If I know anything about you, you'll have all the training you need by the time you finish it."

He laughed. "That's the point, isn't it? Endless training and learning."

Then she started to rise. "I should go so you can eat."

"I can eat around words," he said dryly. "Don't run on my account."

Krystal glanced toward the serving bars and decided none of the trays appeared to be anywhere near empty, so she settled again, leaving the work to the people who had been hired to do it.

"How's *your* work coming?" Davis asked.

"I swear there must be a load of things I'm more capable of than writing a novel."

He swallowed, dabbed his mouth and smiled. "Then why did you decide to write one?"

"I thought I had a story to tell," she admitted.

"You had one to tell or one you *wanted* to tell?"

She bit her lip, hearing the suggestion of truth in his question. "I'm not sure anymore."

He nodded, ate another bite of his sandwich. "The problem," he said, "is turning a hobby you love into a job you're probably not going to love as much."

Krystal couldn't deny that.

"Try taking a break," he suggested. "Take the pressure off yourself for a couple of weeks. I do that as often as I can."

Which probably wasn't very often, Krystal thought. Davis had contracts to fulfill. She didn't have any of her own, though she dreamed of one, so the only way to keep moving was to push herself. Not exactly a good frame of mind for taking a restful break.

Before she could reply, an unmistakable hush spread through the dining room. The clatter of silverware ceased. Even Mason Cambridge's inevitably loud, grating voice fell silent.

Instinctively, Krystal turned to look.

And there in the front doorway stood a hulking man, one she recognized, turned into a threatening shadow by the brilliance of the day behind him. Josh Healey, a man who rarely ventured beyond his own walls. Her heart raced a bit as she wondered what had brought him out of his isolation.

He offered no introduction. He simply made a demand in a deep, angry voice.

"Who the hell maimed and put a seriously injured dog outside my stockade?"

KRYSTAL WAS THE first to move, possibly because no one else moved at all. She felt nearly as stunned as they, but she at least knew who the angry man was: Josh Healey.

"Mr. Healey," she said, trying to sound firm and strong. "What in the world makes you think anyone here would do such a thing?"

"Who else would?" He stepped into the large room, interior light at last casting human features over him. "The guy who raises sled dogs wouldn't have a reason. The couple who have all the horses wouldn't either. Sorry our presence bothers your holy retreat, but none of you is going to drive us out."

With that, he turned on his heel and marched away.

Silence followed his departure, but only briefly as a cacophony of voices rose with every kind of speculation, some with fear of the mountainous man who'd just crossed lines and walked into their quiet, safe space.

Krystal didn't even try to reassure anyone. It was pointless. They needed to talk about what had just happened, and being creative sorts, they'd probably have invented an entire story surrounding this event by nightfall's gathering here.

No way she could stop them, and what would she stop them with, anyway? She had absolutely no idea what had truly happened. Without facts, fiction won the day.

Joan, who'd been in the kitchen, waved her over. Krystal paused just long enough to exchange a smile with

Davis, although he appeared considerably more withdrawn now. *Great.*

The kind of disturbance Krystal and her mother tried so hard to prevent had just occurred. One man. Apparently a badly injured dog. Who the heck would want to harm a dog, anyway, unless it was attacking? Josh was right about that.

It certainly couldn't have been anyone among their guests. Weapons of any kind were forbidden on these grounds.

Which, Krystal supposed, probably didn't mean much at all to anyone who was determined to bring one with them.

Shaking her head slightly, she met her mother in the kitchen doorway. Joan was a lovely woman in her fifties with salt-and-pepper hair always perfectly styled. Every few weeks two hairstylists drove up here from Conard City to take care of the guests and they always did an exquisite job on Joan.

Joan drew Krystal back into her office, away from the two cooks, who were already preparing the dinner menu.

"What just happened?" Joan demanded. "I only caught that man walking away. Everyone out there seemed upset."

Krystal couldn't prevent a half smile. "Not for long. The stories are already growing. Paul Bunyan, anyone?"

"Krystal!" Joan said disapprovingly, but a twinkle appeared in her blue eyes so like her daughter's. "No. Seriously. Is that the guy from across the creek?"

"The same."

"Well, I'm sure he never bothered to cross that creek before. What happened?"

As the moments passed since the scene, Krystal's stomach had begun to sink and now it sank more. The shock was gone, leaving only a fear of what had happened, of where it might lead. Of a sickening disgust over the kind of person who could maim a dog. "Somebody left an injured dog outside the stockade. I gather we're the prime suspects."

But Joan slid right past that thought. "A hurt dog? Did someone try to kill it? My God, Krys, how could anyone be so cruel?"

Krystal could think of a few. Not every person who lived in the little town of Cash Creek Canyon or its environs was naturally kind or good. The artists' retreat might provide a haven from the rest of the world, but beyond it, in Cash Creek proper and the wooded lands surrounding the small town, all kinds of people lived, some of whom she did her best to avoid.

Krystal knew her mother wasn't going to be able to blow the incident off and just enjoy tonight's yarns about it. Nor, truthfully, would she.

"I'll see what I can find out, Mom."

Joan's hand gripped her forearm. "Krys, that man…"

"Hasn't killed me yet," she said. "You know I've talked to him a couple of times."

"Not really," Joan said dryly, forgetting her worries briefly. But she let go of Krystal's arm. "Be careful. Maybe you should take someone with you."

Krystal bridled. "I'm perfectly capable of taking care of myself. Besides, I don't want to make the situation any tenser. I'll just ask what happened, okay?"

Free at last, she headed for the door and grabbed her lightweight jacket from a peg.

This time she was going to get more than a yes or no from that man.

A STORM HAD begun to move in over the mountains. Usually they would get only moderate rain, being in the mountain's rain shadow, but today looked and smelled different.

Krystal sniffed the air, felt the growing chill and decided she'd be unlikely to get back to the lodge dry after she talked to Josh Healey. No, she'd get back to her own cabin and spend the afternoon racking her brains trying to get words onto that damn page on the screen. And she'd believed she could write a novel. Hah!

Maybe some music would help. Sometimes it seemed to focus her brain, turning into a tool she ought to use more often than she did.

But first the issue with Josh Healey. If he'd been making a serious accusation, she had to defuse it. She'd heard he had a bunch of veterans behind the walls of his "sanctuary," but she didn't know what that might mean. Violent types on a hair trigger? Maybe. God knew, she'd heard enough about vets coming back from the war only to commit atrocities.

They certainly must feel paranoid to have built that huge stockade fence. Paranoia reflected in Healey's accusation just a short while ago. Once again, she wondered just what she was dealing with when she crossed the creek. Was paranoia making them dangerous?

As she walked over the stepping stones and drew closer to that stockade wall, she couldn't escape the fear that those walls were enclosing people who were capable of unimaginable horrors. A voluntary prison?

Sheesh! She tried to shake the feeling from the base of her skull, from the back of her neck. They'd been here nearly a year, she reminded herself. They'd made as small a mark on the Cash Creek area as anyone could. No reason to fear.

Unless, maybe, they felt they were under attack.

The dog.

Healey's accusation rode with her. These guys weren't going to be driven away? What had he meant?

Josh Healey apparently saw her approaching. A postern door in the wall opened and he stepped out.

Once again he didn't speak a word to her, just stood there waiting in a camo rain jacket and hood, hands hanging at his sides. His splayed and powerful legs made him look as immovable as the mountains that surrounded them.

At last, realizing she was going to have to start this conversation or stand there waiting until winter returned in a few months, she drew a deep breath. It was more like a sigh, probably because she'd visited this place and this man before. A possibly hopeless task was ahead.

"What happened?" she asked without preamble.

"I told you."

God, she was getting sick of his taciturnity even though their meetings had been few. "Damn it," she said impatiently, "you stomped into our lodge, made something very much like an accusation and offered no useful information!"

His head tilted a bit. His aquamarine eyes showed a

glimmer of interest. "I don't recall leaving out any sa-
lient information."

So Paul Bunyan here was educated. And so what?
"You said someone maimed a dog and dumped it outside your wall. How do you know it was dumped? Why
should you think anyone at the retreat had anything to
do with it?"

"Why shouldn't I?"

Now impatience and irritation were starting to boil
into anger inside her. "Listen, Healey..."

But he interrupted her, his voice as level as a slab of
rock. "How about *you* listen for a change? The dog was
dumped. How do I know? Because it had clearly been
injured elsewhere. Not enough blood right here. It was
a *message*, Metcalfe."

That poked a pin in the balloon of her anger. She blew
a long breath, shoved her inky hair back from her face
and regarded him.

When she came right down to it, the only reasons she
had to be annoyed by this man and his stockade were
her *own* feelings about him and this fortress he'd built.
After a year, some of it noisy to be sure, she couldn't
remember a single thing anyone over here had done to
bother another soul.

Letting go of her anger, she studied Healey in a different light. He'd done not one thing to earn her dislike
since he'd finished building this place. Not one.

What kind of story had she been building about him
during all this time? Well, it would have helped if he'd
made any effort to have a civil conversation. Which was
ridiculous as an accusation. Nobody was required to talk

with her or anyone else. She forced herself to plunge ahead anyway.

"Why are you so sure it's a message to you, Healey? No one around here has a thing against you."

"You think not?" He stared past her, into the woods, into the leaden day that was steadily shrouding the trees with a gray fog. Then those disturbing aquamarine eyes settled on her again.

"The problem," he said flatly, "is that you people think you have a right to an open book. Sorry, you don't. What goes on inside these walls, on *my* property, is no one else's business. Speculate all you want, but it's still the private business of those who live here."

"And that makes you think someone would want to make you leave? Because of one dog? That's ridiculous."

His jaw set. "What's next, Ms. Metcalfe? Another injured animal? A dead one? All to make us look bad?"

She shook her head, wanting to deny it, but unable to escape the sense that he might be right. "How's the dog?"

"I took him back to his owner. Alive. What did you think I'd do?"

Then Josh Healey appeared to tense as he continued speaking, his voice growing hard. "People distrust us because they don't know us. They don't have the right to know us."

"But if you could explain a little…"

"I don't have to explain anything." Then he stabbed a finger at her. "Has it occurred to any one of you, just *one* of you, that these walls have been built not to keep us in, but to keep the rest of you out?"

He pivoted, heading back for the door.

She took one last chance to head this conversation in a better direction. "We've gotten off on the wrong foot."

He paused, glancing over his broad shoulder. "Have we? Maybe it's been indirect, but it's clear to me that you think our mere presence is an invasion."

She nearly winced at his use of the word *invasion* because she *had* been thinking of them as invaders.

He waved an arm. "Ours." He pointed across the creek. "Yours. No reason we ever have to meet. Unless someone throws another wounded animal outside our walls."

She looked down, acknowledging that he was right, fearing she had just received an indirect threat but unsure. This guy kept her off balance somehow, and she didn't like it. "Okay. But *why* are you so sure it's a message, Mr. Healey?"

"Why else would anyone drag that injured animal to our wall? Think about it, Ms. Metcalfe."

Then he turned and walked back into his stockade, leaving her to wonder how she could be so wrong. Or maybe so right?

Maybe someone had a grudge against someone inside that stockade. Maybe the people inside had drawn danger to Cash Creek Canyon.

She turned to recross the stepping stones and tried not to think of someone stalking these woods seeking vengeance.

She looked around as she reached her cabin and shivered, as if the day had suddenly turned colder. The first splatters of icy rain hit her face.

The woods no longer seemed as friendly.

Chapter Three

As Krystal had anticipated, the evening gathering in the lodge's great room turned into a storytelling speculation. Since the food was served by the help Joan hired for those who had paid for the service or self-served by the rest, and since the cash bar was open for its usual several hours, Krystal sat back with a small brandy and watched all the byplay.

It always interested her when these largely reclusive artists actually got together to talk. Usually they separated into small groups, but not this evening. As a storm decided to hurl large raindrops against the tall glass windows, the two fires in the fireplaces made the room feel cozy. A safe place surrounded by the dark and possibly frightening woods. Probably the same atavistic response experienced by humans for hundreds of thousands of years in all its variations.

Krystal wondered with mild amusement just how many of these people were going back to their solitary cabins tonight, and how many would create pajama parties so they didn't need to be alone.

Except for Mason Cambridge, of course, who appeared to believe he had the only correct answers for what had happened that day. He would naturally hold forth for hours, weaving some story or other, and only when his admiring coterie diminished to nothing would he stagger back to his cabin.

Krystal noticed one small woman who avoided Mason's cadre and sat watching from the edges of the group in the room, her face almost frozen. With dislike, Krystal thought, but when she glanced again the woman's way, the expression had eased to one of disinterest.

Mary Collins, she remembered from previous years. A novelist who had evidently published one volume for a romance publisher. She felt as if Mary thought that was a comedown.

From Krystal's perspective, any publication of a novel was far from a comedown. However, Mary seemed bitter in a subtle way, unlike the rest of their guests, most of whom seemed hopeful or at worst frustrated by difficulties with their art.

Shrugging it aside, she returned her attention to a growing, and somewhat unpleasant, myth about the stockade and in particular Josh Healey. Of course, the way he had appeared earlier, looking almost like a threat on the hoof, she supposed it was hardly surprising.

And of course, Mason was leading the darkest version of the story.

Naturally. Didn't he write horror and suspense? Krystal thought shc should be embarrassed to admit she'd never read one of his books. It seemed *everyone* read them but she'd never felt the least inclination beyond a couple of pages.

But in the midst of the growing night's storm, the front door opened again. This time no mountain man appeared, but the more familiar sight of Harris Belcher, slim and work-hardened. Wrapped in rain gear, he made a yellow splash against the orangish glow of firelight and the dimmer glow of electric lanterns and rustic chandeliers. He owned the sled dog business and pretty much knew everyone in Cash Creek Canyon including some of the regulars at the retreat.

He closed the door behind himself, throwing back the hood of his jacket. "Okay," he said. "You should all know. Somebody maimed one of my dogs today. For sure he was in his kennel, so someone took him out to injure him. His romping days are over."

Mason cleared his throat loudly, then spoke equally loudly. "What should this have to do with us? Do you think we hurt it?"

Harris put his hand on his hip. "Aren't you the self-important jackass who comes here every year? Not that I care. I think you all should know because the truth is, in all the decades I've been raising, training and sledding with my huskies and malamutes, no one has ever harmed a single one. And never, ever, taken one out of the kennel to hurt it."

"So?" Mason demanded irritably. Of course, Harris's dismissal of him had annoyed him.

"So there's someone out there being violent in a way I've never seen around here before. You need to be on guard. God knows what'll be injured next."

Krystal rose, ignoring the chill his words seemed to have thrown into the room. He had caused people to glance around at one another almost suspiciously and the mood needed some kind of redirection. "I'm really sorry, Harris. How did you find out about it?"

"That guy from the stockade. He brought Reject to me and explained how they'd found him. They'd given him the first aid they could. Probably saved his life. Anyway, didn't take long for one of my dogs to find the killing spot and it weren't nowhere near my kennels. Or that stockade over there."

Harris dropped his hand from his hip. "No reason to hurt that dog. And no reason, I guess, for anyone to hurt you folks. Won't hurt to be on guard, though."

Joan appeared from the back. "Stay awhile, Harris. Have a drink. This has to have been quite a shock."

"Shock doesn't begin to cover it," Harris said harshly. He pushed his shaggy blond hair back from his face and looked around the room. "I'd like to think none of you might do such a thing."

"Well, what about those guys over in the stockade?" Mason demanded. "If anyone's capable of violence, it's them."

Oh, God, Krystal thought. Something inside her leaped forward like a tiger busting out of a cage. This crap had to stop *now*.

She stood as tall as she could and spoke in a loud voice she seldom used. "What are you all going to do? Start a damn witch hunt? Those vets have been over there in that stockade for a year now and there's never been a problem with any of them. Probably less trouble than some of us around here cause!"

Mason scoffed. "What would you know?"

"I've been living right across the creek from them since the day that Josh Healey first arrived. That's longer than any of *you*. Certainly longer than you, Mason. They're not some horror novel to be written."

Silence answered her. Some of the artists shifted un-comfortably, facing what they had been slowly begin-ning to do.

Harris Belcher, who had begun sipping beer from a handled glass mug, was the first to speak. "I'd say that bringing my dog to me was a kindness so I didn't have to keep wondering, so I could save a lot of his suffering. I'd say giving him all that first aid was true kindness, 'cuz they didn't have to. And I'd say that dumping Re-ject outside those stockade walls *wasn't* a kind thing to do. Somebody's got a grudge going."

Mary surprised everyone by speaking. She was one of the dourest guests they'd ever had. "Seems like those vets might have a hell of a grudge." Then she rose, grabbed her coat and left.

Another silence filled the room. Then, rain or not, people gathered up their gear and began to trail back to their cabins. Few appeared to have anything more to say, even to each other.

In the end, no one was left except a handful of staff, Joan, Harris and Krystal. The three of them settled at the bar, Krystal with her brandy, Harris with his beer and Joan with white wine.

Joan spoke first. "I'm beginning to feel as if I'm caught up in a bad movie. This whole day has been weird, and the rain outside isn't helping. All we need is some thun-der to finish setting the scene."

Harris sighed. "I'm sorry, Joan. I guess I shouldn't have come over."

"You were angry, Harris. And as long as you've had your sledding business here, there's no reason to think anyone would suddenly take exception to your dogs. Of course you looked at outsiders."

"But not the folks in the stockade," Krystal pointed out. Despite her discussion earlier with Josh Healey, she couldn't quite shake her uneasiness about that place and what might go on behind those stockade walls. What they might imprison inside.

The whole place was a strange setup.

"Considering Josh Healey brought me my dog," Harris said, "I'm fairly sure he and his crew didn't have anything to do with it. For God's sake, they could have just buried Reject and never said a word."

Joan swirled her wine in her glass and brought it to her nose for a sniff. "I didn't like what was happening in this room tonight. Krys, have you ever seen the like?"

"Not here," Krystal admitted. "But then, the worst things that have ever happened here were someone stomping off in a dudgeon because they didn't like someone else's opinion."

Harris laughed quietly. "What an image. Well, the truth is, I didn't really suspect someone from here, but…" He turned to Joan. "You bring a new crop of people here every year and have no idea what they might be like. You're not like cops who do background checks."

"No more than a hotel," Joan agreed. "But why should I?"

"Never been a reason before." Harris took another swig of beer.

Krystal had a thought. "You going to call the cops about this, Harris?"

"What good would it do? Reject's an expensive animal, in terms of training and breeding, but what's the sheriff going to do about it? How many deputies can he spare for something like this? Nah, he'll send someone to take a report, maybe look at Reject, and that'll be the end. Besides, I don't want folks getting uneasy 'cuz I brought cops up here to nose around."

"You have a point," Joan said dryly. "God knows how many drugs are floating around Cash Creek Canyon, including here."

Harris smiled. "We got us a funny little town here, don't we? Been funny since the first panners showed up looking for gold. Sometimes I find it hard to believe that was one hundred and sixty years ago. I doubt the place has changed that much, except by shrinking."

"Hard to tell," Joan agreed.

Krystal had to laugh. "Well, there's a gas station…"

The other two grinned. "Got me," Harris said. "Same bank, though."

Now that was hard to believe, Krystal thought. Carrying her brandy glass behind the bar, she began to wash it.

"Leaving already?" Joan asked.

"Bed calls. And I hope I can get some writing done in the morning."

They hugged, then Krystal set out for her cabin with her jacket tightly drawn around her. The rain stung, almost like sleet. Which wouldn't be impossible at this altitude and even in midsummer.

This evening had been quite enough, she thought. The oddness had begun with Josh Healey's unexpected appearance and indirect accusation at lunch, but the evening had grown worse. Far worse.

Something truly ugly had invaded the lodge, however briefly, and it was unnerving. Not her experience of this retreat at all. Not the kind of mood one usually found during an evening gathering.

In fact, that evening's gathering had been larger than usual. A lot of the artists liked to get out for an evening stroll along well-marked paths in the woods. Some had friends they visited in Conard City. Some just drove away for a few hours for a change of scenery. But rarely did it feel as if everyone was in that room at the same time.

Tonight it had. And Krystal had an uncomfortable feeling about the reason. The guests had felt threatened by Healey's visit. They'd instinctively come together like a herd seeking safety. Then the evening had verged not on Paul Bunyan tales but something far uglier.

All started by Mason Cambridge, no doubt. The guy made his living off stories of horrible crimes. Unspeakable acts. Why wouldn't he try to turn Healey's visit into something much darker?

He was going to need some reining in, she thought, but she wasn't sure anyone had ever been able to rein in that man. Bullheaded, pigheaded and egotistical beyond description.

She could almost have believed that Mason had set the whole situation up with the dog just to start a real-life experience of his ugly suspicions of the human race. To entertain himself. Or give himself ideas for a new book.

Then she felt disgusted with herself for harboring such suspicions about anyone, even Mason Cambridge.

No, it hadn't been a good day.

Her cabin still held some of the day's warmth and soon she had a small fire going on her woodstove. Its heat and the glow through the front grating were welcome. She booted her computer and tested her internet connection.

Good, the storm, such as it was, hadn't knocked her antenna out of line. Without it, she'd have been lost at sea. Another way Cash Creek Canyon had changed from the old days: instant connection with the outside world.

Instead of trying to work, however, she began reading articles from some of the science magazines she subscribed to. Interest led her to JSTOR and current research in science publications. By the time she started yawning, she had an idea for an article about some of the recent developments in physics.

Well, she wrote and sold some of those for magazines that catered to lay readers. Another way to put off working on her novel. On the other hand, it would help with her bills.

Satisfied, she washed up, then snuggled into her bed. Only when she turned off the light did she feel the night pressing in.

She didn't feel like that, she thought, annoyed with herself. She never felt the forest as if it were a threat and not a baby's cradle.

But the feeling wouldn't leave her. To her amazement, an image of Josh Healey rose in her mind, and this time she felt only that he was built to be a protector.

Somehow that eased her fears enough to carry her into sleep with one last thought. *God, this is ridiculous!*

JOSH HEALEY SAT in a wooden rocking chair near a fire some of his people had built. They could have had fire inside the refurbished buildings that held fireplaces, but most of them still felt better being in the large, open parade area. Many remained uncomfortable in closed spaces. Hardly surprising given their experiences.

Time within these walls was a deliberately slow and free space. No one got pushed, except gently when necessary. Josh made sure there were always plenty of manual tasks to do, tasks as far away from battle as possible.

They built furniture, like this chair he sat on. When they made enough furniture, he sometimes filled an old box truck with it and carted it to Casper or Laramie to sell. A sense of accomplishment for men and women who had little enough of that.

Flower gardens, well tended. A vegetable garden that might have done better at a lower altitude but was good enough. Repairs around the stockade. There was always work that needed doing.

And of course, there were the group therapy sessions. In answer to his own combat experiences, he'd chosen to become an educated, licensed counselor, simultaneously dealing with his own reentry problems and those of his fellow vets.

Admittedly, he could only help a small group at a time out here, maybe two or three dozen, but getting even these few people away from every possible trigger sure helped.

Inevitably, though, his thoughts turned to that injured dog. To the artists' retreat on the other side of the creek. To the woman who had confronted him.

He kinda liked Krystal's fire. Given his size and his appearance, few people gave him a piece of their minds, but she had. Not afraid of him. A plus.

Still, there were all those people over at the retreat, many of them unknown variables. He gathered some were regular visitors, but what about the rest? Who knew a damn thing about *them*?

He'd learned, too, that those creative types weren't allowed to bring weapons to the retreat. That had been made clear in a magazine ad that had somehow come with his infrequent mail delivery. No weapons of any kind.

What guarantee was there that anyone would listen to that, anyway? He hadn't noticed any metal detectors around the place when he'd gone out on one of his nightly patrols to keep an eye on the surrounding area.

Surreptitious night patrols. Quiet, moving among the shadows as he'd learned to do under hostile conditions. And frankly, he traveled armed with a KA-BAR. He wasn't much worried about encountering an armed hostile human, but there were other things out there, like some large black bears and the grizzly he'd seen once.

He didn't look for a confrontation, but you could never be positive that you wouldn't get between a mama and her cubs. Or just meet an annoyed, territorial grizzly. They didn't always need a reason to attack.

Anyway, he sat on his chair, half listening to the desultory conversation between men and women, some of them edged with the distrust that had its birth in places where you couldn't trust very much except your immediate buddies. None of this group of vets had been his battle buddies except for Angus MacDougall, who'd served twice with Josh. Angus had become a sort of second-in-command inside the compound.

Because there was a reluctance among many to deal with a life that had no laid-out order, some discipline existed. Guidelines to appropriate behavior.

Josh sighed when he considered all the ways a few years in a threatening military environment could affect a soldier. Some simply couldn't give up a sense of order, the one thing they could depend on. Others had taken great pleasure in finding their way around rules, like the military's general order, long since abandoned, that forbade animals to be taken as pets.

Yet, despite minor rebellions, in the service autonomy had nearly disappeared. And Josh had to thread the needle, trying to bring back damaged minds to a place where they could adequately function in a very different world. A world that had been scrubbed from them by training and combat.

Considering that he was trying to protect these vets from a world they couldn't yet handle, he'd probably done a very foolish thing by crossing the creek to tell the people in that damn retreat about the dog. To practically accuse them.

But he'd been angry. More than angry. He'd been furious. The idea that anyone would do this to his vets made him livid. How many may have had their recoveries set back by the implicit threat? It'd be a while before he knew.

But once again his thoughts drifted to Krystal Metcalfe. Easier to think about her than some of the things going on around here.

She owned the retreat with her mother. The magazine ad that had somehow dropped into his mailbox had told him about it. Had painted a truly engaging portrait of the entire Mountain Artists' Retreat. Although why artists needed a retreat left Josh flummoxed.

But the two-page ad had promised private cabins, meals served in a main dining room if you wanted them, a gathering place for those who wanted to exchange ideas. The only restrictions were to bring no weapons and never to bother another guest without an invitation. Apparently no running next door for a cup of sugar.

But that restriction on weapons had caught his attention. Were the retreat owners worried about violence among their clients? Or was it a simple bid to create a sense of safety in a culture that seemed to be growing less so?

Beat the hell out of him. Anyone who'd seen what an assault weapon could do to a human body would never *want* to fire one again—unless, of course, they'd slipped a cog. He'd known a few of *them*, too.

Shaking his head, he rose from his chair and began to walk around the parade ground inside the stockade. Plenty of room in here, even with the two houses and gardens and work shed. Not too big, not offering enough space to make anyone feel that protection was limited, but big enough to allow free roam to the vets.

Not an easy balance. No one would ever know the years he'd spent planning this. The years of research. Not that it mattered. He'd succeeded as well as any man could.

"Josh." One of his female vets emerged from the relative darkness and strode by with a nod. "Carly," he answered. Carly Narth. It had taken three months to get her past calling him Colonel. A small triumph.

When he reached the wooden steps, he climbed up to the walkway that lined the stockade about four feet below its top. From there he could have a view of the woods around and at least part of the retreat across the creek. He walked slowly again, scanning the world, seeing nothing amiss. Halting finally where he had a clear view of Krystal's cabin. She seemed to have retired for the night.

He gave her props for that. After the dog incident, he didn't feel he could let down his guard in the least.

Which might be an overreaction, but he didn't think so. That dog had been placed there for a reason, and there was always the possibility it was an opening salvo against the stockade and the men and women inside it.

The group of soldiers he both honored and had promised to protect with every ounce of his soul until such time as they were ready to return to the larger world.

A few already had, successfully. A handful more seemed to be verging on recovering as normal a life as they ever could. And a new group would arrive this week, recommended by counselors at Army clinics. Men and women who seemed unable to take the final step into their new world, a world without orders and unending violence. A world where they didn't live with constant threat.

These guys had already won most of his heart. He'd do anything to protect them.

Chapter Four

Morning brought brilliant sunshine, dappled by gently tossing trees, and air that held amazing clarity from the night's light rain. The only sign of the passing wetness was the faint, gray fog beneath the trees, a fog that slowly swallowed the stockade. Above it shone a sky like a blue dome, so bright that it almost hurt to look at it.

While Krystal often skipped breakfast in the lodge so she could sit at her computer and try to work, this morning she decided to follow the path through the woods. To her left the creek ran more quickly and loudly than usual, the gorge filled with the night's gift of water. The steep sides contained it safely, though.

As fresh as the air were the forest scents filling it. Krystal drew deep breath after deep breath, savoring it. Rarely did the world seem as perfect as this. Mother Nature's great gift.

But this morning she was also a bit preoccupied, primarily because she wanted to get a sense of how last night's mood might have shifted. Had uneasiness grown? Or had matters quieted down? What she *didn't* want to do was sit alone at her computer wondering, speculating and creating bad stories of her own.

At least the lodge would offer some distraction. She hoped. There had been disagreements in the past that had temporarily divided residents, but nothing like this. Overall, the retreat was exactly that: a retreat. People preferred the quiet. Nature. Their privacy in their cabins. When they wanted human company, they arranged it in their own cabins or in the lodge.

One of the other rules at this place was that you didn't go knocking on anyone's door without an invitation. Peace undisturbed. That's why people chose to come here.

But that didn't mean this morning wouldn't be interesting. Not at all. Some minds would be too fired up by yesterday to think about much else.

Krystal smiled wryly. She seemed to have a case of that herself.

Tucked in a heavy-weight blue flannel shirt and jeans with hiking boots, she felt ready for the day. Well, except for her writing. She wondered when she'd ever get around to calling it writer's block. Calling it that seemed so much more important than she could claim.

Maybe her problem was that she didn't feel enough like a writer to call it a block. Laziness, lack of concentration, but nothing as important as a block.

Then her irrepressible sense of humor took over. What did it matter what she called it? Writing a novel was her pipe dream. Helping her mother with the retreat was her *job*. Big difference.

She was smiling as she entered the lodge, but paused on the threshold, surprised by the emptiness of the space. While it was true many of their residents liked to stay in their cabins making coffee and quick breakfasts of their own, there were usually more people here, reading the news on their laptops or tablets. Some making notes of ideas.

This morning there were only four, Mary Collins of the romance writer school, Lars the sculptor, who claimed to have no second name, and Davis Daniels, the graphic artist.

And one more woman, a quiet academic sort who said she was working on her dissertation. Giselle Bibe, that was her name. Preferred to be called Gizzie. Gizzie or Giselle or whatever, with her mousy, lank hair and big dark-rimmed glasses, could have melted into any wall and drawn no attention. Maybe that worked best for the world of academia. Regardless, the single time Krystal had managed to have a conversation with her, she'd proved to have a bright, flexible mind. Even an occasional touch of impish humor.

Krystal hoped they'd have a better chance to grow acquainted, but Gizzie seemed almost entirely buried in her work.

Joan stood propped and sleepy-looking behind the beverage bar as if she were keeping an eye on the coffeepots. Two other employees, both women, hovered around, walking in and out of the kitchen as if waiting for something, anything, to do.

"So, what's up?" Krystal asked Joan.

"Boredom. This place is entirely too empty even for breakfast."

Krystal nodded and pulled a stool over to sit beside her mom. "You look exhausted."

"As if I could sleep last night, thanks to that uproar."

"Mason wasn't any help."

Joan snorted. "Mason is a walking, talking ad for how a normal mind shouldn't work."

Krystal laughed with delight. "Good description."

"I spent most of the night thinking about all of it." Turning a bit, she filled two mugs with coffee and passed one to Krystal. "That dog is really disturbing me, Krys. We've had neighbors take the occasional potshot at one another, but since we, and the Forest Service, got rid of trapping nearly fifty years ago, animals go unharmed around here."

Krystal answered wryly, "So it'd be better if two guys shot at each other over water rights? Grazing rights?"

Joan frowned. "You know exactly what I mean, Krys. This was pointless cruelty. Everyone knows Harris Belcher's sled dogs around here. Never a lick of trouble, unless you want to count that racket those dogs call singing, but Harris is far enough out of town..."

"That it's no big deal," Krystal finished.

Joan shook her head. "You know all this. It's just my mind's been running in circles, mainly about that poor dog."

"And about it being left outside Healey's stockade," Krystal reminded her.

Joan nodded and sipped her coffee, adding a dab more cream to it. "That bothers me, too. Except no one knows a damn thing about any of them inside that stockade."

Krystal sighed and stared at her cup of coffee. Her stomach burned with acid, probably from talking about the dog. Instead, she reached around and grabbed a cruller wrapped in a napkin, hoping it would help. "How many people in our retreat run around announcing their bios to the world? So those soldiers are private. It's their right."

Joan shot her a glance. "Don't tell me you aren't curious. When did you stop wondering? I've heard you."

For once, Krystal didn't mind changing tack. Pulling a mental U-turn, although she couldn't have said why. "Curiosity is natural. Beyond that it gets sick."

Joan bridled. "Sick?"

"Yeah, Mom. As in rumormongering. As in creating a horror story in here last night, all of it aimed against a group who have done not one bad thing around here." The cruller at least tasted good. She wiped crumbs from her chin.

Joan chewed her lip, then laughed quietly, without any real humor. "You're right, but wasn't it fun?"

Krystal's answer was sour. "Count on Mason Cambridge to start weaving a story that could result in a dangerous mob."

Joan shook her head. "He couldn't do that. Not with all these nice people."

"I have a slightly more jaundiced view of the human race." Which was hardly surprising since she hadn't spent her entire life in these parts and even had a broken heart to show for it. No, she'd gone off to college, a real eyeopener. "Anyway, I'll ask you again. Why do we keep letting that blowhard come here? For him it's just a giant ego stroke to get all those women hanging on his every word."

"Publicity for us."

"Yeah, right. Then people leave here and say bad things about him and by extension about us."

Joan shook her head. "What got into you this morning?"

The same thing that had kept her mother up during the

night. The thought of a dog being brutally attacked. The thought of the poor, suffering thing being left outside the stockade where it might well have died in agony before being found. Left like a message, like a piece of trash.

Which led her to the question: Why? Who out there would have it in that much for Josh Healey's group?

Bright sunlight notwithstanding, Krystal felt a shiver of apprehension.

Then, turning her back to her mother, she reached for the landline and called the Conard County Sheriff's Office. Harris Belcher might think it was a waste of time, but Krystal refused to ignore what had happened to that dog.

Someone in this community needed to be scared into behaving or else discover the risk of a jail cell.

If there was one thing Krystal knew about most people in Cash Creek Canyon, they valued the life of any working animal.

So who were the rest?

IN THE STOCKADE, the morning group therapy ended, followed by a breakfast of homemade bread, orange juice and fried eggs. Everything was prepared by the residents except the juice.

Then everyone, man and woman, scattered around to follow their own pursuits. Some were fond of making furniture. Cleary Howe worked on the plumbing endlessly, slowly bringing hot water to every room in the original house and the scattered outdoor facilities.

Janice Howe, Cleary's wife, took over the garden, sometimes giving orders about hoeing and weeding and fertilizing to anyone who appeared to be just standing around. Around Janice, few stood around.

Elaine Ingall ran a kitchen where they were beginning to put up preserves from the fruit Josh and Angus, Josh's right-hand man, brought back from town by the truckload.

Some of the preserves would probably sell at the county fair. Some of the wooden furniture that was beginning to fill the house would also face the same future.

There wasn't a soul in the compound who didn't take pride in helping the group to be self-supporting. Useful, whatever their other limitations.

But they still suffered from nightmares that tore the night wide open. There were still bouts of loss of self-control, not always caused by anything anyone else could know. There were nights, and some days, when all that would help was staying close, offering comfort, letting the man or woman ride out the horror that memory spewed. On those days a lot of labor stopped as other vets got triggered or hung on to sanity for dear life.

Yet through it all, Josh saw improvement. Maybe only in small increments, but improvement just the same.

The incident with the dog hadn't helped anyone. Josh should have found it on his night patrol, but instead Marvin Damm had snuck out for some reason. Residents were supposed to stay inside at night because the night often brought out their biggest fears, their worst memories. Josh believed it best that none of them was left alone in the dark hours unless they chose the isolation themselves.

But Marvin had gone out and almost stepped onto the shivering, wounded animal that lay right outside the small door.

God! Now Marvin was half a wreck, and nobody in the compound was doing all that well. They all had memories from the military of animals that had been badly injured. Some had been able to endure the general command order to leave the animals be. Others had not. Pet dogs had wound up being concealed in barracks by men and women who found comfort and pleasure in them.

Now they faced an ugly, familiar situation beyond walls that were supposed to keep them safe while they dealt with their demons. A dog had been shot in the hip.

Wonderful.

Finally, overwhelmed by a need to do something simply because he wasn't by nature able to ignore much, Josh loaded himself into the massive Humvee that usually could get them over the worst roads in the worst conditions and set out for the sled dog operation. He wanted to see for himself how that husky was doing. He hoped to be able to carry back some good news to his group.

The road was decent, once he got past the narrow gravel stretch that led to the stockade. Twenty years of abandonment meant the county hadn't spent a dime on road maintenance. At least he'd been able to pay the power company to hook them up again.

As for the road, once he turned out of his property, he found buckled blacktop that had seen better years.

He knew his way to the sled dog operation run by Harris Belcher and his few mushers. The kennels were rarely quiet, and as Harris had explained when Josh had brought Reject to him yesterday, huskies were talkers. Seldom quiet, holding conversations of their own.

Quite different from the quiet Josh had grown accustomed to in his stockade.

Harris Belcher greeted him warmly enough. "Bet you're here to check on Reject. He's actually doing pretty good, but he just became a house dog."

Josh arched a brow. "House dog?"

"His cast." Harris nodded. "Can't be out getting it wet. But to tell you the truth, I think he's enjoying life in front of a warm fire on a soft rug. Spoiled forever now, probably. Jenine, my secretary, isn't helping much."

Josh smiled, as he rarely did. "You sure he won't want to get back on the trail?"

"Hah!" Harris said. "Damn dog is named Reject for a reason. Never been too cooperative in harness. When he was little more than a pup, I thought he was going to make a great lead. Then he changed his mind and wouldn't change it back. Sometimes I wonder if he just hates having all those other dogs behind him."

Josh's smile widened. "I can identify with that."

Harris eyed him up and down. "Reckon you can."

Just then they both heard the grinding of an engine and the crunch of wheels outside.

"Can't be the vet," Harris remarked. "No need." Then he pulled a ragged curtain back. "Krystal Metcalfe, of all folks. Guess Reject has his own fan club."

"After last night," Josh agreed. But he stiffened anyway, wondering why Krystal should be here when she could have just made a phone call. *Most* phones did work out here.

She slipped a bit on damp pine needles as she approached. Harris threw the door open.

"Girl, what you doing here? You coulda called, which I'm pretty sure Joan would have preferred. Reject's doing pretty good."

Krystal unzipped her jacket, revealing a blue flannel shirt, and looked at both men. "Thought I should give you a personal heads-up. I called the sheriff about Reject and he's going to want to talk with both of you." She eyed Josh. "Good thing you're here because I couldn't get a word out of your compound. Wouldn't want the sheriff banging on the door there, would you?"

No, he wouldn't. He didn't need his people getting unnerved by a noisy—and it would be noisy—bunch of deputies banging at the gate. But before he could speak his objection, Harris beat him to the punch.

"If I'd wanted the sheriff I would have called him, Krystal. Like I said last night, they aren't going to be able to do a damn thing. One dog. A dozen or more residents out here with guns. How much time and effort do you think they're going to spend? Waste of resources."

Krystal's chin set stubbornly. "Never. Maybe making a point that this is illegal will make someone else give it a second thought before using another one of your dogs for target practice."

Just then, Reject hobbled out the door of Harris's cabin and pressed himself to Krystal's leg. She bent and scratched him behind the ears.

After a noticeable pause, Harris said, "Looks like you two have just been invited to coffee."

Josh felt more awkward than he liked to admit. It had been a while since he'd been a guest in someone's house, an ordinary house occupied by ordinary people. He should have turned and left, making some lousy excuse, but a remnant of courtesy held him back.

Like it or not, he was soon sitting at a handcrafted wooden table with two other people, total strangers, and a coffee mug in front of him. Along with a plate of small pastries that looked as if they'd been around for a while. He helped himself anyway. Grub of any kind was always welcome.

Krystal addressed the issue first. "I still can't believe anyone would treat a dog that way. You say someone must have removed him from the kennel?"

"Yup."

Reject took that moment to curl as best he could around Krystal's feet. Ignoring her coffee and the dubious pastries, she bent and began to pet him. "Poor baby. Are you going to be okay?"

Harris's face darkened. "Lame. He's going to be lame. But nobody could have hurt him like that unless they managed to pull him out of his run. Damn dog could have leaped any one of those fences like lightning. Danged if I can figure how anybody managed to catch him."

Continuing to pet Reject, Krystal raised her head enough to eye Harris. "Then how do you keep these dogs from scattering all over hell and gone?"

Harris sighed and raised one shoulder. "Huskies are interesting dogs, Krys. They listen as much as they choose. They like sledding, they like the communal nature of the big yard and the runs. If they didn't like it, they'd be gone. But another thing."

Krystal nodded. "Yes?"

"They get attached just like we get attached to them. Can't keep any husky that wants to run, but a lot of them choose to stay. You'd have to ask them the difference."

"Loyalty," Krystal suggested.

"I sometimes wonder. I ever tell you about one of my mushers?"

"Which one?"

Now Harris grinned and shook his head at the same time. "Aaron he was. One of the best. He was training his team and some backups for the Iditarod. Anyway, every single day he'd take them out for a good run with a loaded sled. Tires instead of runners unless there was snow."

"And?" Josh asked.

"Well, now, that got interesting. His team went absolutely nuts somewhere along the trail. You got to understand something about these dogs. They behave until they sense trouble. Saved more than one musher from serious harm by refusing to go over a river that wasn't frozen enough or down a gully that was steep enough to break a neck. They won't go into trouble and won't take their musher into it even when ordered. Smart buggers."

Krystal found herself waiting almost breathlessly. "What happened?"

"Aaron's team came running back here, hell-for-leather, harnesses snapped or jerked out of. Every single dog except one."

"That's a problem," Josh remarked. "Always trouble when a team comes back missing a dog."

Harris nodded. "You got it. So we gathered another team, well rested, and took them out to follow Aaron's trail. They'd find him, for sure."

Harris slugged more coffee. "They found him, all right. Went nuts. We managed to keep them on harness, but they kept yanking to go back home. We knew damn well something had happened there. Finally, handling the team and trying to hunt for Aaron was too much. We let them run home and started bellowing into the woods."

Krystal was now on the edge of her seat. "Aaron? What happened with Aaron?"

"Maybe I should tell you that bears and huskies are sworn enemies. A husky will take off like greased lightning from a bear, and bears hate the dogs just as much. Wanna kill 'em."

Harris shook his head. "Long story short. We heard Aaron call out and found the damnedest thing. He was most the way up a tree, bleeding from a swipe at his hip, and his lead dog was at the foot of the tree, snarling and barking at a damn bear. Don't ask me how that dog survived, or why the bear kept backing off. Six hours of that, Aaron said. Anyway, we made a lot of gunfire to scare the bear off and get Aaron down. He was okay but he was done with sledding."

Josh leaned forward. "Wasn't that unusual behavior for the bear?"

"Yeah. Unusual for the dog, too. Loyalty. Anyway, Cannon, the dog's name, died a couple of years later. Got a hero's funeral here. Not many like him."

Krystal looked down at the dog now sleeping at her feet. "What happens to Reject now, if he's lame?"

"Somebody's house pet, if he doesn't skedaddle on them."

Krystal hesitated only a moment. "Do you think he'd come with me?"

"Do you think those fool clients of yours would tolerate him?"

Krystal felt an instant of rebellion. "I don't give a damn."

Surprising her, Josh Healey laughed. "Go, lady, go. You gotta have *something* the way you want it."

She bridled. This man made her want to fight for some reason. "How would you know what I have?"

He shrugged a shoulder, but his smile never quite faded. "Something about you."

For some reason, Krystal felt as if those strangely intense aquamarine eyes of his had just stripped her emotionally naked. She didn't like the feeling at all and immediately stood.

"Thanks for the coffee, Harris," she said. "I've gotta run. Just keep me posted about Reject. Trust me, I'd like to have him."

"If he climbs in that truck of yours with you, then he's made up his own mind."

JOSH LINGERED A bit longer, thinking the matter over, deflecting some of Harris's questions about the stockade, but doing so carefully. He didn't want to feed the curiosity around here in a way that would be dangerous to his soldiers.

"You know," Josh said presently, "I have some folks who'd love a puppy or two as well."

Harris eyed him closely. "How can you be sure of that?"

"Because I saw them with strays over there in combat zones. I saw them rescue dogs in defiance of general orders. Some worked every angle they could to try to get a dog home with them."

Harris nodded slowly. "I've got a new litter of five. I don't separate them until the bitch weans 'em herself. Maybe four weeks more."

"That's good, not weaning them early."

Now it was Harris's turn to smile. "Guess you know something after all."

Then the crunch of tires on the gravel drew both men's attention.

Harris cussed. "That'll be the sheriff. Why the hell did Krys have to call him? Not gonna do a damn thing about this, I swear."

KRYSTAL WASN'T FAR behind the sheriff's vehicle. As soon as she saw it passing uphill toward the sledding ranch, she pulled a U-turn and followed. Harris had been so dubious about help, she wanted to hear the conversation for herself.

She stopped right behind the official vehicle and climbed out. Josh's Humvee was still here, too, which kind of surprised her. She'd expected him to follow her down the hill within minutes. Of course, where would he have gone that she wouldn't have passed him, too?

Dang, was she scattering all her marbles around here? The obvious sometimes escaped her. Maybe it was time to visit Conard City and her friends there. Fresh concerns, fresh topics of conversation. A livelier world. One that might actually wake her up.

The officer who stepped out of the official Suburban surprised her, however. It was the sheriff himself, Gage Dalton, a man with a long history around these parts who commanded a whole lot of respect. Given his old injuries, however, Krystal was more used to seeing him behind a desk.

He limped when he walked, wasn't always able to conceal a wince when he moved, and one side of his face bore the shiny skin of a bad burn in his past.

He turned as he saw her and gave her his patented half smile, all his scarred face would still let him do. "Riding shotgun, Krystal?"

"Curious, more like. Mind?"

Dalton shook his head as he clapped his tan uniform Stetson on it. "Public service and all that."

She arched a brow and laughed. "Right. All public until you need to keep secrets."

"About investigations in progress? You got that right."

They were now side by side, heading for Harris's porch when the door opened.

"Crap," said Harris succinctly. "What are you gonna do about one dog, Gage? Like you don't have enough to do keeping a lid on this entire county? But get your butt in here. I seem to be having a meeting."

Josh was still at the table, a mug in front of him. Harris, rather gracelessly, ordered them all to chairs, then brought out another plate of pastries, saying, "Well, these are fresh, anyway."

Krystal couldn't suppress a laugh. "I'm heading into Conard City later. I'll get you some fresh from Melinda."

"Good, because I don't get there often."

Which was true, Krystal thought as Harris freshened her mug and poured a coffee for Gage. Then he faced the three of them before boring his gaze into Gage.

"So, Sheriff, what the hell you gonna do and why should you even want to bother?"

Gage leaned back in his chair, wincing a bit but otherwise concealing his discomfort. "Interesting question, Harris. Why should I give a damn about a dog, huh?"

Harris shifted unhappily. "I didn't say it that way. Not exactly."

"But that's what you're thinking. And that's why I'm here instead of one of my deputies."

Harris shook his head. "So tell me."

"Because," Gage said quietly, "I got a hang-up about people who torture animals. And from what Mike Windwalker, the vet, told me, this was torture. Not meant to kill, not even the shooting."

Krystal drew a deep breath. Harris's face darkened like a thundercloud. "No," he said after a few beats.

"I'm sure you hate it, too," Gage continued, now reaching for his coffee and taking a sip. "Damn, Harris, I think you've got Velma beat in the lousy coffee category."

At that Harris delivered a reluctant smile. Velma was the sheriff's chief dispatcher, and her coffee was infamous. "Took lessons, Gage."

"You might give her some yourself." Gage put the mug down and looked at both Krystal and Josh. "You found the dog, Josh, right?"

Josh nodded. "Well, one of my people did. Gave him what first aid we could and brought him up here."

Gage nodded again, pulling a small notebook from his pocket and scanning it quickly. "Says here about two a.m."

"About that. Close enough."

Then Gage turned his attention to Harris. "Your dogs found where the attack happened?"

Harris nodded. "Right after the vet left around three yesterday morning. The dogs were going bonkers, Gage. They knew. So I let out a team of them and they took off hell-for-leather. Found the place where there was blood."

"You gonna show me?" Gage asked.

"Hell yeah, much good it'll do. Dogs been all over it."

"Maybe a lot of *people* haven't. I've got a couple of good trackers. I'll bring them up."

Harris snorted. "Won't find much. Somehow these bastards got Reject down to the stockade and I didn't see a trail of any kind."

"You never know." Gage reached for his mug again, then thought better of it. Instead he took a pastry. "Okay, Harris, I got another concern than just Reject."

Harris's face tightened, but he nodded.

"I'm furious that anyone would treat an animal that way, but there's another issue here. If someone would do that to your dog, they're dangerous to people, too. You follow me?"

Krystal felt her face drain. She hadn't thought of that. Beside her, Josh stiffened.

"Takes a certain kind," Gage said, pushing back his chair. "I'm not going to let this go just because of Reject, Harris. I'm also not going to let it go because of people. You could say this creep just unleashed a two-edged sword. We aren't going to stop."

Soon three vehicles made their way down the slope toward the retreat and the stockade. Toward Cash Creek Canyon, such as it was. Beside Krystal on the bench seat of her truck, Reject lay curled up. Apparently he'd made his decision.

Harris's road was in great shape, thanks to the business he brought. Lots of folks evidently liked the idea of mushing through the winter woods and sleeping in yurts covered with snow.

Nobody in their right mind, Krystal privately thought. Oh, she loved sledding with one of Harris's teams for a day, but for a weekend? Or a week? That much cold didn't appeal to her. Too many winters up here, she supposed.

To her surprise, Josh followed her down her narrow driveway to her cabin. Now, what was she supposed to do about that? She didn't know him well enough to invite him inside, but she didn't want to be rude either.

When he climbed out of his Humvee, however, he stared across the creek at his stockade and didn't at all look like a man who expected any kind of invitation. When he spoke, his direction surprised her.

"Gage unnerved you?" he asked.

She hesitated, wanting to be honest but not sound like a wimp either. "Not completely," she said after a bit.

"Yeah."

Wondering where this all might be leading, Krystal climbed her two porch steps and sat in her favorite Adirondack chair. Then, after the briefest hesitation, she motioned Josh to one of the others. Surprising her, totally out of character from what she'd seen of him, he accepted the invitation, sitting with one ankle on the other knee. A perennial masculine pose. Shrugging, she put her feet up on the railing. Beyond that, she offered no hospitality.

"I suppose," he said presently, "that you have no idea what we're doing across the creek."

"You hardly advertise," she said dryly.

"No. That's on purpose. But given this development, you should know."

She turned her head, curiosity awakening in her. "How so?"

"If anything more happens around here, we're apt to be blamed for it."

Now she pushed forward, sitting up straight. "Why on God's earth...?"

He passed his hand over his face. "Because we're vets. Every damn one of us. You know what some people say."

Krystal drew a deep breath, her hands tightening. "I know what *some* people say. And most of it isn't true."

"Then that makes you a majority of one."

She thought she detected a bitter note in his voice. "But why do you all have to stay over there? Are any of you afraid of what you might do?"

"Goddamn," he swore, sitting bolt upright. "You know, it never occurs to anyone that those walls might have been built to keep the rest of the world out, not to keep *us* in."

Krystal felt slammed as her world tilted in an entirely new direction. No, she hadn't thought of it that way. Not at all.

Josh stood, evidently having had enough of his attempt to be sociable. Krystal felt just awful and jumped to her own feet.

"Josh, I'm sorry..."

"Why?" he asked bluntly. "You're no different from the rest."

Then he strode to his Humvee and took off with a pointed scatter of gravel.

Great, Krystal thought, watching him disappear into the woods along the winding road. This was a guy who'd saved a wounded dog and then she'd hinted at the general view of vets as a threat.

God!

And she'd blown her one chance to get to know the man better. She seriously doubted she'd get another one.

Totally annoyed with herself, she went inside her cabin and switched on her computer. As soon as it booted itself, she turned it off again.

Screw that. Climbing into warmer gear, she grabbed her rumpled pack and headed up the trail to the lodge. Reject limped beside her. Now would not be a good time to be alone.

BACK AT HIS COMPOUND, Josh found his crew considerably quieter than they'd been since they found the dog. Most of them had picked up their regular chores. Those who hadn't sat clumped together, trying to talk in spurts about feelings that didn't lend themselves to words.

He wondered how much the ugly incident had set some of them back. Didn't know exactly how he was going to deal with it. Maybe this was one of those things that would take the entire group.

He found plenty of coffee in the urn and poured himself one of those tall, insulated mugs with a dash of cream. Cream was still a luxury to him.

Then he sat on his usual wood chair in the big room, waiting for the circle to gather. He wondered how many would show, especially since this wasn't the usual time for group. Slowly, however, most of the gang gathered.

For a long time, no one said anything. Silence in this group of men and women often spoke more than words might.

It was Marvin Damm, who'd found the dog the night before last, who spoke first. "Did it live?"

Eyes focused on Josh.

"Yes," he said. "He's going to be lame, but he'll be

fine. I guess the woman across the creek is adopting him." He paused, then added, "The dog's name is Reject."

A few people swore, one man and two women.

"Who the hell names a dog that? Damn it," Carly added angrily, *"we're all rejects."*

Angus MacDougall, who'd become a version of Josh's second hand, spoke. "Ain't none of us *rejects*. Need to remember who rejected who."

Josh nodded, agreeing wholeheartedly and glad Angus had spoken the words, his Scottish burr seeming to add them weight.

"But why *Reject*?" Carly Narth asked. A roadside bomb had left her with a scarred face and patchy gray hair.

"Simple," Josh answered, glad he'd learned this much. "Harris thought he was going to make a great team lead when he was a pup, but then Reject changed his mind about that. Question is who did the rejecting."

That at least brought out a few weak laughs. A couple of the guys gave each other playful shoves. Tension eased from the room.

But Josh knew he couldn't leave it there. It was too important to leave there. But how he hated to give these people another reason for concern.

"There's more," he finally said. Once again all attention fixed on him. "The sheriff is concerned that this could be...something more headed our way. As in someone who might start maiming *people*."

This time there was no silence. A cacophony rose in the room nearly deafening in its intensity. Josh let it run, let the energy burn out as it needed to. There'd come a point when fury and despair would give way to other feelings. None of them good, of that he was certain.

But eventually the noise quieted. A few cusses and nasty remarks escaped, then everyone fell silent. Except for Elaine, their head cook.

"Let me guess," she said bitterly. "They're blaming *us*."

"Nobody's blaming anyone." Which was true insofar as Josh knew. "Not yet, anyway."

Marvin Damm stood up, knocking his chair over. "They'll get around to it," he said, anger creeping back into his voice and posture. "There isn't a one of us in this room that hasn't been picked up by cops for questioning the instant something bad happens."

Grumbles of agreement answered him.

Josh tried to conceal his own growing stress, even though he knew this group was right. All of them. Even himself with his bloody degree and years of training. Easy targets, vets who couldn't readjust. Who had gotten thrown out by their families, who wound up living on the streets because there was nothing for them at a VA hospital except a cup of pills that didn't always work.

Homeless. Unwanted. Until a crime occurred. Then once they'd been picked up for questioning, for any reason, they were on a list for investigation for the next crime. Innocence meant nothing to the law.

There were a couple of former MPs in this group, and they knew the mindset all too well. They dinned a frequent warning about leaving the stockade, especially alone.

Now this.

"Serial killers du jour," one of the former MPs said. Rusty Rodes.

The problem was that Rusty wasn't far from correct.

Chapter Five

Krystal found the lodge busier than it had been that morning. The lunch crowd beginning to gather?

Then she saw the look on her mother's face as she supervised the kitchen help in preparing the buffet luncheon. Krystal went to her immediately. "What's up?"

Joan jerked her head toward the large windows where sunshine spilled into the room, a direct contrast to last night. And there she saw Mason Cambridge, once again holding court, although this time more quietly.

Krystal sighed. "You sure we can't ban him?"

"The idea grows stronger every day. But I've told you…"

"Yeah." Krystal sighed again. "It doesn't help that he gives a seminar every year. More publicity."

Joan cocked an eye at her daughter. "I have no idea how useful many of those seminars are."

Krystal shrugged. "People keep signing up for them."

"Unfortunately. Oh, we're getting a new guest today."

Krystal turned to her. "Do we have room?"

"That empty cottage next to Mason's, the one he insists on renting for the sake of privacy. Anyway, his agent is arriving this afternoon."

Krystal could have snickered. "Poor woman." Darlene Dana, who had been Mason's agent since he was discovered, never failed to look harassed, exasperated and fatigued after a few days with her star client. Krystal didn't envy the woman her job no matter how much it might pay.

"Yeah, poor her," Joan agreed. "Except she *could* kick him to the curb. God knows, I'm tempted."

"So what's he on about today?"

"Maimed dogs, things that creep in the night. He's working up to some real bonfire-type scares tonight."

"Maybe we should light a fire outside and give him free rein." The look on Joan's face succeeded in making Krystal laugh.

At that opportune moment, Davis Daniels showed up, heading straight for the buffet, where Joan and Krystal stood. "Let me guess," he said without preamble. "Our star egotist is setting up a good scare for later. By the time he's done we'll have Michael what's-his-name out there in the trees."

"That ought to keep everyone safely inside," Joan remarked tartly. "No wondering if someone out there stepped off a path and sprained an ankle."

Davis filled a plate with eggs, bacon and pastry, but took a seat at the end of the bar, rather than a table. "You know, Joan, this is a quiet place. I love coming here every year. For a little while I can turn off the world and focus on my art. It doesn't even have to be comic art unless I have a contract. For a little while I can remember the joy that brought me into this field."

"That's really special," Krystal said enviously.

Davis eyed her. "And you can't, at least not right now.

Here's an idea. Unless Joan objects, why don't you come with me on a hike up Morris Trail."

Morris Trail was one of the most difficult hikes around the property. "Takes a lot of energy," she remarked.

"Exactly." Davis's eyes twinkled. "I'm telling you, there's nothing like working your body hard to free your mind."

Krystal found the idea appealing, even though she knew that Morris Trail was apt to leave her dead on her feet by the time they returned. "You're on."

Joan smiled. "Good. It'll get you out of here and doing something refreshing for a while."

Which was how the next morning Krystal came to be wearing a small backpack containing water bottles and rain gear, all the items necessary for safety in a mountain climb where the weather could suddenly change. She followed Davis up the steep, rough incline.

"It'll be easier on the way down," he said over his shoulder.

As if she didn't know. "I'll be too damn tired to care."

He laughed, the sound ringing through the woods.

But halfway up the three-mile climb, the wind shifted and its odor changed, stinging with sharp ozone.

"Davis," she called out.

He, too, had paused and tipped his head up. "End of hiking today," he agreed. "Grab your rain gear."

"Again," she said disbelievingly. Rain, on this side of the mountains, was rare enough to create a wonderful climate for their guests to enjoy. They'd just had that light rain, and now something that looked as if it might become bad. But surely it would blow over because of the updraft against the mountains?

Just then, she thought she heard a buzz in the air.

"Hell," Davis said, just as she recognized the sound.

A charge was building in the air around them. Lightning. Her hair started to stand up. Krystal needed no directions. She dropped low, grabbing her ankles, tucking her head, hoping Davis did the same. There was no time to fool around, not now. Not even to give one another directions.

It seemed like an eternity later that the buzzing eased up, then there was a blinding flash and a deafening crack in the same instant.

But the buzzing remained gone.

She and Davis rose quickly to see a nearby tree smoking. Without another word, they headed back down the mountain as fast as their feet would carry them.

Well, this would make a good story, Krystal thought a bit crazily, not sure if she was more frightened or more relieved. It might even silence Mason.

At the foot of the trail, the lodge was only twenty feet away. Rain had begun to patter lightly and more loud thunder rolled down the mountain. Not until she and Davis were inside did she feel fully safe.

"Thank God," Joan said as soon as she saw them. "I was so scared when that storm broke."

Davis replied, "Not as scared as we were. We just missed getting zapped."

The silence from Mason's table became huge as the group heard Davis. Krystal decided to enjoy it. Maybe there was an upside to being almost fried.

Joan reached out and touched her arm. "Honey?"

Krystal worked up a smile. "I'm okay, really. We didn't have much time to get frightened, did we, Davis."

He twisted his mouth. "Unless you count the fastest run down Morris Trail ever recorded."

With that wry comment, Krystal relaxed completely. Davis, too, looked contented enough and Mason's coterie went back to talking esoterically about writing. Although Krystal was of the opinion that there was nothing at all esoteric about writing. At least not his.

"Not going back to work today, honey?" Joan asked, still looking a bit concerned.

"The lightning didn't kick my brain into high gear."

Just then, along with the freshening breeze and the growing smell of ozone, the front door opened and a woman appeared, looking only slightly ruffled by the wind outdoors. Along with her came the boom of thunder. A perfect entrance, Krystal thought, unable to suppress unexpected amusement.

Darlene Dana, Mason's agent, always looked as if she had stepped off a page of *Vogue*, even as the wind tossed her long auburn hair around. That look wouldn't last long, however. Darlene wasn't above dressing down for the situation. Soon she'd be wearing casual slacks and a T-shirt or sweatshirt.

Right now, though, she made every other woman in the room look or feel dull.

But Darlene smiled her thousand-watt smile at everyone, waving to Joan and Krystal, then heading in a straight line for Mason's table.

Mason might try to worm out of it with an early drink, but Krystal had seen how well Darlene could pretend a friendly conversation while keeping the through line on Mason's next book. Watching Mason holding court,

Krystal sometimes wondered how he ever completed a book at all.

Or why his publisher offered him bonuses just for being almost on time.

And one of those bonuses seemed to be a visit from Darlene.

As usual, Mason spent some time with his followers, no doubt impressing them with his importance in having his agent visit him. Then, with a promise to see them all that evening, he marched off with Darlene into the building storm.

"I suppose," Joan said as they disappeared, "I should have warned them how bad it is."

Davis shook his head. "He heard Krys and me talk about it. If he hasn't the sense to stay in here, then he gets what he might deserve."

"But what about Darlene?" Krystal asked.

Davis laughed. "She probably has the sense to duck."

Thunder rumbled again, as if joining the conversation, but it didn't sound as close as it had earlier.

In ones and twos other guests began to wander in, looking for lunch ostensibly, but likely not wanting to be in their cabins alone for nature's display. If it got loud enough, Krystal knew, it could be hard to concentrate on anything else. It could also be unnerving the way the mountains seemed to amplify the sound and bounce it back and forth like a hard rubber ball.

Washington Irving, she thought. Rip Van Winkle, the bowling gnomes under the mountain. She could understand where that story had been born.

Which brought her to "The Legend of Sleepy Hollow." Irving's tale had been more frightening than the movie, but beyond the windows the day had begun to darken as if night approached, and this night wasn't quieting early.

Joan had already signaled the staff to start building fires in the two large fireplaces. Sizable cast-iron cooking pots waited nearby in case they lost power. Out back a generator stood ready if needed, and Krystal merely shook her head, dreading its use. The lodge's generator beat the vets' hands down when it came to noise, even though Joan had arranged for it to be built into the ground.

All ready, Krystal thought, looking around as the room filled up. Only Mason and his agent were absent, not necessarily a bad thing. Whatever the two of them discussed had always remained private, unlike Mason's endless tales of what it meant to be a published author, what it took to succeed and why he had a gift few else could hope for.

Although Krystal thought rather sarcastically that Mason's success had been bought in part by knowing the right people in the industry.

Oh, man, she thought suddenly. Was she turning into an ugly, vindictive person? Not even Mason deserved such unkind thoughts from her.

Seeking distraction from herself, she turned to helping the staff fill up the food buffet. Mealtime or not, it didn't take long for folks to start seeking the comfort of food.

And beyond the windows the afternoon continued to darken threateningly. Along with it, quantities of carbs began to disappear from the buffet. Cookies, fried potatoes, cakes. Rolls, buttered bread…hell, all the serotonin fuelers.

Now, that was amusing and improved Krystal's mood

considerably. She even joined in the fun with a giant cinnamon roll.

The day continued to darken. The thunder grew louder. Reject wandered around, appearing disinterested.

And suddenly out of nowhere, Krystal thought of the vets down in Josh's compound. This must be god-awful for them, the endless rolling of the noises of war.

DOWN BELOW IN the stockade, the place of safety that Josh and his vets had built, the storm was making matters less safe for each and every one of them. The rolling thunder began to come too frequently, sounding like a determined barrage. The echo off the mountains added to the sense of surrounding danger. Men and women, knowing consciously that they were now safe from the war, nonetheless began to group into knots.

Hell, Josh thought. Hell, hell, hell. He wondered how much hard work was being undone by one overwhelming storm. Past storms had been easier to tolerate, being quieter, less reminiscent of threats of death. This storm embodied the worst.

Then, like a small ray of light in the midst of a nightmare, Angus called out. Angus was the man Josh could rely on no matter what.

"I think that dog is back again."

It was Josh who went out to check, asking no one else to step outside these protective walls, such as they were.

It was indeed the dog they had rescued just the other day. How the hell had he gotten over here on that leg?

This time, however, instead of looking sickly and hurt, the animal seemed determined to get attention. And it wasn't friendly attention, Josh realized, as the husky once again moved away each time he held out his hands.

Turning, he called back through the partly opened door. "Angus? Call that sledding guy. It's his wounded animal."

"Dang, won't the damn thing come in out of the storm? And I thought that woman adopted him."

"Maybe not. Maybe that guy, Harris, I think he is, can come down and get him."

Angus snorted. "Like anyone's going to come out into this crap weather."

Josh had his doubts about that, too, but this dog meant something to Harris, and Josh wasn't going to let the dog suffer needlessly. It went against every bone in his body.

So he stood there, water dripping off his camouflage poncho like a waterfall, and stared at a stubborn dog who was apt to freeze to death if he didn't get warm soon.

And that leg! Mike Windwalker, the vet, had put screws and plates in one of them in the wee hours, then splinted both of them, and now the protective cast on one was getting soaked and probably liable to infection.

"Stupid mutt," Josh muttered. Except nothing about that dog felt stupid right then. Reject bore a message of some kind. He'd known dogs like that in the K-9 Corps. Smart. Never to be diverted from anything it considered to be a duty.

Just as he was getting fed up—he didn't know what to do about it if that dog kept dancing away—Angus stuck his head out. "Phone's out to the sled dog place."

"Sat phone, too?"

"Hell yeah, and you ain't gonna get anyone on the roof to adjust the dish."

Not in the middle of this storm. No way. That left one option. "Call the lodge and tell 'em I'm on the way. Maybe they still got a phone."

Angus's voice became sarcastic. "And just how you supposin' to get that damn animal in the car?"

Josh was past caring. The dog had ridden in the Humvee before. No reason he should refuse today. If he did, Josh couldn't even get his owner down here to help.

So be it.

But Reject had a plan of his own, and it involved struggling his way into the vehicle. This time he even let Josh help him.

Crazy dog.

THE THUNDER HAD grown particularly bad by the time Krystal heard the muffled growl of a vehicle pulling up out front. While everyone else in the lodge remained occupied with card games or conversations, she went to the door and looked. The wide porch roof provided some shelter from the storm.

Krystal immediately recognized the Humvee. What had brought him up here? The hermit and his band of nearly invisible recluses from below seemed unlikely visitors.

But as soon as he opened his vehicle door, she saw Reject leap out and run limping through the lodge door into the great room.

She looked at Josh, who now stood there on the porch in his dripping camouflage poncho, and saw him shrug. "Don't ask me. He wouldn't settle for anything else."

Krystal turned to look at Reject limping across the

room to the big windows. "I hope he didn't hurt himself. And I don't get why he left the lodge."

Josh just shook his head. "Like anyone tells that dog what to do. Anyway, my phone is down, including the sat lines. So I thought maybe you can still get through to Harris, in case Reject damaged his cast, maybe on your landline."

"Well, come on in and we can check. Dry off. Eat. Have coffee. We seem to have become food and drink central today."

He chuckled quietly. "I can get that. My people don't want to be out in this either."

"So that leaves Reject."

Josh stepped inside and shed his poncho, hanging it on a hook with a bunch of other rain gear. "My boots are muddy."

"Join the crowd." But he scuffed his boots on the big entrance mat anyway, removing what he could.

Since he was a stranger to most of the artists in residence, he got only the merest greetings, but no one was impolite. Davis Daniels, the digital artist, greeted him warmest of all and patted the bar stool beside him. "What's with the dog?"

Josh slid onto the stool. "You'll have to ask him. Joan? Did you get through to the sled dog place?"

Joan shook her head, laying the satellite phone on the counter. "Nothing. No landline, no cell, no sat phone. Well and truly cut off."

It wasn't the first time the retreat had experienced this kind of electronic failure, but for the very first time it made Krystal uneasy. She looked from Josh to Davis to her mother and felt no better when she saw a tightness around their eyes. They felt it, too.

Then she looked at the clearly stubborn Reject, who was sitting near the windows. "I guess we don't need to call Harris, anyway. He's supposed to be *my* dog now."

"I was concerned about his cast," Josh said, "but honestly, it doesn't seem to have gotten too messed up."

Instinctively, however, Krystal looked toward the tall windows again, more intently, where Reject had planted himself. "Maybe we should cover the windows." She couldn't have explained her uneasiness even to herself, but watching Reject's attention to the outside world, she felt uncomfortable.

At that, Joan snorted. "Keep that up and I'm going to start thinking we've fallen into a Stephen King novel. It's just a storm, for Pete's sake."

Which was true. But looking again at the two men beside her at the bar, she saw they hadn't lost the tension around their eyes. They didn't like the situation either. It was just a weird storm, though, nothing supernatural or otherwise about it.

Then her gaze trailed back to the window. She saw Reject still sitting there. Erect. Staring out the windows.

"That dog needs some drying off," Josh remarked. "Thing is, he wasn't letting me touch him at all."

"He can find his way to the fire," Joan answered. "That dog never struck me as foolish."

Krystal smiled. "Too true, Mom. None of Harris's sled dogs are foolish, though."

"Too damn smart, if you ask me," Joan retorted.

Almost as if in answer to her, Reject tipped his head

back and howled. It was a wolf's howl, long and haunting and strangely beautiful. Everyone in the room froze.

Without a word, Josh rose and walked over to the window, standing beside Reject. The dog howled again. Then he settled down, nose between his front paws, and continued staring out the window.

The room remained quiet, as if everyone knew something important had happened but didn't know what.

Then Josh spoke, causing a stir. "Krystal? Joan? You got some outside lights? Bright ones?"

Krystal didn't hesitate. They had two kinds of outdoor lighting, one soft and warm for deck gatherings, and a brighter set. Security lights, although they'd never been needed that she knew of. She turned those on, figuring they'd be more useful.

In an instant the totally dark afternoon was flooded with light out to the trees beyond and even slightly past them. But somehow the bright lights made the darkness beyond even more secretive. More threatening.

That made no sense to Krystal, who walked over to the windows and stood beside Josh and Reject. "Light made it worse. How is that possible?"

He pointed. "Deeper shadows. Harsher corners. Makes it easier to see if anything approaches, but that's about it."

Krystal nodded, seeing what he referred to. "Some security lights, huh."

He turned to look at her. "They'd scare most people off from approaching. Animals, too. Regardless..."

"Regardless, we should probably turn them off."

He shrugged. "Depends."

"Meaning?" She looked straight at him, and for once his gaze was steady, not at all distant.

"Meaning whether you're more worried about something coming from the dark or seeing something get close to the house."

At that her stomach did a flip. "Damn, Josh!"

He shrugged and resumed looking outside. Just then, Reject lifted his head and let out another long howl. The room behind, which had just started to make friendly noises again, fell completely silent.

"I'd suggest," Josh said quietly, "that lights or no lights you keep these curtains open for a while. Reject sees something."

A shiver ran along Krystal's spine as she heard her worry validated. "I agree. Can you stay long? What about your vets?"

But now she could feel tension in him, as if every nerve and muscle in his body had stretched to the max. "Josh?"

"How much good do you think I'll be here?"

He had a point. Staring out into those strange woods, woods that had never frightened her before, she knew she didn't want him to leave. Something about the way he stood alert made her feel safer.

But she'd also learned something about those vets down there. Vets who couldn't manage the outside world, at least not yet. Was Josh their only link to this reality? What if the storm pushed them over the edge? What might they do?

"You should go," she said presently. Reject howled again, but this time Krystal managed to ignore it. "You've got people to look after."

But Josh didn't move. "Something has that dog stirred up, and I know better than to ignore a dog's senses."

He pulled a small radio from his pocket.

"What's that?"

"Short-range walkie-talkie. Mostly useless in these mountains, but I'll see if I can get Angus."

But he never moved away from the window, even as he managed a crackly conversation.

Josh was staying. That was when Krystal began to seriously wonder what was out there in the storm.

JOSH FELT BETTER after speaking to Angus. Angus had repeatedly proved he could provide a stabilizing force when memories and fears began to get out of hand. He was trusted by their soldiers, as Josh was trusted. But it was still a lot to ask of one man.

But Josh couldn't leave. Not with Reject howling warnings from time to time, as if he sensed something bad approaching. Not when Josh knew that the people in this lodge very likely had no idea how to defend themselves. No, they'd freak with fear.

Like some of his people in the stockade. God, he felt torn in two.

He knew better than to ignore a dog's senses, though. Squatting down, he lowered himself close to the dog's height. Not touching him, not getting in the way of his senses. Reject gave him a long look from those incredible blue husky eyes, sending a message. Josh heeded it.

"Rock and a hard place," he muttered, not wanting to be overheard. But Krystal, who seemed to be glued to his side, heard him. She spoke quietly.

"Are you sure about the dog?"

"I'd trust a dog's sense of danger faster than I'd trust mine, and mine is pretty damn good."

Several minutes, and one more howl from Reject, passed before she spoke again. "What could be out there? A bear?"

Josh didn't disillusion her by arguing that the husky wouldn't be standing guard because of a bear, not when so many humans were around. No, that was the kind of danger most dogs would avoid, not face off. Good survival instincts, especially when a bear wasn't likely to ignore a dog. Not when dogs enraged them.

No, there was something more sinister out there, and from experience Josh could think of only one thing: a human. A human threat.

He spoke quietly. "How many of your lodgers are here right now?"

Krystal turned to look around the room, scanning with the ease of familiarity. "Most of them. Maybe four or five missing."

"Unusual?"

Krystal faced the window again. "Not really. We have some truly introverted people here and we're likely not to see them much at all."

Josh glanced at her. "How the hell do they eat if they don't come in here?"

"Trips to the grocery for supplies. We lay in some for them, occasionally take them hot meals if they're interested."

"Five-star service."

That clearly irritated her a bit. "We provide a place where artists can work undisturbed. That means in every way they want. It's part of the deal, Josh. Do you do any differently for your prisoners?"

At that Josh turned from the window, feeling his face

turn as hard as rock, his aquamarine eyes as cold as stone. "Has it ever occurred to any of you judgmental people out here that the stockade is to keep *you* out and not my group in?"

That pierced Krystal visibly, sharply. Even though he'd told her that before, this time he could see that it penetrated the distraction of her own thoughts. This time it reached her like an icy jab in her heart.

"I'm sorry," she said after a moment.

"All you people out here who've never faced the horror my vets have faced should at least do them the courtesy of admitting they have more to fear than their own anger."

Krystal hesitated, then said quietly, "Don't they have drugs for PTSD now?"

"Like they work on everyone. No, sometimes the only thing that can work is knitting the holes in the mind. The places you can't see that the violence tore out of them."

True or not, he hated to make the argument. It sounded as if a cure, or any help, was too far away. Reject howled again and Krystal returned her attention to the window. Someone behind her shouted, "Damn it, can't you shut that dog up?"

It was Josh who turned, speaking in a voice that allowed no disagreement. "Good God, Reject is guarding us. Be glad of it."

Well, that unleashed a cacophony of voices behind Krystal, as people began to argue about the dog, but she obviously didn't want to enter the fray. Guarding them against what? people asked. What should they fear in those woods? They'd never feared them before.

But no one again demanded that Reject shut up.

JOAN KEPT THE kitchen staff working constantly. People were eating as much as they were talking, and apparently she felt eating was a better thing.

But Mason's talk the night before last had evidently unleashed something atavistic in these creative people. Krystal wished sourly that Mason was here for it. Maybe he'd catch a dose of his own medicine.

But as the day wore on, people found it harder and harder to ignore Reject's alert posture. Understandably. The dog wasn't even napping.

Joan and Josh both tried to reach Harris to come check the dog, in case his howling had to do with his injuries. They were still cut off, however, except for Josh's dubious walkie-talkie exchanges with Angus. So far everything seemed okay at the stockade.

But if the lightning hadn't continued to rend the air like a maddened firefight, Josh would have climbed up to the roof to pivot that satellite dish to a position where it could receive and send messages. As it was, every time the thought crossed his mind, lightning flashed again and a gale-force gust of wind ripped through to remind him that nothing could make that dish stay in the right position. Not now. Nor could anyone go up there without risking life and limb.

He wondered how long this storm would last. It seemed like an awfully long time already. He wondered how long Reject would stay alert, refusing even to nap as most dogs did.

He wondered how long his own group, which had grown to nearly twenty men and three women over the past few days, would be able to stand this constant barrage of lightning and thunder before one of them snapped back into the past.

He ought to get his ass down there. But Reject kept him nailed here. The dog had managed to come to the stockade to get someone. But he hadn't remained there. No, he'd made it quite clear that he wanted to be here.

He sighed and looked back at the room, so full of people, and thought about grabbing something to eat. Surely he could stand away from the window for just that long. Reject would signal him.

But just as he had the thought, Reject growled. Deep from somewhere within him emerged the most threatening sound a dog ever made.

Instinctively, Josh tensed. He squatted beside the dog and laid a gentle hand on his shoulder. "What is it, boy?"

Reject spared him the briefest glance from those amazing blue husky eyes, then looked out the window and growled again.

All righty, then. Rising, Josh faced the room. "Get in the back. Get upstairs. Get on the floors. Get away from these windows! *Now!*"

For a moment or two, no one moved, but then the flight began. To Josh's amazement, it was a quiet orderly exodus, most likely aided by the way Joan took over and directed traffic as if this were a drill of some kind. She enlisted her employees from the kitchen as well, and Josh gave them credit for remaining calm through it all.

Krystal joined her mother in directing movement, but only briefly. Soon she was back at the window, beside Josh and Reject.

She spoke quietly. "Maybe we should close the curtains anyway. I feel like a target."

Josh didn't disagree with her, but he had a more important matter to think about: the safety of everyone in this building. He couldn't leave all that to one dog. "Get back behind some furniture. I need to keep an eye out."

She nodded but didn't move. "Okay. The threat will have to shoot all three of us."

Josh felt an instant of amusement. "So sure the threat has a gun?"

"I'm not going all Stephen King here. I refuse to. Mason stirred enough of that up the other night."

"Did he?"

"He's a horror novelist. I guess that's the way he runs. Anyhow, he had plenty of people listening to him. I'm kind of surprised anyone went back to their own cabins that night."

"Then the storm."

"Then the storm," she agreed. "We started filling up."

"I'm not surprised, honestly. This is a pretty violent one."

"More than we're used to around here."

Then his walkie-talkie buzzed. He yanked it off his belt and Angus's voice crackled in answer to his.

"Josh, we're on the move. Protection perimeter and don't ask me to stop it."

Josh swore vigorously as he jammed the walkie back onto his belt.

"Josh? What's that mean?"

He looked at her, and those amazing eyes told a different story this time.

KRYSTAL COULD HARDLY stand his silence. That harsh but sad look that reached the corners of his eyes, that brought them down just a bit. He was worried. Unhappy. Not the pillar of stone she had believed him to be.

Then he turned his head back to the window. "The storm's gotten to my people. Angus can't calm them."

Her stomach quivered uneasily. "So? Now?"

"Angus said perimeter. If that's what they're doing, it's okay. It's a protection move. The walls are supposed to do that, but I guess they need to feel more in charge."

Krystal gnawed her lower lip, hesitating to press further into all that Josh had clearly placed off-limits with his silences as much as anything. "Josh? What will they do?"

He shook his head. "Guard the compound. Spread out a little. Keep eyes on each other."

She drew a tight breath. "They feel threatened, too."

"That would be my guess."

"So maybe you should go back to them."

Again he looked at her, shaking his head. "These guys know what to do to form a perimeter. No reason they should go beyond that. At least as long as the woods don't start shooting at them or hurling grenades."

The image was ludicrous. It drew a reluctant smile from her, then she saw Josh smile, too. A smile and a brief snort as he shook his head.

"The woods," he said, "aren't the danger."

She stared out into them, misty now with rain. Understanding filled her with skin-crawling unease. "The shadows are."

"Hence Reject."

NEARLY AN HOUR PASSED. Reject didn't growl again. Josh and Krystal eventually pulled some chairs up to the window so they could sit and watch the outdoors. The change brought them some cover, from the waist down. Hardly enough to keep Krystal's skin from crawling, but somewhat better.

Joan at last appeared at the foot of the stairs. "Can we all come down now?"

Just then Reject growled, a sound so low it hardly seemed possible that it came from him.

"Uh, not yet," Krystal answered.

"So a dog is ruling my day," Joan retorted, but she sounded only a tiny bit sarcastic.

"It could be worse," Josh answered.

"As if. I've got nearly fifty people up there who are getting really frustrated. Yeah, Reject's growl scared them. The first few times. But what does it mean?"

"Trouble," Josh answered.

At that instant a bullet zinged and cracked the window not far from Krystal's head.

Reject raised a howl fit to lift the rafters. Josh pushed Krystal to the floor almost before the sound had died away.

"Joan," he said tautly to Krystal's mother.

"Got it," she answered, her voice shaking now. "Close the damn curtains so my daughter isn't a target!"

"I have to be able to see. Krystal can go hide with the rest of you."

"Like hell," Krystal answered, cautiously sitting up. Josh's shove had been forceful enough to leave her shoulder aching. A few pebbles of safety glass rattled on the floor around her.

And Reject, with a dog's amazing instinct, crawled up on her as best he could, sniffing for damage, lingering for sloppy kisses. Krystal hugged him as tightly as she dared given his injured hind leg.

"Guess he wants to take care of you," Josh remarked. "I need to get out there. In this rain, maybe someone left footprints I'll be able to follow."

Fear seized Krystal, gripping her heart. "Josh, no! You could…"

"Get hurt?" he asked almost sarcastically. "Been there, done that. Fear is hardly on my radar any longer. I'm closing these damn curtains, you pay attention to Reject's warnings, and I'm going to get my butt out there to find the gunman. The silly part just went out of this entire experience."

Krystal couldn't argue with that. A gunshot. Through a window. Maybe intended for her. Maybe intended for Josh. The two of them hadn't been that far apart, after all.

But hadn't they been acting kind of silly for hours now? Wedded to this window and a dog? But she had to admit that the bullet had changed everything. Reject's behavior had given her the creeps, but now it went far beyond some spooky horror novel feeling. This was real.

Josh drew the curtains quickly enough with the electronic controls. At least the generator out back had started running an hour or so ago, but other things could go wrong. Plenty of them.

Insulated curtains approached a near blackout. Other windows had the same protection against the ice of winter. Now protection against something even more life-threatening.

God. She watched Josh pull on his poncho, watched Reject whine a bit as Josh left, then wondered what to do with the curtains closed.

Her mother soon answered that question, coming down the stairs. "I guess we can come down now. Nobody can see in here. Where's Josh?"

"Out hunting a gunman."

Joan just shook her head. "Put men in a uniform and they all think they're invincible."

Krystal didn't think that was fair, but she wasn't about to argue the matter. She watched Reject closely, afraid she might miss a warning, afraid she might see one.

A quieter crowd, minus a few who preferred to stay upstairs, gathered in the great room. Some even had an appetite, amazingly enough. Krystal didn't think she could have swallowed a thing even if she hadn't eaten in a week.

Reluctant to leave the window because of the dog, who still stared toward the curtained expanse, Krystal realized she trusted Reject's senses. She couldn't see anything out there herself. Glancing around the room, she caught sight of Mary Collins sitting alone at a table and went over to join her. Mary had been a late arrival in the lodge today. One of their true introverts, almost always alone by choice.

"How are you doing?" she asked Mary as she slid into a seat facing her. "This hasn't been a fun day so far."

Mary smiled faintly. As usual, the expression was a bit sour and unattractively framed by her oily, thin hair. "The dog has been fun."

"Quite a trip, isn't he?" Krystal was growing fonder of Reject by the minute. "I'm hoping Harris will let me keep him." Although Harris had already made it clear that Reject decided for himself. Maybe it wasn't Harris she was worried about when it came to Reject.

Mary looked over at the curtained window where Reject appeared to still be standing guard.

"He's bright enough. But what do you suppose is bothering him out there?"

Krystal shook her head. "Something. A bullet went through that window. You heard, I'm sure." A hollow sound, echoing in this huge room.

Mary shuddered. "I did. I almost forgot that."

How anyone could forget that bullet surpassed Krystal's understanding, but then, Mary often appeared lost in her own world. Truly involved in whatever she was writing.

Krystal leaned her chin on her hand, trying not to think about Josh out there. Trying not to worry about him. "Got any advice for writer's block?"

At that, Mary's face brightened. "Stop trying to write your book."

Krystal frowned faintly. "And how's that supposed to help?"

Mary shrugged. "It'll take the pressure off. Just spend fifteen minutes in the morning writing about anything that crosses your mind, then walk away."

Krystal sighed. "Seems strange."

"Sure it does. But somehow it takes away the fear and the words start flowing."

"Is that what you do?"

Mary's tone grew wry. "More than I'd like to admit."

"Then I'll try it." Anything sounded better than staring at a blank computer screen. "This doesn't seem like a good time, though."

Mary surprised her with a grin. "Well, you could try one of Mason's horror stories."

Krystal couldn't help it. She looked toward the covered windows and the dog.

Mary asked, "Where's that guy from the stockade?"

"Out looking for a gunman."

"God!" Mary shuddered. "He must be nuts."

"Or a trained soldier."

Silence followed. Then Mary tilted her head. "I hadn't thought of that."

Who had around here, Krystal wondered. Mostly a vague sense of curiosity washed away by their own preoccupations. Not since last year when the stockade had made its final appearance with those log walls had anyone paid any real attention. And that had faded away as some decided the structure simply added to the local charm. People in this retreat weren't especially interested in what was happening outside.

But that was the entire point of this place, wasn't it?

Except that she hated the idea that Josh was out there conducting a lone search. And what the hell had he meant about his group forming a perimeter? A perimeter around what? Against what?

Again that uneasy sensation of something supernatural washed through her. She had to struggle to make it go away. She simply didn't believe that stuff, was willing to suspend her disbelief occasionally for a good novel— the exception being Mason's—but only for that. Things didn't go bump in her night.

But another look at Reject dissolved all her resolutions. The fur along his spine and neck had risen. A silent warning.

Why silent now? God, where was Josh? Should she send everyone upstairs? Had the threat grown closer?

The storm decided to join the act, stepping up the wind until the rain rattled under the porch roof against the windows, sounding almost like a hail of bullets.

Suddenly all Krystal could think of was the way they were cut off from the world, not even a satellite phone. No way to summon help.

Then Reject turned away from the window and faced the front door.

God, what now? Krystal wished for a weapon, any weapon, but she doubted a steak knife would provide much protection. Maybe a chef's knife out of the kitchen.

Then, from out of her distant childhood, she remembered the pilot's voice coming over the loudspeakers on a flight she had taken a few weeks after 9/11. "Just remember there's more of us than them."

Before she could find her voice to repeat that, the front door banged open and Josh entered, a woman in his arms. The agent, Darlene Dana, lay almost unconscious, dressed in jeans and a flannel shirt, her usual costume when she visited Mason. No *Vogue* about her now.

"Get her warm," he ordered, his voice sharp.

"What happened?" demanded a few people.

"She was running through the rain. Mason Cambridge is dead."

THE SHOCK PASSED QUICKLY, possibly because news of Mason Cambridge's demise didn't feel like a major loss to many of them. Regardless, several women moved forward. Josh laid Dana on the sofa near a fireplace and the women quickly stripped her and wrapped her in the afghans that had lain cheerily across the back of every padded piece of furniture in the room.

After a few minutes, Darlene Dana's eyes fluttered open and she groaned.

"It's going to hurt for a few minutes," Josh said, his tone as reassuring as any Krystal had ever heard anywhere. "You got pretty hypothermic."

Joan arrived almost instantly. "Broth okay?" she asked Josh.

"Slowly."

Joan leaned down with a mug in her hand. "It's not too hot, I checked. Let me know when you want a sip, okay?"

Such a small thing, but so important, Krystal thought. Then she looked around and realized the whole damn room was beginning to cluster around Darlene Dana. Wouldn't that make her feel good, to be peppered with questions when she had just run in terror through the most god-awful storm?

She looked around. "Hey, people, back up and give Darlene some room. Give her a chance to recover." At once, however reluctantly, the group backed up and began to sit at tables.

Josh had retreated a short distance to a chair beside a dining table. "Not much she can tell you that I can't, anyway. I reached Cambridge's cabin first. He'd been shot. Then I found Darlene tearing through the woods, sobbing her eyes out, terrified of me. Had to calm her like a scared horse."

Gazes tracked back to Darlene, then once again to Josh.

"Murder?" someone breathed, drawing gasps from everyone.

"Maybe," Josh answered. "I gather this guy wasn't a favorite here. Regardless, I'm no expert. We need the sheriff."

"And we can't call him," Davis said. "Hell's bells."

Bodies shifted. Apparently no one felt it necessary to cluster yet, but their gazes all turned to Reject, who oddly had finally seemed to relax.

"I'll try the landline again," Joan said. "No reason it should be down from this damn storm. I just don't get it."

But something had cut off all communication with the outside world including the landline. Josh gave a slight shake of his head and pulled the walkie off his belt. The sound crackled worse than before. "Angus? You still got a perimeter?"

The answering crackle sounded affirmative.

"Then get 'em up here. This retreat needs more guarding. We found a body."

When he disconnected he looked around at a room of stunned faces. "We still need a sheriff. And y'all are going to have to get used to my vets being out there. They'll make you as safe as possible."

JOSH KNEW HE was looking at a bunch of unpredictable people. There was no certainty about how any of them might act, and how the hysteria of one might transmit to the others. He could keep his people outside pretty much in line, but the ones in here?

Not a person in this crowd was accustomed to discipline, to taking orders. To following directions unquestioningly. Any one of them might go off the deep end.

He drew Krystal aside, giving her the best warning he could. "Watch 'em, Krys. Somebody might get some crazy idea."

"Yeah, like a book I keep trying to forget." She shook her head as if she could shake something out of it. "These are imaginative people, Josh. No telling which way that imagination will run."

"My concern exactly. Besides, the human mind is built that way. I've seen it in a desolate outpost in Afghanistan. Enough darkness, enough isolation, a few weird sounds. Doesn't take much."

Krystal scanned the room again. "How can I keep an eye on so many people?"

"Watch them cluster. Clustering should give you a feel for how people are thinking. Anyway, it must be time to feed them again. That always helps calm people. Ask for your mother's help."

TALK ABOUT SURREAL. Krystal helped prepare a simple meal of soup, roasts, veggies and the last of the bread that had come from Melinda's bakery in town only yesterday. An ordinary meal.

Yet so unordinary. Curtains closed tight against the darkness. They almost never did that because the clients liked the soft glow of the porch lights through the windows. A number always liked to eat at the wooden tables outside on the deck when the evening was pleasant enough.

No one was outside. No one even glanced at the curtains. Krystal could almost feel the awareness of everyone in the room of the hole in the window. A single bullet that might have been directed or might simply have been intended to scare. They avoided looking at the area that had caused them alarm.

Krystal bit her lip so hard she feared cutting it. Avoiding the situation wasn't going to help any of them deal with the reality that they were locked in this building with a killer out there. Or in here with them? God, she couldn't bear the thought, running like ice through every vein in her body. In *here*? It couldn't be. Someone had shot out the window from the outside, not the inside. No, the killer was out there in the dark storm somewhere.

Mason Cambridge dead. Krystal had always thought rather ungenerously that his ego would keep him going another hundred years. Gone. It felt impossible.

His agent, shivering less now, still had eyes so frightened they were terrifying to look into. No one glanced Darlene Dana's way now, as if she had become a symbol of the day's peculiar terror. Surreal.

Surreal that they showed more attention to a dog who lay alert in front of the curtained windows, though he had long since grown silent.

Nothing about the evening felt real. It was almost like slipping into that Dalí painting of the melting watches. Nothing looked quite right. As if everything were distorted.

Krystal tried to shake her mood as she filled the buffet and stacked clean dishes at the ends of it. Tonight there would be no individual service. Too few employees had been able to get to the lodge because of the storm.

Wine and liquor were the first items claimed from the cash bar. Hardly surprising. More slowly, plates of food were filled and people carried their own napkin-wrapped utensils to the table. Evidently not all the factors of real life had vanished in this haven.

But this haven wasn't feeling like one at all. She watched Josh at a distance, talking on his walkie-talkie. It would have been nice to know what was being said.

But finally he approached her. "One of my guys is

taking the extra Humvee down the hill to town to get the sheriff."

"Thank God!"

"It's going to be a rough ride. It looks like some of the road may be washing out."

Krystal closed her eyes. Surreal. More and more surreal. This never happened. "Anything else?" she asked finally, dreading the answer.

"You said some people still hadn't shown up here. Are they still missing?"

Chapter Six

Krystal's heart stopped. Fear raced through her. A murdered man out there and missing people? She scanned the room quickly, trying to make no mistakes. "Oh, God," she murmured. "Four of our greatest introverts. It's not unusual for them to fail to show up here."

She dragged her gaze to his. He was already looking tougher, as if it came as second nature. His voice became hard as steel.

"I guess I'd better look, at least to make sure they're safe in their cabins."

She nodded. "I'll go with you. These people know me and won't be frightened by seeing a stranger. I'll get Joan to take charge here."

Josh scanned the room. "It won't take us long, will it? Just so she doesn't have to handle much by herself."

Krystal shook her head. "We aim for privacy, not distance." Then she smiled slightly. "My mother is tougher than she looks. Trust me."

Joan was frankly unhappy about her daughter going out into this storm with a killer out there somewhere, but she'd learned a long time ago that getting into an argument with Krystal seldom served any use. She spread the map of the cabins, as if Krystal didn't know where they all were, tutting the entire time, but making sure Josh got a good look.

"Just don't take too long," she said sharply. "God, you're going to give me a heart attack."

"You've been saying that for years and you're still here," Krystal teased her. She received only the faintest, tightest of smiles from Joan. Well, that hadn't worked.

Then she and Josh pulled on ponchos, his a camo and hers a bright yellow, and together they prepared to step into a wet, blustery day that seemed more full of rage than a regular thunderstorm. Reject wanted to come along but Krystal eased him back. "Don't want you getting your leg wet out here." He remained, looking droopy.

She tightened the drawstring around her hood and left the snaps down the sides closed. For some reason she ordinarily preferred not to be so enclosed in the garment, but this day offered no alternative.

Then the two of them set out along the stone-edged path. "Paul Aston is out this way," she remarked. "A poet. He *really* doesn't like to be disturbed."

"Let's hope he hasn't been disturbed at all."

Krystal shared his hope. Mason was enough. One death. This wasn't a mystery novel, and she didn't want corpses strewn around the retreat. Although she didn't want to think about it, she was truly distressed by Mason's death. Easier to keep it from the forefront of her mind. As if it would recede.

Paul's cabin was about one hundred and fifty feet back from the main trail. Lights glowed from lanterns and he answered the knock on his door immediately, dressed in rumpled denim with his wisps of gray hair springing every which way.

"What do you want?" he groused. "My computer and power aren't working. Of course, working on poetry by lamplight and with handwriting isn't the worst creative situation." Those benefits didn't keep him from scowling at Krystal, however.

Krystal spoke soothingly. "We just wanted to make sure you're okay."

"As okay as I can be without modern conveniences. I paid for them, you know." Then he slammed the door.

"So much for telling him to be careful," Josh remarked. "Nice guy."

"We don't get paid to entertain only nice people and they don't pay to have us provide less than perfection." A situation that sometimes aggravated her half to death.

Josh snorted. "When you meet perfection, let me know."

They took a turn to the right, heading for the next cabin.

"Don't you have a hand map of this place?" Josh asked.

"The only one is the one you saw in my mother's office. Otherwise we'll rely on my memory."

"A map would sure be useful when my group gets out here."

She turned her head to eye him. His face was only partly visible in the gloom. Then a flash of nearby lightning nearly blinded her. "God!" she said loudly.

"If that was a heavenly comment, I'm sure I don't want to be on the receiving end."

Krystal heard the humor in his voice and felt relieved. If she had to be out here hunting for guests in this awful storm, she couldn't think of a better companion. "So this perimeter thing you mentioned?"

"My people will fan out around this retreat, keeping an eye out for intruders. Like sentries. That's why a map would be useful."

"I can see that. But why should they help?"

"Because it's who they are," he answered levelly. "Still. Despite everything."

Krystal had a strong feeling that she shouldn't ask about the *everything*. This group had been present across the creek from her for a year now and little knowledge of them escaped. Very little. Privacy seemed to be as important across the creek as it was here.

"So where's the name come from," Josh asked. "Cash Creek Canyon?"

"A century and a half ago. Interesting bit of history. A couple of places in these mountains were discovered to have gold. Not so much here, but placer mining continued for a couple of decades."

"Placer?" he asked.

"Rinsing gold from the water. Anyway, that's the Cash Creek part."

"And the creek itself was part of finding gold? And the canyon, too?"

"The placer mining, yes. But there was another advantage to the creek and canyon. It joins up with several other creeks and small rivers that run down the slopes from snowmelt and springs. You might have seen the reservoir up there?"

"Yeah. Kinda big."

"Kinda necessary. For a long time the creeks and rivers joined together to make the larger river that Conard City was built around. Eventually it wasn't reliable enough water and it needed to reach a lot more land, like ranches, so the reservoir was built."

"You're right. It's interesting history," he remarked presently as the lights of another cabin began to show. "Who is this?"

"Giselle Bibe, commonly called Gizzie. PhD student. She's taking a sabbatical here to write her dissertation."

"Tough job, I hear. Better written indoors than out, though." Meant as a touch of humor, she could tell.

Krystal didn't much feel like smiling when the wind chose that moment to blow icy raindrops into her face. Drops that felt almost like sleet, although given the altitude and despite the time of year sleet was entirely possible. As was snow, God forbid.

Gizzie seemed to be doing a whole lot better than Paul Aston. Her half frame readers were perched on the end of her nose and she greeted them with a smile. "You ought to come in for some coffee. And what the dickens are you doing out, anyway? I wouldn't call it hospitable."

Josh let Krystal answer. "Given the severity of the storm and the lack of power, we just wanted to check on people who didn't come to the dining room."

"Well, I'm doing just fine," Gizzie assured them. "Rather nice to be writing in a situation that echoes the history around here. A whole lot more atmospheric, too, without power. No problems, so don't worry about me."

Krystal decided to take it one step further. Hardly knowing what reaction to expect, she clenched her hands tightly. "Mason Cambridge is dead. You might not want to be out here alone."

"Hah! So he finally bought it? I wondered how a man

so choleric could fail to have a fatal heart condition. Well, don't worry about me. I can keep company with his damn ghost, no problem."

As they walked away, Josh spoke. "Maybe we need to be stronger in the warning."

"But we don't know if some killer is after anyone else. Besides, Mason would have been a target for darn near everyone here. The *only* target."

A snort of laughter escaped Josh. "I *do* like you, Krystal Metcalfe."

"I'm being nasty."

"So go for it. Wanna have a competition?"

But she'd heard his suggestion that they make a stronger warning. She decided to be firmer with the others and pick up Gizzie on the way back.

Then he pulled the walkie out from under his poncho and tried again. This time the signal was a little clearer.

"Rusty figures he's halfway down to the town," Angus answered Josh. "As for the rest of us, the perimeter is spreading. Maybe you should let people know we'll be out there. No heart attacks on my watch, please."

"Not likely," Josh answered. "Anyway, there are no comms out here to tell folks about you guys. I mentioned it earlier, anyway. But nobody's going to see you, right?"

"Better not or we'll have a course on using rusty skills around here."

When Josh disconnected, Krystal said, "I like the sound of that man."

"Utterly reliable. Good-hearted, too."

As Krystal had begun to suspect, Josh was as well. After all, he'd been the one to take Reject for help. Some people wouldn't have gone to so much trouble for a dog.

But then, some people didn't value the lives of animals.

"How many more do we need to check up on?" Josh asked.

"Two more, I think. Julia and Sebastian are probably okay, though. A long way from Mason's cabin." Then she bit her lower lip. "I don't suppose I need to go inside the cabins if no one answers?"

He paused midstride and looked at her. She stared at him, once again noting how attractive he was even when he looked like rugged stone.

"Krystal," he said quietly, "I'm going to give you a couple of reasons you don't want to go in any of these cabins. The first is you don't want to mess up a possible crime scene for the cops. I imagine Darlene Dana probably did enough of that at Mason's place."

She nodded. "You're right. I didn't think of that."

"I figured. Then there's the second reason. Take me at my word. Whatever might have happened in another cabin you don't want the images haunting you for the rest of your life."

She stood frozen as unwanted pictures flooded her mind anyway. She was sure her ideas couldn't be as bad as reality. What did she know about it, anyway? Scenes from movies?

Josh reached out and took her forearm gently. "Bad enough what might have happened in there. Absolutely no need for you to see anything. Now let's go make sure the rest of these loners are okay."

And Krystal, very suddenly, didn't want to think about that at all. She'd been assuming only one person had been hurt, and that was a huge assumption under the circumstances.

"Damn, Josh," she muttered quietly.

"Take it easy," he said kindly. "If anyone doesn't open their door, I'll go in. Not you. Absolutely not you. And there's no reason to think that anyone else has been hurt, right?"

Small comfort considering what Josh might find. That they'd have another reason to wait for a deputy. For law enforcement and crime scene teams...

Given the way Darlene had reacted to her discovery of Mason's body, expecting a horrific sight was not beyond belief. She was hardly aware of crossing her fingers inside her gloves.

Julia Jansen, a watercolorist, proved to be all right and more than eager to join the group at the lodge. She didn't even argue when Josh insisted she don her rain gear and come with him and Krystal while they checked on the last absent resident. This storm was clearly upsetting her.

It was certainly one of the most violent Krystal could remember having seen in these mountains. The wind threatened to knock them over as they pushed their way to the last cabin.

Where they found another writer dead. Josh didn't let anyone enter, but Julia began to keen helplessly when she heard that Sebastian Elsin was dead.

"Everybody back to the lodge now," Josh ordered, his voice like steel. "Now!"

Neither Julia nor Krystal hesitated to hurry down the path, their flashlights their only guide. Behind her, she heard Josh get on his walkie again.

"Update" was all he said. A few seconds later, he added one word. "Good."

Then he drew closer to the women. "We're sweeping

up that Aston guy and that woman on our way back. Nobody's going to be out here alone. Got it?"

Krystal gave him a firm yes. Julia sounded fainter. Josh spoke again. "The perimeter is tightening. Eyes are on us. We should get back to the lodge safely."

Chapter Seven

The lodge was unwontedly still, except for the storm that raged outside as if it wanted to wipe the planet clear.

Josh moved to the back room that was Joan's office and Krystal followed, not caring if he wanted her there or not. He was planning and she needed to be part of it. She needed to be able to do something except pace. Except want to scream at the horror of all this. She kept a lid on her self-control, but it wasn't easy.

And Josh was still stuck on the walkie-talkie. It didn't seem possible that communications had been out this long. The handyman, Mel, could usually resight the satellite dish on the rare occasions it got out of alignment. But not in this storm.

People were too quiet, Krystal thought. Joan, in an attempt at cheer, moved through the lodge with her limited staff, serving up menus and drinks. Not much food was being ordered—not that the kitchen could provide much with a short staff.

"All right, I got it," Josh said finally. He had Joan's unrolled map of the retreat spread on the table and was freely marking it up. What the *X*'s meant, Krystal had no idea.

But at last he seemed done with talking in a foreign language, or at least it sounded like it, what with the military jargon he was probably using.

"So, what's going on?" Krystal asked, unwilling to be kept in the dark. At times like these, Josh didn't look like a man anyone should disagree with. A slight shiver ran down her spine. Dangerous. He could be dangerous.

He shook his head. "There aren't enough people in my group to provide a tight cordon. Which isn't to say they won't be working double-time, but they'll probably have to pull in closer, which could make them more visible. I don't like that."

She nodded, understanding that he had to be concerned about a threat to his soldiers. But also about how people in the lodge might react if they happened to see them in numbers. "We'll just remind everyone..."

"Remind everyone of what? That they'll actually *see* a bunch of former soldiers surrounding them? Where's *that* trust supposed to come from?"

Krystal wanted to curse, hating the fact that he was probably right. Over the years she'd heard the casual talk from people who had no comparable experience. People who didn't grasp the price of war. People who distrusted vets because they "might go ballistic" at any moment.

She also didn't miss the bitterness in Josh's tone. "Maybe you ought to make a point of becoming neighbors around here." Even as she spoke she wished she could snatch the ugly words back. As near as she could tell, Josh's group didn't feel like they had neighbors, good or bad.

"Damn it, Krys, how many times do I have to tell you that stockade is protection for my people from the outside world. The world they still can't tolerate. A reality they might never quite join again. A reality that just keeps on wounding them."

She felt an ache deep within her. "I'm sorry. I guess I'm just not getting it."

He tossed a pencil onto the map. "Why should you? It's an alien experience."

Then his walkie crackled and the now familiar voice of Angus came through. "Sheriff's on his way up. He's got a few Humvees so it shouldn't take too long. Body count still at two?"

"Yeah. We think we have everyone rounded up safely. At least for the retreat area. God knows what might be happening in the town." He disconnected.

Krystal's heart had plummeted to her toes. She hadn't even thought of the town, although the oversight was probably the result of the first murder having been Mason. At this point the artists seemed like the obvious targets.

Josh astonished her by reaching out and gently snaking an arm around her. "You look as lost as just about anybody I've known. We'll work the problem. We'll solve it. And reinforcements are arriving, courtesy of the Conard County Sheriff's Department."

Then he gave her a gentle squeeze and released her.

But that hug, brief as it had been, had relaxed a deep tension inside her. Her confidence grew, and she suspected that Josh deserved every bit of her trust.

They left her mother's office, the map remaining behind. Josh made the announcement to the great room, which was still subdued. "The sheriff's deputies are on the way up here. They'll add to your protection and try to find out what's going on. For now, I'd say everyone in this room is safe from an outside threat."

He didn't directly mention his people out there, watching from all sides.

Josh and Krystal sat at a table. Joan brought them glasses of red wine and menus. "Eat," she ordered. "Both of you look like something the cat dragged in."

For the first time since early that morning, Krystal felt truly hungry, as if her mother had given her a subliminal suggestion.

Josh ordered hugely from the menu, offering no apologies for the size of his appetite. Krystal decided to follow suit. Who was going to tell her two hamburgers and fries was too much? Not even herself, not today.

Slowly the room around them began to hum with voices, and meals started to be gathered from the buffet. It was as if Josh had calmed everyone, maybe with the promise the sheriff was on the way.

Halfway through her too-large meal, Krystal spoke to Josh. "I can see one murder. But why would there be two?"

Josh shrugged a shoulder. "That's for the cops to figure out." Then he half smiled. "We can speculate, though."

She had to smile back at him. "Speculation can be fun."

"Sure can. Unless we turn it into some kind of horror conspiracy."

Her smile fled. "That's sort of what Mason was doing the other night. You should have seen our crowd. He had them going almost as much as word of his murder did."

"Not the kind of person you need to have around right now."

"I figured he was rehearsing his next book. It would have been spooky enough."

Seemingly out of nowhere, Joan plopped herself at their table. She kept her voice low, even though the conversation in the room was growing louder, as if from the approach of the sheriff. As if from the approach of the sense of security the news gave them.

"How about you tell me," Joan said to Josh, "just why you were marking up my map? Looked like a ring to me, and I have a right to know what you're doing on my land."

Josh clearly hesitated. His gaze grew distant, as if he saw something miles away, then snapped back to look at Joan.

"My group is out there creating a perimeter of protection. In theory, anything crosses their barrier and we'll know it."

Joan nodded slowly. "And you're not giving us details of them surrounding us because...?"

Krystal spoke. "Because there's an army out there ringed around us. You want to create a panic, Mom?"

Joan drew a deep breath, looking nearly shocked. "Sad to say..." She shook her head. "Okay. I'll feed your people when they can come in."

Josh answered, his voice hard again, "You'll never see most of them. And that's the way they want it."

Even as the room began to recover its life, even as the storm seemed to quiet down a bit outside, a dome of silence seemed to settle over the table where the three of them sat.

"You know," Joan remarked eventually, "I've lived my entire life right here and I can't recall a storm this bad. But then, I can't recall two murders either."

IT FELT LIKE forever to Krystal, but at last flashing blue and red lights appeared, splintered through the stained glass of the double front doors.

Nobody moved. Except Josh. "Stop the stampede if you can," he said to Joan and Krystal, then strode quickly to the doors.

He wasn't far from his description of a stampede. Everyone wanted to get outside to the safety of the sheriff's presence.

Josh paused at the door and spoke loudly, demanding attention. "Stay where you are. We don't know what's out there. We don't want to interfere with the law." He saw Krystal and Joan moving swiftly through the knots of their clients, speaking quietly. Soothingly. The urgent rush to the door eased.

Then he stepped outside into the bath of swirling lights from roof racks and bumpers on three Humvees.

A tall man covered in a yellow slicker, with his cowboy hat protected by an elastic version, stepped out of the first vehicle. He held out a hand to Josh.

"I'm Dalton," he said. "If you recall from the sled dog place. And you're Josh from the compound, as I remember."

Josh nodded. So the sheriff had checked him out beyond the light interview last year from a deputy and since their meeting at Harris's place. Probably knew everything there was to know about the guys at the stockade, too. Well, that would make things easier.

"Two murders?" Dalton asked. As he turned his head, Josh caught sight again of the shiny burn scar that covered most of Dalton's face. The man had clearly known his share of hell. Josh's confidence in the help they'd receive rose a few notches.

"How are you sure they're murders?" Dalton asked.

"Seen enough of it. First one was a bullet to the head. Execution-style from the back."

"So the perp probably knew the attacker."

"Maybe." The thought of Mason's agent danced across his mind. But while the author might be difficult to deal with, why would Darlene Dana cut off her cash cow?

"And the other?"

"A whole lot messier. Stab wounds. One shot that misdirected to a femoral artery."

"Hmm." Dalton rubbed his chin. "Same perp? Different methods. Maybe not so easy the second time. Or maybe the killer was having trouble stomaching the first killing."

Josh shook his head. "Knife wounds hardly indicate sudden squeamishness. But it could have been the other way around, stabbing first. You guys will know better than I can."

"Reckon so." Then Gage faced him directly. "You got your guys out here, that man of yours said when he came down the mountain. Perimeter?"

Josh nodded. "I'll call 'em back if you want. Hell, they'd probably like to get to the stockade themselves. Right now, between us, we've got a lot of folks out there, maybe starting to step on each other with your people."

Gage turned a little to the right, staring into the rain and still-rumbling storm. "If you can keep 'em out there, to help my deputies, I'd be grateful. Up to them, of course. I need to send a few people inside to start questioning the residents here, but I don't exactly have a crowd of deputies with me. Storm's causing trouble down the mountain, too."

Josh hesitated. "My soldiers don't want much interaction, Sheriff. Makes 'em uncomfortable. Sometimes too uncomfortable to endure."

"I get it. I'll tell my units to tread carefully. We just need eyes on this situation. The more the better. Yours would be helpful."

Josh understood from a tactical point of view. But he also knew that coming out to help with this operation had already been a sore trial for his vets. "I can only ask them. I stopped giving orders years ago."

"Fair enough." Then with a hand signal, Dalton began to unload his Humvees. Several deputies he sent inside. The rest he began to arrange in accord with his own terrain map spread under a light in the front seat of one of the vehicles. He asked Josh to point out the two cabins where the murders had happened and where he thought his own troops might be.

Then the criminal part of the investigation began.

COMMS STILL HADN'T come back and Josh was reaching a level of frustration unusual for him. Damn it, he needed to be able to coordinate his unit easily. The sheriff needed that.

And yeah, war had put him in such situations before, but that didn't mean he liked it. Everything became ten times as difficult.

Inside he found two deputies, a man and a woman, dominating the setup, sitting at a table. A couple of other deputies wandered around casually, as if hoping to overhear something that wouldn't emerge in direct questioning. They'd all shed their yellow rain gear, revealing the comforting sight of their police uniforms.

And they *were* bringing comfort. Josh felt as if the air inside the room had changed. As if the pressure had vanished.

This crew of artists might still make it through this situation without developing crazy ideas and opposing plans of operation. No growth of opposing camps that he could see. Plenty of reason to be grateful for that.

Joan handed out insulated carafes of coffee to the deputies along with sweet rolls. Both were received with gratitude.

But the questioning began, as it had to. The smallest piece of information might be important.

And they started with the most terrified witness of all: Darlene Dana. That woman still trembled, as if she couldn't grasp what she had seen that morning. As if it were beyond her to accept the harsh reality.

Some matters could definitely be harder to accept than others. The sad thing was when you started to accept them as a normal part of reality. Soldiers knew that. That's why he had a stockade full of them.

Back in Joan's office, he began to get in touch with his group as best he could. Hardly surprising to him was the way these guys wanted to stay on duty. They were doing something useful, following plans that had once been part of their lives. Becoming themselves again.

Nine steps back in their recovery but Josh wouldn't have deprived them of renewed feelings of usefulness. Not for any reason. They needed it. They could and would catch up later with their work toward recovery. These soldiers were filled with determination and grit.

He joined Krystal at a table out front.

"Hard to believe," she said, "that this has been going on for almost a day."

"Getting late," he agreed, glancing at his watch.

"Nobody is going to sleep for a while."

He smiled faintly. "Does that surprise you?"

"No." She laughed quietly. "It'll be interesting to watch them crash out eventually."

Then she looked around at the room in a way that troubled him. He could almost see her shudder, then she spoke. "I can't believe that one of the people here is a murderer."

"Always the quiet ones." Josh cited a canard he'd never quite believed. He sipped the coffee Joan had swung by to deliver.

"So they claim. But this place is full of quiet types. That one isn't going to work here."

"Maybe not. But why don't you tell me about the people you've gotten to know, at least a little."

She clearly gave that some thought. "Like I might pick up a clue?"

"Why not? That deputy over there, what's her name? Connie Parish? She's going to be asking you for the same information before long."

"Probably. Except you wouldn't let me see much out there at the cabins, so what do I know?"

"Just as well. Trust me. So tell me about the people around us. That's what you *do* know."

Krystal returned her attention to the groups of residents. "Well, there's Paul Aston, over there with the sloppy clothes and almost no hair. You gathered him up earlier."

"Still manages an Einstein look."

Krystal nodded. "You ever figure out how he does that with so little hair, let me know."

"So, what about him?"

"Poet, which doesn't mean anything by itself. Just that he's more introverted than most. In any summer we'll hardly see him, unless he feels a need to walk in the woods. Even then it's a rare sighting."

"I hear poets don't make a lot of money."

Her mouth lifted at one corner. "You hear right."

"So how's he manage to come here?"

"Scholarship. We do a few every year."

Josh nodded, absorbing the information. "What makes him special?"

"He's got a name, if not money. Once in a while he'll even talk to some of our clients who are interested in poetry. Not very often, though."

"So, like a box-office draw?"

Finally he pulled a laugh from her. Quiet, but still a genuine laugh. "Yeah. Good name to have on the annual flyer."

He twisted on his chair, leaning toward her. "What about this Mason guy?"

Krystal leaned back, sighing. "God, that man is—was—a piece of work. I don't think I've ever met anyone with a bigger ego and he didn't care who knew it. Abrasive. I'll never understand why he always had a coterie of followers when he showed up here for meals. It was like he was holding court and loved every minute of it. I honestly don't know how his agent could stand him."

"Money," Josh said flatly. "Bestseller?"

"Always. And if you want my opinion," she burst out, "I never saw a man more likely to become a murder victim."

"Whoa," Josh said quietly.

Krystal looked away, plainly embarrassed by her outburst.

Josh reached across the table and squeezed her hand gently. "I wasn't telling you to stop. Not criticizing you. Just kind of amazed that the guy created such an impression."

"He wasn't forgettable. Ever."

Connie Parish took that moment to come to their table with a notepad. She sat, looking at the two of them. "You were at the beginning of all this?"

"Depends on where you want to begin," Krystal answered. "Someone shot one of Harris Belcher's sled dogs and left it outside Josh's stockade. At least they were able to rescue the animal and Harris was able to take care of it. Then Reject adopted me." She pointed with her chin toward the dog, who was sleeping on a braided rug by the windows.

Connie's brows lifted. "Well, that's definitely a point of interest. Nobody should want to shoot one of Harris's dogs."

"According to Harris, they'd have had to remove him from his kennel. Then they took him a ways into the forest before they shot him."

Connie swore. "Some things I will never understand. Others I know too well." She looked at Josh. "I'm sure you do, too. So you folks saved the dog?"

Josh nodded.

Krystal shook her head. "I can't remember everything in order, Connie. It's been too much today. Josh came over to tell us about the dog. He was pretty angry with all of us, but he also felt it was some kind of message to his group."

That caught Connie's full attention. "Reason for that?"

Josh's mouth twisted. "Give me one reason anyone around here would be happy with our group holed up in that stockade like hermits. Thought maybe someone wanted us to leave."

Connie nodded. "You guys don't strike me as the leaving type."

"We aren't."

Krystal again saw that steel in Josh. The man who could probably handle just about anything. No, he had no intention of leaving or of taking away the protection he was giving his own people.

"Okay," Connie said after she'd made a note. "How did things unfold with Mason's murder? I'm starting to get the impression that no one in this room is particularly surprised by it or very upset by it. Except his agent."

Krystal answered frankly, "You'd probably be right. Not well-liked except by a few. If any."

Connie made another note, then turned to Josh again. "You guys keep to yourselves, if I understand correctly. What were you doing over here when the murder happened?"

That almost sounded like an accusation. Krystal stiffened but Josh remained relaxed.

"I came to bring Reject, the injured dog, to Krystal. He apparently preferred to be with her over me. Understandable." Josh sounded ever so slightly sarcastic. "Anyway, when we got back here, Reject started getting upset at the windows. First howling like he was on watch. Then growling, so I went out to find out what was bugging him enough to growl. That's when I found Darlene Dana a soaked mess at the edge of the woods."

"A *terrified* mess," Krystal added. "I don't think I've ever seen anyone so scared."

More notes for Connie. "So the dog alerted?"

Josh answered, "He acted like there was something out there that he didn't like at all. The growl was such a change, such a deep one, that I became convinced that whatever was out there was seriously bad."

"And your guys started a perimeter."

Josh looked stony, as if he expected criticism. "Yeah. They started closing in around this place."

"Anyway," Krystal said, picking up the story because she understood how Josh must feel, given the protectiveness he'd shown toward his group. She didn't want him to feel attacked once again. "Josh asked me if anyone was missing from our gathering here. Then we went out looking for them. And that's when we found Sebastian Elsin dead, too. Uglier, from what Josh said."

"So it's been a long day for you guys."

Krystal glanced at the clock over one of the fireplaces. Nearly 3:00 a.m. "Slightly."

"And Gage has been out this way twice. Once for the dog report. Then after all the communications failed and you all had your guy come down to town to report murder."

There didn't seem to be any response needed. It was the way things had unfolded. A few days that had grown darker and uglier from the point when Reject had been injured. When the vet, Mike Windwalker, had trudged up here in the middle of the night. When the storm had started a quiet grumbling that now had become almost deafening.

When a message had been left for the vets in the compound? Krystal could understand why Josh might see it that way, but how could a dog's mistreatment be linked to the murder of a man who'd had nothing to do with the dog? That was the only part of this she couldn't add up in some way. Or even Seb's murder. As far as she knew, he and Mason had never even shared a drink.

"Seb didn't know Mason," Krystal volunteered. "I can't imagine any reason both of them should have been murdered."

Connie nodded and scribbled some more in her notebook. "That's interesting. Did they have some kind of problem with one another?"

Krystal shook her head. "Just different people. Seb liked being alone. Mason liked being the center of attention."

Then Connie looked up and asked her last question. "Is there anyone here with a special grudge against Mason Cambridge?"

Krystal couldn't help herself. Even in these horrific times, she couldn't quite govern her sense of humor. "Maybe his editor, but she wasn't here."

Connie almost laughed but managed to maintain a professional demeanor. Krystal could see the humorous glint in her gaze, however. "Should be an easy one" was Connie's answer. "Note that I said *should* and not *will*." Sighing, she shook her head and rose. "You two think of anything else, I wanna hear it. Now back to the emotional mob."

Connie had probably nailed it, Krystal thought. While

the room seemed to have calmed overall, people still grew visibly excited when they were questioned. Close to a mob at times.

"I wonder," Josh said, "what they could possibly have to add to this day?"

"Maybe things we didn't see when we were outside."

"Or maybe a whole lot of speculation."

"Like one of us said earlier, that could be fun. And this damn day needs some fun."

Krystal lifted Reject onto a chair beside her and she began to stroke his silky fur. He looked up at her from blue eyes, the adoring eyes that only a dog could have.

"Why do you suppose Reject wanted *me*?" Krystal wondered.

"Who knows? The dog picked you. That ought to be good enough."

She met Josh's gaze and saw warmth there. Warmth after a day from hell. Recalling his brief embrace from earlier, she wished she could just crawl into his arms and seek that feeling of safety again.

As soon as she had the thought, she yanked herself back from it. She was no weakling to depend on anyone for a sense of security. She was strong enough in herself.

Although today had made her wonder a bit. She thought of the time they'd spent out there in that violent storm. Unseen things whipping around hard enough to tear her poncho in a couple of places. Had she felt fear? Uneasiness? Hell, yes. Like when the lightning nearly struck her and Davis. The power out there dwarfed puny humans. But she'd gone out there anyway. Too brave for her own good?

She put her cheek in her hand and just wished for an easy resolution to all of this. Easy and quick.

A chair pulled back at the table and Krystal looked up to see Julia Jansen joining them. Julia painted mostly abstractionist oils. "I thought it was high time to thank the two of you for rescuing me from the storm. I don't know what I'd have done out there on my own. At first I thought it wasn't that bad, but I'm not used to storms this violent."

"Neither am I," Krystal answered. "I kinda feel like Mother Earth is getting even for something."

Julia nodded, dark eyes framed by long dark hair and high cheekbones. "I keep thinking of that creek out there. Imagining how the canyon is bound to flood."

"It probably will, but we've built high enough to be above the flood zone."

Krystal hoped she sounded sure enough to be believable, because the fact was that she couldn't know for certain. Something in the past had carved that canyon. Something violent enough to carry away rocks and carve the steep walls.

Julia sighed, looking weary. "I'm not going to be able to sleep. I'm not sure anyone will, but I don't mind telling you this is scary. Two people dead and no reason for it. And how do we know that a killer or killers aren't getting closer? Or maybe are somewhere in this room?"

Josh spoke kindly. "Hardly likely anyone can get away with another murder in a room this crowded."

Julia appeared to accept what he said, but Krystal didn't believe it. In a crowd it would be easy to knife someone without being spotted.

Her skin had begun to crawl again. She needed to do something. Anything.

Then she spoke quietly, noting a movement that Josh had warned her to pay attention to. "People are breaking up into groups."

Julia drew a sharp breath. "What's that mean?"

Josh swore quietly. "I gotta get around this room and find out why people are dividing."

Krystal shook her head sharply and stood up. "They'll trust me easier than you." She leaned over and briefly squeezed Julia's wrist. "You stay here with Josh. You'll be safe."

The first place Krystal headed was the small group gathered around Darlene Dana. She appeared to be coming down from her earlier shock and spoke only kindly of Mason. Krystal wondered wryly if Mason had been some kind of Jekyll and Hyde, changing personalities when with his agent.

But the conversation seemed benign enough.

The clustering she was finding around the room didn't seem anywhere near as benign. Some of the clusters were trying to pick out people in the room who they mistrusted. People who might be responsible for this terror. Bordering on ugly, hateful and possibly deadly theories.

Then there were the others, much quieter, less conspiracy-minded. Relying on the sheriff and his deputies to take care of the matter. Inclined to feel safer among so many in this room.

Trouble was brewing, she realized, and she didn't know how to control it or slow it down. A conflict between the opposing viewpoints could get ugly.

Making her way back to Josh, she sat at the table. Julia

had moved on to talk with Darlene. "It's getting nasty out there. Some people are blowing up conspiracy theories and pointing fingers at others."

Josh nodded. "Knew it couldn't be long. People are freaking predictable."

"So, what can I do? What can *we* do?"

"Establish some kind of control."

"How the hell do we do that?"

"I'm thinking."

Well, she supposed that was a good sign. Josh certainly had to have more experience with this kind of situation. She'd never had one in her life.

"Hell," he said finally, and reached for his walkie. The first person he reached was the sheriff. "Gage? What would you say to me asking some of my guys to come in here? Preemptive crowd control."

Gage's voice crackled in the affirmative. "We've found a few things. Tell you when we get back there. In the meantime, some control would be useful."

Josh ended the call, then stared down at his walkie as if it were a snake. "God, I don't want to ask this of my guys. Do you have any idea how far this could set them back?"

He shook his head, then met Krystal's gaze. "No alternative."

She felt her heart breaking as she looked at this man forced to abandon a goal he'd been fighting for for a long time now. Then he changed the channel on the walkie and put through the call.

"Angus? I need a few volunteers to come into the lodge. The place is loaded with people who are on edge, if you get me. Thanks."

Then he jumped up from the table and headed for the privacy of Joan's office. Once there he looked down at the map, then began rolling it up into a tight tube. "There it goes," he said bitterly. "All that striving, all that trying. Back into the war zone."

Krystal's heart went from breaking to shattering. All those lives about to be wasted again because some idiots in the lodge couldn't be trusted to exercise their own self-control.

But what could she say? When Josh surprised her by pulling her into his arms, she had no doubt which way the comfort was flowing.

She'd give him everything she had.

Chapter Eight

Four of Josh's soldiers appeared at the lodge in about twenty minutes. Three men and a woman who looked as if she could carry any load the guys could. The tromp of their booted feet, in cadence, had brought Krystal and Josh from Joan's office.

The room fell silent, staring in amazement at this unexpected invasion. None of the four carried guns, Krystal noted, but the potential threat was hardly less visible as they stood there in a straight line, at attention, in their camo clothing and ponchos.

One spoke. "Reporting for duty, Colonel."

Josh answered, "Thanks, Angus. I appreciate you all volunteering." Then he looked around at a room that had gone from stunned to whispering. "These soldiers are here to protect you. Even from yourselves. If I were you, I wouldn't want to make it difficult for them to provide that protection."

Joan emerged from the kitchen with Donna Carstairs, her chief cook. "Josh? Okay to offer coffee and food to your soldiers?"

"After today, I'm sure they'd be grateful. At ease, troops."

At once the four soldiers broke from formation and

scattered around the room. The effect was to make them appear less of a threat. Yet people remained wary and startled by their arrival.

Krystal, for her part, was grateful that Mason Cambridge couldn't be here. She could just imagine the story he'd weave around the presence of the soldiers.

But people started to talk. Started to hear that these soldiers, so long hidden behind stockade walls, had emerged to protect them all.

Moods gradually became friendlier.

And some of that ugly talk faded away.

Except, of course, the inevitable wondering about whether a murderer was in this room right now. People kept looking around, aware that a threat could be standing only a few feet away.

Soldiers or not, the situation was explosive.

JOSH WATCHED THE soldiers spread out, helping themselves to food but speaking to no one. He wished he could gather them into a group session right now, to help them over this hump of being surrounded by civilians, the very people who had failed to understand them when they needed it most.

Instead of looking as if they needed some reassurance to get through this trial, however, they'd become stoic, revealing nothing of the inner turmoil they must be experiencing from this exposure.

He walked among them, sharing a few quiet words, thanking them. They all nodded, and at least none of them showed the thousand-yard stare that could have warned of trouble. None of this group of four had disconnected in the least way.

And he thought he felt their gratitude when he added an expression of his pride in the way they were handling the situation.

Carly Narth, whose experience had left her with a scarred face, shrugged. "Gotta do what you gotta do, Colonel."

He watched her turn away, changing the direction of her attention again to the crowd they were keeping an eye on. Carly had a terrible story. A roadside bomb had burned her badly. That had been awful enough, but when she'd come home she'd learned that her own family wouldn't look at her. They couldn't handle her injury and didn't want to.

Nor had the rest of the world been much kinder. It was a wonder she showed her face to anyone anywhere. But in this room, her defiance was almost palpable.

KRYSTAL WAS JUST about reaching the point of sleeping upright while leaning against a wall when the sheriff returned along with two of his deputies.

He pulled his hat off, shaking the hair that had nevertheless managed to get wet despite his rain protection. "We've got the crime areas cordoned off. Nobody gets inside those zones. It's a damn mess. Anyway, we'll be back in the morning with more extensive help and the crime scene unit." He glanced around the room. "You gonna need any extra help here?"

He had to have noted the edginess of the room in one sweep of his gaze.

"At the moment," Josh answered, "I'd say no."

Gage nodded, once again sweeping the room with his dark gaze. "Okay. We're starting to get some comms back, mostly landlines, a few satellite phones, but with a telephone tree you ought to be able to reach us from here. Keep people off the internet and off their cells, though."

Josh nodded. "Lousy bandwidth?"

"The lousiest." Gage slapped his hat back on his head and turned to take his deputies from the lodge with him. Then he paused, speaking to the deputy Josh had met earlier. "Connie? You mind hanging around here?"

"Not in the least, boss."

"Just keep me posted."

Then with a sweep, all the deputies but one left the lodge. Connie put her feet up on one table and watched the room over the edge of a coffee cup. She didn't look the least bit weary. And her uniform provided another layer of authority.

Because the room was beginning to seethe again. People were uneasy. Lacking any useful information. Knowing only that terrible things were happening and they were stuck in a virtual cave. No place to run, no place to hide. Faces were growing tighter, more worried. With the sheriff gone there was even less reason for peace.

But the presence of Josh's people in the room seemed to be keeping the cork stuffed in the bottle. As if these seemingly frightened people didn't want to get involved with those hard-eyed veterans. Nor should they.

Reject, who'd been curled up quietly as near as he could get to Krystal, suddenly raised his head, ears perked. He didn't make a sound, not even a growl, but he looked around as if measuring something.

But what?

Josh caught sight of the husky's awareness, too, and scanned the room, following the dog's gaze. Something wasn't right, and it wasn't right in this room.

But how could that be possible? Damn near everyone had been sitting here all day. A few had left only to return as the lousy weather made remaining alone in their cabins an unattractive option.

But could a murderer really be sitting here among them? The question had crossed Krystal's mind and made her no less uneasy now. But how could anyone tell?

She met Josh's gaze, saw the steeliness returning. He wasn't dismissing the possibility.

But even if the killer was right here with them, how could they know? If one more person fell to the blade of a knife, how could anyone know who the killer was? Too many people.

As awful as this day had been, for the first time Krystal felt a real sense of hopelessness. Then there was Reject. He had become alert, and now he jumped down awkwardly from his chair and began to move from person to person as if seeking a pat. Most obliged him.

Krystal looked at Josh. "Could he smell something?"

"God knows. This day would have probably washed away anything but a pigsty."

He had a point, but Reject continued his trip around the room, accepting tidbits of food when they were offered.

Krystal's gaze slipped to the heavily curtained windows again. A bullet had come through that glass. Aimed at no one, it seemed, but maybe aimed at anyone. And the point of that? To instill more terror? To confuse everything more?

"Hell," she muttered.

Josh looked at her. "What?"

"I'm just wishing we were down closer to Conard City. Surrounded by neighbors, all of whom give a damn and know everything on the grapevine."

One corner of his hard mouth lifted. "You feel like that often?"

"Actually, no," she admitted. "I went to school with a lot of people down there and I can drop in for a visit anytime I want. It's not like I'm any more isolated than I want to be."

"So what's changed?"

She twisted her mouth. "Other than a crazed killer?"

He nodded slowly. "Tell you what. You try to catch some sleep on that couch in your mother's office. I'll keep watch over you."

"That's a generous offer," she answered more warmly than she intended. "But you've got more important things to watch."

He shook his head. "I've got four good helpers, and all of them are going to need to cadge their own sleep in stages. You just take yours now. You'll be more useful."

Useful? she wondered as she headed back to Joan's office. Joan had already claimed the recliner and appeared to be out like a light. Good. She'd been going nonstop since early that morning.

Grabbing a blanket, Krystal curled up on the sofa and wondered if she'd be able to sleep at all.

But she did. It was as if Josh's presence out there lifted some of her worries.

At least for a while.

JOSH KEPT AN eye on the lodge great room, and Krystal, all night. He was used to doing without sleep as long as necessary, and this was one of those nights.

Perplexity troubled him, though. Two people murdered by different methods.

And then, what about Reject? Why would anyone attack that dog? And the bigger question: Who the hell had put a bullet through that window? No one had been out there to do that, had they? At least not from the lodge, as far as he knew. And why? Just to terrorize everyone? Or to cause them to close the curtains and see nothing outside.

That latter thought gave him heartburn. Reduced visibility was a dangerous problem.

How many killers might there be? Who might have been missing in the hours before anyone suspected there had been murders? He was ready to discount the people they had gathered up from their cabins. None of them appeared capable of such killing, although anything was possible.

God. He rubbed his eyes and resumed his study of the room. He noticed his own unit was just as busy watching, even as the clients in the room began to fall asleep with their heads on tables, their bodies spread on area rugs. Filling whatever comfortable chairs they might have found.

The thunder, at least, had finally drawn into the distance. Maybe morning, bringing the sheriff and his experienced teams, would shed light on everything. Maybe they'd even have some *actual* light to see by. Not that he was eager to see any more detail in those two cabins.

He didn't need imagination to fill in what his flashlight beam had missed.

Reject evidently finished his survey of the room, keeping his secrets in the way of a dog, and struggled up onto the chair beside Josh. Josh reached out to pet the animal. Dogs were such wonderful companions that he often thought people didn't deserve them.

He eventually noticed one person who seemed more restless than the others. Mary Collins, wasn't it? A romance novelist who'd been published. Was fear keeping her awake?

Damn, he'd never imagined that he'd get to know any of these people, let alone by name. His whole purpose in being in this area was to provide a refuge and psychological care to vets most in need.

Being a psychologist didn't necessarily give him special insights, but his time in uniform had given him a connection few who had only sat behind desks as professionals could have had.

Maybe he was kidding himself that he was doing these vets of his any particular good. But some at times felt ready to move on, which he counted a victory. Others might never be ready.

Josh never judged them. Judgment was the last thing any of them deserved or needed. They'd know when their own time to leave came.

And right now, this group looked filled with purpose and determination. That had to be a good thing. Maybe. Or it could be slashing old wounds open. No way to guess at this point.

Then his thoughts drifted to Krystal and he closed his eyes briefly. She was the most attractive woman he'd met in years, and it wasn't just her natural beauty. Her intelligence. Her courage. She'd insisted on going out with him into that storm earlier, even knowing the possible dangers they faced.

It was the kind of behavior he expected from women in uniform, not from quiet, inexperienced civilians who weren't on a steroid rush.

Krystal embodied a lot of things he admired. And felt attracted to.

And he was wasting his time daydreaming. He'd chosen his path in life, an important one, and he wasn't about to start shredding it. Too many people relied on him.

Their faces floated before his mind's eye, faces that he'd come to know well for the most part. Faces that hid the unending internal battles they fought. He couldn't possibly tear that group apart in pursuit of selfish ends.

All of it was pipe dreaming anyway. They had a much more immediate issue to deal with: murders. One or two perpetrators? The idea of a single killer seriously bothered him, given the difference in the crimes, and he wondered if he could possibly get some of Gage's impressions about the murders. Although he'd learned cops were pretty silent about ongoing investigations, there was always the hope Gage might be of a different mind under these circumstances.

But then morning brought a new list of troubles. Of course, these artists wanted to get back to their cabins for their computers, for a change of clothes. For some semblance of normal life.

And of course, they started convincing themselves the threat had passed. No more murders so far. A great metric. Not.

Josh drew a steadying breath and began to make plans for a new problem, one that at least probably had the sense to wait until after Joan had served breakfast. Then this crowd would try to move out.

LYING IN THE middle of the room, Mary Collins thought about how easy she had found it to locate a coconspirator in the murder of Mason Cambridge. Enough people around here hated the man with a purple passion.

But only Mel Marbly had a desire as strong as her own to end the existence of Cambridge. Mason had spent a lot of time insulting Mel Marbly about his gardening work. Called him a dirt pusher, a mud rat, a stupid sod farmer. Criticized him constantly for dirt under his fingernails. Called him a dolt.

More insults than any man should have to take and Mel had been taking those shots for years now. It was as if Mason Cambridge needed to look down on anyone who actually worked with their hands. And somehow Mason had managed not to toss his insults when the Metcalfes were around, and Mel hadn't complained to them.

But Mary had heard. The whole thing disgusted her until her stomach turned over every time she heard Mason. She'd often seen hate glowing in Brady Marbly's eyes as well. Perhaps more than her husband Mel's.

But Mary knew neither Brady's nor Mel's feelings of rage for the insults they'd endured could come close to her own feelings of hatred. Her *justified* feelings of hatred.

For Mason had stolen from her. Had taken her dreams and claimed credit for them. Had used them to launch a career that should have been her own.

Mary hadn't stopped seething in years. The calmer voices of friends, who reminded her that ideas couldn't be copyrighted, made her feel no better. Reminders that a book never would have been written since Shakespeare if no ideas could be copied helped Mary not at all.

None of it meant a thing to her. Vengeance meant everything and that man deserved to pay for treating her like dust beneath his heels. She hadn't mattered to him, not even enough to give her credit for her ideas.

She'd been useful. Nothing more. Catapulting him to a career as a bestseller when he stole her idea, leaving her nothing but life as a mid-list romance novelist.

Because even though her ideas were better than Mason's, they got brushed aside by publishers because Mason was going to do it better. Or maybe not so much better, but he was guaranteed huge sales.

Right. He'd stolen her chance and wouldn't give even part of it back to her.

But Mel was serving her well. He'd wanted to kill Mason, but he'd decided to stab Sebastian to death to make it look like a different kind of crime. Then the bullet through the window at that damn dog. A brilliant touch, if she did say so herself, although she feared Mel was getting his own ideas, might mess things up. Too many victims. Too many possibilities now. Would that cause confusion or lead the cops right to Mel?

She hated dogs, but this one had become a freaking nuisance. He was next on her list if Mel didn't mess things up. Still, she needed to find a private minute with Mel in order to make sure he was still largely in line with her. Especially since he wounded the damn dog in the first place, without clearing it with her. Still, it had proved to be a touch that had added to the terror. Maybe not a mistake on Mel's part. She still hadn't made up her mind about Sebastian, much as his murder must be muddying the waters.

But Mel was beginning to make her seriously uneasy.

In the meantime, she sat back, pretending occasionally to join the general fear, and just enjoyed all that she had unleashed. She hadn't expected quite this much uproar over one dead author.

She should have guessed. Mason would do everything in the biggest way possible, even die. But never had she guessed that she could enjoy the reaction to his murder as much as his murder itself. Life *did* offer some gifts, few though they were.

Then she looked at the soldiers, including that one who had appeared to be in charge. She hadn't expected them. Since a year ago when the stockade had started to be built, she had known they liked to be left alone. They wanted no part of the rest of the world except the two or three who occasionally went shopping for essentials in Conard City.

Now they were out and about, at least some of them, and they made her skin crawl. Unpredictable creeps, likely to explode into violence without warning. Wasn't that what these PTSD guys did?

Even the sheriff and his jerks didn't worry her as much. Then she forced her attention away, for fear she might draw notice by focusing too much. She had more important matters to deal with anyway. Much more important.

Like making sure she took care of the Marblys before they could talk. Then to get out of here unscathed.

She had confidence in her abilities to escape. After all, look what Mason had achieved just because of her. *Mary* was the one with the brilliant, devious mind.

She ordered another coffee and half dozed as she watched the room. Not long before something would start happening, she felt. The only question was whether she should take advantage of it just yet.

THE COMPOSITION OF the room started to change as the few remaining deputies, cold and exhausted from a long night in the rain, began to rotate through to take advantage of the hot coffee and sweet rolls Joan and her staff provided.

As near as Krystal could tell, the crime scene units were out at the cabins, but no information could be shared yet.

The room did calm, however, as if the growing desire to escape eased, at least for now. As if the presence of those uniformed deputies changed the mental landscape. Even those who had been talking of returning to their own cabins decided to delay in favor of coffee and rolls.

Josh's soldiers switched off duty then, too. Grabbing something to eat, then heading out, four more to follow them into the lodge.

When Krystal had the chance for a quiet word with Josh, she murmured, "I thought these guys didn't want to be out here with us."

"They don't. But they feel a duty."

In those few words he offered a flood of information. Krystal studied the soldiers with new respect, noting for the first time how many of them were visibly injured. Regardless, they all showed backbones of steel.

"What exactly do you do for them?"

"I'm a psychologist. I'm also a veteran."

Another few words containing a flood of information. And for the first time he shared with her his purpose. His meaning. More than just providing a sanctuary for the wounded.

Her respect for him deepened. This task of his was momentous.

But what had she done with her own life? Dabble at a novel? Help run this writers' retreat, some of which managed to seem awfully indulgent. Although she had to admit her own indulgence in her private little cottage on the creek canyon. Sure, she had duties at the lodge, primarily helping her mother and the staff, but what else of importance did she accomplish?

Hours of scribbling a few words on an otherwise empty computer screen.

"Write anything at all," Davis Daniels had suggested. That didn't seem to work well for her. She needed something more organized to focus on.

Hah! Maybe she should start at the middle or the end of a story and see where that got her. When she'd first started writing, that had been a problem for her: a vivid beginning, then the end too clear not to write immediately, both of them surrounding a big, gaping hole she couldn't figure out how to fill. Some part of her simply felt the story was completed even though it clearly wasn't.

She'd had a lot of those false starts in her bottom drawer until she'd finally thrown them on her fireplace. No point in keeping useless ideas.

But sometimes she missed them because they had been

so much fun to write. So absorbing they'd carried her totally away.

She was having no such luck this time. Rising, she went to help Joan and the kitchen staff churn out enough food for a suddenly hungry army. The night's storm had begun to drift away, letting patches of sunlight through, and only the dripping of rain from the leaves remained as a reminder.

Even some of the curtains had been drawn open to let in the freshening light. People avoided the open ones, which was kind of ridiculous to Krystal's way of thinking, given that she suspected a whole lot of them were wanting to get back to their cabins, which would expose them far more than the windows.

The urge to return to private cabins grew even stronger when Angus MacDougall and Josh climbed up to the roof to realign the satellite dish. After a few false starts, computers came on again, and people started using their cell phones and satellite phones.

The world had returned to normal.

Except for two corpses lying out there. Except for the inescapable presence of one or two murderers.

Yeah, normal, Krystal thought. Not the kind of normal any of them should want.

THE COPS WEREN'T off duty, however. As they warmed up and ate, they moved among the residents, talking quietly, explaining that, at this time, the other cabins appeared safe.

"No signs of breaking and entering," Krystal heard more than one of them say. "But that doesn't necessarily mean there can't be."

Uneasy looks passed around the room, then the remaining poet, Paul Aston of the crazy hair, raised his voice. "Then just what the hell are we supposed to do, Deputy? Hang around here all day with no good reason? We have *work*."

Sheriff Gage Dalton had come into the room unseen, but when he lifted his voice he claimed everyone's attention. "Stick it out a few more hours," he said firmly. "You don't know what's out there and why this happened. But if you really want to race out there by yourselves, be my guest. I can't stop you. Just stay away from the areas marked off with yellow crime scene tape." He stepped outside, probably to speak to some of his deputies.

Well, that dampened the growing restlessness, although probably only temporarily. At some point these people were going to honestly decide the threat was over. That someone had a grudge against Mason Cambridge, easily understandable, and Sebastian Elsin had just gotten in the way of a vendetta.

It sure made more sense than any other explanation.

But what were they going to find when they got out there?

DARLENE, MASON'S AGENT, was having the hardest time of anyone. That, too, was understandable. She'd found the body. That alone would have seriously shaken anyone to the core. But to have it be the body of someone she knew well? Far worse.

Darlene didn't seem to want any physical comfort, not a hug or a pat on the shoulder. She remained curled up in a padded chair, wrapped in a blanket and sipping hot chocolate whenever Joan, Krystal or the staff thought to bring it to her. And her hands had never stopped shaking, most especially when Connie had interviewed her about what she had seen.

The woman needed an ambulance, Krystal thought, but getting one up here right now seemed difficult. Mud and more mud layered the road outside, and then came the first low rumble. Landslide. Inevitable. Krystal prayed it would remain in the confines of the canyon, where it would do less harm. Usually such floods did, although they could make a mess of the canyon for a while.

"Okay," Gage Dalton announced as he reappeared, grabbing all the attention in the room. "It's a mess out there. You've already been told it's bad, but now we have landslides. I have no way of knowing how long they'll last or how bad they'll be. If anyone here decides to venture out, then you'd better take someone with you. I'd prefer you didn't, though. I'm having to bring up a lot of heavy-duty equipment from the county, and from neighboring counties as well, and we're going to need some of it at lower elevations."

He paused, looking around, clearly gauging the responses. "You go out there on your own, you're going to *be* on your own. I don't have the manpower to dig you all out."

Krystal shuddered. Frankly, she couldn't imagine much worse than being buried alive in mud. Inevitably, she looked toward the porch windows and wondered if they'd hold against an onslaught, especially the one with the bullet hole in it.

But the impatient swirling in the room had started to settle down again, and Krystal had reached the end of her rope. Using her jacket as a pillow, she gathered it up and used it on the table as a place to rest her head. For a little while, she woke occasionally as if she couldn't quite rest with all the people around, but at last sleep claimed her in a deep embrace.

Dreams of Josh followed her, however. Dreams of the confident way he moved, the force in his voice when it was needed, his surprising gentleness with his vets.

Hard and soft. She liked both.

Chapter Nine

Josh kept an eye on Krystal as she slept bent over the table, thinking she was going to ache like hell when she woke.

But he had other concerns running alongside thoughts of her. Sheriff Dalton was of the opinion that the landslides were pretty much stopping. He sent some of his Humvees out to check and they came back with reasonably good news.

Which left the crowd in the lodge great room. Their urge to get out of the place was growing by the minute. But what would they find when they got out there?

Then Angus appeared, radio in hand. "How much help you want?"

"How much you got?"

"Damn near everybody. Any of their reticence has vanished."

Of course it had, Josh thought. The kind of emergency these people had trained for, had faced for so many years. They knew what to do in this situation and right now needed no plans or directions for the unknowns of the civilian world.

This could also throw them back into their personal

hells, but Josh couldn't bring himself to deprive these men and women of their renewed sense of purpose.

He suggested, "They want to escort people back to their cabins? Because there's no guarantee these artists will be able to find them easily after this storm. Paths washed away and so on. But our troops found them all last night and a look at the map will be all they need for guidance. Plus, the residents have to be provisioned if they want to stay."

"You know we can carry the provisions, except the most disabled among us. Just get the crap together."

Joan was happy to open her larder. The food had been meant for these people anyway.

It was settled. Part of Josh even felt good about it. His people out there helping these artists hike safely home would create a more tolerant environment for them all. A win-win. Maybe.

Of course, as life had taught him, anything could get worse.

THE ARTISTS PROVED initially surprised that soldiers in camo ponchos, carrying heavy packs, insisted on accompanying them to their cabins. Some wanted to object out of mistrust, but most quickly saw the advantage in it. Some even managed to offer their thanks.

Still, the stone-faced soldiers who accompanied each of them were intimidating. Nor did they appear to have any desire not to be. They marched out with their charges and they looked ready to handle anything.

Krystal sat up, rubbing her eyes, and having missed the departures, she took a belated trip to the kitchen to find out if she could help. The small staff seemed to be doing all right and assured her they'd taken shifts to sleep. That left Joan, who looked as if she hadn't slept a wink.

"Mom, you can let me take over for a little while. You need some sleep."

Joan put her head in her hands. "Do you know what this is going to do to us? To the business?"

That had been the farthest thing from Krystal's mind, but considering how much of her effort, time and life Joan had put into this retreat, Krystal could understand her mother's concern. Or maybe it was a partial concern, unwilling to deal with the murder issue.

"We'll come back," Krystal hastened to assure Joan. "Awful as this is, it's a single incident out of years of success."

"Right." Joan rubbed her eyes. "Guess what headline is going to follow us."

"Headlines don't last long."

"But they can be brought up at every opportunity on the internet. Nothing ever dies anymore." Then Joan closed her eyes. "Except people," she murmured. "Except people. Mason I can almost understand, but Sebastian? He practically faded into the background."

Krystal leaned back in her chair, knowing her mother was right, but not knowing what she could say about it. Sebastian couldn't have been any more inoffensive. Who could have a grudge against him?

The question gave her a renewed chill. Cops and soldiers notwithstanding, something was very wrong out there. Terribly wrong. And Krystal couldn't be sure they had enough protection to deal with a sick grudge of some kind. How many people would it take to turn this entire lodge into a deadly fishbowl? She'd bet not very many.

Josh's mind was running along a similar but different track. He and the sheriff were hitting it off well, sharing as much information as they could, but it wasn't a whole lot. They staked out coordinates on the map, presuming the killer or killers must still be out there, but neither of them quite believing it.

"Two killers," Gage decided.

Josh agreed. "Methods too different."

"But why?" Gage spoke the question that neither of them could answer. Why two murderers?

The sight of his soldiers marching out with civilians, determined to protect them, filled Josh with pride. Not all chose to go with the civilians but he could understand what this might be costing them whether they chose to remain behind or take the dangerous trek. Memories. Horrors. Risks to themselves and friends.

A trek that could be more dangerous in many ways. He wished he could go out with them, but they were separated, one soldier to two civilians, and he'd be useless.

So he stayed at the lodge, patrolling outside. Reject, that tough little husky, limped with him everywhere but gave no signs of concern. That much was good, anyway.

Even though the rain had stopped and patches of blue sky showed between the trees, leaves still dripped water, a constant patter. Then every so often came a rumble in the distance. More mountain sliding? He hoped the trees would be able to withstand most of it.

The heavy equipment Gage Dalton had promised began to arrive, although exactly what it was supposed to do at this point beat Josh. Maybe just stand at the ready in case a dangerous slide happened.

Josh's own experience of such things had been mostly limited to drier terrain, although Afghanistan was by no means a dry country for the most part. But rains like yesterday? A whole different ball of wax.

He took a few minutes to check on Krystal and her mother. They looked about as depressed as two people could. Well, they were watching a life's work be washed away and murdered away. He could get it.

As if the situation wasn't bad enough all by itself, regardless of the future.

Two murders, so very different. That was bugging the hell out of him. There had to be a point. Not just that two murderers might be involved, but that the crimes had been staged to be so different. A message there? He and Gage were left scratching their heads.

And did Reject fit in somehow? He glanced at the fluffy husky and couldn't imagine it. Yet the dog had been seriously injured, then dumped as if he were some kind of message at the stockade.

No sense in any of it.

Given his background, Josh didn't necessarily need things to make sense. War sure as hell rarely did. Act and react. Except right now there was little to react to.

Two bodies, ostensibly being pored over by a crime scene unit. Two bodies unrelated except they were both clients of the retreat.

Two bodies, making no sense at all. Nor did patrolling the outside of the retreat lodge. Gage had as many deputies as he could spare, and while they hardly created an impenetrable wall, neither did Josh's men and women.

Nothing could protect totally.

Hell. He went inside with Reject, sure the dog would cheer Krystal at least a bit. He'd noticed how that animal managed to bring small smiles to her face.

Although very few of the original crowd remained in the great room of the lodge, they were making use of the kitchen staff and waitpersons, who appeared to be glad to be occupied.

Who wouldn't be right now, Josh wondered. The ugliness of this whole situation carried him back into times he would much rather forget. Times when those he'd cared about had paid the price of war. When Carly Narth had become too wounded to join so-called polite society again. He remembered that awful scene all the way to his gut.

Limbs had been lost. Men and women had been crippled. And for some of them, prosthetics provided no answer.

Then there were the spouses who could no longer take the changes in their husbands and wives. Those who feared having them around their children. The ultimate rejection.

God, he hated to think about it. Hated that he could do only small bits for people so terribly wounded.

But Krystal looked happy to see Reject and that made him feel somewhat better. He was coming to care for Krystal as much as he cared for his own people. He could see she was going through hell right now, but it was more than that. He admired her innate strength she seemed so unwilling to let go of.

Where had that come from? Did it matter? She stroked Reject, who decided to give her his belly, a true honor.

Poor little doggie with a cast on his leg and two legs splinted. So badly mistreated by some human. But then, humans had a way of doing that. Bitterness crept into his thoughts, an unwanted visitor. He shoved it away, burying it in a deep place he never wanted to visit again.

He didn't like the sight of the deputies wandering in the woods, seeking scattered clues. On all those police vests yellow showed out like a target. A protection from accidental misfires by fellow deputies but a damn bright announcement to anyone out there who wanted a target.

He pulled on his poncho again, making sure his KA-BAR was firmly tucked into its sheath. In his hands that knife was just about as good as a pistol. Or a rifle. He could throw with enviable accuracy.

But to get outside again, that was important. To keep an eye on those deputies who announced their presence. In his camo he could remain damn near invisible and so could the people of his unit.

He paused, giving Krystal a kiss on her cheek that obviously surprised her. Hell, it surprised him, too, as did the instant flood of desire that slammed him. God, not now. "I'm going out for a little while. Don't worry."

She eyed him up and down, and the faintest of smiles edged her face. "You'll be invisible out there?"

"That's my hope. Plenty of practice."

Joan didn't look any happier about his foray but offered no objection, as if she knew a protest would be wasted. Evidently she got it.

Rain still dripped from leaves, recreating the sound of the storm that had just passed. The ground was a mess of runnels, and washed rivers of pine needles and leaves. Useless for tracking.

But maybe not everything was. Tree limbs had snapped at a man's height, too low for the wildness of the storm. Some had broken even lower. Stealthy this guy was not.

Yet what real purpose could he feel in killing two so unrelated people? Mason he could understand. Damn near everyone at the retreat understood that one, but Sebastian? No one appeared to even speculate about that.

So what was the link? There had to be one beyond a rental at this retreat.

Those who remained at the lodge great room appeared as unhappy as those who had left. People who had determined they must work even in the face of such threat.

Hell. One more round of the wide porch, one more check on the deputies he could pick out, then he returned to the lodge to sit with Krystal and Joan. Two people who needed reassurance. Two people for whom he had none to offer.

Joan brightened a little as he joined them. Krystal's face was a bit gloomier, but not entirely. She managed a faint smile.

"What now?" Krystal asked bluntly. "There's no way to come back from two murders. None."

Joan sighed and the brief brightness she had shared abruptly vanished. "Screwed by the internet."

Josh, gathering their meaning was about their business, couldn't exactly argue that. He already had some experience of what a few typed lines on a social media note could do. Didn't matter if they were malicious. They just had to be personal in a way that revealed secrets anyone ought to be able to keep.

Privacy. Crap. No longer possible.

But he looked at Joan and tried to find some way to reassure her. Even the slightest thing.

Then a thing, a small thing, occurred to him. He pulled out his cell phone.

Joan drew a sharp breath. "The cells are working again?"

Josh shook his head sharply. "Sat phones only, and intermittent at that. Angus is out there with a deputy trying to get it all up and running. Anyway, this is on my phone, not a signal. I want you to see this."

Then with a flip he ran through photos until he came to the one he wanted. "This is Carly Narth. One of my best soldiers. And you can imagine what she's been through, thanks to the internet."

And there, unmistakably, was Carly's horribly scarred face, a testimony to the atrocities of war. A testimony to man's inhumanity to men.

"Oh my God," Joan breathed. Krystal bit her lip and seemed to stop breathing.

Joan raised her horrified gaze. "What can she do?"

Josh flipped his phone away from the photo and shoved it into his pocket. "What *can* she do?"

Krystal shook her head. "I saw her last night but I never dreamed she'd been injured so badly. She kept her face turned away or under her poncho hood. My God, Josh. How do you ever live with that?"

Josh simply shook his head. "Her family couldn't. Threw her out. Too upsetting for the children. *Her* children, I might add."

"How could they..." Krystal's voice trailed off.

"Because they *could*," Josh said harshly. "Because social services workers agreed that it was too awful for the kids to live with. Never mind that their mother is a hero. Evidently that doesn't count."

The women exchanged looks, small nods. Krystal faced him. "You're telling us something."

"Damn straight. Carly never gave up. She's still fighting for a normal life despite her appearance. She's going to make it, too. But what about the two of you? You gonna fight or are you gonna give up?"

He had no doubt of their answer, not after seeing Carly, but how long would they stick to it? "Anyway," he continued almost harshly, "you can give yourselves excuses or you can fight. I suggest fighting, and that starts with the damn internet. Sure, anyone can find out about you if they want to, but the question becomes who is going to bother. After these murders pass, nobody is going to care since you're not involved. Sure, there'll be a brief flurry of Mason's books on the shelves because he's dead, but that won't make much of a difference. He was a lousy writer anyway. People read him only because they ran out of other horror writers to read."

Krystal smiled. "You've read him?"

"Much to my embarrassment. He was awful, always awful, and he was coattailing on someone else's work if you want my opinion."

Mary Collins had been listening, and now she sat upright, trying not to be obvious about it. So others agreed with her about the theft of her work. That Mason had made it only because of her.

Joan sighed heavily. "You're saying to just ignore this. And Mason."

"It won't be easy at first. Reporters will be everywhere. Nightly news will want to see you. Thing is, don't give them what they want. They want shock. No way. I'll help you with figuring that out."

Krystal surprised him by reaching across the table to lay her hand on his. "You've had to go through this."

"Damn straight. More than once. I'll help."

MARY COLLINS FELT a strong urge to get rid of Josh just then. She didn't want Mason to get away with any of his misdeeds. None. Getting even with this retreat was part of her plan, too. After all, they'd made Mason a star guest for years.

"Damn it all to hell," she muttered under her breath. This damn soldier was going to be a pain in her butt.

She knew she could shoot a man. She'd gone with Mel to make sure they took out Mason. She hadn't anticipated Sebastian's murder, though. However, Mel Marbly had proved useful in taking out Sebastian—although he'd been a lot messier about the job—and helped create a distraction, for which Mary forgave him for getting his own ideas. Of course, thinking about this caused Mary a small smile. Clearly Mel had enjoyed Sebastian's killing, and had certainly made it different enough from Mason's murder.

Unfortunately, she'd have to get rid of Mel now, and maybe his wife as well. Still, given a little time, she could get out of here before two more murders were uncovered. Murders she couldn't possibly be linked to.

Still hiding a smile, she sipped fresh coffee and played solitaire. Across the room she could clearly see the damn Metcalfes alone with Josh Healey.

She hoped the Metcalfes' business suffered a setback, but Josh Healey was a different concern. She hadn't planned on his unit emerging from behind their walls to get involved in any of this. From everything she'd heard about them, they never showed their faces except for one or two guys driving into town for supplies.

No, she hadn't planned on them guarding this place, hunting for killers.

She swore silently again, but then realized these guys wouldn't be hard to take care of. No, from what little she'd heard, they didn't like to be out of their stockade. Given a small opportunity, they'd head back to their hideout.

A bunch of sickos.

Satisfied, she flipped another card in her deck.

She'd get 'em all. Every damn one of them. She was smart enough to plan all of this.

Chapter Ten

Josh noticed that Reject never entirely slept. All the while he appeared to be snoozing, his ears never stopped perking, twisting. He was listening every single moment.

Josh couldn't have asked for a better guard. He'd seen what K-9s could do in the military, knew how alert they could be to sounds and smells. Reject apparently had the same instincts.

Which meant Josh didn't hesitate to send Joan to her bedroom and Krystal to a spare room. He swore to them that Reject would warn them of anything, and recalling the husky's attention to the window and his growling just before the gunshot, they believed him.

But Krystal was a different matter. Somehow he followed her into her small, private room. Somehow she turned into him, surrounding him with her arms, drawing him into a snug embrace. He closed his eyes, trying to remember the last time a woman had made him feel this way.

Sadly, he couldn't. Other women had passed through his life, but Krystal was unique.

He could no more have stopped himself than he could have stopped an incoming missile. He wrapped his own arms around her and held her as snugly as he dared. Bent his head and risked a kiss of her soft, warm lips.

Heard the sigh escape her. Felt her move even closer into his arms. "Oh, Josh," she murmured.

His head nearly exploded with desire. God, he wanted her. His entire body flamed for her. A throbbing drove him toward completion, ignoring the clothes between them, ignoring every impediment.

Then he heard Gage's roughened voice from the great room.

At once he leaned back. Krystal, too, leaned back.

"Damn," he muttered. Then, "Soon. I promise." It was a promise that would require more than the threat stalking them now for him to break. A promise nothing could keep him from fulfilling at the first opportunity.

Reluctantly, he left Krystal. Gage was looking for the murderers and couldn't be ignored. Not even for the heat of desire.

He stepped out of the back room. A few people still sat around tables, that Mary woman playing endless rounds of solitaire.

Not everyone felt safe with cops and soldiers roaming the area.

Gage waved him over and Josh soon bent his head close to the sheriff's. "CSU found something," he murmured. "A woman's small boot print. Nothing like that agent was wearing."

Josh glanced over at Darlene Dana, Mason's agent. The woman seemed to have taken up permanent residence on a sofa, still staring blindly at her mental image of what she had seen when she found Mason. "You got impressions?" Of the shoe pattern. Could be the most useful thing of all.

Gage nodded. "Believe it or not. Rain helped some."

Josh rubbed his chin, thinking. "Okay. I'm not sure how we'll start a shoe hunt, though. And can you be sure it's a woman's print?"

"Smaller than most men's, although not impossible. Thing is, the tech doesn't think the person could be very heavy, not in that mud."

"But still possibly a small male."

Gage simply shook his head. "Not easy. Never thought this case would be. Hell's bells. Two murders and every sign that they were committed by different people. Find me a reason for that, Josh. Any reason will do at this point."

Josh sighed, frustrated beyond belief. "Nobody's told me a useful thing except about Mason Cambridge. Maybe I should look into this Sebastian Elsin some more. People seem to think he was pretty invisible. Then there's Paul Aston, another poet. Maybe he knows something more about Elsin."

Gage nodded. "I'm about to get truly shorthanded. A lot of folks downstream of these mountains are running into major trouble. They need us."

Josh understood perfectly. "I'll try to keep my unit out here as long as I can. But this situation is hell for them."

"I'm surprised they showed up. Well—" Gage slammed his hat on his head "—I'll keep you posted as I can. Sure would be nice to have full comms back, though. Although we're doing better, up here at least."

Josh couldn't have agreed more.

He looked around the room and finally caught sight of

Paul Aston over in a far corner, working on a computer with what had to be a lousy internet connection, especially with comms still unreliable. Hah. Josh remembered the days when an internet connection hadn't been required for the use of a computer. Fancy typing machines for the most part. Boy, had that been a long time ago. He probably shouldn't advertise his age.

He wended his way to the other side of the room and without an apology sat with Aston. Paul looked up, startled by the interruption. "What...?"

"I need a word or two about Sebastian, if you don't mind. Sheriff is curious."

Paul hesitated only a minute before closing the laptop. "I didn't know him very well. Most people didn't."

"But you're both poets, right?"

Paul's smile was crooked. "And we're all humans sharing the same planet, right? About the same relationship."

Josh shook his head, managing an amused shrug. "Can't blame a guy for trying."

"Of course not." Paul leaned forward, elbows on the table. "So, Sebastian. What did I know about him? Give me a minute. It's not like I keep notes on everyone I meet here."

Josh was glad to give him the time. He accepted fresh coffee from Donna Carstairs, who worked out of the kitchen and was apparently doubling as a waitress. "Something to eat?" she asked. "Even a guy like you has to eat sometime."

"What's on the menu?"

"Burgers and more burgers. My second line cook bailed yesterday. Oh, yeah, I think I can make some fries, but it'll take time to heat the deep-fat fryer."

"Then just the burgers, please. Two of them. Mustard and ketchup."

"Ah, a man with my tastes. What about you, Paul?"

"Just some of those wheat crackers if you have them, with some cheese. Not very hungry."

Donna moved on, leaving Josh and Paul alone at the table.

"Okay," Paul continued, "Sebastian. Total introvert, worse than me. But sometimes he'd try to be humorous."

"Tried to be?"

Paul shook his head. "I don't know where he learned to be funny, but a lot of people around here didn't take it that way. Offensive, like. Anyway, it was only once in a while, kinda like he figured out he wasn't making anyone laugh."

That was worth noting, Josh thought, making a mental note.

"Anything else?"

"A bit of a misogynist." Paul sighed. "Not so terribly overt that it couldn't be ignored much of the time, but it was still there, and these days women notice it."

"As well they should," Josh answered.

Paul gave him a half smile. "I imagine you've served with women who wouldn't stand for a bit of it. Anyway, like I said, he mostly soft-pedaled it except with a rare joke that wasn't terribly funny to anyone, except some of the jerkier guys."

Josh lifted a brow, amused in spite of himself. "Jerkier guys?"

Paul sighed. "I'm sure you know exactly the type I mean. Mason led the lot. Thought women existed to serve his needs, treated 'em like they were beneath him. Jerk-

ier than most, but he got away with it, the holy and al-
mighty Mason Cambridge. Those same women hung on
his every word."

"I guess you didn't like him either."

Paul just shook his head. "Best to start with a little
respect for others. I don't think that man ever felt any."

Donna put two burgers in front of Josh, buns looking
a bit stale, burgers more gray than brown. The second
plate held Paul's cheese and crackers. "Sorry," she said.
"Stove isn't heating up well. Maybe low on propane.
Anyway, I promise I can do a better burger than that."

"These are good enough," Josh told her. "If I got picky,
I wouldn't have made it all those years in uniform."

Donna flashed a grin. "It'd be nice if everyone else felt
the same way. Well, I'm off to see what I got left to do."

Individual soldiers guiding people back to their cabins had worked, at least enough to cut the crowd in the
dining room by two-thirds, or so it appeared to Josh as
he scanned the area. It struck him that an awful lot of
people had somehow decided they weren't at risk from
the killer or killers.

How had they managed that? As if he didn't know.
How many patrols had he led into death-defying situations with young people who believed they were somehow invincible?

Until the first bloody fight, anyway. Seeing your
buddy blown into a cloud of blood and detached limbs
had quite a sobering effect. Eighteen-year-olds became
men overnight, not always in a good way.

So a lot of these artists had convinced themselves of
their own invincibility. That only Mason and Sebastian
had been targets—never mind that bullet through the

window. Nothing had happened in hours, and that was all they needed to persuade themselves of their own safety. He knew his people would check out the cabins and surrounding areas, but that was no proof against a lurking killer. No way. A single man or woman could slip through those woods unseen if they knew how.

Trying not to grind his teeth because all that ever did was give him a headache, Josh left Paul to his work and began to slowly make his way around the room. Fewer people, easier task, and apparently his frequent appearances at the lodge had eased the fear of him.

Most of it, anyway. Some uneasy looks still darted his way, but then some of them were directed toward Reject. Apparently the dog's preternatural senses yesterday had made him a thing that wasn't quite earthly.

Which could be half-true, Josh thought with mild amusement.

Krystal fell into step beside him before he'd wound his way through half the room.

"People are foolish," she remarked and didn't try to keep her voice down. "I can't believe how many people went back to their cabins. Like making themselves offerings to a killer in the woods."

He didn't disagree, but there was no way to agree with her when others could hear. "My people will check out their security."

"I'm sure they will. But since they don't have Reject's senses, they could miss a lot. Crap."

He glanced at her, reading the strong annoyance in her face. "Cops all over the place, too."

"Not enough of them." She shook her head and came to a dead halt. "They can't *know* they're not out there with a beast who just wants to kill for the joy of it. They can't know that, Josh."

He sighed quietly and looked around, thinking about the scene differently. "Maybe people started to feel like fish in a bowl. Easier to attack while gathered here."

"We mentioned that, didn't we? I hate to say you're probably right. God, *Mom's* right. She's worried about people getting killed—she's not some kind of monster—but she's also worried about what this can do to the business. Sheesh, Josh, she's spent decades turning this place into a reputable artists' retreat. This'll kill it. Make it visibly unsafe. A kind of reputation you can't claw back, not with the internet."

Josh had no counterargument for that. He'd already said all he could on the subject.

"We'll probably attract the thrill seekers now."

He asked dryly, "The Mason Cambridges you mean?"

At last a smile tickled the corners of her mouth. "Maybe so. But I'm not sure we want to be a retreat for wannabe horror writers, at least not mainly. Damn, we used to have such a nice, peaceful environment."

"It'll come back. It might just take some time." He spoke with more surety than he felt, however. He had only to look at his group of soldiers to know how long bad publicity could last.

Krystal stopped walking and faced him. Their eyes met, and Josh felt an overwhelming *zing* of attraction for her. In an instant he wanted to pull her away to a private place and discover every inch of that body she concealed beneath jeans and loose Western shirts.

Because he was sure it was a perfect body. Even in

loose clothing she couldn't hide it all when she moved. But it wasn't just her body.

He wanted her to smile at him. Sigh at him. Murmur his name. Share that strong inner core of hers, one he felt matched his own. A woman to meet him as an equal. A true partner.

He caught himself just before he did something stupid. He didn't want to offend her, and he certainly didn't want to draw attention to her and the way he was feeling about her.

But did he see, in those blue eyes of hers, an answering heat? He could only hope because the time for any of this frankly sucked.

She shook her head a bit, as if in answer to some internal discussion of her own, then faced forward, making it clear she intended to continue the survey of their remaining guests.

She was better at it, too, maybe because the clients here knew her, unlike him. Even though he'd had a highly visible profile here since yesterday, he was still the unknown. A pretty large unknown, he admitted to himself. One of his nicknames in the Army had been Giant. Total exaggeration, but it had given him some idea of how he appeared to others.

Krystal slipped easily into chairs at occupied tables, greeted warmly by everyone. Josh stood back, creating space for her and the people she needed to talk with. When it seemed wise, he seated himself nearby.

Krystal, he discovered, experienced no hesitation about coming right to the point.

"We've had two murders," she said bluntly. "Very different murders. I know the cops interviewed you yesterday, but this is today, guys. I want to know if you remembered something in the meantime. Some little thing that didn't seem important enough to bring up yesterday."

Well, she certainly got the four people she was with to exchange looks. He didn't get their names. Didn't matter. If they needed them for some reason later, Krystal would know.

"Well," said one of the women slowly, "I thought it was weird how Mason started that creepy story before his murder. Were you listening, Krystal?"

Krystal gave a half shake of her head. "I was busy."

"We *all* should have been," said one of the men.

"I hate to admit it," the woman said, "but that man could spin quite a tale. Anyway, a couple nights before he was killed…didn't you notice it? Sebastian mentioned it at the time." Then she paused, shaking her head, a tear running down her cheek. "Poor Sebastian. He didn't deserve what happened."

Who does? Josh thought a trifle sourly.

The woman dabbed at her eyes. "Anyway, we were sitting there listening to Mason tell his tale and Sebastian turned to me and said, 'Carrie? Doesn't it sound like he's plotting his next book? His next murder?'"

Carrie shuddered. "At the time I thought it was amusing. Of course that's what Mason was doing. He was always doing that. But that night I could only joke that the only thing missing from his story were the fools who ran out into the night woods, instead of staying safely inside, only to meet the killer with the axe. Like all those movies." Carrie shuddered again. "It was exactly like that."

She raised a watery gaze to Krystal. "Is it possible he planned his own murder?"

Josh stiffened. He saw a small shudder run down Krystal's back.

"Hardly likely," Krystal answered firmly. "Besides, he wasn't out *in* the woods, was he?"

That leavened Carrie's face somewhat, and the others at the table became more relaxed, as if they had feared something worse.

"Nah," Krystal said, rising, "he just went back to his cabin and ran into a killer. Didn't have to be him. Could have been anyone, like what happened to Sebastian."

Heads nodded. Then one man said, "Although I have to admit—Mason seemed the likeliest person someone would want to kill."

An uneasy laugh passed around the table.

"But not Sebastian," Carrie reminded them.

As they walked away from the table, Josh fell into step with Krystal. "Thoughts?"

"Nothing except that people seem to be finding their own relationship between Mason's storytelling and what happened. How unlikely is that?"

"Very. Unless Mason Cambridge was suicidal."

"Always a possibility, I suppose."

Just around then, soldiers returning from their escort duties began to come through the door. As was usual, given their training, they fell into step, a heavy tread.

"Packages delivered, sir," one former corporal said, stepping forward. "Just a few more to go."

"And nothing unusual?"

"Nothing we saw, unfortunately. Whoever was behind this has gone to ground."

Not good news, Josh thought. Looking at Krystal he saw his doubts reflected there. Nothing but a possible woman's boot print, which he well knew could mean anything or nothing. Men came in smaller sizes and weights, not just women.

He spoke to Krystal. "So Mason was popular with the ladies?"

"Flies to honey and all those aphorisms. Yeah, they hung on his every word."

Josh repressed a smile at Krystal's evident dislike of the writer. "Not one of his fans, huh?"

"Hardly. I kept telling Mom not to let him come, but he was a drawing card. The kind of headliner that was good for business."

"Didn't you agree?"

Krystal faced him, hands on her hips. "I could have tolerated him in smaller doses."

Then they resumed their walk around the room. Sunlight had begun to give way to the hints of another stormy day, and the remaining guests had begun to look uneasy again, as if they wanted to pull the curtains closed.

Except that made keeping an eye out for a threat almost impossible.

Gage had said he was shorthanded, looking for help. Josh eyed the troops who had come in to warm up and eat and decided to take a risk with their reaction.

He joined them, a roll in hand, coffee in the other. "I'm looking for some volunteers," he said quietly. "No one who's uncomfortable with the idea. Hell, that's why we built the stockade, so we wouldn't have to deal with this crap."

A half dozen nods answered him.

Josh drew a long breath, acutely aware of what he'd already asked of these vets. "I need some patrols out there. The sheriff is shorthanded."

He wasn't surprised by the hesitation. These people had already left their safe zone to face hazards they knew all too well. Hazards they still had trouble dealing with.

Then one of them nodded. Rusty Rodes, a former MP. "I'll do it," he said. "There's something going on out there that needs to be stopped. I'll see who else will join me." Then he held up his mug with a half smile. "Heating up first, boss."

In the back office, opening the slatted blinds on the window that offered a view of the large lodge room, Krystal watched. Josh joined her and surprised Krystal by wrapping his arm around her. A secure feeling without a sense of encroachment. She had to fight an urge to rest her head against his powerful shoulder.

"What do you think?" he asked presently.

"That no one knows a damn thing about what's going on out there. Not a thing."

"Yeah. Some help."

Krystal sighed and scanned the room once more. "Another storm. I wonder if we'll get crowded again. We're not exactly stashed with enough provisions for days of this."

Josh understood the logistical problem. It was written into his genes after his war experiences. "Count on Gage Dalton."

"This entire county counts on that man. You'd think he'd have had enough of us by now."

"Is there often trouble up here?"

Krystal shook her head with a restrained laugh. "Usually we're pretty much boring. People just want to work."

"A different summer, then."

But, unable to help himself, Josh turned toward her. He didn't wind her in his arms much as he wanted to—that damn window blind was open.

He caught Krystal's gaze, drinking in her delicate features, even that small nose some people would have killed for, and smiled the warmest smile he still had in his heart.

"Lady," he said quietly, "I want to have sex with you right now. I want to strip you naked and fall into your depths and never emerge again."

He heard her sharp gasp of indrawn air, then she didn't breathe at all. Her face softened in every inch, but she said nothing.

He raised his hands and took her gently by her upper arms. "That's a promise," he said quietly. "You can kick it back in my teeth, but it's my promise to you."

"Oh, Josh," she murmured. "Oh, Josh. Please. But when this stuff is over."

He could have swept her into a tight embrace, to answer her need with his own, but that damn window...

Reluctantly he stepped back. "Soon."

"Not soon enough."

At that moment Joan chose to enter the office. She scanned the two of them as if she'd missed nothing at all, then nodded. "Wondered when" was all she said about them.

Krystal flushed faintly. "No news?"

Joan shook her head. "Nada. But there's something weird about that Mary Collins. Can't put my finger on it, though."

"The romance novelist?" Josh asked.

"The same. Never saw such a bitter woman in my life. At least she published a book." Joan sighed. "Of course, some folks will *never* be happy."

Josh stood looking out the window. "She's the one with the stringy dirty-blond hair, glasses, right? I swear she's been playing cards by herself this whole time."

His head tipped back a bit. "An interesting response to all of this, wouldn't you say?"

Krystal couldn't help but agree. "As if she feels she has nothing to fear."

"Yep. Except she was on *this* side of the glass when that bullet came flying through." He rubbed his face. "Hell, my kingdom for a decent clue."

"Well," Krystal said, "I'm all for talking to Mary right now. I'll tell her I need a touch of her zen." With a steady stride, she headed that way.

Josh decided to hang back, sitting with Donna Carstairs, who was eating a thin peanut butter sandwich. "Want one?" she asked, holding a half out toward him.

"I think I can smear my own peanut butter."

Donna chuckled. "Bread's getting stale, though. You'd best toast it."

"I've eaten bread so stale I could see where Fleming got his idea for penicillin."

Donna's laugh rose from her belly and Joan's laugh joined hers. Joan said, "I bet you and your group have quite some tales to tell, if they ever want to."

"Maybe so. Depends on how people around here feel about us."

Donna nodded and shoved half her sandwich his way. "A spread of opinions. Eat anyway. I'm sure you've heard them all. Some people want to think you're dangerous even though you've done nothing to scare them. Others figure it's none of their business. Then there are some who feel sympathy, at a safe distance. The whole gamut."

Josh nodded and turned his attention to Krystal. He couldn't tell if she was getting anything at all out of Mary.

"Now that one's interesting," Donna remarked. "Mary. She comes nearly every year, and nearly every year she pretty much avoids Mason. Not that she's the only one."

Joan snorted. "Not everyone liked that literary lion. Comes on too strong for some. But to kill him?" Joan shrugged. "What would that gain?"

Josh had an idea. "A lot of money for his agent and publisher. Nothing like a dead writer."

Joan nodded slowly. "Won't say that hasn't come up before, but I'd remove that agent, Darlene, from the list. If that woman ever stops shaking it'll be in her next lifetime."

Then Josh spoke heavily. "Or maybe she didn't know how awful it could be to kill another human."

Joan's gaze met his directly. "So tell me, Josh. Is it awful?"

Josh closed his eyes, stomping down on a flood of memories he needed to control, resisting his urge to yell at Joan for even daring to ask such a question. "Yeah," he said finally. "It's that god-awful."

Joan at least didn't offer any fake sympathy. "I figured" was all she said.

"It's better that way. To feel that way."

"Maybe. Maybe we wouldn't go to war as often."

Joan sighed and turned to Donna, whose face had tightened. "How much can we feed this small mob?"

Donna jerked her chin toward the darkening day. "It'll be pretty thin unless Gage shows up with the supplies he promised."

Joan snorted. "Like he doesn't have a thousand other people to take care of right now."

Donna answered quietly. "Like he doesn't have a couple of murders to take care of right now." Then she looked pleadingly at Joan and Josh. "What the hell happened here? This isn't our kind of place, not anymore."

Josh leaned forward, claiming Donna's attention. "It'll be okay when we get this done. Something crazy happened, but it won't happen forever."

He wished he believed that. None of this was adding up to any kind of sense. Murdered SOB author? Possible. Even likely. But that poet guy, so inoffensive he faded into the background? Paul had been pretty clear about that.

He was relieved when Krystal finally ended her conversation with Mary Collins. Maybe she'd gotten some useful information.

Krystal paused to speak to a few people who were ensconced at their own tables. Outside, the storm began to blow again, though not as wildly as yesterday.

At last she reached the office, grabbed a cup of coffee and sat with the others.

"Well?" Joan demanded.

"Mary absolutely didn't have the highest opinion of Mason Cambridge, I can tell you that for sure."

Josh leaned forward. "As in?"

"As in she thought he was a disgusting creep not above stealing the works of others."

Josh leaned back immediately. He hadn't expected such a bold accusation. "Stealing?"

Krystal merely shook her head. "The woman doesn't get the difference between copyright infringement and copyright in general. She's not the only one on the planet."

"How so?"

Krystal accepted a roll from Donna. "How long will these rolls last?" she asked Donna.

"Let's just say I'm about to remember how to bake again. You can help."

Krystal smiled and nodded. "I remember those lessons when I was a kid. Messy."

"You can't make fresh dough without being messy."

Josh had reached the point of tapping his fingers impatiently on the tabletop. "Mary?" he prompted.

Krystal bit into her roll and wiped her mouth. "Nothing in particular except I don't think she'd have trusted Mason further than she could throw him."

"Why not?"

Krystal dropped her roll half-eaten. "A lot of writers, and not just Mary, from what I gather, believe there's a copyright on ideas. You come up with a brilliant idea and it's yours. Nobody can take it. Except that's not true. Take Star Wars, for example. Anybody can use that term, but it's the graphic way it's presented that's copyrighted and trademarked. Regardless, no idea is copyrighted, and to prove that one is actually stolen would be a hell of a legal task. Hell, a writer can't even copyright her own name."

"So there are a lot of people running around with the wrong idea?"

"A lot who don't seem to understand just how limited copyright protection is. Regardless, Mary isn't the only one, from what she said."

"Well, that lengthens the list," Josh remarked, looking out across the room, a room that was slowly becoming more occupied.

"I guess that depends on who you think would murder over it." Krystal pushed her cup and roll aside. "I don't like Mary."

Joan stiffened. "Why not? She's never been a problem in the past."

"I don't know." Krystal shifted her attention to Josh. "You know what I mean, I bet. Something in the eyes."

He knew all too well exactly what she meant. "Hell" was his only answer.

"What should we do?" Donna asked.

"Keep an eye out," Josh replied. "And I'm going to ask the same of some more of my troops. I just need to know how many we need to watch."

Krystal reached impulsively across the table, understanding now some of what Josh dealt with. "Would that be good for them?"

"Their choice," Josh said evenly. "Nobody gets forced. Maybe for some it will even be good." Hadn't he caught a glimpse of that earlier? Glad to be on task again? Glad to have a purpose. Maybe it would be the best thing in the end for some of them.

He rose. "I'm going to go talk to some more of my soldiers. See what kind of response I get."

Krystal rose, too. "Can I come?"

Josh scanned her. "For what purpose?"

"Maybe a woman would give all this more purpose."

What the hell did she mean by that? Josh scowled but didn't prevent her. As if Carly Narth, a woman, didn't already do that with her scars. Or maybe Carly just seemed too tough.

Mentally shrugging, he led the way to the door, to where a few of his people waited. Then out the door and onto the porch. The wind blew, but not as stiffly as yesterday. The rain even seemed gentler.

And they waited, six of them, milling around, looking for orders.

As soon as Josh appeared, they gave him their full attention. They hardly seemed to see Krystal.

"I'm looking," Josh said, "for some who are willing to stand guard, keep an eye out. Something is going on out there, although at this point I can't be sure it isn't inside."

He noted that Carly Narth stepped closer to Krystal, whether in a protective posture or in recognition of a kindred spirit, he couldn't tell. Regardless, as tough as he believed Krystal was, he had to feel better about Carly's experience. At least Krystal didn't seem to notice the gesture.

Soon he had even more of his soldiers ready to move out on a quiet mission. Garbed in the mountain camo clothing, they wouldn't stand out at all, and experience had taught them how to be stealthy.

Camo ponchos were gone, though, getting rid of any possible rustle of that fabric. Experience. Troops as prepared as they needed to be for the cold and wet. Admirable people. With a rough plan of action, they were ready.

He watched them filter into the woods singly, nearly

invisible unless he had known what to look for. Only Carly remained and she looked at Krystal. "Ditch the yellow poncho. It's a target. You got any camo?"

"Some. From back when I used to hunt."

"Then get it on now. Don't need you sticking out like a sore thumb."

Krystal offered no objection, apparently recognizing the sense of the order. Stubborn as she could be at times, she showed none of it now.

Ten minutes later she returned in old-fashioned camo, none of the modern infrared reflective gear. It would nonetheless serve its purpose. He doubted the killer in the woods was supplied with the right kind of goggles. Too freaking expensive.

At least he hoped he wasn't wrong. He knew he and his soldiers had a few of the temperature-sensitive goggles between them, hardly a big supply but enough.

Hell. A killer or two on the loose in woods which provided major protection for him or them just by itself. Or one or two hidden inside the lodge, where matters could get ugly in an eyeblink.

He looked at Reject, who had followed him to the open door. "Stand guard," he said, hoping the dog understood that much.

He could have sworn the husky did, standing up taller on his damaged hind legs. Dogs and pain. He wished humans could tolerate it as well.

Josh hated being on duty inside, but then he had a thought, a thought that should have occurred to him sooner: *he* was the psychologist. He was constantly evaluating his own troops for their mental stability, but maybe he should be observing the people in the lodge much more closely. Hell.

Then out of the misty day emerged Harris Belcher, the owner of the sled dog teams. He headed straight for Josh. "Want any K-9 help?"

Josh started to shake his head. "You can't risk your dogs, Harris. Expensive, well-trained..."

"I wasn't thinking about risking them all. I can take a team out the way I did looking for Reject. And trust me, they all remember that odor of the bastard who hurt Reject and they don't like it."

"But the killer might have moved on, might be seeking targets from a different location."

Harris shook his blond head. "Won't make any difference. These dogs are able to smell weak ice. They won't have forgotten this odor. Damn near as good as bloodhounds."

Josh hated the idea. His troops had a choice whether to take these risks, but the dogs didn't. On the other hand, they'd be useful, very useful.

"Just don't risk too many," he said at last.

Harris gave him a crooked smile. "You ever seen how fast these dogs can escape danger?"

"I hope I don't have to."

But then he watched the dogs head for the woods. Might as well have been wearing white targets on their tails, although not all of them. Some had fairly dark coloration. Regardless, after a whistle from Harris, the pack seemed to get the order to spread out. No pulling in a team this time.

Carly and Krystal weren't far behind. He hated not being able to follow them, but he needed to keep an eye on the interior of the lodge. No idea in the world where these threats had come from, not if the killers could have moved inside with the group of clients.

Still, he would have preferred to be out there with Carly, doing something more useful. Except that he knew Carly well enough by now to realize how she would take offense at that. After what she had been through, she wasn't about to allow anyone to suggest she wasn't capable in even the smallest way.

So two women he cared about marched into the treacherous forest and he was forced to stay behind. That didn't suit his personality at all. He especially hated to see Krystal marching into that dangerous darkness.

The protector in him was emerging full-time and his fists kept clenching and unclenching. God, he hated having his hands tied like this.

And scanning the room for someone acting odd seemed like hardly a great use of his time.

KRYSTAL WAS GLAD to be moving through the forest with Carly. No telling how much they'd accomplish, given the acreage out here, but it was better than nothing. She suspected Josh wasn't feeling any better.

"Josh doesn't like being stuck like this," Krystal murmured.

"No. Shh."

Carly was right, of course. This was no time for gab that might give them away. The deeper they sank into the dimly lit forest, the further they seemed to slip into danger. At one point Carly held up her finger, freezing them both in place, listening intently.

Then a husky raced by, tail fully raised and fluffed.

Carly pointed and the two of them did their best to follow the dog. It wasn't easy.

The dog leaped easily over obstacles that tried to trip the two women. It soon left them behind and Carly and Krystal stopped and looked at each other, panting.

"I'd like to know what he smelled," Carly whispered.

Krystal nodded.

Just then, a loud crack, only slightly smothered by the wet trees, tore the air wide open.

The two women exchanged looks, then started hurrying back toward the lodge, keeping low.

A gunshot. Almost impossible to tell where it came from, but they worried about the people in the lodge.

THE BULLET CAME through the window from the outside. A second shot rent the air. Reject sent up a howl fit to raise the dead. The lodge's clients hit the floor as fast as Olympic divers.

Josh swore, lowered himself to a deep knee bend and inched toward the window. From outside. That meant the killer was still out there. Now to hunt him while keeping the people indoors safe.

As soon as he could, he pulled his walkie off his belt and raised his team.

One didn't answer. "Rodes," he said again, his voice sharp.

"Got him" came the voice of Angus. "Hit through the thigh."

"Bad?"

"Not an artery. Cleary and Janice are moving in to help carry him."

Josh felt as if a bomb were about to explode inside

him. Rusty, of all people. A former MP with a spine of hardened steel. A steady personality despite his demons.

But Josh had another, more immediate concern. He looked around at all the civilians crouched on the floor, lying face down. Terrified, as well they should be.

"I'm going outside. Joan, you still got that shotgun?"

"Believe it. Nobody's getting in here."

Donna edged toward Josh. "You can't go out there alone. Don't be a damn fool."

With a murderer out there? No, he wasn't a damn fool, but he didn't want anyone else to be one either. Everything about Donna said that there was no way possible to keep her inside short of tying her up. She even carried a chef's knife, for the love of Pete.

Joan spoke quietly. "Donna," she said warningly.

Donna answered just as quietly, "You do your job in here. Joan, there's a killer out there. Protect these people."

Josh eyed Donna. "Why should I make an exception for you?"

"Two years of infantry training before I busted a knee. I'm good enough."

Joan fell silent.

Protecting these people was what it was all about. Josh crept toward the door as Reject let out another bone-chilling howl.

Why, he wondered, had nature given huskies the same howl as wolves. Because it sure made the blood want to curdle.

ALSO LYING ON the floor was a woman scared out of her wits and wondering what the hell had happened to her careful plan to get rid of one lousy writer. Just Mason Cambridge. Had she asked so much?

The guy was a bald thief without the least bit of shame or compunction. He deserved to die. Maybe Sebastian had been a brilliant diversion.

Or not. Because a second bullet had come through that window and she became convinced this time it was directed at *her*.

Because only *she* could identify the perp. The guy with the trigger finger. The guy who had stabbed Sebastian.

God, the thought of a stabbing made her sick to her stomach. One gunshot, neat and clean, should have been enough. But not for this jackass.

She'd had nothing against Sebastian, anyway. He'd always been respectful. Unlike one man who thought he was God's gift to the literary world.

Not even Mary thought her writing reached that level, of being God's gift. She wrote to entertain. She wrote to distract people from the realities of life. To give them a break.

And Mason had stolen all of that for his own, then acted as if *he* mattered. As if he were the only one who mattered.

Now here she was, lying on a floor, scared out of her mind and wondering if her coconspirator was coming to protect himself by killing her before she could talk.

As if she'd ever admit anything. But he didn't know that.

Then another bullet cracked the glass, this time leaving a crazed web of cracks all over it.

The shots were getting closer. She looked around, wondering if she could find a better place to hide.

CARLY AND KRYSTAL heard the next two gunshots, seeming louder this time despite the dripping leaves. Carly leaned close to Krystal's ear. "We need to circle in around the sound."

Krystal nodded, understanding. Assuming one shooter, their only chance of catching him was encirclement.

If there were two shooters, they were out of luck, but better to take down one than none.

Krystal was also developing the sickening feeling that this shooter had a target in mind inside the lodge. Why else would he be shooting from the outside? But who could that target be?

Mason made sense. Sebastian hadn't, of course, but who knew that man very well? But to go after someone else in that building? More secrets? More ugliness? Did any of them really know each other that well, despite some of the artists having visited for years?

Hell, no. Mason had, as far as she knew, been the only resident to run around advertising himself, his success and his abrasive personality. But who could know what might have been running beneath among the quieter of the others?

God, she thought as she and Carly crept through the wet woods, separating slowly from one another as they tried to localize as best they could where they'd heard the shots come from.

Krystal wasn't at all used to this kind of searching and hunting. Never had she felt her civilian inexperience as much as she did then. She got the principle, but she didn't have the practice. Keeping low to the ground, belly-crawling a couple of times, she could only hope she was doing this correctly.

And noticing, for the very first time, that a forest floor that had always seemed smooth enough when she walked over it now held a million little tortures in the form of sharp broken branches and twigs. At least that helped focus her on something besides crawling toward death.

Chapter Eleven

Josh surveyed the indoor scene, the people glued to the floor. He prayed that one of them didn't panic enough to stand. So far, none had.

And Joan looked quite businesslike with her shotgun. Anybody who tried to get in might not live to talk about it. Donna had at least subsided, taking an order to keep an eye on Joan.

But there was a shooter outside. One, as far as he could tell. The sound seemed mostly centered, although it was moving around a bit. It had to have been to get Rusty.

Reject let out another low growl, hunched on the floor but appearing ready to spring.

The dog recognized the size of the threat out there.

Josh made a signal to Joan, who nodded from her guard-post near the kitchen.

With everyone on the floor, Josh felt he needed to get outside and try to locate the shooter. God, wildly pumping bullets into a room like this was madness. Anyone could have been wounded or killed. How could there possibly be a target among all these people?

He looked around the room at frightened faces, at bodies plastered to the floor, and began to signal with his hand for everyone to remain low. All he needed at this point was for someone to lose their head and leap upward in an attempt to flee. And there was simply no way to prevent it.

He kept low, to be invisible from the windows, hating the way it slowed him down. He hoped the rest took the hint.

But Josh had to try to locate the shooter. He needed to be proactive, not simply wait here for the next step in the shooter's plan—if he even had one.

Josh signaled once more for everyone to remain low, away from the line of sight from the windows. Out of harm's way insomuch as possible.

Then he opened one of the two front doors as quietly as he could, given that the rain had made hinges want to squeal. This time nature favored him. Not all the lubricant had failed.

Slipping out that door seemed almost too easy to do. The day's attempt at sunshine had already failed. Then to his utter annoyance, his sat phone beeped once.

Hell, he should have silenced it. But anything coming over it was likely to be important.

It was Angus. "Can't send you any more help. Mudslide downslope, sheriff and every spare hand are digging people out."

"Copy," Josh answered quietly, then put the phone on a quiet vibrate, kicking himself for not having done it sooner.

He waited for any sign that the call had been heard, but no sound came back at him. Maybe the shooter wasn't listening for anything so minor. Maybe he was more absorbed in his beastly task.

Regardless, Josh's heart squeezed until he felt the breath was being stolen from him. Krystal was out there. Carly had plenty of experience and would look after her, but not every possibility could be accounted for.

He might lose Krystal before he even got the chance to really know her.

Of all the losses he'd faced in his life, that one loomed as being among the largest.

KRYSTAL WASN'T DOING much better emotionally as she crept along the forest floor. She was terrified for all the people inside the lodge but she was even more terrified for Josh.

It seemed wrong, somehow, to value one person over another, but her heart wasn't listening anyway.

Josh had come unexpectedly, unwantedly, into her life, and she wasn't ready to let him go. Even if he wanted to go back to hiding in his stockade with his soldiers she doubted she would let him.

Not that he'd been hiding, she reminded herself. But he'd closed himself off so completely from the outside world that she could scarcely believe how quickly he'd melded himself into her life.

In just a few days, Josh Healey had emerged from privacy into the wider world of Cash Creek Canyon and had become respected by many. Maybe even liked. Her mother sure liked him.

She eased farther along the wet ground, ignoring a sharp stick that poked her thigh. She knew she was distracting herself with thoughts of Josh. Those could come later.

Right now there were a whole lot of people who needed protecting.

At least the shooter seemed to be focused on the lodge rather than individual cabins. Whether that might change was enough to make her heart jam into her throat.

All this open space. All these residents essentially unprotected by anyone. Even Josh's soldiers and the deputies creeping around out here couldn't possibly create a tight enough noose to prevent a single shooter from getting through.

Faintly she heard Carly moving through her part of the pincer movement. At least that's what Krystal thought it was called. She began to wonder if the retreat's "no guns" rule had been a wise one after all.

Except, she thought in a moment of irrepressible humor, imagine all these artists taking potshots from their cabins because something frightened them. This place would become a shooting gallery. If it wasn't already.

JOSH EASED ALONG the porch of the lodge, then down onto the wet ground. Twice now the shooter had chosen to blast holes in the windows and once had hit Rusty. What other area might he choose?

It would sure as hell help to know what the guy was after. What he was hoping to accomplish. Fish in a bowl was hardly a guide.

Could the guy just be interested in killing? He wouldn't be the first. Josh had seen those broken minds before. Minds that had crossed some internal barrier between respect for life and total disregard for it. Some even became excited by it. Justified by it.

He was also sure it wouldn't be long before fingers started to be pointed at his soldiers, albeit wrongly.

People wanted to believe vets with PTSD were dangerously violent, even when most of them only suffered from pain and misery and an attempt to block it from their own heads. Many were better off left in solitude or the company of others who shared their experience. Almost none wanted to hurt anyone else. They hurt enough within themselves.

He slipped farther along into the semidarkness of the still-dripping woods, listening for any betraying sound. Maybe this guy had discovered his own true nature when he killed Mason Cambridge.

Because something about the wildness of this attack seemed to have come from nowhere. Whoever the shooter was, it was highly unlikely he'd ever done this before. Nothing about this seemed carefully planned, merely carried out.

So what here had brought this all about?

Mason Cambridge? The epicenter of a lot of hate and anger. The man more than one person had pointed to as likely to be hated enough to be a victim.

But that wouldn't explain Sebastian, unless he was meant to be a diversion. Then there were these random gunshots through the windows. There had to be a point.

Surely this creep must have a point in all this, however nonsensical. Surely he must realize he was making a bigger target of *himself.* That far more people would be hunting for him now.

So what might make him not care? Or did he think

all of this confusion would protect him? Protect him from what?

Josh's mind was running overtime, trying to build some kind of profile that would help him hunt this killer.

And running overtime worrying about Krystal.

KRYSTAL FROZE AS another sharp crack tore through the air. Then, after a terrible moment, it was followed by a scream. Maybe two of them. Oh, God, had someone been shot?

She began to crawl more quickly through the undergrowth, heedless now of all the poking and hot ripping of her skin. This had to be stopped at any cost.

JOSH HEARD THE fourth shot as he was edging his way into the thicker woods. He still had a view of the lodge windows through the tree branches, though it was broken now by the greenery, the glass crazed by the earlier shot.

It was still enough. The scream caused his heart to freeze for just an instant. He knew that sound: someone else had been shot. He could only wonder how this might be affecting his people, who had had enough of those sounds to haunt their lives forever.

God! Trying to hurry his steps toward the last sound of the rifle without giving himself away slowed him down, made him feel like a charging bull who could race through any obstacle to reach the shooter except that he was continuously blocked.

Except the shooter could escape in these dense woods. Josh pulled his KA-BAR off his belt, ready. No crawling, not now. Only crouching as necessary.

Out there were his own soldiers, those who could face

this threat. Closing in, he was sure. These people knew how to tell where a gunshot sprang from. As long as the sound didn't reawaken horrors that had driven them to these woods.

But Krystal was out there, too, knowing nothing about how to handle such a situation.

God, he was torn between getting that damn shooter and racing out to help Krystal. Although Carly must be keeping her safe. Must have made it clear how to move surreptitiously.

He paused, fist clenched around his knife, and listened.

The falling of remaining raindrops from the trees didn't help at all, but faintly, just faintly, he believed he heard someone sliding over the ground, judging it had to be one of his soldiers. Few civilians knew how to be that quiet.

Approaching as quietly as possible. With any luck, the shooter wouldn't recognize the sound.

Nor should he, given his rampage. He was out for one thing only, and it didn't involve worrying about quiet sounds in the woods. In fact, Josh would guess at this point that the guy didn't care at all if he got caught.

A vendetta. But against whom? Who the hell had triggered this guy into this shooting spree?

Josh couldn't even imagine what might be the trigger, although given his psychological training he ought to be getting a clearer picture by now.

But all of that seemed to be escaping because of his determination, his concern about Krystal and the other guests.

And damn it all to hell, Krystal was out there unarmed except for a chef's knife he thought he'd seen her carry out. But how could she know what to do with it? Unlike Carly, unlike himself and others in their group, Krystal had no knife training.

He could have cursed a blue streak, but that all had to remain silently locked in his mind, where it offered no release at all.

Moving closer to where he had heard the last shot, he hoped he would get there before anyone else did. He'd gladly lay down his life before anyone else got hurt.

He'd lay it down for Krystal in a heartbeat.

Then there had been the scream from within the lodge. Someone had been wounded. God willing, someone in that place knew how to provide decent first aid.

He sped up his steps as much as he dared. Maybe it was time to draw the killer's attention. Right at himself. Away from everyone else.

KRYSTAL FORGOT EVERYTHING else when she heard the scream from the lodge. Her mother. All their friends. If that SOB had hurt or killed someone…

Forgetting everything Carly had been trying to teach her, Krystal shoved herself up from the wet ground and began to run toward the lodge. To hell with caution and catching the guy. That could come later. Right now someone had screamed from within those supposedly safe walls.

Someone might be dying while tree roots hampered her every step.

SHE REACHED THE front door at last and burst into the lodge, ready for almost anything. Or so she thought.

What she was not prepared for was the sight of Mel

Marbly, their longtime handyman, holding the entire room captive at the point of a rifle.

"Get in here," Mel growled. "But before you do," he shouted, "you tell those jackasses out there that if one of them comes through that door now I'm going to shoot your mother."

Krystal's legs weakened, but she had no doubt Mel could do as he threatened. Her mother lay in plain sight on the floor.

As did so many others who could be killed.

Having no choice, her hands shaking, she opened the front door and called out, hoping everyone heard her.

Then she heard a distant walkie crackle, followed by another. The word was being passed. Thank God. Reassurance that the situation was known helped her even though she knew it might do no good. At least she wasn't facing this alone.

Then she looked at the threat, trying to figure out if there was anything at all she could do. Especially since Mel held the deadlier weapon.

"Drop that knife," he said. "Now. Kick it away."

She dropped the chef's knife, certain it had been practically useless in her hands anyway. She kicked it aside, then faced Mel, hoping to take his attention from everyone else.

"Why are you doing this, Mel?"

The man sneered, actually sneered. In all the time Krystal had known him, she was sure she had not seen that expression on his face.

"Mel? Did something happen? Did something make you really angry?"

Mel snorted. "Like you didn't all see it. Like any of

you did a damn thing about it. Except one of you. One of you hated him enough to take action."

Her chest tightening, Krystal scanned the floor, wondering what collaborator Mel might be hiding here. Someone who might be as much of a threat? *God!* Then Mel snapped her back to the moment.

"Big-deal author," Mel growled. "Except he didn't have a new thought of his own during his entire career. He stole ideas like cherries to be plucked off a tree. He even stole some from that famous writer, what's his name? It's a wonder other writers didn't sue the pants off him."

Krystal's nerves tightened as she watched the way the gun barrel jerked around, as if Mel couldn't focus on a single victim.

"Why didn't any of you sue him?" Mel demanded of his hostages.

Nobody seemed to want to answer, understandably, given the way things were. Raising a voice might be the last thing anyone did.

So Krystal took it on herself, not caring if she sounded irritated with Mel. Caring only that she grabbed his attention.

"Sheesh, Mel, do you have any idea how expensive it is to sue for copyright infringement? How long it takes? And how freaking hard it is to prove?"

"If you steal…"

Krystal was already well tired of this argument. "For God's sake, Mel, how do you prove something was stolen? Seriously. *Your* idea? Shakespeare probably already had it. Your words? How many of them will it take before a judge will decide it's no accident? Then there's you, the writer. You make that kind of trouble, chances are no publisher will want to touch you with a ten-foot pole. So you kill your own career."

Mel's hand wavered, but only a bit. He was staring at someone, but Krystal couldn't tell whom.

"How would *you* know?" he demanded.

"Because every so often someone is an idiot enough to try to sue a big-name author. And if you follow the story you see the same thing. It can't be proven for a lot of reasons. Oh, once in a while someone succeeds, but not often."

Mel glared at her and Krystal didn't like the look in his eyes. Death seemed to be written there and she feared for everyone in the room.

Where were Josh and his people? Too far away in the woods to be of much help? Yet she was counting on him with her whole heart even though she knew she had to find a way to act herself. Who knew how far away he might be, and all these people depended on her.

Trying to think of another distraction, she spoke again. "Mel? Can I sit down? I hurt my leg out there."

He gave a short laugh, as if he didn't care, then waved the gun barrel toward an empty chair. Far enough from others that she couldn't protect anyone. Not what she wanted, but her only choice.

"Thank you," she said, feigning a gratitude she didn't at all feel. A quick scan told her the chef's knife was still too far away. God, she needed this man to make a mistake. An important one.

Mel continued to wave the gun around, a danger to everyone if his finger slipped on that trigger. It might, Krystal thought, gripping the seat of her chair with her hands until they felt white-knuckled. How could she prevent that, especially when Mel appeared to have started sweating.

"You feeling okay, Mel?"

He scowled. "That ain't gonna work on me. I'm just fine and you quit saying I might not be. I could decide to shoot *you*."

Krystal drew a long, shaky breath and put her life on the line. "Then why don't you, Mel? Just kill me now."

Joan made a whimper from where she lay near the kitchen, but Mel didn't glance her way. "Your mom could be next."

Krystal bit her lip. "Is something special about me, Mel? Why you don't want to shoot me this very minute?"

He shook his head, but the gun in his hands shook with the movement, just slightly. "Ain't got no problem with you, ladybug. You've always been nice to me. Nice to every damn person in here, even them that don't deserve it. Nah. I'd rather kill your ma. She's the one who keeps bringing that Mason back every damn year."

Krystal caught her breath. It was true. She saw her mother's eyes, saw the terror in them. *Do something*, Krystal told herself. *Do something before this guy gets out of hand.*

Mel raised the barrel of his gun just a bit. "Six shots in here, ladybug. Six. Then I got a clip with another ten. That's a lot of these idiots I can get rid of."

"But why should you want to?"

"Because that man treated me like crap! Every time he saw me. You think I give a real damn that he stole other people's work? Everyone complained about it, but not one of these cowards tried to do a damn thing about it. Not one. Bunch of scaredy-cats, sucking up to a man they think is a thief. Or maybe he wasn't so much the bad guy. I only know of one book he stole."

Quiet settled over the room.

"Whose?" Krystal demanded. "Whose book?"

Mel shook his head. "Why should I tell you if she won't?"

That was when Krystal began to scan the faces on the floor. A woman. Maybe that woman with the strangely dead eyes. Except those eyes looked terrified now, not dead.

What the hell was going on here?

OUTSIDE, JOSH WAS wondering pretty much the same thing. His soldiers were steadily gathering, along with deputies who'd been left behind to help. Gathering, ready for a large attack if one seemed warranted. But those damn windows might as well be opaque. No heads could be seen except that of one man, waving a rifle. A rifle that could get off six shots in quick order, more if he had a clip. A lot of people injured or dead.

More curses filled his head. Angus reached his side.

"Not looking good, boss," Angus muttered.

"Yeah. Civilians."

"Civilians were always the problem."

Too true. There were a lot of lives in there that had to be protected without setting off that creep with his dangerous rifle.

Josh closed his eyes briefly, trying to draw a mental image of the situation inside, trying hard not to picture Krystal in the middle of it. One person, no matter how loved, could inadvertently cause a distraction that led to chaos. Given his growing feelings for that one brave, lovely woman, she could cause that distraction.

Reaching deep within himself, Josh sought the detachment that had carried him through so many dangerous, deadly times. A detachment that could make decisions without overweighing the consequences.

People mattered, individuals mattered. But then there was the mission.

BESIDE HIM, ANGUS STIRRED. He had his radio set to as low a volume as he could get. Josh barely heard the murmuring between the troops.

"Soon," Angus said to him. "Everyone's pulling together in a tight cordon."

"Then what?" Josh asked almost sharply. "Yeah, we can storm the place but what about all those people in there? Hell, Angus, you don't need me to draw a map."

"Nah," Angus muttered. "I wish you could, Colonel."

So did Josh. He stared at those messed-up windows. Too bad he couldn't see more from here. Which left only one choice, a choice that might cause harm all by itself. If his soldiers became protective of him. If he got noticed by the bad guy inside. A dangerous choice but none were left.

"Angus, let everyone know I'm going on a solo recon. Don't anybody move. We gotta have some idea what's going on in there. Damn, we don't even know how many armed people are holding those hostages or who might be where."

"No kidding. Keep low, boss."

A reminder so obvious it could only be said out of caring. He gave Angus a friendly punch to his upper arm, then began creeping through restarting rain.

Damn, when had this forest floor become so full of tree roots?

Distracting question and he knew it. He'd had plenty of experience with using distractions to distance himself from the deadly trouble approaching. Distractions, but not any that would reduce his focus.

Focus was the one thing he couldn't afford to sacrifice now. Krystal. He clenched his teeth until they ached. She was his focus, though not his only goal.

The leaves and pine needles beneath his feet felt nearly greasy with the rain. Only his tactical boots kept him from sliding.

For the first time since this mess had begun, he found himself wishing for a rifle. It would have given him more control at a greater distance.

Unfortunately it might also set off the gunman or gunmen inside. A spray of bullets out of their semiautomatic rifles could be fast and deadly. Too fast to counter until the damage had been done.

Swearing under his breath, he crept forward toward the windows, his only hope of getting a decent view of the inside. At least most of the curtains were still open because the morning—had it only been *this* morning?—had seemed so bright and cheerful.

Now the gray pall of the rain had settled in again, killing useful light, washing everything in depth-defying shadows.

Damn weather.

Finally he reached the porch. Now he had to move

even more silently. Old wood creaked. Someone paying attention inside might hear it.

At least he heard no loud sobbing from inside the building. If someone had been shot, it hadn't been bad. Or maybe they were dead. The urge to kill was growing in him.

Creeping along the porch also filled him with a familiar anxiety. The kind that made him more cautious, that eased away any unnecessary fear.

Because there were some things he had ceased to fear at all, including his own death.

KRYSTAL'S MIND RAN at top speed as she sought to find an additional way to distract Mel. The man seemed to be enjoying waving that rifle entirely too much, as if he were looking forward to using it again.

Against the wall sat Julia Jansen, her leg grazed at the calf muscle, a tight bandage around it. Julia had grown pale, but she didn't appear to be losing a lot of blood. That was good.

But what had made Mel choose her for his first blast of death? Anything in particular?

"Mel," she said, drawing the man's attention her way again.

"Yeah. Why can't you just shut your damn mouth? You're gonna get one of these people shot."

She drew a long breath and closed her eyes. No, she couldn't leave Mel undistracted while he held that unsteady rifle.

"I get," she said quietly, opening her eyes, "why you hated Mason. But whatever did Sebastian do to you? He was so quiet and inoffensive."

"That's what *you* thought," Mel growled, waving the barrel around again as if it were nothing but a firecracker. "The guy pissed me off. Always creeping around. Always being nice to Mason. Weak, that's what he was. A suck-up."

Krystal nodded, not sure she was understanding this part at all, but what did it matter as long as Mel thought she did. With great effort, she didn't look at the windows although she was hoping to see half an army swing through them, guns blazing.

Except for everyone on the floor. Josh had to be thinking of them, too.

But as she listened to Mel, a conviction steadily grew inside her: Mel had not acted alone. He'd been provoked. Urged. In some ways Mel was a weakling himself, as she'd seen from time to time over the years.

Someone *could* push him. He might even get creative on his own, but the original driving force? Not Mel.

Desperately she looked around at the faces hiding beneath tables and chairs. Did one of them hide a truly ugly secret? Would it help if she could get Mel to spill the identity or just make it worse?

God, she wished she had some kind of experience to measure this against.

Then her gaze settled on Mary Collins. She remembered all the hard-eyed looks Mary used to send Mason's way, but right now Mary appeared as terrified as any of them.

But why wouldn't she, even if she had started this? She might be the one who had unleashed the monster. But she certainly had every reason to be terrified of Mel now.

God, Josh, where are you?

JOSH WAS STILL creeping along the windows, peering through the cracked glass to build the necessary map in his head. Damn, there were so many people in there, people who needed protection. But so far he'd seen only one shooter, one guy waving his gun like he didn't know what it was good for. Waving it too close to Krystal.

Muttering another curse, he turned away from the windows and covered his mouth, speaking quietly into his sat phone. At least it didn't crackle like the walkies.

He laid out what he could see as best he could see it, focusing on the shooter. Making sure everyone understood that Krystal was sitting alone in front of the door.

From what little he could hear inside, he could tell she was doing her best to keep the shooter distracted.

Brilliant, tough woman. Admirable.

But now he had to work his way around to the front door and try to line up the troops in the safest way possible.

KRYSTAL WAS REACHING the end of patience and, along with it, fear. Oh, she feared for everyone in this room but was losing fear for herself. Each time she glanced at her mother, the ache was piercing. Somehow she had to protect Joan no matter what it cost.

Taking a stab in the dark, she looked directly at Mary Collins, speaking directly to her. "Why'd you have Mel kill Sebastian? What did that man ever do to you?"

"I didn't make anyone kill him," Mary said, her voice leavening with fear.

"Nah," Mel agreed. "Except she thought it was a good idea after. 'Cuz then it wouldn't make any kind of sense about Mason. She liked my idea good enough then."

At that, Mary stood up, hardly seeing all the people scattered around her. "I never should have trusted you." Her voice quaked but her eyes had grown hard again.

"Maybe not," Mel said, waving the gun her way. "But I was smarter than you. All these folks running around wondering why these two guys should get killed. Didn't make no sense nohow. Puzzle piece that don't fit. Remember I told you about them? You thought I was smart then. Smarter than you because you never figured it out yourself."

Mary kept her hands still, as if she knew she faced serious danger from Mel. Krystal tried to judge if she could move fast enough—would she be able to wrestle that rifle from Mel's hands? Before he killed half the people in this room?

She readied her muscles, but even as she did so she realized she didn't have the leverage to leap that far.

"Guess you were going to get away," Mel said. "Leave me behind to face it all. Bet you didn't think I figured that out, did you?"

Now Mary was looking fearful again. "We had an agreement."

"Didn't have an agreement that you'd skip out and leave me behind."

"Damn it," Mary said, bursting out from her fear. "You were supposed to leave, too. And if you hadn't killed Sebastian…"

"If I hadn't killed Sebastian, what? You coulda sued Mason for years, but you spent your time just hating him. Nursing a need for vengeance. You got your vengeance, lady. And maybe you're the one I should be leaving behind."

Mel raised his rifle, pointing straight at Mary.

Then, after being silent all this time, Reject let out the most frightening howl, long, almost endless. Krystal's skin tingled as Mel became startled enough to aim his rifle at the dog.

But Reject had already leaped, flying toward Mary as if he had picked out a threat. Just as Krystal felt this was her only chance to take a leap at Mel, the doors behind her burst open with a loud bang. Glass from the windows finished shattering all over the floor.

Josh and his soldiers had arrived and in no time at all had Mel zip-tied. Mary tried to run but Krystal was having none of it. Changing her trajectory, she headed straight for the woman who had started all of this.

And Reject stormed along right beside her.

Chapter Twelve

After the hellish hours that had just passed, Krystal felt as if time sped up to almost overwhelming speed.

Mary Collins had managed to scratch Krystal's cheek, which the paramedics insisted on treating even though Krystal thought it was superficial.

She spent a long time hugging her mother, the two of them alternately crying and laughing with relief. They stood beside stretchers as Julia and Rusty were carried out by paramedics. They watched as Mary and Mel were carted out in handcuffs by Gage Dalton and his deputies. As it should be.

But she could scarcely believe the anger and rage that Mary screamed as she was carried away. All these years Mary had hidden those feelings so well that all Krystal had recognized of her before was that she had ice in her eyes when she saw Mason. Hardly a surprising thing, given Mason.

Still, it was shocking to see what had been right under her nose, a threat almost beyond imagination. And the saddest thing of all was that Sebastian had paid the price of his life merely to provide a distraction.

The minds of some people would always be beyond her grasp. Always.

THE LODGE BEGAN to quiet down. Voices that had been filled with disbelief and excitement gave way to a deeper silence as events began to sink in. They'd been held hostage at gunpoint.

Two among them had been killers.

Krystal thought she saw distrust in some of the faces as the artists looked at each other. Only Julia Jansen had received none of that in the minutes before the ambulance had been able to sweep her away along with Rusty.

Krystal felt the sting of that distrust herself. She and her mother. They had created this place. They had made it possible for killers to thrive here.

They were as guilty as anyone.

Krystal felt her throat tighten as she looked at her mother. Joan sat in the chair beside her and the two women held hands tightly.

"That's it," Joan whispered. "They'll all leave soon and I doubt many will come back."

Krystal would have liked to argue the point but looking around she knew her mother was right. The Mountain Artists' Retreat at Cold Creek Canyon would bear this stain for a long time. Too long for the business to survive.

Not even a bear attack five years before had dried up the business. That was a natural threat, one they were all warned about before coming here. One that could be controlled by proper behavior, such as never ever feeding the bears.

This was entirely different. Unnatural. Something that could have been prevented, although just how Krystal couldn't imagine. Should they have allowed their clients to bring their own weapons? Hardly. The "no weapons" rule had its basis in protection of wildlife, prevention of accidents and even a genuine, if unstated, concern about a client who might get too drunk and too angry in some kind of argument.

No, that rule had been meant to protect, and the fact that it hadn't this time was not her mother's fault. No one could plan for a Mel or a Mary. But it wasn't going to matter where the fault lay, was it?

Krystal smothered a sigh and wished she could find a single word to cheer her mother up. None came.

Joan shook herself finally as the room nearly emptied. "We need to staple those curtains closed," she said briskly. "Keep the night out."

And the fears.

To her surprise, the remaining veterans immediately stepped in to help with the job. Two staple guns were dug out of the equipment storage room at the back and willing hands went to work. The dark curtains rippled forlornly even as they were stapled tight over broken glass.

The chandelier lighting still worked, creating its rustic glow as it always had. One of the vets started a fire in one of the fireplaces.

In a surprisingly short time, most everything looked natural again. Although it never would be.

Joan's kitchen, with the help of Donna and one of her helpers, began churning out frozen cinnamon rolls and biscuits for the vets and those who remained. The coffee machines began working overtime.

The remaining vets ate quickly, then sifted away into the outside world, a world they didn't want to share anymore, but a world they had just saved. Even Carly Narth, who had spent the dangerous hours beside Krystal, vanished as well. Krystal had wanted to thank her sincerely, but the opportunity was lost, for now.

Reject, happy with a biscuit, curled up on a chair and looked quite content. Krystal stroked him, thinking what a hero that husky was.

Maybe a dozen of their residents remained, talking quietly now, eating cinnamon rolls and drinking coffee.

Deciding the fate of the artists' retreat? Sharing the million reasons they would never return?

Joan walked over to them, pausing at each table for a conversation, although what her mother could say to change any minds after this Krystal couldn't imagine. But maybe she could. Some of these relationships stretched back for years.

And after a bit she saw a few faces smile. Okay, then. Maybe Joan could work a miracle.

For her part, the day was getting to her. Reject had curled up and gone to sleep and she so very much wanted to join him.

Except that after today she suspected her dreams would be nightmares, filled with all the horrors Mel and Mary had brought into her life. Into everyone's life.

They'd probably need to get a full-time psychologist just to deal with this aftermath.

Then she thought of Josh. He was a psychologist and apparently he now devoted his life to helping people who'd been through traumatic experiences. Although she suspected that what had happened at this lodge would never in any way reach the level of horror those vets had known.

Just look at Carly Narth with her badly burned body

and head. God, the option of suicide had probably sounded good to her at times.

Despite not being able to fully relax, however, Krystal rested her head in her hand, elbow on the table, and began to drift into an uncomfortable sleep.

Then a voice drew her from the dawning of a nightmare.

"Krystal?" Josh, his voice quiet, almost gentle.

She pried her eyes open.

"I have to go. My people may need to help each other deal with what's just happened. I don't know how long it might take. Several days?"

Krystal managed a nod even as her heart sank. "They were brave," she said, although she could scarcely imagine how emotionally brave some had been, given their backgrounds and the troubles they faced now.

"Yes," Josh said. "They are. Do you want to stay here or do you want me to walk you back to your cabin?"

Oh, the peace of her cabin sounded so good just then, but she still saw Joan across the room.

"I need to stay," she told Josh. "There's an aftermath here, too. I don't want my mom to face it alone."

He nodded understanding. "I'll see you in a few days."

Then he was up, striding toward the door, his remaining two soldiers following him.

Back to their stockade. Back to the place where they had been trying to keep the world out.

God, it all stank.

Two people with a grudge had just psychologically wounded dozens. And to what end?

Chapter Thirteen

Josh saw Krystal often over the next week, but only from a distance. She had returned to her cabin and her habit of sitting outside with her morning coffee.

A plank walkway, chest-high, lined the interior walls of the stockade and he, too, returned to a morning ritual of pacing it with his coffee.

Between him and Krystal, Cash Creek roiled, still muddy from the storm, still carrying some debris from higher up. The stepping stones had vanished beneath racing water.

A boundary. Probably a good thing, given the thoughts that had been plaguing him.

His people were doing well, considering. They felt proud of what they had done, proud of facing their personal demons to do it. But pride notwithstanding, none showed the least inclination to leave the stockade walls again anytime soon.

The morning was chilly. Josh had found an old shearling jacket buried in his belongings and wore it instead of his usual camo jacket. Warm. Soft with age. The mug of coffee in his hands was growing cold, but he didn't care.

He was staring too much and too often at Krystal and she probably knew it. People always knew when someone was staring at them. He just hoped he wasn't making her uncomfortable. He kept looking away, training his gaze on something else, pretending that the forest out there was the most fascinating thing he'd ever seen.

And in a way it was. He had come here only because his family had owned this land and that piece of forest for generations. Then he got the letter from the Forest Service saying that the land appeared to be abandoned and would become part of the forest if no response was made within a year...

Well, it hadn't taken him long to come up with a great idea for this place. Isolated, the beauty of being surrounded by woods, the opportunity to perform tasks that suited each individual? Yeah. Perfect.

And so far it had been. Well, until the events of the last week. At least those seemed to have caused mere psychological ripples rather than the emotional tsunami he'd feared.

A few phone calls with Gage Dalton assured him the wheels of justice were grinding for Mel and Mary, but there'd be an inevitable need for testimony from his troops. Maybe they could take care of most of that out here? Gage said he'd make that possible insofar as he could.

Problems. Problems upon problems, but his gaze drifted back to Krystal again. So near yet so far. Maybe the biggest problem on his plate. Years ago he'd learned to let go of things to the extent that he could. Let go of people because they'd go away eventually.

Although there were faces and names he carried in

his heart like burning brands. They'd never go away. But he'd made an uncomfortable peace with that.

So he ought to be able to turn his back on Krystal Metcalfe, right?

Except he didn't seem able to, even when he castigated himself with awareness of his own problems and limitations, and how little he had to offer a woman. A normal life? Hah. A family? He didn't know if he would dare.

Comfort and security? Well, security maybe. Comfort wasn't likely in this stockade. Nor would he consider leaving this structure or asking her to live here. People here depended on him and they had every right to. He'd given them the right.

He looked down at the central parade ground where his group had begun to move on to their daily chores.

His *friends.*

But the force that was drawing him toward Krystal was growing stronger by the hour. More irresistible.

KRYSTAL ORDINARILY LOVED Cash Creek, but right now she loathed it. Sitting on her porch, booted feet up on the railing, coffee in hand, all she could see was a muddy gash that cut her off from Josh's stockade.

She was aware that he watched her sometimes. She watched him, too, when she thought she could avoid detection. Part of her felt extremely foolish, sure this was nothing more than the kind of crush she'd experienced in high school.

But her heart kept telling a different story. Even though she hardly knew the man, she knew she wanted him.

And not just physically. Something about Josh had reached past old barriers constructed to protect herself from heartache, a heartache experienced so long ago that she had all but forgotten it.

Apparently she hadn't. A boy she could barely remember, a summer romance shorter than the summer itself, had left a deep mark on her, a scar that had stayed with her although she rarely thought about it.

Until now. Now it rode her with warnings of heartbreak, barely remembered though it was.

Josh couldn't possibly want her anyway. She was nothing, a young woman who couldn't quite get her career on track, a woman whose life seemed tied up with a now dying business. A woman with a very limited future, it seemed.

What did she have to offer? He was a man of the world. He'd seen things she didn't even want to imagine, had lived a breadth of experience that made her own comfortable life dull by comparison. More importantly, he had devoted his life to an important cause. She certainly couldn't claim that.

Hell, what did she even have to talk to him about?

Separate worlds. Separate lives.

Divided as much by Cash Creek as anything right then.

She hated that creek. Then she shook her head at herself and headed inside for fresh coffee and another stab at a blank page on her computer screen.

What if she wrote about the nightmare they'd all just survived? At least it might clear the lingering cobwebs of the horror from her mind.

JOAN CALLED A few hours later. The mountain afternoon was turning chilly as it often did, and Krystal had wrapped herself in a blue fleece sweater, one long enough it reached her knees.

"Well," Joan said, "you'll be amazed to know that I'm getting some reservations for this winter. From some of last year's visitors. And some, believe it or not, from people who were here with us during that horror."

That horror. Neither of them seemed able to describe it any other way.

Krystal's heart leaped happily. "That's great, Mom. I guess some folks aren't thinking that any of that was the fault of the retreat."

Joan sighed. "I could easily see how some of them might. You were right when you said I should have stopped inviting Mason."

"As if anyone could have predicted this. Really? I just wanted him gone because he was so irritating. Too irritating apparently."

"Mary Collins must have thought he was more than irritating. Anyway, I still can't believe that a resentment could flower into that horror."

That horror. "I think flower might be the wrong word."

Joan laughed. "You are *so* right. So when are you coming up here again? I know there's going to be a lot of banging for a few days to repair those windows, but *I'm* here to entertain you."

"Tomorrow morning," Krystal promised. "After my morning coffee."

After the call, she once again regarded the roiled creek with displeasure and peered over her coffee cup at Josh Healey.

Oh, man, did she have it bad. And he probably hardly knew she existed anymore, even though she caught him sometimes looking her way from his stockade. Nope. He was probably thinking about other things. As proved by his disappearance from the walkway, gone on to other occupations.

A week. Slightly more. Not even a wave across the canyon.

Sighing, she threw hope to the winds and returned to that blank screen in front of her. Where to start writing about those terrible events?

Before she could think of a single word to type, however, someone knocked on her door. Startled, she jumped up. In an instant she realized her sense of safety had been badly damaged by the events with Mel and Mary.

It was just her door. Just her *door*. She'd never hesitated to open it before, but now she stared at it as if a poisonous snake waited beyond.

God, she couldn't allow this to continue, to allow her entire life to be permanently altered by those two beasts.

It was just a knock on the door, for heaven's sake. It was probably someone from the lodge bearing some food gift from Joan's kitchen, where Donna and her help seemed to be determined to produce menus fit for a king, few guests as they had at the moment.

The knock came again. "Krystal?"

It was Josh. Her heart nearly stopped and she froze in place. Part of her wondered how he'd crossed the creek, part of her skittered around inside her head trying to figure out what he could possibly want here. Most of her was afraid of what he might *not* want here.

"Krystal? Are you okay?"

At last she managed to shake herself free of conflicting

thoughts. Just a neighborly visit. Nothing more. Maybe he needed a cup of sugar?

At that, the last of her tension seeped away and she grinned at herself. Much better.

She took the three steps and opened the plank door. Josh stood there, wearing jeans and a shearling jacket and muddy rubber boots up to his knees.

"Hi," he said with a half smile. "You busy?"

"Um…no. But how'd you cross that creek?"

His smile widened. "I found a place upstream that wasn't too bad. I'll keep my muddy boots out here, though."

"Coffee? I can bring it out."

"Sounds great." He moved to sit in one of her Adirondack chairs.

But before she stepped inside, she turned to look straight at him. "Why," she asked nervously, afraid of his answer, "did you hunt up a way to cross the creek?"

He tilted his head slightly, then shrugged, his expression growing inscrutable. "Seemed there was this lady on the other side of the creek and I couldn't stop thinking about getting over here to see her."

Her heart stopped for the second time in just a few minutes and she slowly sat on the edge of the other chair, coffee forgotten. The creek rushed below, swallowing sound, nearly silencing a breeze that began to blow in the treetops.

"Josh?" Her voice trembled, then her hands shook as well.

"I know this is nuts," he said, his face still unreadable. "You have every right to tell me to swim back across that creek and never show my face again. I mean, look at all those people across the way that I'm working with. Who'd want to take that on?"

Krystal caught her breath and her hands knotted together. She hardly dared to allow her imagination to fill in the blanks in what he was saying. Or what he hadn't said.

But small tendrils of hope began to grow in her heart. Josh... She couldn't even explain to herself what was happening inside her.

He waved a hand. "Sorry. I'm naturally ham-handed when it comes to talking about my feelings. Wouldn't have thought this would be harder than a group therapy session."

"Harder?" Her nails were beginning to dig into her palms as every bit of fear and nervousness tiptoed its way to hope.

"I get that you don't know me," he continued almost roughly. "How could you? We're basically strangers to each other."

She couldn't dispute that and hope began to slip away. Just a little.

"But we have time to talk ourselves blue in the face if we want to. The thing is, Krystal, do you want to?"

Something sucked nearly all the air from the universe. Krystal's heart hammered, her voice grew thready. "Want to?"

"Get to know me. Me to get to know you. I know it won't be easy because I won't give up my soldiers for any reason, but we can cross that line if we get to it. In the meantime, we need to talk to each other. We can give those damn stepping stones a real workout."

Then he astonished her, rising from his chair to come

kneel right in front of her and take her cold hands in his large, warm ones.

"Like I said," he repeated huskily, "I'm ham-handed when it comes to stuff like this. But, Krystal, you're haunting my dreams and damn near every waking moment. You have me thinking about things I haven't considered in years. Things like a family. A future. And I want them with you."

That's when he let go of her. "I guess this would be a good time to leave."

She reached for his hands, grabbing them tightly as she pulled them back. "Why?"

"Why should I go?" He shook his head. "Dang, Krystal, I'm damn near a perfect stranger, I just marched into your house and threw a whole bunch of emotions at your feet and I have no business to expect anything but a heave-ho."

But every barrier, every fear, every uncertainty inside Krystal washed away like the crashing water on Cash Creek. She rose to her feet, wrapped her arms around his shoulders and pulled him close to her as an indescribable joy rushed through her.

"Damn it, Josh, don't you dare think of leaving, I've been craving you, too, and you'll break my heart if you..."

He didn't let her finish. He stood, sweeping her off her feet, a huge smile on his face. "Screw the mud," he said as he headed for the door and the interior of her house, "I'll clean it up later. The only thing I care about right now is loving you with every ounce of my being."

"Oh, yeah," she said, leaning her head into his shoulder and grabbing the front of his shirt tightly. "Please. And promise never to stop."

"Never," he said as he kissed her deeply.

Only the second of many, many more to come.

"I love you," she whispered, surprised at the words that escaped her heart, words she had been for so long afraid to say.

"I love you, too," he said gruffly. "Impossible, yeah? No. It's here, it's now."

Then he added, "It's here forever."

* * * * *

PERIL IN PINEY WOODS

DEBRA WEBB

Chapter One

Pampered Paws
Piney Woods, Tennessee
Saturday, May 4, 10:00 p.m.

Megan Lewis was exhausted, but she smiled at her favorite pooch. "You got some nerve making me stay in the shop this late."

Raymond, her ten-year-old border collie, gazed up at her with those eyes that she could never resist. He lay on the floor next to the kennel door where the newest pet abandoned in front of her shop cowered in fear. Fortunately, incidents like this didn't happen very often—at least not at her shop. But when they did, she refused to let the animal down any more than it already had been.

She had no choice. Her heart wouldn't allow anything else.

The beagle that had been left on her doorstep early that morning wasn't a young animal. Meg suspected she was eight or ten. She'd found the poor baby at the front door before dawn. Couldn't be a local. Everyone in Piney Woods knew Meg lived upstairs. The only reason she hadn't heard the culprit's arrival or departure was because she'd been in the shower. But when she'd stepped out, Meg had certainly heard the animal's howl. Beagles had a distinct yodel-like sound.

Unlike most animals abandoned on the sides of roads or at vet clinics or even businesses like this one, there had been a note attached to the beagle's collar. The owner had explained that Pepper was not doing well, and the owner had no money to take care of her. She or he hoped that the owner of such a charming and caring place would be able to give Pepper the love and help she needed.

Certainly, Meg would try.

Just after lunch, Lonnie Howell, the local vet, had stopped in for a look. He would need to do more testing, but he suspected a heart issue. Meg was to drop Pepper at his clinic on Monday for the necessary testing and a more accurate diagnosis. Lonnie hadn't made any promises, but Meg knew him well enough to understand he would do whatever was necessary to help the animal whether there was money involved or not.

Meg crouched down and smiled at Pepper. "Don't worry, girl. We're going to take very good care of you, and once you're well enough, we'll see that you get a proper home. Just bear with me until then."

Pepper's sad eyes tugged at Meg's emotions. This career was definitely tougher in some ways than her former one. She gave Raymond a good scratch between the ears. She doubted he would be coming upstairs tonight. Raymond sensed when other animals were in an elevated state of stress. He stayed close when he felt his presence was needed.

"You're a good boy," Meg said before pushing to her feet. She'd already locked up, but before going upstairs she made a final walk-through. The lobby was secure. The computer and drawers at the check-in counter were locked up. Since she wasn't open on Sundays, she used the day for a deep clean. She and one of her two employees—they alternated Sundays off—would spend the afternoon making the place shine. Cleanliness was important to Meg and to the animals. Folks trusted her with their beloved pets, and she wasn't about to let them down.

The kennels were all secure. Only three dogs and one cat were staying overnight. Pampered Paws was primarily a grooming service, but they did some boarding too—like the four presently registered for the weekend. No matter that Piney Woods was a small town, Meg actually had five customers whose dogs were on a weekly day care plan. The owners worked long days in the city of Chattanooga and had no one to look after their pets. Meg's shop was the first in Piney Woods to offer the service, and it had gone over far better than she'd anticipated.

In the beginning Meg hadn't expected to take on any extra services beyond grooming. She'd arrived in Piney Woods after having already purchased the small two-story building on the main street that cut through the center of the little town. After exiting her former career in a hasty manner, she'd decided her only other marketable skill had been with pets—mostly dogs. She'd grown up on a farm with lots of animals and no shortage of dogs. Her father, too, had taken in every stray that came along. Meg had shown a real knack with the lost animals. Her father had called her the dog whisperer. The term was a bit exaggerated, but she'd never met a dog—or any animal really—she couldn't get along with.

They bonded quickly and easily. God knew she'd had all kinds of dogs and numerous cats throughout her life— particularly growing up on the farm, which made her well acquainted with the art of grooming. Seemed like the perfect fallback plan after her first choice fell apart.

She checked the back door and then headed upstairs to a studio apartment the former owner had used as a rental for extra income. The place was perfect for Meg. She didn't need much space. Just the basics. She unlocked the door and went inside, relocking it behind her. Crime in Piney Woods was basically nonexistent, but old habits died hard. Having a locked door between her and the rest of the world was the only way she could sleep—that and the one weapon she kept on her person at all times. No matter that in Tennessee it wasn't uncommon to see folks carrying a gun or knife, Meg preferred the element of surprise, which meant keeping hers carefully concealed.

Certainly, life was different here, but she liked it. On the farm in Bakersfield, California, where she'd grown up, she had learned to appreciate solitude. Not so much as a kid but certainly as an adult whenever she'd visited. The family farm hadn't been one of the massive multi-million dollar operations. Just a small vineyard and end-less acres of fruit trees that had at one time provided a decent living to their little family.

Her heart squeezed at the memory of running through the orchards with at least one dog on her heels and her father grinning at her for once again escaping the house when her mother had grounded her. She'd sneaked out so many times before age twelve that her mother had in-sisted she was going to be like Dorothy in *The Wizard of Oz*. One day she was just going to disappear, and no one would know where she'd gone. Her mother had warned that there might not be a yellow brick road to guide her to where she needed to go, much less to a wizard who could get her back home. Meg shook her head. She had loved that movie as a kid. She'd learned every line by heart and often played out the part of Dorothy, complete with running away. Not that she ever went very far or intended to stay gone. Looking back, Meg could only think that it was a good thing she'd been an only child. She wasn't sure her parents could have survived two like her.

Funny how her mother, may she rest in peace, had been more right about her daughter disappearing than she could possibly have known. Disappearing had become her job...

You can never go back.

Meg turned off the thought and flipped on the lights. That had been another time, another life.

She banished the memories. This was her life now. No point looking back.

She crossed the room and stared out the front window at the deserted street below. Piney Woods was the quintessential small town. One main thoroughfare, Pine Boulevard, which was really just a two-lane street with vintage shops lining the more "downtown" portion. Upon entering Piney Woods proper, there was a full-service gas station and convenience store just before reaching the sidewalks and vintage shops of the old downtown strip. Meg's place was the first shop on the left. A two-story brick building with a canopied entrance and meager parking out front. The parking slots along the boulevard were few and first come, first served.

The downstairs portion of her shop had long ago been

tiled with a commercial grade product which made for the perfect flooring for a pet grooming service. She'd had some substantial plumbing upgrades completed, along with the framing up of separate spaces for kennels. Also lucky for her, since her shop was the first in the row on this side of the boulevard, she had a good-sized area in the back that could be a patio or extended parking. Instead, it had become a pet playground and had only two extra parking spots—one for her and for whichever of her two employees was on duty. Just over a year later, it turned out to be the right decision since five of her favorite clients had asked for pet-sitting services.

Another perk of her shop's location was the fact that she could see everyone who drove into town if she wanted to stand at the window and watch. There was a single main street that led into Piney Woods, and it dead-ended at the cliffs that overlooked the city of Chattanooga and the valley below. There were lots of little side roads in and around Piney Woods, but none led directly in or out of town. It was either come back out along Pine Boulevard or go over the cliffs at the other end or down the mountain along rugged trails on the two remaining sides. It was the perfect setup for someone who needed to meld into the background while monitoring the comings and goings around her.

Meg picked up the binoculars she kept on the deep windowsill. She eased onto it and used her binoculars to scan the street. The street lamps allowed her to see the sidewalks and any pedestrians who might be out and about. Folks who lived in Piney Woods were in for the night. She smiled. It wasn't like there was anything to do at this hour anyway.

The shops along the boulevard were closed. Most had dim exterior lighting. Some left a single low wattage light on inside as well. No one on the mountain wanted bright lights obscuring the view of the stars. The diner, the post office, a local pharmacy, a tiny bookstore and a small organic market were on the side of the boulevard opposite Pampered Paws. Another reason Meg had chosen this spot. At the time of her purchase, one year ago, the bookstore had been just a vacant shop. But it was on the wrong side of this little main thoroughfare for her use. She preferred being on the side with the small urgent care and the vintage furniture store.

Meg had wanted to be able to see folks coming in and out of the diner and those other more often visited shops by the folks passing through. She had made it a point to know the backgrounds of as many of the locals as possible—not that there were many. Keeping tabs on any new faces was important. Made life more comfortable for Meg.

She shifted her attention to the right, to the part of Pine Boulevard that transitioned into a county road where the Gas and Go, the gas station and convenience store combo—another key operation to keep an eye on—was lit up like the beacon of a lighthouse reaching out to anyone wandering in the dark. It was the only all-night gas and food service available for several miles. Further along that same county road was the fire station and a Hamilton County sheriff's substation. The bigger stores and supermarkets were a half hour or more away. Apparently, this was the way the citizens of Piney Woods liked it, because they had kept out all big business operations that showed interest in the area.

Another reason Meg had chosen this little town. Made her life all the easier.

She hoped things stayed the way they were.

Did anything? Ever?

Meg dismissed the troubling idea and zoomed in on the one vehicle parked at the Gas and Go.

Dark blue or black truck. Dented tailgate. Georgia license plate.

No surprise—they were very close to the Tennessee-Georgia line.

Jennifer O'Neal was on duty. Alone. The Gas and Go always had two employees on duty except for the late shift. Meg rolled her eyes. Sure, there might be less business at this hour, but it was prime time for trouble. Worse, the girl had just turned twenty-one. She was as thin and elfin as Tinker Bell.

"You should look for a better job, Jennifer," she muttered.

Meg zoomed in on the young woman behind the counter. Jennifer's eyes were wide with something like fear… her mouth opened slightly as if preparing to scream. *What the hell?* Meg's heart thumped as she zoomed back out far enough to take in the man who now stood at the counter.

Gun.

The gun in his hand sent Meg's heart into her throat. She put aside the binoculars, grabbed her cell and headed for the stairs in a dead run.

By the time she reached the back door downstairs, she had Deputy Sheriff Ernie Battles on the line. "Ernie, this is Meg. There's a—" Meg bit her tongue to hold back the code "—what looks like a robbery happening at the Gas and Go. The perp is armed with a handgun."

"On my way," Ernie said quickly, then he swore. "I'm maybe ten minutes out."

The rumble of the cruiser's engine roared over the line as he obviously rammed the accelerator.

"Should I call 911?" Meg had to do something. She couldn't just stand here.

"They won't get there any faster but go ahead. I need to drive."

The call ended.

Meg's gut clenched hard, and drawing in a breath was nearly impossible as she unlocked the back door and slipped out. As she moved through the darkness to the front corner of her shop, she called 911. She provided the necessary info, then hung up and shut off the ringer of her phone. The operators and dispatchers preferred to keep a caller on the line or to call back under certain circumstances. Meg didn't have the time for additional conversation, and she certainly didn't want her phone ringing or vibrating in the next few minutes.

She flattened against the building, held perfectly still and watched the movements of the two inside the Gas and Go. The guy with the gun was shouting. Jennifer was cowering in fear.

Ten minutes. Another twist to her gut at the idea that Jennifer did not have ten minutes.

Meg glanced both ways. The street remained empty.

This guy would be long gone, and Jennifer could be dead in ten minutes.

Meg swore. Then she sprinted across the street.

She hunkered down as she reached the perimeter of

the well-lit parking lot. The truck—obviously the one belonging to the man with the gun—shielded her to some
extent from view.

Keep going.

Meg moved closer.

Though she no longer carried a gun on her person,
she did keep a sheathed knife at the small of her back. It
was easier to conceal than a handgun. She reached for it
now. Small, lightweight. Made for survival.

On the driver's side, since it was shielded from view,
she stabbed both tires, twisted and dragged the blade to
ensure the job was done. Stabbing through the sidewalls of
tires wasn't an easy task but her knife was very sharp and
it wasn't her first time. Plus, she was strong. She may have
left her former career, but she hadn't walked away from
staying fit and prepared. It was too essential to her survival.

With that done, she eased to the front fender to get an
update on what was happening inside.

The perp had pulled Jennifer from behind the counter
and was dragging her toward the short corridor that led
into the back storage area of the building. Meg had only
been back there once. She'd come over for paper towels,
and Jennifer had been too busy to leave the counter to
go into the back for more since she hadn't had a chance
to restock that night. Meg had a general idea of the lay-
out. There was a back door. The guy could do whatever
he had in mind and then slip out the rear of the building.

Dread swelled in Meg's chest.

There was only one reason for him to take Jennifer
into the back…before taking off with whatever cash had
been in the register. He either wanted to play with her,
or he intended to kill her…maybe both.

Deputy Battles absolutely would not get here in time to stop either situation.

"Damn it," Meg muttered.

She tightened her grip on the knife and lunged toward the entrance. With her free hand, she grabbed the door handle and held her breath. Opening it wouldn't be the problem. It was the door's closing that would trigger the little bell that sounded off with each customer's arrival.

She released the door, raced to the counter. She launched herself over it, landing quietly on the large black rubber antifatigue mat as the bell jingled. Crawling quickly, she made herself as small as possible at the end of the counter closest to the front of the store, where she would be able to watch for the deputy's arrival.

Assuming she was still breathing when that happened.

The near silent tread of rubber soles on the shiny tile floor blasted across her senses.

The guy with the gun was coming.

She didn't have to see him to know he would be scanning the aisles and surveying the parking area around his truck. He'd heard the bell on the door.

He stopped at the front of the counter and leaned across, expecting to find the trouble hidden behind it.

Meg didn't dare breathe.

She had, at best, one shot at this.

As he walked toward the end of the counter where she was hiding, her muscles bunched in anticipation of lunging for him.

Tension vibrated inside her, fingers tightening on her knife.

A scream from the back of the building stopped his momentum.

"Help me!" Jennifer's trembling voice. "Please help me."

He swore, and that single, muttered word told Meg that he was nearly on top of her—just around the corner of the counter—maybe two feet away from her position.

Meg dared to move her head, leaning back just far enough to see him from the shoulders up. His back was turned to her. He was torn between shutting up his hostage and ensuring no one else was inside the store with him.

Jennifer screamed again.

Meg readied to move.

Now or never.

She shot upward.

He twisted…the weapon in his hand leveled on Meg.

The logo of a rock band on his tee, ragged jeans and biker boots flashed through her brain in that single second before she propelled herself forward. She swiped her knife across his throat. Twisted her body into a roll. Hit the tile and rolled.

The gun went off.

The ping of the bullet hitting the floor next to her had her scrambling farther away.

Then the gun bounced on the floor.

Meg scrambled to her feet.

His hands were at his throat, blood spewed between his fingers and flowed down his torso in a river of red.

His gaze connected with Meg's for a split second— damn, he was young—before he crumpled to the floor.

No matter that he was a goner, she kicked the gun across the floor before rushing toward the storage room. She bypassed the restrooms and the entrance to the cooler and rushed through the open door that led into the back, into the storeroom.

Jennifer, her clothes half ripped off her body, huddled in the floor next to boxes of paper products.

Her left wrist was tied to a metal pipe that snaked up the wall. Meg cut her loose and then tucked her knife away. She reached toward the terrified young woman. "You're okay now, Jennifer. Deputy Battles is on the way."

Jennifer's eyes remained wide with fear. Tears and mucus streamed down her face. "He…he…"

"He won't hurt you now."

Meg sat down on the floor next to her and held her until help arrived.

Chapter Two

Gas and Go
Pine Boulevard
11:50 p.m.

The blue lights from the two sheriff's department SUVs throbbed in the night, sending flashes through the glass-fronted store. Meg couldn't say for sure how long it had taken for Deputy Battles to arrive. Long enough for the adrenaline that had been coursing through her body to recede, leaving her to face the reality of what had just gone down in a colder, harsher light. Long enough for her to understand that there was a strong possibility this would change everything.

There had been no alternative. She'd only done what she had to do.

Another deputy had cordoned off the half of the parking lot nearest the entrance with yellow crime scene tape. A sedan bearing the county's CSI team logo had arrived maybe half an hour ago. The sergeant, probably the leader of the team, had glanced at Meg as he entered the shop.

The coroner had taken the body away a few minutes after that. There was a lot of blood on the floor.

A *lot* of blood.

Meg blinked and turned her face away to prevent staring at the spot on the shiny tile floor where the perp had expired. She hadn't seen that much blood in a while.

She'd hoped never to see or to be involved with this sort of thing ever again.

This was so, so not good.

Her nerves jangled as she allowed the idea of what had just happened to sink in a little deeper.

Not good at all.

Damn it.

The perp had been identified as Zyair Jones, a career criminal from just across the state line. Though only twenty-five, he had a long line of offenses, not the least of which was armed robbery and sexual assault. Jennifer might not feel like it just now, but she was lucky to be alive. Men like the perp who'd dragged her into that storeroom typically escalated, and judging by his extensive rap sheet, an escalation had been due any time now.

Meg shifted in the stiff plastic chair next to the counter at the farthest end of the shop where she'd been sequestered by Deputy Battles. Since there were no other seats in the building except for the one she'd seen at the desk in the storeroom, she supposed this one was for the clerk on duty to take a load off when the opportunity presented itself. When someone like Jennifer was on duty alone, going to a breakroom was not really an option. The entrance would need to be locked for her to even go to the restroom for a personal relief break. Meg imagined the boss didn't want that door locked any more than necessary.

The owner had been called and, like the rest of those interested in what had occurred tonight, waited beyond the crime scene perimeter. She'd spotted the lady who owned the diner and the man who'd opened the book shop. There were several others, but none she recognized from this distance.

Meg had already given Battles a quick overview of what happened while the paramedics examined Jennifer. But he would be back when he completed his questioning of the victim. Meg had watched his face as she answered the questions he posed. He'd tried not to look surprised when she'd told him about swiping the knife across the guy's throat, but he'd failed to keep his face clear of the reaction. There were other questions he would have for the next round. Like why did she carry a knife? What had prompted her to react so violently? What had made her think to slash the truck tires before coming inside? Etcetera.

She gave her head a little shake. Providing answers that would assuage any concerns or uncertainties he had would be easy enough for now, but the notion of what she'd done would linger in his thoughts. Every time he saw her from this moment forward, he would remember this night. The neighboring shop owners would talk among themselves about how she'd been able to take down the would-be robber and rapist. And there was no question what Jones had intended. The cash from the register had been in his pocket, and he'd torn at Jennifer's clothes while he regaled her with his intentions. Still, there would be talk.

Nothing she could do about that.

For now, she was just thankful she was seated far enough away from that expansive wall of glass to avoid the prying eyes. The last thing she needed was someone taking her photo and putting it on the net or, God forbid, in the news.

"Meg."

She glanced up at the sound of her name. Battles stood at the entrance to the short corridor that led into the back. He motioned for her to come with him.

Careful to keep her back to the front of the shop, she did as he asked.

Now for the second round of questioning.

When she reached him, he turned and walked with her toward the storeroom door. "One of the deputies from the Dread Hollow substation is driving Jennifer home, but she wanted to see you before leaving."

"Is she okay?" Evidently so, but asking was the appropriate response.

"She's shaken up," he said, "as you can imagine, but she sustained nothing more than minor physical injuries."

She got it. The horror of what happened would be the only mark that lingered. For how long would be entirely up to Jennifer and her ability to bounce back from trauma without developing PTSD. Hopefully she would be one of the lucky ones. With the right kind of support, it was possible.

When Meg walked through the door, Jennifer rushed to her and hugged her hard. "Thank you so much for saving me." She drew back. Tears flooded down her cheeks. "Deputy Battles told me I was so lucky that you spotted the trouble and came to help since he couldn't get here fast enough." She looked away a moment. "He said he was going to kill me."

"But he didn't get the chance," Meg assured her, then she produced a smile. "And what kind of neighbor would I be if I didn't help?"

Jennifer's lips quivered as she managed a dim smile. "Thank you." She scrubbed at her face with her hands before resting her gaze on Meg's once more. "You saved my life."

Meg nodded. "We both got lucky."

"Your parents are waiting for you," Battles said. "You go on home and take it easy for a while, like I said. And call that counselor."

Jennifer promised she would then the other deputy ushered her away. When the back door closed behind the two, Battles said, "Let's go over a couple more things, and then I'll have Deputy Porch escort you back to your place."

Porch was the deputy from Dread Hollow who'd just left with Jennifer. Meg made it a point to know all members of law enforcement in the area. Knowledge was power as well as protection.

"That won't be necessary," Meg insisted. "I'll be less conspicuous if I take the long way around through the alley and avoid all those folks gathered out front."

"You're not worried about going that long way around in the dark?"

Her answer had surprised him, and now that nagging little suspicion that something was off here was bugging him again. There were people who noticed little things like that, particularly cops and those working in the fields where the extra effort of paying attention were crucial. A good cop didn't miss much.

"No, sir," she insisted, mentally scrambling for the right answer to head off a deepening of his curiosity. "I take my runs at night along those same paths. I've never bumped into any trouble."

This was pretty much true. Though she had been observed by a bear once. A fox more than once. And a coyote twice. Never another human, which is what she suspected he meant. She had no fear of the local wildlife, just a healthy respect. That was all any animal needed. She spent so much time with dogs she imagined she smelled more like a dog than a human on those rare encounters with wildlife anyway.

Battles nodded slowly as if he wasn't entirely sure he was okay with the idea but couldn't think of a good enough excuse to argue her point. Finally, he hitched his head toward the desk and chair. "Why don't you have a seat at the desk, and we'll go over a few things, and then you're free to go."

Meg returned his nod. "Sure."

This was where things would get tricky.

She walked to the desk, pulled out the chair and settled into it. Same hard plastic as the other one. Most likely, the owner didn't want any employee getting too comfortable sitting down. Battles leaned against the wall next to the desk. He looked exhausted as he flipped back a few pages in his notepad. He'd probably been on duty well past his shift at this point.

"You stated," he began, "that you were at your window and noticed the trouble across the way." He lifted his gaze to hers. "Meaning here."

"That's right." She made a sound, a kind of soft laugh. "I'm a watcher. Birds, animals and people. I keep a pair of binoculars at the window. My apartment upstairs faces the street. In the mornings when I first get up and at night before I go to bed. It's relaxing. I like watching the world around me—no matter where I am. It's a habit I developed during all my travels. You'd be surprised what you notice just watching the world go by."

He grunted an acknowledgment as he made a note of her answer.

As far as anyone in this town knew, she had spent most of her adult life traveling the world. This was the first place she had stayed for more than six months, she had told anyone who asked. But at almost thirty-five, she had decided it was time to settle down. She'd always loved animals, and going into the business of taking care of them was the perfect career. The cover story had sounded good to her and, so far, to whomever she'd told it.

"Is that why you carry a survivalist type knife?"

This was the biggest sticking point for the deputy. Understandable. A woman carrying a knife like the one she had wasn't the norm.

"It is. I've never been very fond of guns, but I've spent a lot of nights in a sleeping bag on the ground under the stars. Keeping a knife handy felt like a healthy habit. These days, it helps with all sorts of menial tasks, like opening all those boxes delivered to my shop. Once in a while, a pet will get hung up in its restraint loop, and I never want to cause an animal anxiety by taking the time to untangle it. I'd much rather just cut the restraint and start fresh."

Battles made another note before meeting her eyes once more. "So, you don't carry it for protection?"

Meg turned her hands up. "I suppose I do. I mean, I have it with me on my runs, and if confronted by trouble, I would do what I had to. Like tonight. But injuring anything or anyone—much less taking a life—is never something I want to do. I'd much prefer to avoid the trouble altogether."

The deputy's brow furrowed as he considered her for a few seconds more. "Just one last question."

Meg braced herself. This would be the one that required the most finagling.

"Why didn't you stab him? Why go for the throat that way?" He shrugged. "Just seems like an unexpected move for someone such as yourself."

Meaning a woman who wasn't a cop or self-defense expert. If Jones hadn't been wielding a gun, she would certainly have gone a different, perhaps even less lethal route. But her only hope had been to go for the swiftest deadly strike.

Meg took a moment, although she already had her answer prepared. "I was attacked once." She drew in a deep breath. "A very long time ago. After that, I decided it would be in my best interest if I took a self-defense course. According to the instructor, when your weapon of choice is a knife and you are faced with certain death, it's best to go for the jugular. Anything else is like trying to swat a fly with a tennis racket. Too much leeway for a potential miss."

He held her gaze for a long moment without responding. Obviously he wanted more.

"He had a gun pointed at my head. If I'd tried to stab

him, I would have been dead before the point of my knife pierced his skin. My only viable option was to lunge, swipe and go into a rolling dive for the floor in hopes of avoiding the shot he would no doubt pull off."

Battles gave one of those vague nods. "But how did you slit his throat before he could fire the weapon?"

A reasonable question from a man who thought Meg to be a throwback to the days of hippies and flower children. She supposed she did sort of dress the part. Old jeans, vintage tees. She kept her long dark hair in a braid. It was a good cover.

"I was hunkered behind the counter," she explained, "as I said earlier. When he reached the end of the corner, his weapon aimed at me, Jennifer suddenly screamed for help. He turned to stare toward the storeroom—instinct, I suppose—and I took the only opportunity I believed I would have."

A firmer nod this time. "You were lucky."

"I was lucky." She blinked. "I'm just sorry I had to… do what I did."

Battles tucked his notepad away. "I'm sorry to have to confiscate your knife and scabbard, but I'm sure you've watched enough TV and movies to know we have to keep all evidence until the investigation is concluded."

"I understand." She had a backup. No need to tell him that part. For now, she was just thankful not to have aroused his suspicions further.

"I'll be in touch if we have more questions." He straightened from the wall. "You sure you don't want someone to walk you home?"

Meg stood, relief sliding through her body, immediately followed by exhaustion. It was late and she was tired. "No thanks. You've got your hands full here. No need to take someone away from their work to walk me around the block."

"You did a good thing, Meg," he said softly. "I know this may be difficult to live with for a while, and you'll question yourself over what you had to do, but, bottom line, you did the right thing and there's no question in my mind that you saved Jennifer's life. You're a hero."

Oh, good grief. She was not a hero and the last thing she wanted was that label in the report. "I just did what anyone in my shoes would have done." She shrugged. "It's not like the guy gave me a lot of choices."

"Still," Battles insisted, "you took a great risk, and now it's time to take care of you. See a counselor. This was a traumatizing night, and the full impact won't have set in yet. Taking a life—no matter the circumstances— comes with a truckload of emotional baggage. Don't ignore the impact to your psyche."

"Thanks, I'll keep that in mind."

Deputy Porch called for Battles, and before he could say more to Meg, she turned and walked toward the back door. The door closed behind her, and she took a moment to draw in a chestful of air. She closed her eyes and drew in another breath, exhaled it, then she started to walk. She weaved her way through the woods for the short distance before it turned into the narrow alleyway that lined the back of the old shops. Rather than step into the alley, she kept to the woods. The going was rougher, but the likelihood of running into anyone was greatly diminished.

When she reached the end of the first block of the old shops, she made her way up to the alley and around the corner to the side street. At the end of each of the four blocks that constituted the old town portion of Piney Woods, a short, narrow cross street led into residential areas. There weren't that many houses actually used as homes. Two had been transformed into bed-and-breakfast operations, one was a doctor's office, another was a dental clinic and most of the others were now retail shops.

The few that remained residential holdouts were those of founding families. The annual Christmas tours featured those homes, and members of the families told stories of how their ancestors had come to choose this portion of the mountain as home. All the shops participated. Last Christmas, even Meg had opened her shop to the tour. She'd had her employees do the hosting. Putting herself in the limelight was not something she liked doing.

Not to mention it was dangerous.

Not going there.

A glance down the boulevard and Meg surveyed the crowd that still lingered in the Gas and Go parking lot. Emergency lights still strobed in the darkness. Excitement like this almost never happened in Piney Woods. Folks would be out until it was wrapped up in hopes of learning the full details.

The idea that trouble had shown up tonight worried Meg just a little.

Not that she really thought the dead guy who'd attempted to rob the Gas and Go had anything to do with her past. *Nah.* The idea was pretty ridiculous, in fact. Frankly, he'd been an amateur. His long list of crimes indicated nothing more than a scumbag who preferred not to work for a living. He opted to take what he wanted because he was too damned lazy to earn it.

She'd met plenty of stone-cold killers in her life, and he had not been one of them.

Sadly, however, had her reflexes been any rustier, she would be the one dead on that slab in the Hamilton County Morgue. She'd barely outmaneuvered the thuggish punk.

"You gotta stay in shape, Lewis," she muttered as she ducked into the alley on her side of the block. It had been just over fifteen months since she'd been in a position to need to protect herself. She imagined even if it had been fifteen years, muscle memory would have had her doing the same thing. There were some things that couldn't be forgotten. But speed and accuracy were another story. Those required regular training.

Beyond ready to get home, she walked faster now. She wanted to wash the night's events off her skin and burn her damned clothes.

When she at last reached her shop, she entered the code into the gate and stepped into the fenced perimeter of her back yard. The area was a like a kid's playground, except the equipment was designed for dogs. There were a couple of doggie ramps and slides. Tunnels and balance beams. Shade houses. Her favorites were the water fountains and the toy boxes. And she hadn't overlooked the cats she served when designing the playground. Two state-of-the-art cat condos had been installed. A little something for everyone.

At the back door, she entered the code, and the lock released. Once inside, she toed off her sneakers and stripped off her clothes. She frowned, remembered she'd shut off the ringer on her cell. She switched it back on and tucked the device into the waistband of her panties and walked to the laundry area, where she grabbed a couple of garbage bags. For now, hiding the clothes would have to do. She was too tired to burn them tonight. Besides, the last thing she needed was the crowd at the Gas and Go seeing smoke behind her shop. She'd take care of it tomorrow, but she didn't want the animals picking up the scent of the dead guy. She double-bagged the trash and stuffed it into the front-loading washing machine and closed the door.

She made it up the stairs before her cell erupted into the short, soft bursts of her chosen ringtone. Too tired to answer anything but a true emergency, she tugged the phone free of her waistband and checked the screen.

Griff.

He'd already called seven times. She should have noticed when she turned the ringer back on. Apparently, she'd been too tired, and no doubt he'd heard about the trouble.

She hit Accept and said, "Hey. What're you doing up so late?"

"Checking on you after learning about the robbery at the Gas and Go."

Pain arced through her shoulder as she reached for the nightshirt draped on her bed. She grimaced. "I'm okay. Just about to go to bed."

She didn't like blowing him off. Avery "Griff" Griffin was a good friend—one of the first she'd made when she moved here last year. She liked him. Maybe too much. But the less he knew about this, the better.

Like that was going to happen. Griff and Deputy Ernie Battles had been best friends since they were kids.

"Well, that's a shame because I'm at your front door."

She closed her eyes and held back a sigh. "Why didn't you say so? I'll be right down."

Meg considered changing out of her nightshirt, but she needed it to back up her story. Besides, it wasn't like Griff hadn't seen her in shorts and tank tops. Not that different really. That thought introduced a long line of images into her head that she could have done without just now. Memories of Griff pulling off his shirt during a long hot afternoon of work at his farm. A T-shirt plastered to his chest after helping to give a dozen dogs baths.

Not somewhere she needed to linger. She exiled the memories. They both loved animals and worked hard to rescue as many as possible, but that common bond was as far as the thing between them needed to go.

She hustled down the stairs and padded silently across the cool tile floor. He waited at the front entrance, looking all sleep tousled and far too sexy.

Don't think about it.

Without turning on a light so as not to draw attention, she unlocked the door and opened it. "Wild night," she said with a glance at the ongoing spectacle at the Gas and Go.

"Yeah." He closed and locked the door.

So, he planned to stay a while. Which meant he'd already heard most of the story about her part in what happened. The downside to living in a small town—everyone knew everyone else. Nothing stayed secret for more than a minute.

"You want a beer?" She folded her arms over her chest.

He shook his head. "You gonna tell me what happened?"

"First." She held up a finger. "There's something I need to show you."

She turned and headed for the kennels. He followed. No need for her to look back and check, she could feel his closeness. This would buy her some time to calm her jangling nerves. A few minutes of distraction to take the edge off.

As she entered the doggie hotel—as she liked to call the kennels—Raymond raised his head. He still lay next to the abandoned beagle's kennel.

Meg crouched down and gave Raymond a scratch between the ears. "Hey, boy."

Griff eased down next to her and reached over to do the same. He and Raymond had a very close relationship. This did not help Meg's ability to keep the man at a safe distance. The scent of his aftershave—even at this hour—made her want to lean closer and take a long, deep breath.

He smiled at Raymond, then shifted his attention to the beagle. "Hey there."

"She's about eight or nine," Meg said. "Her name is Pepper. She has some health issues. Lonnie's going to run tests. Try to get to the bottom of the situation."

"Where'd you find her?"

His gaze locked on hers, and for a moment, Meg couldn't speak. She chalked it up to the insane night she'd had. Truth was, he did that to her sometimes. His hair was that blond color that wasn't really all that fair but was still way too light to call brown. More of a mix of caramel and gold. His eyes were the kind of gold you rarely saw. So pale, so distinct. But the trouble didn't lay in those gorgeous eyes or in the six feet of perfectly formed masculinity. No. The trouble was his incredible kind and giving nature, especially toward animals. Meg had never met anyone quite like him.

The fact that she was seriously attracted to him was not such a big surprise, all things considered, but she respected him and just plain old liked him in ways she had never expected to like anyone. The latter was terrifying on some level. She'd never been attracted to anyone in the way she was to this man. It was as much intellectual as it was physical.

Griff was making her soft, making her want things she could never have.

Somehow she had to remedy that situation. Problem was, she hadn't figured out a way to do that—not in the twelve months she had been here.

Don't think about it right now.

She pulled her mind back to the moment and the question he'd asked. "The owner couldn't take care of her anymore and left her at my door with a note."

Griff smiled. "Then it's someone who knows you and realizes what a good person you are."

She looked away from that incredible smile and focused on Pepper. "Except I don't have the space for allowing the reputation for taking on extra pets to become a common belief. I wish I did." This was the truth, at least most of it. She would take them all if she could. The problem was if she had to disappear—and that was always a possibility—what would become of them?

She couldn't live with the probable answer to that question.

"I've got the space. When she's on her feet—" he

turned to Meg, the pull of his eyes forcing her to look at him "—I'll take her."

She managed a smile, mostly because the effort prevented her from analyzing the details of his face more deeply. The lips...the jawline. *Stop.* "You already have a lot of animals, Griff."

He chuckled. "Doesn't matter. I have a big farm with a barn big enough for my herd of dogs and cows and horses—as well as plenty more."

"Not to mention no shortage of cats and chickens."

His smile turned to a grin. "Those too."

He hadn't purchased or been gifted a single animal that lived on his farm. All had been abandoned. Every cow, every horse. Even the chickens. Folks would call him when someone had moved away and just left one or more animals. Griff would go pick them up and bring them home. If they were sick or injured, he would nurse them back to health, and there they would stay. It was the perfect life for the animals and for him. Meg could never tell anyone, but it was her dream life.

Not ever going to happen, she reminded herself.

"Why don't you tell me about what happened over there?"

This was the question she'd dreaded. She pushed to her feet. "I need a beer."

He stood. "That bad, huh?"

He already knew the answer. Ernie might not be able to give him ever little detail because of the ongoing investigation, but he would have passed along all he could.

"Yeah. That bad."

The worst part about Griff knowing was the idea that

it would likely change his opinion of her—and not for the good.

Griff was the first person in her adult life—besides her parents—whose opinion mattered so very much to her.

This was bad, and nothing in her vast survival repertoire gave her any suggestion on how to stop the momentum.

Chapter Three

Griffin Residence
Sundown Road
Sunday, May 5, 8:30 a.m.

"Listen up," Griff said to the dogs eagerly waiting at the doors of their kennels. "Dr. Howell is coming this morning for checkups, shots or whatever any of you need. I expect you all to behave."

Sad, gloomy eyes peered up at him as if they'd understood every word.

"Don't give me that," he argued. "You behave yourselves and you all get treats."

Ears perked up and tails wagged just a little, and he smiled.

"All right then. You'll be staying in your kennels until after Dr. Howell has seen you, so just chill for a while."

As he walked away, the animals began to settle in for the wait. Though some had been abused and all were castoffs, they trained easily and well. Even Petey, the newest arrival. Griff gave the old bloodhound a nod as he passed his kennel. Petey had settled down, following the lead of the others.

Griff couldn't remember a time when he wasn't surrounded by dogs and other animals. Every morning he spent hours feeding and filling water bowls and troughs. But he loved every minute of it. He shook his head at the idea that he'd ever thought for one minute he could be happy in the world of high finance in the big city. But as his grandmother had often told him, if he hadn't given it a go, he would still be wondering. Now he knew.

Outside the veterinarian's truck had arrived. "Morning," Lonnie announced as he headed Griff's way.

Griff opened the gate to the large pen that surrounded the barn. "Morning, Doc. The day been good to you so far?"

Lonnie chuckled. "As good as it can when you've got a calf in distress during delivery. We had a rough go of it for a bit, but luckily, we managed all right. Mama and baby are just fine. Henry's wife even made me breakfast."

Henry Bauer was a neighboring farmer. His family had owned their farm almost as long as Griff's had.

"Good to hear." Griff gestured to the doghouse, which was actually a two-thousand-square-foot building with forty dog kennels and a storeroom. The kennels were all inside, but there were plenty of windows, and each kennel had access to this large fenced area in back of the building. "Your patients are ready. If you need me, let me know."

"I always look forward to your crew. And I appreciate you letting me come on a Sunday morning. The better part of the upcoming week is looking a little crowded."

Griff understood. Lonnie's partner had retired due to health issues, and so far he hadn't found a replacement.

The man was swamped. "No problem. I'm just thrilled you could get to us."

Lonnie paused before moving on. "By the way, I may know someone who's interested in the bloodhound."

Griff liked nothing better than finding loving families for the animals, but *loving* was the key word. "You made them aware that she's old?"

"I did. He already has a dozen of his own. Like you, he likes giving them a good life—age or condition is irrelevant. Trust me, Griff, he'll take good care of her when you're ready to let her go. And she'll be with others like herself."

How could he say no? Bloodhounds were pack dogs. She would be happiest with a group of her own kind. "Sounds good. Have him give me a call at his convenience."

"Will do."

Lonnie wandered on to the kennels. Griff was caught up for now, so he headed to the house. Meg had promised to come and have a late breakfast with him. She'd managed to persuade him to go home last night without providing details about what happened at the Gas and Go. He hadn't been thrilled about the idea, but she'd been exhausted, so he'd given in. Part of him had wanted to park outside her place and keep watch all night. But that wouldn't have helped. She wasn't in any danger. If he'd ever had any doubts about her taking care of herself, he had none now. He was the one who had an issue.

He wanted to take their friendship to a different level, but she insisted she wasn't ready for that sort of relationship just now. Not exactly the answer he wanted to hear, but he couldn't deny understanding where she was at.

He'd been there. Leaving Nashville eight years ago hadn't been just about being unhappy with his career choice. His whole life had been turned upside down when the woman he'd expected to marry and spend the rest of his life with had announced she had a new vision for the rest of her own. Even more surprising was the reality of how little he'd missed her. Then had come the unexpected relief. Looking back, he realized he had come way too close to making the mistake of his life.

He walked through the back door and into the old farmhouse kitchen that badly needed an update. He hung his hat on the hook by the door and headed to the coffee maker. He'd had a quick cup at 5:30 a.m. this morning, but he needed another desperately just now. While he waited through the hissing of the machine doing its thing, he considered the cabinets, counters and appliances that were the same as when he'd been a kid. Until recently, he hadn't thought much of the aged interior. It was all serviceable. Clean. What else did a man need? Except his sister had suggested he might want to update if he ever expected to lure in potential wife material. What woman, she'd insisted, wanted to see herself in this kitchen?

Griff shook his head and barely restrained a laugh. His sister, on the other hand, couldn't stop renovating. Louise Griffin Alvarez had married a mere twelve years ago, and already she'd renovated her house twice. Good thing her husband had a sense of humor and a healthy bank account.

Griff loved his little sister. She was so much like their mother. In fact, Louise had built an in-law suite during her last renovation, and their mom loved living with her daughter and her grandkids. Louise teased that if Griff would just get around to having kids of his own, maybe he too could enjoy some nana time. Griff glanced around the old kitchen and couldn't stop the flood of images and sounds that echoed in his brain. He and his sister had been happy growing up here. The only bad memory was when he'd found his father down by the pond, and even that one wasn't all bad. His father had died the way he'd wanted to. He'd been working in the yard and gotten overheated. He'd taken a break in the shade by the pond—one of his favorite places.

Taking walks down memory lane happened more and more often these days. Maybe because his sister reminded him every chance she got that he wasn't getting any younger. And it was hard not to visit the past when he lived in the house where he'd grown up. His grandfather had built the home and the barn. His father had grown up here too. His parents had planned to live here until they passed, just as his grandparents had. Though things hadn't worked out exactly as planned, Griff intended to go for that same goal. He just hadn't expected to do it alone. When he'd come back eight years ago, he'd figured that eventually he'd meet someone and start the rest of his life. So far that had not happened—he hadn't even come close. He shook his head and pushed away from the counter.

He scrubbed a hand over his face. Maybe he did need to renovate. Shake things up. New paint colors and all that.

Too bad the woman his heart seemed intent on wasn't interested and likely wouldn't be impressed by a shiny new kitchen.

Speaking of Meg, he spotted her truck coming up the drive. Meg had insisted on bringing the food. All he had to do was provide hot coffee and orange juice. The scent of the fresh brew lingered in the room. He opened the fridge door, grabbed the carton of orange juice and placed it on the counter, where he arranged a couple of glasses and mugs. He considered pouring a cup of coffee to take to Lonnie, but the knock on his front door derailed the notion.

He ran his fingers through his hair, took a breath and headed through the home. The place was a typical farmhouse. Two stories. All the bedrooms and a bath upstairs. The common rooms and a half bath that was added in the fifties downstairs. Nothing fancy. Hardwoods on the floors. Painted plaster on the walls. All in need of a refresh, according to his sister.

Still, the place suited him. He was happiest in a pair of jeans and boots. He wore a cowboy hat the way his father and grandfather had. When his ex-fiancée insisted the hat had to be saved for the proper occasion, he should have realized things between them would never work. He'd grown up with cows and horses and chickens and such. The proper boots and hat were more important than any other attire he'd worn.

Meg liked his hat. He smiled at the memory of her saying so.

He opened the door and the woman standing on his porch made him smile even wider. Meg Lewis had the brownest eyes he'd ever seen. So dark they were like gazing into midnight. And the hair. He loved her hair. Long, dark and thick, but she almost never allowed it to hang free. It was always in a single braid hanging down her back all the way to her waist or draped over one shoulder with a cute little ribbon tied at the end.

Today there was no ribbon.

His gaze roamed back up the pink tee that sported images of blooming botanicals then to her face. She smiled, and that alone had his heart stuttering.

He almost laughed at the reality of just how pathetic he was. Maybe it was the idea that forty was looming in the not-so-distant future and the wife and kids he'd expected to have were still nothing more than an expectation. Or maybe it was the idea that he'd finally met the *one*, and she only wanted to be friends.

Meg held up a brown bag with the diner's logo on the front. "Katie insisted we try her new breakfast burritos."

Griff hummed a note of anticipation. "If Katie made them, they'll be good." He hitched his head. "Come on in."

Meg stepped inside. "How's your herd this morning?"

"Nervous."

"Guess so. I saw Lonnie's truck out there."

"Yep." His stomach rumbled. "Man, those burritos smell good."

MEG COULDN'T AGREE MORE. She hoped the food would help stave off his questions about last night. She'd tossed and turned the few hours she'd spent in bed wondering how to get past the questions he would no doubt have. To some degree, Griff saw through her facade. His ability to view her so clearly made her a little nervous.

Deputy Battles had been happy to accept her explanation of what happened—or at least he appeared to do so. But Griff would have other concerns. Like how had she managed to react so exactingly? How had she recognized how deep the knife should go to inflict the necessary result?

Worse, she hadn't been able to suppress the worries about her photo ending up in the media. All this time, she had been so careful to ensure she stayed below the radar. To her knowledge, not a single photo had been taken of her since her arrival in Piney Woods. But if this rescue of hers picked up too much steam in a slow news cycle, the reporters involved would go to great lengths to find something on her.

If that happened...

Just stop. She cleared her head. She had no control over what others did. All Meg could do was take this one step at a time. Maybe the whole thing would fizzle out today. Maybe Griff wouldn't ask as many questions as she feared he would. And maybe he would accept her answers without wanting additional clarifications.

Yeah, right. She'd never get that lucky.

Whatever happened, she would do what she had to.

The trouble was Avery Griffin had spent seven years as a forensic auditor in one of Nashville's top financial groups. He was trained to look beyond what he saw and to find the reasons behind the results. Actually, she suspected his university training had little to do with this ability. She firmly believed the man instinctively saw what others didn't. For the past year she had worked extra hard to keep him at arm's length.

Not an easy task. She took in his crisp white cotton shirt and faded blue jeans. The boots...she resisted the urge to sigh. Too distracting, too desirable. The man just got under her skin somehow.

He was just too good-looking. Too nice. Too…*good.*

In the kitchen, he gestured to the counter. "Coffee's ready. Orange juice is handy."

Meg placed the bag of burritos on the table. She liked this house. The big farm-style kitchen with the table in the center made her want to bake bread, and she'd never baked bread in her life. It just felt so homey. "Should we invite Lonnie? I'm sure we have enough food."

Griff frowned before he seemed to catch himself and fix his smile back into place. "He mentioned that Mrs. Bauer made him breakfast this morning. He was helping out with the birth of a calf."

"You have a sick animal, or is he here for routine examinations?" She opened the bag and removed the warm wrapped goodies. It was Sunday after all. Not the usual office hours even for a country vet.

"Just vaccinations and checkups." He poured two steaming mugs of coffee. "He has a big week coming up and wanted to get a head start."

He didn't have to ask how Meg took her coffee. They'd had coffee together enough times that he knew she liked it black. They'd made fast friends only a few weeks after she got her shop going. He'd gone out of his way to send business in her direction. He brought two or three of his dogs each week. She doubted he'd ever bothered with a groomer before, but he was thoughtful like that.

By the time she had the food on the plates he'd provided, she was salivating at the delicious smells of peppers and onions and cheeses. The eggs and spicy sausage and all those other juicy ingredients were rolled into homemade tortillas. She was ravenous this morning. She wouldn't mention this though since most people wouldn't likely understand her having any sort of appetite after what happened last night.

Griff placed the mugs of coffee on the table and filled two glasses with orange juice, then they sat.

"You feeling okay this morning?" he asked as he unwrapped his burrito.

His first question was simple enough. She relaxed a little. "I'm good. Not as sore as I expected after that dive to the floor." Realizing her missed opportunity, she added, "I'm working on not thinking about the other part."

"I'm sure that part will just take time."

"Hope so."

They ate for a time. Whatever question he had next waited. Suited Meg. The burrito was so good she devoured it in record time. Felt a little guilty about wolfing it down. She toyed with her napkin a bit, finished off her orange juice and considered whether she wanted another cup of coffee. The man brewed good coffee. Or maybe she'd go for another burrito.

"You ready to talk about it?"

No. Absolutely not. But she had promised to talk to him this morning, so refusing was not an option. Not to mention how worried he looked. Her goal was to alleviate his concerns without prompting his curiosity. Always a fine line.

"Sure." She took a deep breath and launched into her practiced story. "You know how I love watching my little part of town. I could just sit at my front window and watch all day—or night—long."

"You spotted the trouble," he suggested as he reached for a second burrito.

"I usually take a look before I go to bed." She made a

face, a bit embarrassed. "It's just a silly routine of mine. I swear I'm not nosy or some sort of peeping perv."

"I always take a walk around outside before going to bed. Check on the animals." He laughed. "Say good night. So I understand."

He really was such a nice guy. She would never want him to know how she'd had to lie her way into this life. "I do that too—say good night, I mean. Some folks might think that's a little strange, but it feels like the right thing to do."

His smile faded, and he held her gaze for a long moment. Her pulse reacted. "I think that's part of why I like you so much, Megan Lewis. You're my kind of people."

The want in his eyes, the sound of desire in his voice— every ounce of strength she possessed was required not to give in. How many times had she thought about taking him to her bed? Or joining him in his? God, she didn't even remember how long it had been since she'd had sex. Forever…it seemed.

But she would not—could not drag this man more deeply into her life. The potential for a bad outcome was far too great a risk.

Friends. They could be friends.

"Anyway," she went on, "I spotted the guy with the gun and immediately called Deputy Battles. He was ten minutes out and there was no one else, so I did what I had to do." She stared into her empty coffee mug for a long moment. "By the time I got across the street, the guy was dragging Jennifer into the storeroom. I knew what would happen. I had to do something. She didn't have ten minutes."

The unfinished second burrito went back onto his

plate. He reached for a napkin and wiped his hands as if needing time before speaking. "Ernie said you saved her life."

Meg shrugged. "I'm just glad I spotted what was happening."

"I take it," he ventured, "you've had self-defense or survival instruction of some sort." He glanced away. "Ernie mentioned you'd been attacked before."

She'd known the two would have this discussion. Not only had they been best friends since their school days, they'd been on the basketball team together. Theirs was a tight bond.

"Mugged," she said, going for the less complicated scenario. "He roughed me up a little. Bruises, broken wrist. I decided that was never going to happen again, so… I made myself smarter, more prepared for the unexpected."

The relief on his face was palpable. "I think that's smart. I've urged my sister to do the same. Everyone should know how to protect him-or herself."

"It's important." Meg had met Louise. And his mother. He'd taken her to Thanksgiving dinner last year. He'd wanted to take her to the family's Christmas gathering as well, but she'd pretended to be sick. Family Christmases were far too intimate.

Her decision hadn't been about not wanting to spend time with his family. Like him, they were all very nice. It was about protecting herself and him from the mistake he so badly wanted to make.

She could not be what he wanted, and to pretend otherwise would only do harm.

"I need you to promise me something, Meg."

She held her breath. Hoped this was not going to be one of those things that would make remaining friends even more difficult.

"I'll try," she offered.

"Next time, call me. Let me help."

That she could agree to. "I will. There just wasn't time last night. It all happened so quickly."

"I understand, but I want to try and be there whenever you need me for whatever reason."

She relaxed just a little. Maybe he wasn't going to go after answers the way she had feared. "I appreciate that."

He cleaned up the remains of their breakfast while she washed their mugs and glasses. She adored the vintage sink with its attached drainboard. It was all so homey. So comfortable.

"You can never change this sink," she said as she dried her hands. "It's amazing."

He leaned against the counter and grinned. "Don't ever say that in front of my sister. She thinks I need to gut the place and have all new everything installed."

Meg's mouth dropped open in dismay. "No. This kitchen is perfect. The cabinets are perfectly imperfect. I love the pale green color." She put a hand to her chest. "And the stove. It's a Wedgewood. You can never ever change the stove either."

"I'm glad you like it."

The amusement in his tone and in those gold eyes made her feel far too warm. "Sorry," she offered, "I get a little carried away when people talk about ruining something as awesome as this kitchen."

"Since we're on the subject," he said, "what about the paint?"

It was yellow. Nice. Very light. "This must have been your mother's favorite color."

He grinned. "It was. She repainted it this same color every few years."

Meg's cell sounded off from the back pocket of her jeans. Saved her from having to say that she'd never really cared for yellow. "Excuse me a moment." She checked the screen. Jodie Edwards. "It's Jodie. I have to take this."

Griff knew both her employees, Jodie Edwards and Dottie Cowart. One or the other usually worked with Meg on Sunday afternoons to get the weekly deep cleaning done, but today they'd suggested the two of them handle the shop for Meg. After last night's misadventures, Meg hadn't argued. They would also hang around for the pickup of the boarded animals. Prevented Meg from having to answer the questions the owners would no doubt have. Frankly, she was glad to have the day off.

She accepted the call. "Hey, Jodie. What's up?"

"There's a couple of reporters hanging around outside," Jodie whispered. "One from the *Chattanooga Times* and one from the *Tennessean*. They've knocked on the door wanting to talk to you."

Meg suppressed a groan. She had been afraid of this. "Tell them not only are we closed but that I won't be around today." She made a face. Tried to think how she would manage to stay out of sight until this whole thing blew over.

"Actually, I was thinking that I can handle things for a couple of days," Jodie offered. "Dottie is happy to come in and help if I need her."

Meg wilted with relief. "That would be great, Jodie. Are you sure you don't mind?"

She laughed softly. "Are you kidding? My kid has a birthday next month. I can take all the extra hours you want to give me."

"You are a lifesaver," Meg assured her. "But don't hesitate to call if you need me."

"Just relax," Jodie insisted. "I've got this."

The call ended, and Meg tucked the cell back into her jeans pocket.

"Problem?"

She turned toward Griff. Now for the next issue. If she couldn't go to work, what should she do?

Spending too much time with this man was not a feasible option.

That would only get her into more trouble, and she was in enough already.

Chapter Four

Meg parked at the medical clinic and walked the block and a half back to her shop. Most of that distance, she kept to the woods behind the alley. Griff had lent her one of his trucks. He had several vehicles that sported the logo for Sundown Farms. Her own truck carried the Pampered Paws one, too easy for the reporters to spot.

It would have been better to avoid coming back for a few hours more, but she really could not stay with Griff any longer. At least not without the risk of crossing a line she did not need to cross. She'd learned to keep their alone time to small windows. Besides, Jodie and Dottie had finished for the day, and the boarded animals had been picked up. Meg could sequester herself to the second floor and just stay stashed away at least until tomorrow.

Sadly, three news vans were still parked in front of her shop, taking up customer parking. Except that it was Sunday and the shop was closed. No doubt at least one of the three would hang around for a long while despite Jodie and Dottie having left and no one else being inside—at least to their knowledge. The upside was that eventually all would give up and go away.

Keeping a close watch on the far end of the alley as well as the corner of her shop, Meg eased through the back gate and into the doggie playground. When she reached the back entrance of her shop, she waited for a while and just listened. The street was quiet at this hour since folks who lived in Piney Woods were either at home or church or gathering at the diner, which was open seven days a week. Some would be lunching or shopping in Chattanooga. The vague sound of chatter from the reporters apparently still hanging out on the sidewalk in front of her shop kept Meg on her toes.

She slipped her key into the lock, gave it a twist and hurried inside. She closed the door, disarmed the security system and locked the door once more. Again, she waited and listened. All quiet. Rather than risk having a look out front, she hustled up the back stairs. They were narrower and steeper, but they were perfect for a moment like this. There was a door at the bottom and at the top. Most people assumed the one on the first floor led to a closet or another room. When she opened the upper door, Raymond lifted his head and stared at her.

He lay at the top of the stairs, where he waited whenever she was away. From that vantage point, he could see her if she came up the main steps or the back ones. She was surprised he wasn't still hanging near Pepper.

Meg squatted and held out her hand, and the old fellow got up and came over to greet her. She gave him a few rubs and a hug. "Hey, boy." She smiled down at the animal to which she had grown far too attached. "We have things to do."

Meg surveyed the studio where she had grown to feel at home. When she'd landed in Piney Woods, she really hadn't expected to feel that way—so *at home*. Growing up an only child and then losing both her parents by the time she was thirty, she hadn't expected to feel at home anywhere—not even in the place she'd lived since leaving for college sixteen years ago. She'd been comfortable in Los Angeles, but she'd never felt that same sort of hominess she'd felt in Bakersfield.

Funny how she'd ignored the idea for all those years.

When her mother had died, at least she'd still had her father. Then, just before her thirtieth birthday, her father's heart attack had changed everything. The farm in Bakersfield had felt like a foreign land. She and her on-again-off-again boyfriend had parted ways. Her place in Los Angeles had felt like…a motel room—not that it ever really felt like home. A place to sleep and shower. Nothing more.

For two and a half years, she had existed in that numbing place. She'd worked and that was about it. Work had consumed her existence. Her tolerance for risk-taking had expanded into territory that more and more resembled carelessness, indifference. Her colleagues had noticed. She'd been warned more than once that she was dancing on an edge.

The warnings and the close calls hadn't changed one thing.

And then came the final act—the end of her story as she knew it.

Meg pushed the thoughts aside. She'd done what she had to do. No going back now.

She opened the bottom drawer of the dresser where most of her clothes were stored. There wasn't really a closet. Anything she wanted hanging did so from the three hooks she'd added to the wall. She removed the layer of socks and undershirts and lifted the false bottom she'd added.

Meg stared at the items she'd hidden there. A passport and driver's license with another name—one she'd hoped not to ever have to use. Stacks of money for emergencies. Keys to the car she kept in a storage unit in town. And the key to the safety deposit box that contained the only proof of the whole truth—not that the truth would ever save her.

"You are beyond saving," she muttered.

Raymond whimpered and eased closer to her. He sensed her distress. She hugged him and scratched him behind the ears. "Don't worry, boy. I'll make sure you and Pepper are taken care of."

Meg thought of Griff. He would take care of them. She didn't even have to ask.

She rounded up a backpack, threw in a couple of changes of underthings and an extra tee. She added the cash she kept on hand and the other items from her hidden compartment to the bottom of the bag.

"Just in case." It was always better to be safe than sorry.

Moving with caution, she eased toward the front window and checked the street below. All but one of the news vans had left.

Good.

All she had to do was wait out the last one.

Until then, she did a final recon of her place. Made sure she hadn't left anything incriminating. Not much she could do about the fingerprints and DNA. By the time anyone had analyzed all that, she would be long gone. The downside to having to take that step was that everyone she'd come to view as friends would then know she wasn't who she'd said she was. She supposed that was better than just disappearing and leaving them to wonder.

Who was she kidding? The only person whose opinion mattered was Griff. She really hated the idea of him thinking badly of her. But that was inevitable at some point. Even if this whole business blew over without her being outed, he would continue to pursue a closer relationship, and she couldn't allow that to happen. Eventually, he would grow tired of the effort and move on.

An ache pierced her. She closed her eyes and shook her head at the ridiculous reaction. How had she gotten so sloppy over the past twelve months or so?

Her parents had always warned that her internal clock would catch up to her. She hadn't believed them. She had been all about her career. Work had become her life. Sex was just a perk—not something she intended to allow to guide her existence.

As for kids, that was never going to happen. She could never ever put another human being in the line of fire. It was bad enough that she'd allowed Raymond to get attached to this life. But he would learn to be happy with Griff. The real trouble was with her learning to be happy *without* Griff.

Meg rolled her eyes. Though they had never even so much as kissed, she felt closer to him than any other man in her whole life—besides her dad, anyway. But that had been a whole different sort of connection. This thing with Griff was…

"Don't go there." Meg set her backpack next to the door that led down the backstairs.

Dissecting this thing she felt for Griff would be like poking needles in her eyes. Whatever *this* was, it was irrelevant. If she intended to stay alive and protect the people in her wake, she had to keep her head on straight.

One last pass through her desk, and she was satisfied she hadn't overlooked anything. She placed a letter for Jodie on top of her desk. Inside was the deed to the property and the title to her truck. Both of which Meg had signed over to her. Jodie was a young single mom and she had no one. Her parents were junkies who cared only about their next fix. Jodie was a good person. This place would give her a future she might otherwise have difficulty achieving.

Meg hadn't forgotten Dottie either. Dottie was a retired school teacher who simply loved animals. She had an adoring family and grown kids who were there for her. Dottie was set. Still, Meg appreciated her friendship, and she'd left her a tidy bonus for being a good friend. She'd always talked about wanting to take a cruise with her husband but refused to spend the money. The bonus would take care of several cruises without Dottie having to dip into her savings.

These things Meg left handy just in case. As long as she didn't have to disappear, she would put the items back into her hiding place until that status changed.

Meg made a clicking sound and motioned for Raymond to follow her. She needed to check on Pepper. Jodie would have fed her and let her outside for a while. But if Meg had to disappear, she didn't want to leave without saying goodbye to Pepper.

If she was really lucky all these preparations would be for naught. The next few days would pass, and the story would be forgotten by all but Jennifer and her family. Some other event would top the news, and Meg would just be a distant memory for any interested reporters.

But she couldn't risk not being prepared.

Preparation was the key to survival.

Pepper stood at the door to her kennel. She actually looked better today.

"Hey, girl." Meg opened the kennel and sat down on the floor. Raymond took a position next to her. Damn, she was going to miss this dog.

Pepper joined them, laying her head on Meg's lap. The three of them sat huddled together for a long while. Meg really didn't know how long. She opted not to look at her phone. Instead, she leaned against the wall and allowed her eyes to shutter. She had barely slept last night.

Her eyes drifted closed, and her mind wandered to the farm in Bakersfield, where she ran through the orchard. The air felt cool on her cheeks and her laughter echoed off the trees. She hadn't been home in so long…

Griffin Residence
Sundown Road
2:30 p.m.

DUST ROILING IN the distance had Griff putting a hand over his eyes to see who was headed toward his place. The driveway was a long one, and anyone who'd gotten that far from the road was no doubt looking for him. Either that or they were lost.

Then he spotted the markings on the truck: Sheriff's Department. His pulse quickened. He hoped nothing new had come up with last night's trouble. Instinctively, he checked his cell to ensure he hadn't missed a call or text from Meg.

The truck pulled to a stop in front of his house, and he recognized the driver. Ernie.

Griff relaxed a little. He threw up a hand as he waited for Ernie to emerge from the vehicle and head his way.

"Afternoon," Griff said. "I'm afraid you're too late for lunch." He patted his stomach. "That peanut butter sandwich is long gone."

Ernie laughed. The two of them used to live on peanut butter sandwiches in the summer. Griff's mother warned they were going to go nutty if they didn't learn to like some other lunch besides those sandwiches. She'd finally persuaded them to add bananas. They had laughed and teased his mom that now they were going bananas. She had pretended not to be amused, but he'd seen her secret smiles.

"I could go for a cup of coffee," Ernie said with a grin. "I had lunch at the diner, and it was way better than a peanut butter sandwich."

"Lucky you." Griff hitched his head toward the house. "Come on in." He glanced at the laptop his friend carried. "What's with that?"

"Something I need to show you."

Maybe it was Griff's imagination, but his friend's face blanked and his tone turned serious. Whatever was up didn't seem to be good.

While Griff started a pot of coffee, Ernie settled at the kitchen table and placed the computer on its surface. One hand rested on the device as if he feared it might run off or vanish. He talked about the weather and the blind date he had agreed to on Saturday. Griff laughed and nodded at the right times, but nothing about this felt right.

When the coffee was brewed and cups were filled, Griff joined him at the table. "So, what's up?"

"I'm sure you've spoken with Meg about what happened last night."

"I did." Ernie was aware Griff had a thing for Meg. Ernie had been divorced for two years. He and Griff often discussed their relationship woes.

"How did she seem?" Ernie shrugged. "I mean, was she upset? Calm? What's your take on her reaction?"

Griff's unease escalated. "What's going on, Ernie? We've known each other for a long time. What's with the beating around the bush? If you've got something to say or to ask me, then just do it."

Ernie set his mug aside. "Something's off with Meg. I know how you feel about her and that the two of you are close, but I just have this bad feeling that there's something I'm missing."

Griff digested the words. "Okay. I saw her for a few minutes last night, and we had breakfast together this morning. She stayed awhile to avoid going back to her shop. A couple of reporters were hanging around." He shrugged. "She seemed fine. Last night she was a little shaken, but she was handling it well."

"That's the thing," Ernie said. "She's handling it really well. Even right after it happened, she was as calm as a cucumber. She'd just killed a man, and I would have expected her to be, at the very least, shaken up."

A hint of anger mingled with Griff's uneasiness. "What does that mean?"

Ernie held up both hands. "I'm not accusing her of anything, it's just odd. That's all I'm saying." He exhaled a big breath. "Look, we're like brothers, man. I'm just worried. There's something off, and I can't pretend I didn't pick up on it. I hardly slept last night for mulling this over. It just won't sit right with me, and my gut kept telling me that I needed to talk to you about it."

Griff felt a little irritated. "I've known Meg for about a year, and I've never seen her overreact to anything. Maybe she's just not the type that lets all her emotions show." He had to admit that being forced to kill someone to protect yourself was a big deal, but still, if hiding her emotions was her way, then it was possible...

Ernie just listened and said nothing, but his face told Griff the tale. This was not good.

Hell, Griff didn't understand how to excuse this, whatever it was. What he did get was that his friend was worried. Griff had known Ernie his whole life, if he had a bad feeling about this, it wasn't just his imagination.

"Explain it to me," Griff prompted.

"I wouldn't generally do this," Ernie said as he opened the laptop. "But I think this video explains it better than anything I can say."

"What is this?" Griff studied the screen, recognizing the inside of the Gas and Go.

"This is the video footage from the store's security cameras." Ernie looked straight at him. "It's a clip of what happened between Meg and the dead guy—Zyair Jones."

Griff nodded. "All right. Let's see it."

"I'm going to play it in slow motion. Otherwise you'll miss the things I need you to see, because it happens really fast."

Griff nodded. Ernie pressed Play and the video started.

The clarity wasn't the best, but it was good enough to see the intent on the guy's face. Gun in hand, he was walking toward the checkout counter, prepared to do whatever was necessary. The camera view showed Meg huddled at the end of the counter. Griff's chest constricted.

A scream echoed in the video.

Jones looked over his shoulder toward the back of the place.

Meg had moved ever so slightly to see what he was doing. Suddenly she sprang upward.

Jones turned back toward her.

She was already moving through the air like a ballet dancer. The knife she held sliced across the man's throat even as her body started to turn in midair.

Blood spurted.

The gun fired.

Meg hit the floor, right shoulder first.

Jones staggered, then crumpled to the floor.

Meg got up. She kicked the weapon away, and then, staring at the man, she backed a couple of steps away. The next instant, she turned toward the back of the store and started in that direction.

"That's pretty much what she told me happened," Griff said. His gut was in about fifty knots, and drawing in a breath was as difficult as hell. None of this he intended to let his friend know. His mind kept replaying that twirl, slice and dive maneuver.

Ernie nodded. "Same story she told me."

Griff studied the image on the screen of the paused video that showed Jones face down on the floor in a pool of his own blood and Meg midstride as she walked away. He looked to his friend. "So, what's the problem?"

Ernie scrubbed a hand over his jaw. "There are a couple of things. First, she kicked the gun away."

Griff shrugged. "Smart move. The guy could have grabbed for it as she walked away. If he wasn't dead, I mean."

"Except," Ernie countered, "she didn't appear concerned about him being able to do that since she didn't check to see if she'd completely disabled him. She didn't nudge him, check for a pulse, nothing. She just kicked the gun away from his reach and walked away. Like she knew for sure he was done."

Griff blinked. "Are you suggesting she didn't care that she'd killed this guy?" What the hell was he saying here?

Ernie held up his hands again to show he wasn't here for a fight. "I'm saying she understood that he was dead. She didn't need to check because she recognized the fact by the amount of blood or simply because of the blow she had landed."

Griff shook his head. "Okay, so then what's the problem?"

"There are two problems in my opinion. One," Ernie said, "she killed the guy—obviously in self-defense— and had no visible issue with having done so. I guess what I'm saying is if you had just killed a guy, wouldn't you have some sort of reaction?"

"I can see how it looks that way," Griff agreed, not wanting to sound as if he was talking against Meg. "But that doesn't mean she didn't have an issue. What we're looking at could be shock."

"Maybe," Ernie relented, frowning as if he hadn't considered that possibility.

"What's the other problem?" Griff couldn't keep the frustration out of his voice.

Ernie backed the video up just a little and let it play again, showing the part where she kicked the gun and headed toward the storeroom. "She kicked the gun without stopping to consider what to do with or about it. She just kicked it away." He pointed to the screen. "That was instinct. The kind of thing you do without thinking because you've done it a bunch of times before."

Confusion furrowed Griff's brow and signaled a distant headache there. "You saying she's an ex-cop?"

It was possible. She'd told Griff that she'd had a grooming service in Arizona before her father died and she'd decided on a change of venue. Maybe she had been a cop, and she just didn't want to talk about it.

"I'm saying," Ernie said slowly, "that she was either a cop or...or that she has killed before—" he held up his hands again before Griff could light into him "—and is familiar with the routine of doing the job."

"What the hell, Ernie?" Griff leaned back in his chair and stared at his lifelong friend. "You're suggesting she was not just some sort of killer—but one who had done it enough times to form habits, like kicking a weapon away. Like she was some serial killer or whatever, is that what you're saying?"

"You're taking me all wrong," Ernie argued. "I'm not

saying she's a serial killer or something." He rolled his eyes. "My money is on cop."

Either way, worry nudged Griff at the idea. "Play it again."

Ernie started the clip over, once more in slow motion. This time, Griff focused on Meg's face. What he saw was focus, intent. What he did not see was fear or uncertainty.

Whether Meg was a cop or a killer, she had—without question—done this before.

The knots in his gut turned to stone.

But how was that possible? A hurricane of emotions whipped through him. He knew this woman. Had spent hours and hours with her. She loved animals. She loved life. She was one of the nicest people he'd ever met.

"One more time," Griff said, his words barely a whisper.

He had to be missing something. This could not be what it looked like.

Chapter Five

Pampered Paws
Pine Boulevard
3:00 p.m.

Meg jerked awake.

Raymond and Pepper had alerted. Heads up, bodies tense.

On alert herself now, Meg eased to her feet. Listened intently.

Banging on the front entrance made her flinch.

Since it was Sunday and the shop was closed, it wouldn't be a customer. More reporters, she figured. Banging on the door was not acceptable. She'd just have to call Deputy Battles.

Muffled shouting and cursing echoed through the wall that separated her position from the lobby.

Maybe not reporters.

"Come on," Meg murmured to Raymond, ushering him into the open kennel. Pepper followed without prompting. Meg closed the door, careful not to make a sound. If trouble was here, and obviously it was, she didn't want the two elderly dogs getting caught in the fray.

Her first instinct was to call 911, but a part of her worried that if this was the trouble from her past, she feared that she'd only get someone killed. She didn't want Deputy Battles's blood on her hands. If her photo and last night's holdup at the Gas and Go had somehow hit social media or the internet news…

She shook off the idea. Didn't want to go there yet. Instead, she eased forward, all the way to the door that stood between this room and the lobby. Dropping into a crouch, she peered through the keyhole in the old-fashioned door. She'd never felt the need for a key to lock up between the kennels and the lobby. Maybe she should have. A little late now.

Glass shattered.

As she watched through that keyhole, a man's hairy arm reached through the now broken front entrance door and flipped the dead bolt. Her muscles steeled for battle.

Damn. She should have set the security system. She hadn't meant to fall asleep.

One man, then another entered the lobby. The larger guy—tall, thickly muscled—was older, fiftyish. The other was a few inches shorter and a good deal thinner and maybe in his midtwenties. Both wore jeans, tees and biker boots.

A memory of the guy who'd bled out on the floor at the Gas and Go flashed in her brain. Jeans, tee and biker boots.

No doubt these were his friends.

Damn. Just when she thought her biggest worry was Griff's opinion of her.

"Come on out!" the older man shouted. "Don't make us have to hunt you down."

Using a bat, or maybe it was a club he carried, the skinnier guy swiped most of the items on the checkout counter off for emphasis. Thankfully, the vintage cash register teetered near the edge without crashing to the floor. Meg didn't see any firearms, but that didn't mean one or both wasn't carrying. The bigger guy had a sheathed knife, the sort a hunter carried, on his belt. The feel of cool leather at the small of her back was reassuring.

"You got to the count of three," Big Guy warned, "then we're taking this place apart."

No need to let things get out of hand, she decided. Besides, now that it was clear the trouble wasn't what she'd feared, she could handle things. Hopefully without too much fanfare. Just to be sure she didn't have to take this too far, she sent a text message to 911. Maybe no one would have to die before the police arrived. With that out of the way, she tucked her cell back into her pocket and did what she had to do.

She opened the door and walked into the lobby, closing the door firmly behind her.

"Can I help you, gentlemen?" She looked from the older guy to his friend and then to the mess on the floor. Shattered glass and the items that had been on the counter. Nothing irreplaceable. Just a nuisance.

Big Guy glared at her. "You killed my son."

So this was Zyair Jones's father. Regret pricked her. "I'm sorry for your loss, sir. But he didn't leave me a lot of choice. He had a gun pointed at me."

"You mean like this?" Skinny Guy tossed his bat/club down and drew a weapon.

Meg glanced at him. Nine millimeter. *Damn.* She

had hoped neither one was carrying. Oh well, just made things more interesting. The fact that he held the weapon sideways told her he didn't have a freaking clue what he was doing. Just trying to look tough like the thugs in the movies. Did that mean he wouldn't shoot her and, with sheer luck, hit her? She wasn't taking the risk.

Before she could respond, Big Guy growled, "Put that away. I told you I'm doing her the same way she did Zy."

As he spoke, he whipped the knife from its sheath. "Let's see how you like bleeding out alone on the floor."

Meg stared directly into his eyes. "Your son robbed the Gas and Go and was in the process of sexually assaulting the girl who worked there. When I interrupted his criminal activity, he aimed a loaded weapon at me and appeared intent on using it. What would you have done?"

Renewed fury twisted his face. "You think that makes me feel any better? You." He took a step toward her. "Killed." Another step disappeared between them. "My." One more step closer. "Son."

She held his gaze, gave a single nod. "I did. And I guess I'm going to have to kill you too."

While the shock of her daring words startled him, she sack-tapped him with enough force to send him doubling over. The howl of pain that erupted from his mouth echoed through the lobby. She grabbed the vintage cash register—the one thing that remained on the counter—and crashed it against the back of his head. The register hit the floor, and using all of her weight, she shoved the addled man backward.

Skinny Guy jumped astraddle of his downed friend—maybe to protect him, maybe because he was just reckless like that—and waved his weapon. Aiming sideways again. "You are dead, bitch."

Apparently regaining his bearing, Big Guy suddenly lurched upward.

Meg dove for the floor.

Skinny Guy flew forward, and his weapon discharged.

Meg scrambled around to the front of the counter. She grabbed the abandoned bat and shot to her feet just as Big Guy turned toward her. She swung the bat at his head with all her might.

The impact of the hard wood against his skull vibrated up her arms.

He stared at her a moment, his nose gushing blood, his eyes unfocused, then he dropped onto his back. The floor shook with the impact.

A scream rent the air and Skinny Guy threw himself at her.

They tumbled to the floor.

Where was his weapon? Her frantic gaze zoomed from his right hand to his left.

No weapon.

She rolled. Got on top of him.

His hands went to her throat and squeezed.

She punched him in the throat.

His hands dropped immediately to his neck as he gagged and fought for breath.

Rubbing her hand, Meg got up and backed away from the guy now curled into the fetal position.

The sound of sirens in the distance had her breathing a sigh of relief. She went to where the nine millimeter laid on the floor. She picked it up and removed the magazine. Once she confirmed the chamber was clear, she placed the weapon on the counter. One by one, she removed the rounds from the magazine and tossed them over the counter. When she was done, she hurried back to the kennels to ensure Raymond and Pepper were okay. Both stared up at her with worried eyes.

"Good dogs," she murmured, reassuring them before rushing back to the lobby.

The sheriff's department SUV squealed to a rocking stop outside her shop. Two deputies, including Ernie Battles, barreled through the door, weapons drawn. Both surveyed the damage and the wounded.

Battles turned to Meg. "You okay?"

She nodded. Shook her right hand. "I'm good."

The Big Guy roused and scrambled to his hands and knees. Then he puked.

Battles nudged the man with his weapon. "Mr. Jones, you are under arrest…"

The rest of what the deputy said was lost on Meg. Her attention had zeroed in on the reporter with her face pressed to the glass. Worse, her cameraman stood in the open entrance, filming the whole thing.

Holy…

"Back off," the other deputy warned as he moved toward the doorway. "This is a crime scene. I need you back on the street."

The reporter shouted Meg's name.

She turned her back.

"How does it feel to know you killed a man?" The words echoed through the air.

Meg glanced toward the woman being ushered off the sidewalk and back to her van. Two more news vans arrived while she watched.

Dread welling inside her, Meg walked to the counter and sat down on the floor behind it.

Whatever privacy she had hoped to keep intact after all this was gone now. Her face and this new story would be all over the internet by tomorrow. Any hope of maintaining anonymity was gone.

The jig was up.

Two other deputies arrived and hauled the perps away in separate cruisers. By then, Battles had taken Meg's statement and she had started the cleanup. The other deputy, Hershel Gardner, had rounded up a box from the dumpster in the alley and was helping with the glass pickup.

The best part of this, Meg decided—looking on the bright side—was that it had occurred late in the day. No way would it hit the news before morning. The minutes that had elapsed also had her thinking that if she was really lucky, the story wouldn't get picked up by a big network or the Associated Press. No reason for it to, in her opinion. There was plenty of bad going on in the world to keep her issues way down at the bottom on the interest barrel.

"Can we talk?" Battles asked.

"Sure." Meg propped the broom she'd been using against the wall and followed the deputy over to the counter.

Battles searched her face before saying whatever was on his mind. Meg hoped he wasn't going to ask more questions about her self-defense techniques.

"I need you to rethink this thing about not wanting to press charges," he suggested. "I get that you feel bad for Mr. Jones because his son is dead, but you did what you had to do. It was self-defense. Jones has to get right with that. To be honest with you, he's likely part of the reason his son was always in trouble. If Jones gets away with this, it just gives him more power."

Meg understood what he was saying—better than most probably—but she also understood that Jones had been operating on emotion. "The breaking and entering should stand," she agreed. "But not the assault. I think he already got the short end of the stick on that one."

"No question," Battles granted. "But what about the next person he gets riled up at? Will that person be able to fend him off the way you did? If he gets away with what he did to you, then down the road, someone else may end up paying the price."

He had a valid point. Maybe too valid. Meg should have thought of that. Maybe she was operating on emotion a little too fully as well.

"You're right. He should face the full ramifications for what he did, and maybe he won't be so bold next time."

Battles nodded. "Good." He chuckled. "You know, I'm still trying to figure out how you handled a guy at least three times your size. Not to mention he had an accomplice with him who was armed."

She laughed. "I think what really helped was the element of surprise. They didn't see the potential for a real fight."

Battles shrugged. "Maybe so. But the way you emptied that magazine on the weapon and…" He shrugged again. "I don't know, just the way you handle yourself reminds me of my own training."

"Maybe I watch too many cop shows. Picked up on

some of the moves. You know how television and social media can influence our thoughts and actions."

He nodded slowly. "Yeah, I guess you're right."

Voices outside drew their attention to the street. The first reporter was gone. Had to get her story in before anyone else, no doubt. The other two were shouting questions at a new arrival.

Griff.

Meg's heart reacted and she silently chastised herself.

He climbed out of his truck, then reached into the back for what appeared to be a sheet of plywood.

"I should give him a hand," Battles said.

The deputy hustled outside and helped Griff bring in the four-by-eight sheet of plywood. Once they'd propped it against the wall, Griff glanced at her before going back outside. Meg blinked, considering if she should have said something.

While Battles ushered the two reporters and their cameramen off the sidewalk and back to the street—again— Griff returned carrying a toolbox. This time, he walked all the way back to where she stood.

"Hey."

She sighed. "Hey."

"We're going to secure your front entrance," he explained. "Then I'm coming around back to pick up you and Raymond. You should pack a bag. I plan on keeping you for a while."

"But—"

He shook his head. "No buts. Jodie and Dottie can take care of things around here. You need to disappear for a few days until the smoke clears."

He was right. She understood this. The problem was

he didn't, not really. For now, this was her only real option. "Okay."

She climbed the stairs, the receding adrenaline making her feel as if she'd run a triathlon. Since she'd already packed her go bag, all she needed was another with a couple changes of clothes and a nightshirt. Well, and her toothbrush and hairbrush. A few toiletries. She could hang out at Griff's for a couple of days and see how this was going to shake down. Maybe she'd get lucky, and the story would go unnoticed. After all, small-town Tennessee was a long way from big-city California.

She could hope anyway.

Truth was, she probably wouldn't feel safe going forward, whether the story made headlines or not. The life she lived was uncertain enough without layering in the extra issue of not one but two very public situations.

If she dared to stay, how would she ever stop looking over her shoulder after all this?

Staying was a less than optimal idea. But going filled her with a kind of sadness she'd never expected to feel again.

She had allowed herself to get far too close to this place. She walked to her beloved window and watched Griff get something from the back of his truck and head back into her shop. She was way too close to this man.

It was dangerous, too dangerous.

There was no guarantee she could protect him if her past caught up with her.

Chapter Six

Griffin Residence
Sundown Road
7:00 p.m.

Despite all that had happened, Meg smiled when the truck rolled to a stop at the end of Griff's long driveway. The herd of dogs that had been lying on the porch all stood, ears perked up, tails cautiously wagging.

As soon as Griff opened his door and the dogs got his scent, they were yapping and rushing toward him. It was the closest thing to heaven she could imagine in this life.

Meg parked her truck next to his and climbed out. What was not to like about a man who loved dogs—animals in general—this much? More telling was the fact that the animals clearly loved him. That they had a haven here was just icing on the cake.

He joined her at her truck and grabbed her overnight bag. "You mind if I get this bunch fed before we make dinner?"

She picked up her backpack from the floorboard. "As long as you don't mind if I help."

He grinned and reached for the backpack. "I never turn down a helping hand."

Meg opened the back door and helped Pepper from the back seat. Raymond managed to hop down all on his own. The two followed her to the front of his truck where they waited while Griff took her bags into the house. He hadn't been too happy about her insisting on driving herself over here, but she couldn't imagine being stranded in the event she had to leave. An exit strategy was far too important to be caught with no wheels.

When he went into the house she noticed he hadn't locked his door. Not a good idea, especially with her around. She'd have to talk to him about that. Or maybe she'd do him a big favor and disappear. It would be in his best interest.

The way her gut clenched made her regret having been so foolish. She should never have allowed herself to get so comfortable here, to believe for one second that she might be able to have a real fresh start the first time around. The move and then the acceptance of people in this town had been far too simple. She should have known it was too good to be true.

The herd, as Griff called them, followed him down the steps. A few low growls were exchanged as they eyed Pepper and Raymond, but Griff gave the command for the group to behave and the growls stopped. The animals, including the interlopers belonging to Meg, followed Griff and her to what looked like a barn but was actually a very large state-of-the-art doghouse. Dozens of kennels and all else that his herd might need was inside. He called each dog by name as they portioned food into their bowls.

"Pepper," Griff said as he opened the door to a vacant kennel, "I was thinking you might like this one."

Pepper sniffed the door, then wandered into the kennel and over to the bowl of kibble.

Griff closed the door. "Raymond, you come on with us."

Griff was aware that Raymond slept at Meg's bedside, and though none of his many animals stayed in the house with him, he'd insisted he wouldn't mind Raymond doing so. The sweet Lab he'd had for fourteen years had died last year, and so far Griff wasn't ready for another one to get that close. Meg understood. It was like losing a family member.

Once the dogs were settled, they moved on to the "cat barn." The four-legged furry animals seemed to come out of the woodwork. Raymond stuck close to Meg. Though he was around cats at the shop, never so many at one time.

The cat barn had once been a smokehouse used by Griff's grandparents for curing meat before the common availability of freezers. Inside were all manner of climbing areas that led to cozy little nooks. A total of fifteen cats pranced about, taking a turn at rubbing against Griff's legs. They too adored him.

Once the cats were served, Griff and Meg moved on to the big original barn where they fed the eight horses and four cows. There were two large pigs rooting around in a smaller pasture beyond the barn, and they got a little something as well. Raymond was quite curious about the snorting creatures. Meg was fairly certain he'd been around horses and cows before but never pigs.

As they headed to the house, Meg surveyed Griff's

farm. No matter how many times she came here, she was still impressed by the well-thought-out setup and the enduring relationship between Griff and the animals. It really was a special place. She glanced at the man next to her. A special man.

Who deserved a woman without secrets, who could share this wonderful life with him.

She blinked away the notion. Certainly not her.

Inside, he picked up her bags and said, "I'll take these upstairs."

She nodded and did what she knew needed to be done. "I'd feel more comfortable if we locked the doors."

He studied her a moment, then gave a quick nod of his own. "Course."

She locked the door and he headed up. She moved on to the kitchen and locked the back door as well. The urge to search the house gnawed at her, but she ignored it. There was no reason for her to suspect an ambush at his address. At least not yet.

Sad. Very sad.

He joined her in the kitchen. "Your room is the second door on the right upstairs. There's only one bathroom up there. I hope you don't mind sharing."

"Not at all. I'm grateful for your hospitality."

He waved her off and headed for the fridge. "Rhianna Glen dropped off a casserole this afternoon." He withdrew a white covered dish embossed with pink flowers. "Chicken, broccoli and rice, I think she said."

Meg grinned. "I see. Rhianna Glen, huh? That's nice." No matter that she kept a teasing lilt in her voice, jealousy poked at her. This was the sort of woman who would end up wrangling Griff. Someone who had no secret past, someone who had the option of staying forever.

He laughed as he set the dish on the counter, removed the lid and prepared to put it in the microwave. "She's just trying to be nice."

Now Meg laughed outright. "I know you aren't that naive. She's recently divorced and you are a very…" How did she put it without sounding overly interested? "A good catch."

He pressed the Start button and the microwave hummed to life. "Good catch." His forehead furrowed and he executed a slow nod. "Makes me feel kind of like a largemouth bass."

Meg barely suppressed another round of laughter. "You know what I mean. Rhianna is a woman of a certain age whose upbringing has taught her that having a husband is the only way to be happy, and therefore, she must replace the old model posthaste."

Now Griff was the one laughing. "I guess so. Plenty of that going around lately."

Meg leaned against the counter next to the sink. "So, you're saying Rhianna isn't the only one."

Rhianna and her husband had divorced after four short years. No children. Rhianna was a lifetime resident of Piney Woods. She no doubt felt she should have first dibs on the town's most eligible bachelor.

He shrugged, reached into the cupboard for plates. "There may be a couple of others who bring me food. It's nothing new."

Meg decided she wouldn't mention people did that for funerals too. "They say the stomach is the way to a man's heart."

He placed the plates on the counter next to her. "Not this man."

He held her gaze for several seconds, and the look in his eyes somehow prevented her from breathing. "Sorry," she said in the lightest tone she could muster. "I wasn't aware you liked casseroles so much."

"I don't…really." He searched her face as if looking for answers to something he wanted to ask.

Uh-oh. Back to the questions. She shifted away, opened the utensil drawer and grabbed a couple of forks. "It sure smells good." He said nothing but it was true. "I've never been much of a cook," she rambled on. She'd tried since getting settled in Piney Woods, but her heart had never been in it.

When she turned back to him and passed the forks, he said, "Clearly you have other skills."

His gaze held hers in that probing way again, and somehow, try as she might, she couldn't look away. "Most animals love me, so I guess that's my superpower."

"That's not what I meant." He laid the forks on the plates without taking his eyes off hers. "How in the world did you disable two men all by yourself?"

"I told you about the self-defense classes." Was it her imagination, or was he standing purposefully closer, searching her eyes a little more intently?

He moved his head slowly side to side. "This was more than self-defense classes. Ernie says you put both down without a weapon. That one guy was huge. I couldn't have put him down. Not without some sort of advantage." His eyes narrowed. "What kind of advantage did you have?"

"The cash register," she said, struggling to prod answers from her brain. She'd foolishly lapsed into some trancelike state prompted by nothing more than Griff's nearness and his eyes. "I slammed it over his head after I kicked him…well, you know where."

Griff winced. "And what was the other guy doing during all this?"

"Watching, I think." She allowed the events to play out in her head. "He waved his gun at me, but the big guy got up and knocked him over. It was a total accident but really worked to my advantage."

This time Griff frowned. "I'm not following."

"When the big guy first went down, the skinny guy jumped to stand over him." She shrugged. "I don't know, maybe it was some sort of couldn't-get-it-right ninja move to protect his friend and at the same time confront me. Then things got a little chaotic. I dove for the floor. The gun went off." She shrugged. "I found the bat the skinny one had brought in with him and used it on the big guy. He went down again. But the skinny guy jumped up." She rubbed her forehead, trying to recall the precise chain of events. "Next thing I knew, he had me by the throat and I punched him in his throat." She looked at her right hand. Her knuckles were swollen and her fingers were a little blue. "Hurt like hell, but it hurt him worse."

Griff took her hand in his and rubbed his fingers over hers. "You need something for that?"

She watched his fingers on hers, savored the feel of her hand in his. "It's okay. I've suffered worse, believe—" She caught herself too late, squeezed her eyes shut for a second. "I mean, I was in an accident once and broke my arm. That hurt a whole lot worse. I've had a…"

He was watching her so intently that she couldn't continue speaking. She wanted to, told herself to, but the words would not come.

"It feels like there are things you need to tell me," he said softly. "Things that are relevant to how you can take down two men all alone. How you can stop a man carrying a gun with nothing but your wits and a knife."

"Self-defense classes." The lie was sounding weaker all the time.

"You can tell me anything," he said, his gaze pressing hers with an insistence that made her weak. "You know that, right?"

She nodded. "I do. We're friends."

"Then why aren't you telling me?"

The images of him being tied to a chair and tortured then shot loomed in her mind. She drew her hand from his and steadied herself. Not an easy feat.

"You're overthinking this." She manufactured a smile that no doubt looked as fake as it felt. "I just got lucky. Those guys weren't nearly as tough as they work at appearing. The younger guy got all his moves from thug TV, I think."

The microwave dinged, and she had never been so thankful for Rhianna Glen's casserole.

Griff hesitated but then finally turned to take the casserole from the microwave. He placed it on the counter, then tossed the oven mitts aside and searched for a serving spoon.

Meg grabbed a couple of napkins from the holder next to the salt and pepper shakers and placed them on the table. "What're we drinking?"

"I have beer, tea, water," he replied as he placed their plates on the table. "Take your pick."

Though she rarely allowed anything that might alter her ability to think clearly, Meg decided she deserved a beer. Like last night, this had been a hell of a day. "I'll take a beer. How about you?"

"Sounds good," he agreed.

She grabbed the beers from the fridge and settled at the table. For a while, they ate and chatted about the dogs. The casserole was actually very good. They both laughed at the idea that Rhianna likely wouldn't appreciate him sharing her dish with another woman. Then they cleaned up, grabbed another beer and headed into the living room. Meg relaxed a little and decided that maybe he was going to let the whole issue go.

Deputy Battles hadn't really given her much trouble when she gave her statement. No doubt he had been a little shocked by the scene and the fact that she'd been the only one left standing but chose to overlook it, considering the two men had invaded her shop and had done considerable damage. After all, she had been lucky to survive. But time had cleared his head, and judging by the questions Griff had asked, he and Ernie had discussed what went down in her store. The more they talked, the more questions came to mind.

Now, obviously, they were both suspicious. And who wouldn't be? The question was, could she alleviate their concerns?

The ways she might accomplish that goal twisted inside her. Just another reason the life she had built here was in all probability over. Even if her past didn't find her, *this* would haunt her. No one would be able to just feel grateful she'd survived. There would always be questions just because she had come through unscathed, not one but two close calls. It was human nature. People were curious. They needed reasonable explanations and her explanations had not been anywhere near reasonable enough.

The quiet went on for longer than was comfortable. Guilt heaped heavier onto her shoulders and Meg struggled with something to say. She didn't like that her closest friend—and Griff was that and, if she were totally honest, more—was disappointed in her or whatever it was he felt.

But she could not go down that path with him. His life would be changed in ways he couldn't possibly understand, and she refused to be responsible for altering his entire existence to that degree.

Griff set his can aside and turned to her as if he'd finally landed on what he wanted to say next. "Are you concerned those two men will come after you again?" He studied her a moment. "I mean, you did agree without much persuasion to come home with me. I'm guessing you're at least a little worried, whether you want to admit it or not."

Meg chose her words carefully. To tell him that an abrupt exit from his place would likely be simpler and cleaner than from her shop wouldn't be the response he wanted to hear.

"I suppose I was in a sort of shock. The idea that the man's family would seek revenge never even entered my mind. Apparently, it should have." This was frankly an oversight on her part. She wouldn't have made such a rookie error in the past. Maybe she was getting soft.

"Ernie's worried there will be others, even though the two involved in today's attack won't be giving you any trouble anytime soon. Sheriff Norwood is working with the sheriff in Dade County to get a handle on the situation."

Meg nodded. "Good to know."

"Someone could confront you on the road," Griff added. "At the market. It's something you need to give some thought to."

Wait. Wait. She got it now. This was more than just about her. "Is there something about the Jones family that you and Ernie haven't told me?"

"There are a lot of good people out there who belong to very cool, very nice biker clubs. But the Jones folks are not nice, and they don't belong to a club like that. This is a criminal biker gang. Sheriff Norwood mentioned there was an FBI investigation into these guys. We're talking bad guys, Meg. Really, really bad guys."

As if she needed the situation ramped up. The FBI? Really? This just got better and better.

"Okay." She finished off her beer. "This is why you're so worried?" On some level the news was a relief. If this was the primary factor troubling Griff, then maybe he wasn't as suspicious of her as she'd believed. Somehow that made her feel a little better. "I just have to watch my back until this is sorted."

"We," he corrected. "We watch your back."

She grinned. Toyed with her empty beer can. "You may not find the job as interesting as you think."

The ghost of a smile tugged at his lips, but he wasn't ready to shrug off the seriousness just yet. "I'm willing to find out."

Again, she carefully selected her words. "You're a

good friend, Griff. I appreciate your consideration of my welfare."

"I appreciate," he teased, "that you keep my life interesting."

Meg laughed. She wasn't sure if that was a compliment. "I wish I could say I try, but to be honest, the interesting part just barges in."

"Ernie wondered if you had ever considered keeping a handgun for protection."

If she'd had any other question about the idea, this was clearly confirmation that they had indeed been discussing her. "I'm good with my knife."

Handguns, if done legally, involved background checks. Not doable. If she told him she already had a weapon, then she'd have to reveal that it had not been legally purchased. Either way, this would create a problem. It was best to insist she didn't like guns. And she didn't. Not really. That said, they were a necessary evil sometimes.

"I have a rifle you could keep at your place."

"I appreciate the offer, but I wouldn't feel comfortable with a rifle."

"We could do some target practice with it tomorrow. Get you comfortable with it." He grinned. "See how bad you really are."

"Couldn't hurt, I suppose." What else could she say? Not that she was an expert marksman. Not that she could disassemble and reassemble any firearm he chose to put in front of her in record time.

"Good. I, for one, will feel better knowing you've got a little firepower handy."

"I'm tired of talking about me," she said, curling her

legs under her and settling deeper into the comfy sofa. "Tell me about how you decided to become a keeper of discarded things."

"Didn't we talk about this before?"

"I've asked, and you've always given me the abridged version. I want the details."

He leaned back, draped an arm across the back of the sofa. "I guess I had that one coming."

For the first time since before she'd spotted the holdup at the Gas and Go, she relaxed and waited for him to continue. Just avoiding further discussion about her was a significant boost to lowering her tension.

"I was working sixteen-hour days," he began. "Not that I didn't love my job, but there's a fine line between love and obsession. I think it was easier than coming home and facing the discord there."

"Relationships can be difficult sometimes." Meg was well aware. Her one serious relationship had crumbled under the tension of high-pressure work. Hers and his. Man, that had been so long ago. *Another life.*

"I guess I didn't want to see the end coming, but it came anyway, whether I was here or not. Once it was over, I had to ask myself why I was pouring my whole life into something that should only occupy a small portion of it." He glanced around the room. "I wanted to be here doing something that mattered at least part of my time. One evening, I went out to get my car from the parking garage, and there was a dog. It looked alone and sad, neglected. I gave it a scratch behind the ears and the bag of chips I had in my car." He stared at his hands a moment. "The next evening it was still there. So I loaded him up and took him to a shelter. That was when my eyes were really opened. There just aren't enough shelters—worse, there aren't enough decent humans, in my opinion—to care for the animal population. I decided I had to do something."

"You could have donated funds for building more shelters. That's what most people do. Throw a little money at it. Sometimes it's the best they can do. Sometimes it's just easier that way because you don't have to look too closely."

"I did that too," he said with a pointed look in her direction. "And I still do. But I had all this land, and since farming wasn't my thing, I decided to use it for something that mattered. I can't save the world, but I can do all possible to save the part of it that I live in."

"Wow." She had known part of that story, but this, this was the sort of tale real-life heroes were made of. "That's amazing."

"I still enjoy the work I do on a professional level at the firm, but most of my time is spent here doing what matters."

"I'm sure your mom and your sister are very proud of what you're doing here." How could they not be? This was amazing.

He chuckled. "Mostly, I think they believe I'm in denial about barreling toward forty with no wife and no kids and nary a prospect."

Meg wanted to laugh at the idea, but she got the distinct impression that he was serious. "I'm sure your family would love to hear about your casserole queens."

"I think they'd enjoy hearing about you."

Their gazes held for a long moment. Every ounce of

will power Meg possessed was required not to pursue his motive behind the statement.

Instead, she stood, stretched and yawned. "I'm beat. I hope you don't mind if I hit the shower and call it a night a little early."

"Right." He pushed to his feet. "I'm sure you're exhausted. Make yourself at home."

"Thanks." She backed away a step. "See you in the morning." She headed for the stairs.

"Night," he called after her.

"Night," she said without looking back. She couldn't trust herself to look back without running right into his arms.

Chapter Seven

Griffin Residence
Sundown Road
Monday, May 6, 7:30 a.m.

Meg flinched. Shook her head.

The cold touched her again.

She jerked awake.

Raymond sat beside the bed, his muzzle resting on the quilt. Even as her gaze focused in on him, he nudged her with his cold nose again.

Meg laughed and swiped at her eyes. "Morning, boy."

The light filtering in through the window had her frowning. What time was it? She grabbed her cell from the bedside table and sat up. 7:30 a.m.

Her eyebrows reared up. She *never* slept past 5:30 or 6:00 a.m. Ever.

She threw the covers back and bounced out of bed. "Raymond, why didn't you get me up sooner?"

He stared up at her with a questioning look as if to ask how he was supposed to have done that.

"You're right," she agreed as she dug through her overnight bag for clothes, "I should have set the alarm on my phone."

But she usually woke up on her own. Maybe knowing someone else was in the house with her had helped her sleep more deeply. She dragged on her jeans. Not just someone but a friend. A good friend.

She pulled on a tee, finger-combed her hair and pulled it back into a ponytail using the scrunchie she wore as a bracelet whenever it wasn't in her hair. Not just a friend, she admitted. A guy she respected, thought was sexy and was kind of attracted to. Truth was she'd lain in bed for hours last night thinking about him just down the hall. Wondering what it would be like to be in his bed. Wishing she could just enjoy that opportunity and never worry about consequences.

That was the reason she'd overslept. Even at thirty-four, a girl could be kept awake by fantasies.

"Not smart," she muttered, slipping on her favorite sneakers.

She straightened the covers on her bed and hung her nightshirt on the footboard. She folded yesterday's clothes and set them on the bed. Maybe she'd have a chance to launder them later. She didn't have many things with her and she had to stay prepared.

At the door, she opened it wider and peeked out. The hallway was clear. She hurried to the bathroom, freshened up and did necessary business. Then she headed for the stairs. Raymond followed her to the top of the stairs. As they descended the staircase, the scent of coffee had her moving faster. Downstairs, she headed for the kitchen. The smell of toasted bread and maybe bacon had her stomach rumbling. If the man cooked too, she might just have to marry him.

Even the thought had her feeling an odd little jab in the center of her chest.

Not possible.

Approaching the kitchen, she paused and grinned at the scene. An apron was cinched at Griff's waist. He carefully lifted pieces of browned bacon from the pan to a plate lined with a paper towel. The light in the oven showed a tray of biscuits. The man made biscuits? Then he turned to another pan and gave it a stir with a spatula. Eggs? Grease popped and he swore. Meg leaned against the door jamb and folded her arms over her chest to watch.

But Raymond had other ideas. He scooted in around her and gave a single deep-throated bark.

Griff turned around and looked from Raymond to Meg. His face flushed a little. "Morning."

"Were you just going to let me sleep all day?" She pushed off the door and joined him at the stove.

He shrugged. "I figured you didn't sleep much the last couple of nights and needed a little extra."

A reasonable conclusion. "Thanks." She surveyed the bacon and eggs. "Looks and smells great. What can I do to help?"

He turned off the oven, removed the pan of biscuits and gestured to the table. "Have a seat. It's all done."

"Then it's only fair that I do the cleanup." Meg crossed to the coffee maker and poured herself a cup.

Griff plated the eggs and bacon, then added a biscuit to each. He settled the plates on the table and then rounded up forks and napkins. "You may have noticed I don't have a dishwasher."

"Neither do I." Truth was, she mostly used paper plates. Not to mention, she ordered from the diner really often. Cooking for one was not so much fun. She took a seat at the table and savored a taste of coffee. So good she moaned. "You make really great coffee."

"I'm glad you like it." He sat down in the seat opposite her. "How about we do the cleanup together, and then I don't have to feel guilty about my guest washing dishes by hand."

She laughed. "I certainly wouldn't want you feeling guilty."

Raymond decided he wasn't getting a treat, so he stretched out on the floor next to Meg's chair.

"Please tell me you didn't make these biscuits from scratch." She bit into the soft, fluffy baked good and moaned again. She might just moan and sigh through this entire meal.

"My mama's recipe."

Meg rolled her eyes. "You put me to shame, Avery Griffin. I couldn't make a biscuit from scratch if my life depended on it."

He chuckled. "I guess I'll just have to teach you."

The suggestion filled her head with all sorts of notions that had nothing to do with baking.

"Speaking of family," he said after a few minutes of devouring the delicious meal, "my sister called this morning. She insists that we come to lunch at her place on Sunday. You have any plans?"

She would so love to say yes, but she couldn't even be sure she'd still be here. Yet, the hope in his voice, in his eyes, had her agreeing. "I do not have plans. I would love to go."

"Great." He dove back into his meal, but not before she noticed the sparkle her answer had put in his eyes.

She really hoped she didn't have to disappoint him.

Determined not to borrow more trouble than she already had, she put all else aside and just enjoyed the moment. It felt good, maybe too good, chatting with Griff over the breakfast he'd made and then washing the dishes together. She imagined this was how it would be if they were together.

Do not go there.

She knew better, but it was impossible not to imagine how it would feel to live this life, this partnership with the two of them working together and laughing and feeling just like a team. What would it hurt to let herself dream for a few minutes?

In her back pocket, her cell vibrated, drawing Meg from the fantasy. She stilled, withdrew it and checked the screen. Long ago—right after she exited her former life—she had set up notifications for anything that appeared online related to who she was previously. For a while, the notifications had come frequently and furiously. She'd topped the headlines on the West Coast for a few months.

Eventually, the notifications had dwindled to nothing. Since moving to Piney Woods, she hadn't received a single one. She was gone, probably dead, and there wasn't a soul on the planet who cared.

But this notification wasn't about the person she used to be. This was about Megan Lewis, owner/operator of

Pampered Paws in Piney Woods, Tennessee. This was about her life now.

The one that was, as of this second, officially over.

Her heart sank to her knees.

Her name and, worse, her photo filled the screen. Several news outlets in both Tennessee and Georgia had picked up the story. That was troubling enough, but it was the pickup by the Associated Press that sealed her fate.

No One Messes with This Woman

The story explained how Megan Lewis of Piney Woods, Tennessee, was a hero. Not only had she rescued a young girl from a savage fate, she had taken on the would-be killer's vigilante family, kicking butt and taking names.

Cold seeped into her bones as she read several versions of the same story. Her face appeared over and over—images all credited to the one reporter who'd lingered after yesterday's invasion at Meg's shop.

"You okay?"

Meg blinked. Shoved her phone back into her pocket. "I'm sorry, what?"

Griff had moved in toe-to-toe with her. He searched her face. "You look like you've seen a ghost."

She had. Meg swallowed back the dread rising in her throat. Her own.

"It's nothing." She forced a smile. "What's next on this morning's agenda? I'm guessing there are a lot of animals ready for their breakfast."

She couldn't think. Couldn't kick the voices from her

head. *They will see this. They will come. Your life here is over.*

She had to get Griff moving into his day so she could figure out the best plan for exiting this life, for leaving everything behind. She thought of Raymond, and her heart hurt.

Griff's worry shifted into a grin, somehow dragging her from the painful thoughts. "Mornings are my favorite part of the day."

She forced a smile, hoping he wouldn't see through it. "I can't wait to see what makes you say so."

He led the way to the barn, where they hayed the horses and cows. Added a bucket of feed to the pig trough. Meg struggled with keeping this new reality at bay so that she could enjoy this last morning with Griff and the animals. After the big animals were done, they moved on to the cats and then the dogs, all of which were freed to roam. Griff allowed the cats and dogs free range all day every day. He preferred putting them back into their kennels at night. The animals seemed to feel more comfortable that way, he explained. Maybe because the routine of it felt comforting. Then Meg and Griff gathered a few eggs in the chicken coop and restocked their feeders. She understood exactly why this was the best part of his day.

Meg felt so grateful for having been able to share it with him.

"I should drop Pepper at the vet clinic." She reached down and rubbed Raymond on the head. He'd followed every step they had taken. She suspected he sensed something was wrong. "Is it okay if I leave Raymond here until I get back?"

"Sure. I have some work to do in my office." He grinned at the dog. "Raymond can keep me company."

"Thanks. I'll just get my wallet and keys, then I'll load up Pepper."

He hitched his head toward the house. "You get your stuff. I'll load Pepper into your truck."

"I appreciate it."

Meg walked back to the house, holding back the urge to run. The longer she stayed at this point, the more dangerous for anyone who had been associated with her. Trudging up the stairs, she considered that leaving Griff a note would be a nice gesture, but there was no time to explain. No time to say the things that had swelled into her throat. How did she tell him that all he thought he knew about her was a lie? Whatever suspicions he had about her based on the events of the past two days would never in a million years live up to the truth. The truth was far scarier and far uglier.

Some secrets were better left buried.

Except hers was about to be exhumed in the worst kind of way.

The friends she had foolishly made, the reputation she had built would all be shattered when the truth came out, and it was coming. There was no holding it back at this point. She couldn't stop the hurricane. Her only hope was to try and limit the devastation.

She picked up her backpack. Leaving the overnight bag was necessary so as not to draw suspicion from Griff when she walked out. She descended the stairs and hesitated at the front door. A last, lingering look around and she was gone. Allowing herself to get so attached had been a bad move on her part. She had known better.

Griff waited at the driver side door of her truck. When she reached him, he opened the door for her. Why did he have to be so nice? So caring? Her entire soul ached. So damned handsome?

"I should drop by the shop," she said, hoping to extend the time she had before he started to wonder why she wasn't back.

"Just be careful," he said. "I called Ernie, and he says there's no one else in the Jones family you need to worry about, but they haven't interviewed all the members of that biker club yet. You need to be careful until we know if the threat is over."

He had no idea.

Meg gave him a little salute. "Yes, sir."

He caught her hand when she lowered it. "It's important to me that you're careful, Meg. To tell you the truth, I'd feel better going with you."

If he hadn't stared into her eyes that way, she might have been able to ignore the way his hand held hers so protectively. "I appreciate that and I promise I'll be careful. You have plenty to do here. I'll be fine."

And then the final nail in her coffin. He leaned down and brushed his lips across hers.

If she had been smart, she would have drawn away, but she simply could not. She wanted more. If she never saw him again after today, at least she would have this one kiss to remember him by.

So not smart.

But oh so sweet.

She melted into him, her backpack hitting the ground and her arms going around his neck. His arms went around her waist and pulled her closer.

The desperation that clawed through her was nearly more than she could bear, but she had to resist. She would not allow the danger to find her here, where he could be hurt. She had to go. She had to go now. Drawing the trouble away from here—away from him was paramount.

She drew back. Pressed her forehead to his chin because she didn't dare look into his eyes again. She might be strong, but she was not that strong.

"I should get going."

"I wish you didn't have to go."

Her hands slid down to his chest, and she levered herself away. Somehow managed to meet his eyes. "See you later," she lied.

He nodded. "Later."

She picked up her backpack and climbed into her truck. Before pulling out, she waved. He waved back, and then he watched until she was driving away. She watched too as he grew more distant in her rearview mirror.

Gripping the steering wheel as hard as she could, Meg kept going. She glanced over at Pepper and smiled. "Don't worry. Griff will bring you back home after all your tests."

He would take care of Pepper and Raymond.

Meg didn't have to ask or to wonder, she knew he would. That was the kind of man he was.

Dropping Pepper off at the vet clinic was easy enough. She told Lonnie if he couldn't reach her with the test results to call Griff. Lonnie assured her that he would, and Meg headed into town. A truck parked in front of Pampered Paws sported a glass repair logo. She was glad Jodie had found someone who could come so quickly. Meg parked in the alley behind the shop next door. She needed to talk to Jodie—and Dottie too if she was in. She wasn't sure just yet how the conversation would go, but it had to be done. She could simply rely on the letter she'd left, but this way would be better.

The usual crew of dogs were in the back play space. Meg gave individual attention to each of the animals as she made her way to the back door. She entered the code and stepped inside. Pop music played softly. Meg smiled. Jodie was in for sure. Dottie preferred country music. If she was in, she would insist that customers preferred country as well. Jodie never argued with the older woman. Whether it was respect or friendship, she always allowed Dottie to have her way.

Jodie was just outside the newly repaired front entrance and was handing a check to the repairman when Meg entered the lobby. The man thanked Jodie and went on his way. Jodie came inside, closing the door behind her. Her face brightened when she spotted Meg.

"You're here. Everything okay?"

The urge to tell her no and all the reasons it wasn't okay surged into Meg's throat, but she couldn't go there. Now or ever.

"Everything's fine. I dropped Pepper at the vet's. Griff is going to take her in when she's ready to be picked up."

"Aww, that's great. Pepper will love it there. Griff is such a great guy." She waggled her eyebrows as she joined Meg behind the counter. "You know he's really stuck on you. I mean, seriously stuck."

Meg smiled sadly. "He's a great guy for sure."

Jodie rolled her eyes. "Just pretend I didn't say the rest."

Now or never. "There's something I need to show you."

Her friend and employee picked up on the nuance of disquiet in Meg's tone. "What's going on?"

"You know," Meg began, "I don't have any family."

Jodie nodded slowly. "You told me, yes."

"After what happened on Saturday night, I got a little worried about things."

Jodie's face scrunched with worry. "Not to mention those guys busting in here yesterday. That had to be terrifying."

Meg nodded. "A little."

Jodie grinned sheepishly. "But you did kick their butts."

"I did." Meg pushed aside the images that immediately popped into her head. "Anyway, I wanted to make sure you knew about this." She reached into the cash register, lifted the cash tray from the drawer. She set it aside and picked up the unmarked envelope she'd tucked last year. "About six months ago, I started thinking about this, and I decided to do something about it."

Meg opened the envelope and removed the three-page document. She handed it to Jodie. "If anything were to happen to me or—" she shrugged "—if I just disappear, this shop and the business are yours."

"What in the world?" Jodie looked from the document to Meg. "Are you going somewhere? Has something happened that I don't know about?"

"No," Meg lied. She'd grown very good at lying over the years. "I just don't have anyone to leave things to, and I wanted to be sure that if I died or if I just decided I was done with things here that you take over. I see how good you are with the animals and the customers. I feel comfortable leaving all of it with you—if something happens. I also left something for Dottie. It's all upstairs on my desk. This is more or less a letter of instruction."

Jodie shook her head, refolded the document. "This isn't right. There's something you're not telling me."

Meg took the document from her, tucked it back into the envelope and placed it in the register drawer. "You don't need to worry," she argued. "Just know that it's here. I want you to take care of this place if I'm not here. Got it?"

Jodie blinked, emotion shining in her eyes. "Well, of course I will. But this sounds like—I don't know—something permanent."

"Hey," Meg said, "it's just insurance. Smart business-women don't take chances."

Jodie did another of those slow nods. "Okay. I guess I understand."

Meg hugged her. "Good. Now I have stuff to do, so you carry on." She gestured to the door. "Great job getting that taken care of first thing."

Jodie smiled, her cheeks a little flushed. "Thanks. I love this shop. I hope you know that I will do my very best to run it just like you, if ever the need arises."

Meg smiled. "See. I did the right thing."

With that out of the way, Meg went upstairs and checked her studio one last time just to make sure there was nothing else she needed, then she used the back stairs to leave. A female voice she recognized as one of the shop's regular customers told her Jodie was preoccupied. Just as well, Meg wasn't so good with goodbyes. She loaded into her truck and drove away.

Her eyes burned, but she refused to cry. She had enjoyed her life here. She'd hoped it would last, but there had never been and never would be any guarantees.

Not this time or the next.

Griffin Residence
Sundown Road
11:00 a.m.

ALL MORNING GRIFF hadn't been able to shake the feeling that something bad was about to happen. That overwhelming sense of doom just lingered and lingered. Especially after Meg had left.

When he spotted Ernie's SUV rolling along his driveway, he understood his instincts had been right. Whatever news his friend was here to deliver, Griff suspected it was not good.

He waited on the porch, one shoulder propped against the post on the right of the steps. "Morning," he said as his friend climbed out of his SUV.

"Morning." Ernie glanced around. "Is Meg here?"

Griff shook his head. "She had to drop off that rescued beagle at Lonnie's, and then she was going to check in at Pampered Paws. What's up?"

"Good. I was hoping I could speak to you alone," Ernie admitted. "There's something you need to know about Meg."

"All right. Come on in."

Ernie followed him inside. "Do we need something stronger than coffee to do this?" Griff asked, bracing for what he feared was going to be the bad he'd sensed coming. He wasn't usually one to drink in the middle of the morning, but his entire being was poised on the edge of panic.

"Another time maybe," Ernie suggested.

"I'm guessing we should sit."

Ernie nodded. "Yeah. That's probably a good idea."

Griff took the few steps to the living room and dropped into his favorite chair. It was an old one, had belonged to his daddy. At some point, he needed to consider getting it recovered.

Ernie picked a spot on the sofa. "I did something I wouldn't generally do after the scene at Meg's shop yesterday."

"What's that?" However hard he tried to relax, Griff's gut just tied in bigger knots.

"Truth is," Ernie went on, "that video in the Gas and Go just kept eating at me. I couldn't get it out of my head. It…" He shook his head. "It didn't feel right."

"Meg said she'd been attacked before," Griff countered. "She took her self-defense classes very seriously. That seems pretty reasonable."

Ernie nodded slowly. "Maybe. But then when I walked into her shop and saw those two men on the floor, I realized I couldn't ignore what my gut was telling me. Something was off. This was way more than self-defense classes. This was professional."

"I can see how it looked that way," Griff admitted— he'd been a little stunned himself. "But she didn't do anything wrong. Meg is a good person, and she had every right to do what she did."

Ernie held up a hand. "I'm not trying to say she did anything wrong. I'm just… I don't know." He shrugged. "I was worried she wasn't telling me the whole story. That maybe there was something she didn't want me to know."

Griff stood and braced his hands on his hips. "Just say whatever it is you gotta say, Ernie. This conversation isn't going to get any easier."

Again, Ernie held up a hand. "Just sit down, Griff. Don't get all riled up until you hear me out."

Griff took a breath. His friend was right. He swallowed his pride and dropped back into his seat. "So, what did you do?"

"I ran her prints."

Anger pierced Griff. "Like a criminal or a suspect of some sort?"

"I felt it was my duty," Ernie argued. "And I was right to believe something was off."

Griff's anger wilted a bit. "What do you mean?"

"Meg's real name is Angela Hamilton, better known as Angel—as in the Angel of Death. The reports I got back says she's a contract killer, Griff. She worked for this ruthless drug lord out in LA. Apparently, he did something she didn't like, and she killed his son. That's why she went into hiding—which I suppose is what she's doing here—hiding. If those people find her, she's dead. Maybe anyone around her too."

For a couple of beats Griff couldn't speak. Then he snapped out of it. "That can't be right." He shook his head. He knew Meg. She was too kind and too caring to be a cold-blooded killer. Even as his mind insisted that he knew this, the video from the Gas and Go played in his head like one of those social media reels stuck on a loop, then the images from the scene at her shop.

"Man," Ernie said, "I'm sorry as hell to bring this to your door, I know you like her, but this is scary stuff. *Dangerous* stuff."

Griff thought of the backpack she'd carried when she left and how she'd looked at him after that kiss with such regret. Dread welled in his throat, and he fought to swallow it down.

"What else did you do?" He looked at his lifelong friend and waited to hear the rest.

"Nothing." He held up both hands as if to prove his innocence. "I thought I'd talk to Meg, hear her side of it before…"

"Before what?" The anger was back, like acid burning a hole inside Griff's gut.

"Before doing what I have a sworn duty to do."

Griff's mouth worked before he got the words out. "What is it you expect me to do with this information?"

"If she comes back," Ernie said, his voice subdued with the guilt he no doubt felt, "I need you to let me know so I can come talk to her."

"You're going to arrest her," Griff tossed at him. "That's your intent, isn't it?"

"No," Ernie rebutted. "I'm going to talk to her, and we'll all figure it out from there." He stared hard at Griff. "Meg Lewis is a good person, you're right. And I like her too. But we have to figure this out, okay? She's a wanted criminal."

Griff nodded. "Okay."

Ernie stood. "Thanks. I realize this is hard. Just let me know when you hear from her."

Griff nodded. "Sure."

But not until he knew the whole story. No way was he throwing Meg under the bus until he was convinced there was no other choice.

No way in hell.

Chapter Eight

Meg had almost made it down the mountain when her cell rang.

Griff.

She couldn't answer. He would want to know when she was coming back, and she couldn't tell him that she wasn't. Not on the phone.

Or maybe the truth was she just didn't want to hear the disappointment and then the anger in his voice. She didn't want to field the questions and tell him more lies. It was better this way. *Just go.*

He and the others she had foolishly allowed herself to grow close to would be safer with her gone, where she could draw the trouble away. The less they knew, the better for all involved. Once anyone who came looking for her realized she had left town, they would follow. She'd already started the process of leaving a trail of bread crumbs to lure them after her.

She'd transferred ninety percent of the cash from her bank account to an online account based in the UK. Her readily usable assets were one of the first items that would be checked. Relocating cash was a huge tip-off that a target was on the move. She hadn't needed to move any assets to disappear; doing so was only for pointing those who came after her in the right direction she wanted them to go. Smart targets never made elementary mistakes such as that one. Those looking for her would believe she'd gotten soft or rusty, maybe both.

No matter that she'd only been in the running game for fifteen months now. She had learned from the best—from a man who'd spent his life playing the game. Those he sent to retrieve her would be looking for the sort of mistakes they expected her to make after being out of the game for more than a year.

In reality she had made only one mistake. Her cell vibrated against the seat next to her. Griff had left a voicemail.

And he was it.

Meg pulled over at the next gas station. She would fill up here using her one credit card, adding another crumb to the trail. To fill up at this gas station was a reliable indication that she was headed out of town. She climbed out, tucked her card into the slot, then made her selection and placed the nozzle into the fuel filler neck of her truck.

She watched the digits flash on the screen as the tank filled. Listening to the voicemail wasn't necessary. He probably just wanted to know if she would be back in time for lunch. Hearing his voice wouldn't benefit the necessary efforts ahead of her.

Staying wasn't an option.

Leaving was the only choice. A trail would keep her past from endangering Piney Woods, and then she would ghost her followers like a bad boyfriend. Nothing she hadn't done before.

Preparation was everything, and she was prepared.

The flashing digits stalled and the nozzle clicked, indicating the tank was full. Meg removed the nozzle, twisted on the cap and climbed back into her truck. She tossed her cell phone onto the seat, started the engine and reached for the gear shift.

She closed her eyes and fought a losing battle for about five seconds, then she gave up. Snatching up her cell, she clicked the icon for her voicemail and listened.

"Hey, Meg, I know you're probably headed back this way by now. I just wanted to remind you to grab some bread on your way. We used the last *two* slices at breakfast this morning. We need bread for lunch. See you soon."

Worry drew her face into a frown. He'd made biscuits for breakfast, not toast. The idea that his voice had sounded a little odd and that he'd emphasized the word *two* nudged her hard.

He was trying to tell her something.

She swore. Had someone already made it to Piney Woods and determined her most recent location to be at Griff's house?

Shoving the gear shift into drive, she spun out of the gas station parking lot. Once she was on the road headed back up the mountain, she called Jodie at the shop.

"Pampered Paws."

"Jodie, it's Meg."

"Hey, your old friend Darlene was here looking for you. She said the two of you went to school together."

Meg's heart stuttered to a near stop.

"I was a little hesitant to tell her anything—you know you can never be too careful these days—but she showed me a pic of you two back in high school. Loved the wild hair!"

"Wow," Meg choked out. "I haven't seen her in years." Her heart now thundered at breakneck speed. "Did she say where she's staying?"

"No but she left here headed to Griff's place to catch up with you. She couldn't believe you were living in such a small town. She said you'd always been a big-city girl."

Meg forced out a laugh. "Yeah. Darlene knows me well."

The sound of the bell over the shop's front entrance jangled.

"Oh," Jodie said. "Gotta go. Mr. Jolly is here to drop off Princess."

"'Kay. Thanks."

Meg ended the call and jammed the accelerator to the floor. She had to get to Griff. If she was lucky, it wouldn't be too late.

Sundown Road
12:10 p.m.

GRIFF DESPERATELY HOPED Meg had gotten the message he'd attempted to pass along. There were two people here looking for her. He watched the man pace back and forth at the windows framing the front of the living room. The woman, Darlene O'Neal, sat on the sofa smiling at him. She'd claimed to be an old friend of Meg's. The man was her husband, Ted, she explained. Except Ted didn't seem the least bit friendly, much less warm toward her. He'd flashed a fake smile at Griff when he'd been introduced, and then he'd taken up watch at the front windows.

Darlene, on the other hand, had settled on the sofa and proceeded to ask Griff a thousand questions about Meg. He'd answered as vaguely as possible. He nodded and smiled now and then as Darlene waxed on about all the good times she and Meg had shared back in high school.

Griff wasn't buying any of it.

First, the jeans and plaid shirt the man—Ted—wore were obviously new. He wore his shirt unbuttoned, tail hanging out with a T-shirt beneath. The slight bulge Griff had noticed at the small of his back wasn't likely a cell phone.

The woman wore khaki colored slacks and a loose tee that sported one of Chattanooga's aquarium logos. She hadn't turned her back to him, so Griff hadn't spotted a similar bulge, but he suspected she was carrying a weapon as well. There was just something about the two that made him worry about their intentions.

"Where is your vacation taking you next?" Griff asked when the woman paused in her lengthy monologue about Meg. The man had said they were on a cross-country vacation. They'd both taken leaves of absences from their stressful jobs and were seeing the sights wherever the road took them.

Darlene smiled. Ted glanced over.

Not a question either had expected.

"Gatlinburg," she said. "We can't wait to do a little mountain hiking."

Griff hummed a note of question. "I would've thought

you'd be dying to visit Nashville first. Everyone seems to love that scene."

"Already been there," Ted said. "I don't like country music."

Darlene smiled another of those big fake smiles. "We're more into the rock thing. Meg and I used to pretend we were groupies for whatever the hottest rock band was."

Funny. Meg had told him that she'd loved country music since she was a kid. It was all her parents ever listened to. It was all he'd ever heard her listen to.

Next to Griff, Raymond made a distressed sound. He, too, was aware something wasn't right. Maybe he sensed Griff's tension.

"I should let him out," Griff said, standing.

Both Ted and Darlene visibly tensed. Ted shifted to face Griff, his frame rigid. Darlene straightened from the relaxed position she'd taken on the sofa.

Griff shrugged. "He's an old dog. Probably needs to pee."

Darlene stood abruptly. "I changed my mind about the water. I'd love a glass."

"Sure." He headed toward the kitchen, patting his thigh so Raymond would follow. He didn't have to glance back to know Darlene brought up the rear. She had no intention of allowing him out of her sight.

In the kitchen, Griff opened the back door. "Go on, buddy."

Raymond stared up at him as if to ask if he were sure.

Griff hitched his head toward the yard. "Go on. Do your business."

Reluctantly, Raymond moseyed on out. Griff closed

the door behind him and turned back to his guest. "Ice or no?"

"Just water," she said.

He rounded up a clean glass and ran it two-thirds full of tap water. "Here you go." He passed the glass to her.

"Thanks." She took a sip and made an appreciative sound. "We don't have water right out of the tap like this back home."

Griff wasn't sure what he was supposed to say to that. "Big cities come with their own issues, I guess."

"They do," she agreed.

He said nothing else. She said nothing else. After about a minute, she sat her glass on the counter and looked expectantly at him, so he headed back to the living room. She followed.

"She should be here by now," Ted said, seemingly to himself.

"I'm sure she'll be here any minute. She had to stop for bread," Darlene reminded him as she settled back on the sofa. "Be careful that she doesn't see you," she warned her supposed husband. "We don't want to ruin the surprise."

Ted had already moved their car to the back of the house. Griff hadn't bought the surprise thing either. He was no lawman or detective, but he knew an ambush when he saw one.

Frankly, his head was still reeling at the information Ernie had passed along. He wasn't entirely sure he bought the story. Not that Ernie would lie. For that matter, he'd shown Griff the records or so-called rap sheet he'd printed out. Meg's prints had matched this Angela

"Angel" Hamilton's. Didn't matter. He knew Meg and she wouldn't...

Kill anyone...

But she had. She had killed Zyair Jones during the Gas and Go robbery. She could easily have killed the two that broke into her shop.

Griff swallowed back the bitter taste of dread and regret. He couldn't have been that wrong about her. He'd always considered himself a fairly decent judge of character. Surely he hadn't been that far off the mark with Meg.

Ernie had been flabbergasted as well. He kept saying none of it made sense. Although he'd suspected something was off, he hadn't anticipated it would be something straight out of a spy movie. Griff studied the two people seated in his living room who waited for Meg to arrive. But these two, they gave off exactly the kind of vibe he would expect from a hired assassin. Had these two obvious imposters come here to assassinate Meg?

His gut twisted, and the ability to draw in a breath grew more difficult. He had to do something. He couldn't just sit here and allow Meg to walk into a trap. He'd done the only thing he could on the phone when the two had urged him to make sure Meg was headed back. Honestly, he hadn't expected her to come back after what Ernie had told him. And maybe she wouldn't have if he hadn't called her and left that odd voicemail. If that was the case, then whatever these two had planned was on him.

His cell vibrated. He reached into his back pocket. Again, the two visitors came to a new level of attention. That wasn't suspicious at all. Ignoring their reaction, he pulled out his cell.

Meg.

He answered the call. "Hey."

"Hey," she said. "I'm almost there, but I had a flat tire just as I turned into your driveway. I can walk to the house, but I just wanted to let you know why it was taking so long."

"I can drive out there and help you fix the tire," he suggested.

Darlene leaned forward. Her eyes narrowed.

Ted surveyed the yard, then glanced at Griff before returning his attention to the window.

"That would probably be better," Meg said. "I'll just wait here then."

"Be right there." Griff ended the call as he stood.

"Has something happened?" Darlene asked, rising to her feet as well.

"No big deal." Griff slid his cell into his back pocket. "She has a flat on her truck, but she's just down the driveway at the road. It'll take ten minutes maybe to change the tire."

"I'll help." Ted stepped away from the window.

Griff made a face. "You don't need to do that. If you've ever changed a tire, you know it's a one-person job. You two can wait here and—"

"We'll go with you," Darlene insisted. "We can take the surprise to her."

"All righty then." Griff looked from one to the other. "I can get my keys or we can walk. It's only about three quarters of a mile."

"We should take your truck," Ted suggested.

Griff went to the kitchen and snagged his keys from the rack by the back door. When he turned to go back to the living room, he wasn't surprised to find Darlene watching him from the doorway.

"I simply can't wait to see the look on her face," she said, feigning excitement.

Or maybe she was excited by what she had planned for Meg. Griff felt sick at the idea.

"I'm sure she'll be happy to see you." It was the best he could come up with, given what he expected was about to go down.

Raymond had stretched out on the porch along with the other dogs.

"You have a lot of pets," Darlene noted.

"I rescue pets," Griff explained. "These are all animals that have been abandoned."

Ted grunted as he scanned the dogs. "I never understood why someone would abandon a dog when it's far easier just to put them out of their misery."

If Griff hadn't already disliked the guy, he damned sure did now. "Some people shouldn't have pets."

Another grunt was the guy's only response.

Griff climbed behind the wheel. Ted opened the passenger side door and waited for Darlene. It was a flat-out miracle in Griff's opinion that the guy had any sort of manners.

"Maybe I'll just walk," Darlene said. "It's a nice day. You two go on and get a head start on changing that tire."

Griff didn't like the idea, but there was little he could do about it. Instead, he started the truck and backed toward the barn, then headed to the road. He drove slower than usual and kept an eye on the woman strolling along the gravel road behind him.

"You don't need to drive so slow because of her," Ted mentioned. "She'll catch up."

"I'm driving slow," Griff said, resisting the urge to clench his teeth, "to prevent leaving a cloud of dust for her to walk through."

He could drive faster without that concern; the road was mostly gravel after all. But he was banking on this guy not knowing the difference.

Ted didn't argue the point.

A couple of the longest minutes he'd ever experienced later, Meg's truck came into view. Sure enough, the left front tire was flat. He parked. Scanned the area for Meg. Didn't see her, but the jack laid on the ground next to the spare tire. A part of Griff hoped this was some aspect of her plan to evade this bizarre couple. But maybe it was just all the movies he'd seen that put the notion in his head.

Griff parked and got out. Ted did the same. Darlene hadn't rounded the curve in the long driveway just yet.

When Meg didn't appear, Griff called her name. "Meg?" He walked over to the truck, surveyed the deflated tire. He frowned. Looked as if the sidewall had been punctured.

"Where is she?" Ted scanned the surrounding woods.

"Meg?" Griff called again. "She has to be here—"

The blast of a gunshot silenced him. He shifted to see Ted preparing to fire a second time.

Griff started toward the other man. "What the hell?"

A second shot exploded in the air.

Ted stood for a moment, looking startled. The weapon he'd been holding slipped from his hand and clattered on the gravel. Griff blinked, stared at the hole in the man's forehead.

Ted dropped to the ground.

"Run!"

Griff shifted his stunned gaze toward the trees.

"Run, damn it!"

Meg.

He couldn't see her, but the voice was definitely hers.

Darlene appeared in the distance.

She was running now.

Gun.

Her arms were extended and she was holding a gun.

Griff lunged for the tree line.

Another gunshot sounded.

The bullet nicked a tree to his right.

Griff darted behind another larger tree. He held completely still. Listened.

Another gunshot.

A scream.

"Oh God." He peeked past the trunk that concealed him. If Meg was hit…

He eased from his hiding place and moved carefully toward the road in the direction of the scream.

Darlene sat on the ground. Meg stood over her, the weapon in her hand pointed at the downed woman.

"Get up!" Meg ordered as she tucked something—another gun—into the waistband of her jeans at the small of her back.

The images that had filled Griff's head when Ernie told him he suspected Meg was this Angel, this assassin, flooded his brain now.

Before he realized he'd stepped from the tree line, he was moving toward her.

"Get. Up."

Meg stepped back as the other woman struggled to rise. Blood had spread from her right shoulder toward her chest. She cradled her right arm which hung against her side.

"Don't come any closer, Griff."

He stalled. Needed a moment to find his voice. "What the hell is going on, Meg? Who are these people?"

"Who sent you?" Meg demanded of the woman who'd called herself Darlene.

Darlene, or whoever the hell she was, grinned. "Who do you think sent me?"

Meg aimed her weapon at Darlene's face. "Answer the question."

"Your old friend. He wasn't happy to find out you were still alive, so he sent us to rectify the situation." She turned up her left hand. "You understand. He can't have you continuing to breathe under the circumstances."

"That's too bad for you," Meg said.

Griff moved a step closer. "What're you going to do?"

Meg suddenly reached back with her left hand and whipped the weapon from her waistband and pointed it at Griff. "I said don't come any closer."

He froze. Something like fire rushed through him—a weird combination of anger and disappointment.

Darlene laughed. "You going to shoot him too? I'm guessing your Goody Two-shoes friend here has no clue who you are." She looked past Meg and directly at Griff. "You don't know a killer when you meet one?"

"Shut up," Meg growled as she lowered the weapon she had aimed at Griff. "Turn around," she said to Darlene.

The burn of anger roared hotter through Griff, over-riding the other emotions. He might not have seen past whatever facade Meg had built, but he wasn't a fool. She was not a bad person, no matter what his eyes were telling him right now.

Was that his heart talking or his brain? If it was the former, he could be in trouble here.

Darlene reluctantly turned around. Meg shoved the extra weapon back into her waistband and approached the other woman. She checked her waistband, ran a hand down and then up her legs from the tops of her shoes to her pockets. Then she checked her pockets. She removed something.

Griff peered harder to try and see what Meg had taken from the woman's pocket, but he couldn't make it out.

Meg glanced back at him. "I need your help."

Her words hit him square in the chest. "What?"

She hitched her head for him to come there. "I need your help," she repeated.

He made his way to where the two stood, stepping over a fallen tree.

Meg handed the object toward him. "When I get her to my truck, use this to secure her left hand to the steering wheel."

Zip tie. The object was a nylon zip tie. He took it from her and nodded.

"Start walking." Meg nudged Darlene.

They walked through the woods back to the two trucks abandoned on his driveway. His gut clenched at the sight of Ted whatever-his-name-was still lying face up on the ground, a hole in his forehead.

"You killed him."

His own words startled him as if his brain hadn't realized his mouth was speaking.

"I did."

He met her gaze. "Why?"

"Because he would have killed you if I hadn't."

"Don't believe her," Darlene shouted. "Ted and I are cops from Los Angeles. We're here to take her back. She's wanted for murder."

Griff blinked once, twice.

"If you believe that," Meg said, urging the other woman toward her truck, "I have some oceanfront property in Arizona to sell you."

Griff nodded. He knew Darlene was lying. If she and Ted had been cops they would have said so up front and showed some ID.

When they reached Meg's truck, she opened the driver side door and nudged the woman in the ribs with the muzzle of her gun. "Get in."

Darlene did as she was told, though her glare was lethal. It was clear she wanted to tear Meg's head off.

Meg glanced at Griff then. "Secure her."

While Meg held the gun aimed at Darlene's head, he secured her left wrist to the steering wheel. The keys weren't in the ignition, and the tire was flat, making an escape unlikely unless she chewed off the zip tie. It didn't appear she could move her right arm. The bleeding was worse.

Griff stepped back. "She needs medical attention."

Meg stared at the other woman. "But she doesn't deserve it."

Griff started to argue with her, but she faced him. "Let's go. You drive."

Griff glanced at Darlene one last time before doing as Meg said.

"You just going to leave me to die?" Darlene shouted after them.

When he and Meg had climbed into his truck, he noticed she had at some point grabbed her backpack, and more importantly, she still had the gun, and it was aimed at him.

"You going to shoot me too?"

"Just drive. Toward Chattanooga."

He started the truck.

"I need your phone."

He gave her his cell, fastened his seat belt and then shifted into Drive.

When he was on the road heading away from his place, she took her eyes off him long enough to do something on his phone.

Several thoughts zoomed through his mind. He could wreck the truck, and that would stop whatever this was. He could just stop and demand answers.

She tossed his phone onto the middle of the bench seat between them, then fastened her seat belt.

He glanced at her again as he drove.

"I sent a text to Ernie," she said. "Told him there were two thugs from LA in your driveway, one dead, one injured. He should call for backup because the woman is incredibly dangerous and an ambulance because she's injured. So don't look at me that way."

Before he could say anything, his phone started to vibrate. He glanced at it, saw Ernie's name on the screen. "You should let me talk to him."

Meg grabbed the phone, accepted the call and set it to speaker. Ernie's voice shouted, "What the hell is going on, Griff?"

"This is Meg," she said in answer. "Listen to me, Ernie. Don't be fooled by the injured woman. She is very dangerous. She will kill you if she gets a chance. Keep your weapon trained on her until the paramedics arrive, and then do the same while they attend to her. She will kill whoever she has to in order to escape."

"Meg, where is Griff and what the hell is happening?"

"I'm here," Griff said. "I'm okay. I don't know exactly what's going on…" He glanced at Meg. "But what she said is true."

"Remember what I said, Ernie," she reiterated, then she ended the call and threw the phone out the window.

"What the hell?" Griff demanded, dividing his attention between her and the road.

"Take the next left," she said. "We don't want to meet Ernie on his way to your place."

Griff gritted his teeth and tightened his grip on the steering wheel. "Where are we going?"

"As soon as I figure that out," Meg said, "I'll let you know."

Griff wanted to believe those people back there were the bad guys—just like she said. And that she was actually not this Angela Hamilton.

But the fact that she kept her weapon aimed in his general direction warned him there was a good chance he was wrong.

Chapter Nine

1:30 p.m.

How had this happened so fast?

Meg had known time was short after that reporter managed a shot of her. But that had only been last night. Even as it was picked up on the AP, Lorenzo's people couldn't have seen it and gotten here this fast. It wasn't possible. There had to be another explanation.

Damn it. She'd wanted to lead the bastards away from here, not bring them in like long-lost cousins.

"Is it true?"

The sound of Griff's voice snapped Meg from her musings. "Is what true?" She shook herself and realized she was still holding the weapon at the ready. She lifted the top of the console and placed it inside. She had to shake this haze of disbelief. She had to be better prepared. On her toes. His life—she looked at him—depended on her.

Griff glanced at the console, then at her. "Is your name really Angela Hamilton?"

Anger stoked in her belly. "Did she tell you that?"

Lizbeth Franks, aka Darlene, whatever she'd called herself today, was one of Lorenzo's top guns. Being female and on the petite side worked to her benefit. Opponents always underestimated her physical ability and her intellectual ruthlessness. The woman was utterly heartless. She would shoot her own mother if it served her purpose.

"You mean the woman you shot?"

So, it was that way, was it? "At least she was still breathing," Meg allowed, "unlike her friend."

Griff looked at her again, and this time his gaze lingered long enough for her to wonder if he'd forgotten he was driving.

"You killed that man."

"We discussed that already," she pointed out. "If I hadn't, you would be dead now. Me too, assuming he could catch me."

She understood that Griff did not fully comprehend any of this. Who would? How many people experienced this kind of situation in their lifetimes? Sure, there were criminals out there who shot each other up on the street. Thugs who robbed places like the Gas and Go all the time. But this was a whole different level. That part he obviously got. *This* was something only those who lived in the world she had once lived in fully grasped. It was glamorized, badly, in movies and in novels. But this was not a movie or a novel. This was real life, and fearlessness along with finesse would be required to survive.

Griff braked for a traffic light that had turned red. He turned to her. "Who are you?"

Meg considered this for a moment before she answered. Part of her desperately wanted to tell him everything. To make him understand her situation so he wouldn't look at her that way. But that would put him in more danger than he'd already fallen into. The truth was too dangerous. Just being close to it had already put his life in jeopardy.

Still, she needed to give him something. As much for herself as for him, she didn't want him to feel about her the way she suspected he did right now. She couldn't bear the way he looked at her.

"You can call me Elle." Her father had called her Elle. She'd been named after her grandmother Eleanor.

"So, you're not Angela Hamilton, aka Angel, a cold-blooded assassin?"

"I recognize that it may seem like I am when you consider what's happened the past couple of days. But I have never taken a life unless mine or someone else's was at stake and there was no other option except to intervene with deadly force. If I was a merciless killer, those two men who invaded my shop would be dead. Lizbeth—Darlene—would definitely be done. She doesn't deserve to keep breathing, but I chose not to make that decision since I had the situation under control without having to end her life."

Griff pressed her with those golden eyes that made her want to say whatever was necessary to reverse this situation.

"Then why are your fingerprints connected to that name?"

Her jaw dropped. "How do you know that?" She had figured Darlene or her dead friend gave him that name.

A horn blew behind them.

Meg put her hand on the console as she whipped her head around. The driver behind them threw up his hands in question. Meg realized the light had changed back to green, and they'd just been sitting there. Griff realized the same and hit the accelerator.

"Ernie worried there was something else going on after the attack on you by the Joneses, so he ran your prints. The Los Angeles Police Department responded almost immediately."

Of course they had. Great. No wonder Lorenzo had gotten someone here so quickly. He had eyes and ears in the LAPD. Same with the sheriff's department in Los Angeles County and numerous others. The man owned the West Coast.

When Lorenzo didn't hear from Lizbeth in a timely manner, or if he did, assuming Ernie allowed her a phone call, he would send others. He wouldn't stop until she was dead.

She had to get out of here.

"Where are we going?"

She needed to think. Things were complicated now. There would be no slipping away with no strings, leaving this man and all else behind. Lizbeth would believe that Griff was in this with Meg. She would hunt him down and use him for luring Meg back.

"We need to hide for a bit." She considered the options. "I need to figure out my next move."

Silence radiated between them for a mile or so. Meg wished it hadn't come to this. She wished Griff had never needed to know about her past. If she hadn't seen the guy at the Gas and Go—but then Jennifer would likely be dead—maybe she would still have her carefully structured quiet life.

But her life was not more important than Jennifer's.

Meg had done the right thing, and she would do it again. *Damn it.*

"I might know a place."

Meg waited for him to go on.

"Ernie has a cabin."

She laughed. "I'm not sure that's a good idea, considering he thinks I'm some sort of hired killer, and this woman who called herself Darlene will spin an even nastier tale—assuming she doesn't kill him."

"Ernie won't do anything if I tell him we need time."

Meg wondered if he really believed Ernie would go along with the idea. "Ernie is a lawman," she reminded him. "I'm not so sure he's going to want to go along with this idea, even for a lifelong best friend."

Griff sent her a look. "He's worried about you. About us. He will give you a chance."

Meg contemplated his statement for a moment before saying more. "Does that mean you're giving me a chance as well?"

She might be getting soft, but she wasn't a fool. This could be a ruse to get her captured and him free of her. If she were in his shoes, that was exactly what she would do.

"Why wouldn't I?"

That was the big question. Why wouldn't he? Because he was a good person.

No question. She knew this with complete certainty. Ernie was a good person too.

"Okay. We'll go to Ernie's cabin and regroup."

It might be the last decision she ever made, but she was willing to take the risk.

Deep Woods Trail
3:20 p.m.

ERNIE'S CABIN WAS, as the road leading to it suggested, deep in the woods. Perched on a creek bank and miles away from Piney Woods. Miles away from basically anything actually. As long as Ernie stuck by his word, Meg could live with the situation for long enough to pull together a workable plan.

They'd stopped at a convenience store and grabbed a few things well ahead of arriving in this area, paying cash. A quick call from the store's landline to Ernie took care of a few loose ends and garnered a bit of an update. But she made sure Griff gave his friend the least amount of information necessary. Not that Meg expected Lorenzo to have access to someone inside the Hamilton County Sheriff's Department, but she couldn't be sure of anything. The man had money and power, and he was the epitome of ruthless. He wanted Meg nearly as much as he wanted his next breath. She doubted the scumbag had ever wanted anyone dead as badly as he wanted her that way.

The cabin's front door opened, and Meg jumped in spite of knowing that it was only Griff.

"I parked the truck behind the cabin."

So far, Griff hadn't asked any additional questions and he'd cooperated without hesitation. She imagined that would change as soon as the initial shock and denial had worn off. There was a lot she wanted to tell him, but she still wasn't sure it was the right thing to do.

And even if it was safe to do so, how did you walk back more than a year and multiple layers of subterfuge?

She had lied to him repeatedly. Nothing about the tale she'd spun had been true. Well, except for growing up in Bakersfield on a farm and her love of animals. All of that had been the truth.

"Thanks." For however long it lasted, she genuinely appreciated his help.

They should eat. That would buy her some time before he thought of more questions and would hopefully calm her jangling nerves. Bologna sandwiches had never been among her favorites, but the selections at the convenience store hadn't been that great. She could eat a dead rat if it was roasted just right—if the need arose. She'd only had to do that once. She doubted sharing the experience would help her build her case about not being a ruthless assassin.

Since Griff leaned against the counter saying nothing, she opted to take the initiative. She removed the bologna from the fridge, where she'd stored it only moments ago. Next, she grabbed the mayo and mustard and bread. A couple of soft drinks and chips.

He watched as she prepared the plates. The cabin's kitchen area, which was actually a corner in the main room, was well stocked as far as dishes and utensils, pans and dry and canned goods were concerned. There was electricity and running water, including hot water. So, not so rustic as far as the necessities were concerned. A bathroom with a shower. But only one bed that stood in another corner of the big room.

This should be an interesting night. The way she saw it, her biggest problem would be not allowing her desperation to guide her. Desperation never led to anything good.

Her gaze landed on the man who complicated an already complex situation even more. In more ways than he could fathom.

"We should eat," she suggested as she pulled out a chair.

He moved away from the counter and took the seat across from her. They ate. No talking. Just eating, drinking and glancing at each other and then away. It was somehow disturbing and yet oddly sensual.

When he'd eaten every morsel on his plate, he pushed it away and stared directly into her eyes. "Who are you?"

She downed the last of her drink. Made a decision. "I can't tell you all you want to know because that information could be a problem for you later. I don't want to create more problems for you."

"I've got Lonnie taking care of my animals and Ernie keeping watch for any new arrivals in town," Griff said.

Ernie had agreed to covertly inform Jodie to close up shop and lay low for a few days.

With that one call she and Griff had done things they hadn't wanted to do. The difference was that this was her problem, not his. The steps he had taken were out of the goodness of his heart, not necessity.

She owed him for giving her the benefit of the doubt.

"You owe me the truth."

He'd read her mind. "You're right." She stood, stacked their plates and headed to the sink. She washed the plates and the utensils she'd used to make the sandwiches, then dried her hands and turned to face him.

He waited, still seated at the table, watching her every move.

"My name, like I already told you, is Eleanor, Elle.

I'm from Bakersfield, California. Both my parents are dead, just like I told you before. I have no siblings. No ex-husbands or serious relationships. All the things I told you about my personal life were true. I grew up on a farm, etcetera."

"You lied about everything else," he countered. The distrust and disappointment in his voice and expression was a punch to the gut.

"Only about my career. Everything else was all true."

"Is your former career the reason these people came after you?"

She nodded. "The man they work for is very power-ful. If you believe in heaven and hell, good and evil, then he's the devil. The one you heard stories about as a kid."

"What does that mean exactly? The devil?" Griff's voice warned that she'd lost ground with the analogy.

Okay, back it up. She took a breath. "It means I took something that belonged to him, and he's spent nearly a year and a half trying to find me so he can have his revenge. Now, because of Ernie running my prints, he knows where I am."

A scowl claimed his face. "You stole something from him?"

"In a manner of speaking." She wasn't prepared to ex-plain. She'd already told him too much.

"You want me to go along with whatever this is, but you won't tell me the whole truth."

She braced her hands on the counter on either side of her. "I'll be out of here by morning. I just need you to give me until then."

He stood, turned his back on her and walked to the door. "I need some air."

She hated like hell to say this, but she had to. "Leave the keys to your truck."

He glared at her for a moment before tossing the key fob on the sofa, then he walked out the door.

That move hadn't gained her any ground either.

Nothing she could do about that. Maybe he would understand later.

Doubtful. She closed her eyes and pressed her fingertips there. How the hell was she going to keep him safe from what was coming? If she took off, Lorenzo's people would just find him and torture him to death in hopes of getting information on her.

Really, how could she possibly save him now without taking him with her?

He had family. A mother. A sister. Friends. A life. He wasn't going willingly. She was a fool to even consider he might.

But if she left him here…

She knew what would happen. There was no question.

He would die, and his death would be her fault.

GRIFF WALKED TO the end of the narrow drive that twisted through the trees along the creek bank. He and Ernie had come here as kids. Had poker nights here once a month to this day. It was quiet, way off the beaten path and very few people knew about it. It was their getaway. Their man cave. Only now it felt like a prison, like hell on earth. Griff wanted to do the right thing. He wanted to help Meg.

But what if trusting her was wrong?

Ernie wasn't so sure about Griff bringing Meg— or whatever her name was—here, but he'd deferred to

Griff's judgment. So far, no one else had shown up asking for Meg. At least not as far as Ernie knew at this point. The woman, Darlene—Lizbeth, Meg had called her—wasn't talking. Ernie hadn't given her a phone call yet. He intended to put it off as long as the law allowed. All because Griff had asked him to trust him.

But what if trusting Meg and, by extension, him was a mistake? What if he got Ernie killed?

His gut twisted hard.

If Griff still had his phone, he'd call and ask Ernie what the chances were that the criminal record he'd pulled up on Meg was somehow faked. She insisted that wasn't her name and that she wasn't a hired killer.

Griff had to admit he believed her, but what if his emotions had clouded his judgment? He had feelings for her, feelings not so easily dismissed.

Damn it.

She said she needed until morning and then she would be gone. Could he let her go like that? Pretend she never existed? Go on with his life like he hadn't met her?

He thought of the way she took care of the animals, of how she took care of the people around her. What he knew about her just didn't fit with what he'd witnessed the past couple of days. It sure as hell didn't fit with what Ernie had found.

Griff paused and recounted the facts.

She had dropped that guy—Ted—from a serious distance with a handgun. She was no amateur when it came to firearms. Then there was the way she'd handled herself. Having him secure the woman to that steering wheel. The way she'd taken down the guy in the Gas and

Go. Then, she'd taken down the two in her shop without a weapon.

No question her actions could fit with a hired-gun type. On the contrary, she could just as easily fit the description of a well-trained cop. He toyed with the idea for a moment. Made sense. Fit with her caring personality more so than the idea of an assassin.

If she had been a cop, why not just tell him? Why all the lies and the running?

Maybe she'd been a witness to a crime. It was possible that was why she was on the run. But that scenario wouldn't explain her special skill set. Or why she wasn't in some sort of witness protection program.

Griff ran a hand through his hair, turned and stared at the cabin. If she had been a cop, why wasn't she willing to tell him?

He walked slowly back to the cabin. Maybe if he gave her a little more time, she would decide it was safe to tell him more. He recognized that on some level, she didn't trust him enough to tell him the truth. Or maybe it was like she said—too dangerous to tell him.

He'd thought they were friends. Had hoped they would become more than friends. That kiss they had shared sure seemed to suggest there was more.

Moving with more determination now, he approached the cabin. She had come out onto the porch and settled into one of the rocking chairs. Same ones that had been here for more than three decades.

"I've been thinking." He climbed onto the porch and settled into the other rocking chair. "Where did you learn to shoot the way you do? I mean, there's good and then there's really good. You are really good. Most folks on farms learn to shoot rifles. You took Ted out from a hell of a distance with a handgun."

"Lots of training." She sighed. "I was the best in my class."

He'd like to believe he was so charming she hadn't even realized he'd been questioning her, but he knew better.

"Same class as the self-defense one?"

"In a manner of speaking."

She wasn't going to make this easy.

Time to ad-lib. "Ernie says the training for a cop is intense like that. Focus on marksmanship skills and self-defense."

She said nothing.

"So, this guy—the devil, you called him—he was a bad guy. You were working on an investigation involving him. You took something from him in an effort to bring him down, but something went wrong and you ended up burned."

She smiled. "That's a hell of a story, Griff. You might want to pitch it to a movie producer."

Frustration lit across his senses. "You could at least tell me if I'm getting warm."

She watched him for a long time before she responded. He had decided she wasn't going to when she finally spoke. "You're a good guy, Griff. I truly regret being the reason you've been dragged into this. I had a plan. Sadly, it just didn't work out."

"Because Ernie ran your prints." He got it now. "His doing so tipped off someone who informed this super bad guy, and he sent his people after you."

"Something like that."

He was getting closer. "If this Darlene character gets a chance to call him, he'll know he needs to send someone else."

"Unfortunately. Even without a call, he will be suspicious by tomorrow. He has no patience for lingering. He expects results on the immediate side."

"Does he want you brought to him, or does he just want you dead?"

"Based on Lizbeth's appearance, I'm guessing the latter. She isn't known for her finesse with targets. She's much better at terminating than transporting."

Griff had come to that same conclusion as well. "Is there anything I can do to help?"

She leaned forward, pressed her forearms to her knees and clasped her hands. She stared at her hands for a moment before meeting his gaze. "I'm afraid there isn't anything anyone can do. I'll either outmaneuver him or I won't."

The barrage of emotions that churned inside Griff were impossible to isolate. The anger and frustration and worry and regret coalesced into something resembling dread and fear, but far more potent.

"I want you to know that whatever you've done, my opinion of you has not changed." He fixed his gaze on hers. "I believe in you, Meg—Elle. I will do whatever I can to help you through this."

She smiled. "You're a really nice guy, Griff. You deserve a good life and a romantic partner who can give you as much as you give everyone in your path. But there is nothing you can do to help me. There's nothing anyone can do."

She'd said those same words before, but he had decided that was one part of her story he wasn't going to believe. She wasn't the only one who could develop a plan.

Chapter Ten

Deep Woods Trail
9:00 p.m.

It was dark.

Time to move.

Meg—she'd focused so hard on calling herself Meg for the past fifteen months that she couldn't even think of herself as Elle now that she'd been outed—had made a decision on her next step. For the plan to work, she had to find a way to keep Griff out of sight for a while.

She glanced at him. He'd insisted on heating up a can of soup and then that they both ate said soup. The crackers he'd found were a little stale but not so bad. She wasn't complaining. The ability to perform critical thinking and to physically outmaneuver the enemy required two things: sleep and sustenance.

The one thing she understood with absolute certainty after spending the past few hours shut up in this small cabin with him was that he was determined to help her survive this situation. This was exactly why she should never have allowed herself to get so close to the folks in Piney Woods. People like Jodie and Dottie, and certainly Griff, cared about her and wanted to help with whatever she needed.

But they didn't adequately comprehend the situation. This was not about picking up an extra shift or taking home a few dogs to foster. This was about facing people who killed for a living. People who enjoyed killing. People with no conscience. Unfortunately, there was no simple solution to her dilemma.

The one thing she needed right now was to be alone— to be abandoned by those who cared about her. It was the only way to ensure their protection, and even then she worried that might not be enough.

But if she got away clean and Griff laid low for a few days while she laid out a new trail for her pursuers to follow, he might just survive the coming storm.

She glanced at his back as he put away the bowls they had used and he'd washed and dried. She should have helped, but she'd been staring out the window in deep thought and hadn't known what he was doing until he was done. Since it was dark, it was time to put her plan into action.

"Do you think Ernie has any flashlights around here?" She strolled toward the kitchen area. "If the generator runs out of fuel, we'll need flashlights."

He glanced around. "I'm sure there are some around here somewhere."

"Mind if I poke around?"

"Be my guest." He tossed the towel onto the counter. "I'll help."

Meg started with the side tables in the living room area. She found poker cards and game chips. A lighter. Pens, pads of paper. Scissors. A couple of cans of beer. She laughed, held up a can. "Someone was hiding his stash."

Griff grinned. "That would be Joey Hurt. He used to be a deputy here. He joined us a couple of times. That was his favorite brand. No one else liked it, so he always brought his own supply."

Meg placed the beer back in the drawer. She stood, stretched then moved on to the bedside table. She dropped to her knees and pulled open the first drawer. Right on top was a pair of binoculars. "These could be handy." She placed them on the table.

"We like watching the deer come to the creek for water."

"Birds too?" She glanced at him. She imagined there were lots of bird species and wildlife.

"Sometimes." He shrugged. "Mostly the four-legged animals."

"Aha." Meg lifted a pair of metal handcuffs from the drawer. "Did you use these in your poker games?"

Griff laughed as he closed the last of the cabinet doors. "I can't answer that question. You'll have to ask Ernie. He's the only one who ever comes here with a romantic interest."

"A romantic interest." She nodded. "Did you ever bring a romantic interest here?" None of her business, but she couldn't help herself.

"Not me." Griff opened a drawer next to the sink. "I prefer…" He stopped talking as if he'd realized he was about to say something too personal.

She shrugged and placed the handcuffs on the table. These could definitely come in handy. The fact that he hadn't used them on someone like Rhianna the casserole queen was all the better. Funny how she had absolutely no right to feel anything remotely resembling jealousy, and still she did. Just one more indication of how far over the line she had allowed herself to go. Doing a mental eye roll, she shifted her attention back to going through the drawers.

"I've been thinking." Griff walked over and sat down on the edge of the bed.

She erased the immediate reaction from her face. The last thing she needed was for him to pick up on any impatience or regret at the idea that he wanted to help. She needed him to believe his help and advice were welcome. She also didn't want him picking up on her possessiveness toward him.

"About?" she asked innocently.

"About the situation." He let his impatience show a little.

"Okay. Tell me your thoughts." She sat back on her heels, gave him her undivided attention and waited for him to go on.

"Ernie can go to Sheriff Norwood. She's good. She might be able to help."

Why couldn't Meg make him see that the more people drawn into this, the higher the body count would rise? Ernie, the sheriff—no one could fix this. No matter how good, no matter how well intentioned. This was not that simple. "I wish she could, but that isn't likely. I appreciate the suggestion though."

"Sit with me." He patted the mattress beside him. "You've been pacing the floor and staring out that window for hours. Now you're prowling around in drawers.

You need a break. I know you're worried, but you keep blowing off my suggestions."

Meg moved up to the bed. "Really, I appreciate your suggestions. I appreciate your friendship. I just don't want anyone else to get hurt by this, and that's what will happen if other people get involved. I keep telling you this, but you're not listening."

"The sheriff's department is already involved," he reminded her.

Not that she needed a reminder. "I wish that wasn't the case."

"Don't you think it would be helpful if they understood what was happening? Isn't being in the dark more dangerous to folks like Ernie?"

It was, and that was exactly why she had to get out of here as quickly as possible. She'd stayed too long after the first strike as it was.

"You're right." She made a final decision. "Maybe I should meet with them first thing in the morning to make sure they understand the situation."

The relief on his face was palpable. More guilt heaped on her shoulders. She hated lying to him.

"Great. You can call him first thing, and we'll make that happen."

"Speaking of which," she stood, "I should charge my phone."

Anything was better than staring into his hopeful eyes. She dug her charger out of her backpack and found an outlet. It wouldn't take long, so she didn't have to wait on moving forward with her plan. The sooner she was out of Griff's life, the sooner his was back on track. Distance was crucial right now. She would get out of Tennessee and let Lorenzo know she was headed his way. That should shift focus quickly enough from Piney Woods. This was the only way.

Maybe she'd head northeast and disappear into New York City. Lorenzo had contacts there as well. The bastard had contacts in every city of importance in the country. A little place like Piney Woods had felt relatively safe in the grand scheme of things. If Ernie hadn't run her prints, maybe—just maybe—she would still be safely ensconced in her made-up life.

Moments with Griff flickered through her mind like last week's recap of her favorite series. Jodie's laughter and Dottie's mothering. The best meat loaf she'd ever eaten at the diner. Raymond. God, she loved that dog. The idea of never seeing him again…

She really had to get out of here before she lost the ability to stay focused.

The longer she waited, the harder it would be to walk away.

As if he sensed her emotional struggle, Griff joined her at the window. He pulled down the worn shade. "You should relax. We'll take this to the sheriff in the morning and go from there. There's nothing else you can do tonight. Worrying won't help."

Meg braced herself. "You're right." She turned to him, looked deep into his eyes. "I think I need something to take my mind off the fact that I might never be safe, no matter where I go."

The words were for him—to garner a response—but sadly they were all too true.

He cupped her face in his hands. "I can do that," he whispered as his mouth lowered toward hers.

Her heart surged, her body trembled as his lips brushed across hers. He kissed her softly then, carefully, as if he worried she might shatter. Her hands found their way to his chest, flattened there, molding to the strength she felt beneath his shirt. His body was solid from long days of hard work. His muscles flexed beneath the pressure of her touch. She wanted so badly to unbutton his shirt, to feel the heat of his skin against her palms.

He pushed his fingers into her hair and deepened the kiss. Meg's body caught fire, reacted so intensely she barely remained standing. Her fingers were unfastening the buttons of his shirt before her brain realized what she was doing.

She just wanted to touch him, to feel him.

Catching her breath no longer mattered, slowing down was not happening. Her fingers fumbled, couldn't move fast enough. She tugged open the final button and pushed the shirt off his shoulders, and then her hands slid over his bare skin. Every nerve in her body reacted.

His fingers tangled in the hem of her tee, pulling it up and over her head. She should slow this down, but she couldn't. She wanted to feel all of him, wanted to taste him. To have him taste her, to touch her all over. They moved toward the bed. Whether he took the first step or she did, Meg couldn't be sure. Didn't matter. All that mattered was that they shed the rest of their clothes as quickly as possible.

She unfastened his jeans.

He stopped kissing her, drew back just enough to look into her eyes. "We really doing this?"

He was right. What had she been thinking? Reality

slammed into her like a bucket of icy cold water splashing over her body.

You need him disabled.

Meg blinked. "Yes." She kissed him hard on the mouth until his resistance melted away. Her fingers went to his zipper again, and she slowly lowered it. He reached around her, unfastened her bra. She gasped. He dragged it down her arms and tossed it aside. Then his hands closed over her breasts. Her body seized with pleasure.

She moved his jeans down his hips, purposely leaving his boxers in place—as difficult as that task was. She so wanted to feel that part of him too. She lowered to her knees, and his eyes closed as if he couldn't bear to watch. Tugging his jeans down, he lifted first one foot and then the other so that she could pull them free.

When she stood once more, she ushered him down onto the bed. She straddled his waist, immensely grateful she still wore her jeans. She slid her palms over his chest, leaned down and caught his lower lip between her teeth.

He massaged her breasts, tugged one toward his mouth. She cried out, barely held on to her wits. While he focused on driving her crazy with his mouth, she grabbed the handcuffs, quietly fastened one to the vintage iron headboard. He stilled, looked up at her, but she didn't give him time to react. She snapped the other cuff onto his left hand.

Then she kissed her way down his chest to distract him from what she'd just done. When his eyes closed once more, she quickly climbed off him, off the bed and stepped back.

Distracting him with the promise of sex was low. No question about that, but it had been necessary.

She grabbed her bra and put it back on.

His languid expression shifted to one of wariness. "What're you doing?"

"You'll be glad I did when all this shakes down."

"What the hell?" he growled as he sat up and attempted to tug free of the headboard.

God, she had never seen that much of him. His body was pretty perfect. She almost sighed. Instead, she grabbed her tee and yanked it over her head, which she badly needed to get on straight.

"I have to go," she said, finger-combing her hair. "The sooner I lure Lorenzo's thugs away from here, the sooner you'll be safe."

"You said," he snapped, "we'd go to the sheriff in the morning."

She stuffed one foot into a sneaker and then the other. "I lied." Why pretend? He was no fool.

He yanked at the cuffs one more time. "I guess I shouldn't be surprised."

"No." She drew in a big breath. "You shouldn't. I've been lying as a way of life for a long time now. It was necessary to my existence." She turned away, couldn't bear the look in his eyes. "I'm sincerely sorry that my decision to come to Piney Woods has hurt you and others. I'm sorry you and Jodie and Dottie trusted me and were nice to me. I should never have allowed you to get so close." The emotion burning at the back of her eyes escalated her frustration. What the hell was wrong with her?

She had to be stronger than this. Smarter. Or they would all end up dead.

"So, you're just going to run." The anger in his voice was unmistakable.

"I'm not running," she argued, her ego bruised. "I'm navigating the coming storm to a different location. Away from you and the people here who I care about."

"I'm supposed to believe—" he banged a fist against his chest "—you care about me." He tugged on the handcuff again. "I can't imagine how you show your deeper feelings for a guy."

He had no idea just how deep her feelings for him went. *Big mistake, Eleanor.*

Her mother had always called her Eleanor. Only her dad and her school friends had called her Elle. That life—her real life—felt so far away. She had no one left. She'd abandoned those who hadn't died. She had thrown herself into her work and ignored all else. She had purposely chosen not to have so much as a goldfish, much less a dog or cat. She'd had nothing and no one who could slow down what she had to do. No one and nothing that would prevent her from taking the next big risk.

One year ago, she had allowed herself to start caring again, to care about another person or thing, like sweet Raymond. Now she had to walk away.

You have to do this...have to do this.

"Disappointment you'll get over," she offered. "Dying doesn't provide that option."

She unplugged her phone, tossed it and the charger into her backpack. She remembered the binoculars and tucked those into her backpack as well. Then she grabbed Griff's truck keys. She walked to the door, paused. As difficult as it was, she turned to face him. "I'll call Ernie in the morning and let him know you're here and in need of his assistance." She moistened her lips. "Goodbye, Griff."

She started to turn away again but hesitated. "Take care of Raymond for me."

"Elle—Meg, wait."

She couldn't. She twisted the button on the knob, locking it and then closing the door behind her. He shouted after her, but she kept going, didn't want to hear his words. She stepped off the porch and slipped into the darkness.

The truck was parked behind the cabin. She took a moment to listen carefully to the night sounds. The whisper of the breeze sifting through the trees, the trickle of water in the nearby creek. The chirp of crickets, faster tonight because it was cooler. Her body adjusted to the outside temperature, to the night sounds.

The bump and clomp coming from the cabin warned her that Griff was attempting to disassemble the old iron bed. Not an easy task, and the probability of breaking it was a serious zero. It was one of the older real iron beds.

More of that regret and guilt piled on. She should go before she screwed up and changed her mind.

Going was essential. It was the only way to see with any measure of certainty that he was safe. She told herself this over and over as she moved away from the cabin and deeper into the darkness.

A soft thud down the road caused her to stop. Every muscle in her body froze. Another gentle whump.

Car door.

A good distance away. Sound carried in the dark. Her breathing slowed as her instincts elevated to a higher state of alert.

Moving slowly, listening intently, she removed her weapon from the front pouch of her backpack, then hung the backpack on her shoulder. The cold steel in her hand sent her pulse into a faster rhythm and her heart into a firmer *bump, bump*. She closed her eyes a moment and isolated the sounds she heard. Silenced the roar of blood in her ears. Ignored the thumping in her chest. Listened beyond the breeze, the trickling creek and the crickets.

A voice, possibly male. Too distant to make out the words.

Someone was here. Near the road, she thought. At least two people. She had heard the distinct sound of two different doors closing.

If there were only two, she could take them before she vanished. She had the element of surprise that they no doubt believed they possessed.

How had they learned their location?

She swore silently. Property records, of course. Ernie Battles was a friend of Griff's. Looking him up in the county database was easy peasy.

Damn it.

Moving soundlessly, she kept to the edge of the drive, near the tree line. Slowly, one careful step at a time. *Listen...listen.* The faint echo of a spoken word. Not moving closer yet.

Vague thump, then another.

Not two, four.

Her hopes sank deep into her gut, making her feel ill.

That was a risk she couldn't take. She was more likely to be overpowered by four thugs. That would leave Griff bound and vulnerable.

Meg did an about-face and moved quickly, silently back to the cabin. As soon as she hit the clearing, she leaped into a dead run. There was no time for explanations. No time to argue. She hoped like hell she could convince him without a lot of words or actions.

At the door, she turned the knob. *Damn it!* She had locked it. She wrestled with the keys on the ring with his fob. Stuck first one and then another into the lock until she had the right one. She twisted the knob again, and the door opened. She stepped inside, her finger immediately going to her lips. He had managed to drag his jeans on as well as his shoes. He stared at her now but kept his mouth shut. She grabbed his shirt from the floor and passed it to him.

"They're here," she whispered. "We have to go."

He tugged at the handcuff.

Oh hell.

She tucked her weapon into her waistband, opened the drawer, her heart pounding, and felt around inside. Where the hell was the key?

"Check the next one," he murmured.

She closed the first drawer, careful to do so quietly and then dragged open the bottom drawer. She felt around, not daring to turn on any additional lights.

Her fingers moved over something cool. Metal. She picked it up. The key. *Thank God. Thank God.*

Fingers fumbling, she fought to get the key into the slot. They were both breathing hard by the time the cuff came loose. She lowered it to the bed to prevent the clink of metal.

She pointed to the back door. Hoped like hell the trouble hadn't reached the cabin yet. She pressed her finger to her lips once more. They had to be quiet. So quiet. These people had the same training as her. They would be listening.

Her weapon in hand, she moved in the direction of the back door. She turned the knob and slowly opened the door, wishing it not to squeak. Had it squeaked when she closed it? She couldn't remember. No squeak. *Thank God.*

She stuck her head out far enough to peer around. Listened hard. No new sound, no movement.

She eased out the door. Rested each foot in the grass with care.

Griff slipped out behind her, pulled the door to without making a sound. Smart guy.

She grabbed his hand with her free one and tugged him close enough to whisper directly into his ear. "We're going into the woods. We need to go far and fast. But I don't know these woods. I need you to get us as far away from here as quickly as possible while making the least amount of sound possible."

His lips pressed against her ear. She shivered in spite of herself.

"I understand." He squeezed her hand. "Trust me. I won't let you down."

His words wrapped around her chest and squeezed. She nodded, turned her face up to his. "Lead the way."

He'd been in these woods before. Many times as a kid, he'd told her. She had no idea when he'd last hiked in the area, but he was the only shot they had of escaping.

She was counting on his recall not only to get them out of here but to get them out of here fast.

Otherwise, they were dead.

Chapter Eleven

10:15 p.m.

Griff was still buttoning his shirt as they slipped deeper into the woods. The sound of the cabin's front door being kicked in had his heart banging harder against his sternum. He wasn't sure how many there were, but he suspected more than two.

How long would it be before they realized the cabin was empty and his truck was still there?

Five, six minutes at most.

His heart rammed harder with worry. Had to get Meg out of here. He ran faster, dodging trees and clusters of shrubs in hopes of minimizing the noise from their desperate race. The stars and the moon weren't providing much in the way of light to see where the hell they were going. But the longer they were in the dark, the easier it was to see. Meg stayed close behind him. He gave himself a mental shake. Not Meg, Elle—Eleanor.

Not that it mattered what he called her. She had planned to leave him. Disappointment and no lack of hurt twisted inside him even now with trouble not far behind them.

That whole make-out session had been about getting him in a vulnerable position. The reality added anger to the emotions throttling inside him. *Damn it.*

As if she'd sensed his anger, she grabbed him by the arm and pulled him to a jarring halt. He glared at her as she leaned close. Close enough to have his body reacting as if she hadn't shown her cards already, as if he were a fool and would fall for her tricks again—and he was.

"We need to hide now," she murmured against his ear.

He forced back all those distracting emotions. Had to think a moment. The sound of air sawing in and out of his lungs had his brain struggling. Or maybe it was just her. Didn't matter. *Focus!*

Where exactly were they? He closed his eyes and pictured the area in daylight on one of those many summer days he and Ernie had played here as kids. Had prowled around like hungry bears as teenagers. The images flashed one after the other, and then he knew. There was a good hiding place nearby. It was not exactly the safest place to hide, considering snakes were on the move this time of year, but it beat the hell out of the hired guns who would be coming up right behind them any second now.

He took her hand, held it tight in his and moved more slowly, this time going westward. Whenever a twig cracked or undergrowth brushed his leg, he flinched but didn't stop. He paused at a massive tree he recognized the dark shape of, felt over the bark for the place he had carved his and Patty Hall's initials into the bark. *There.* His fingers traced the letters. A smile nudged his lips. They were close now.

He eased forward, free hand extended until he hit the

outcropping of massive boulders. Large clumps of eerie grayness in the near darkness. There were all manner of stories about how the giant stones had ended up piled in this spot, but Griff wasn't sure which, if any, of those tales were true. He and Ernie had used the pile for everything from a pirate ship to a castle. He knew all the gaps between the rocks and all the hiding places beneath the overhangs of ones levered atop others.

Moving cautiously, he reached into the gap he knew provided the best cover from anyone passing by. He locked his jaw and held his breath as he felt around inside, swiping at overgrown weeds and what felt like spider webs. He encountered nothing that reacted—like a snake or raccoon or maybe a possum that might have taken refuge inside. The spot wasn't ideal for a bear or bobcat.

He tugged her closer. "Feels clear in there."

"Go," she muttered, the single syllable a frantic sound.

He climbed in, twisting his body so that he eased through the slot between rocks.

She moved in next, nestling her bottom against his lap. Not that there was any other way for two of them to fit together in the space. Then she tucked her backpack next to their legs and leaned against his chest. Instinctively, his arms went around her waist in a protective manner, despite the weapon nudging into his gut. He doubted she would appreciate the effort. She didn't need his protection. She was more than capable herself. Maybe he just needed to feel the comfort of her body in his arms.

As if he'd said out loud that her weapon was poking him, her hand slid between her back and his stomach and retrieved the weapon. A few seconds later he understood that the move hadn't been about his thoughts. The sound of undergrowth brushing fabric and boots crushing wild grass whispered across his senses.

The bad guys were close.

His arms tightened on her waist. She placed a hand on his clasped ones and squeezed reassuringly. He realized then that she had been only too glad for him to climb in first. Of course she had. That way her body shielded his. He locked his jaw and barely resisted the urge to shake his head. He should have thought of that—not that it would have done any good. She didn't take orders from him. She'd made that clear. If she had her way, she would be long gone and he'd never see her again.

For his protection.

He closed his eyes and focused on controlling his breathing. No need to allow his anger and frustration to show more than it already had. He damned sure didn't want her mistaking his tension for fear. He wasn't afraid, damn it. He blinked. Maybe he was. But not for himself. *For her.*

Given that these people from her past wanted to kill her—at least that was what she'd said, and he had no reason to believe she was lying about that aspect of all this—she would be safer if she could disappear. Rather than selfishly wanting her to stay, he should work harder to help her escape, to disappear. These scumbags would follow. No question about that. Griff and Meg were hiding in a pile of boulders with two or more armed killers tracking them like deer in open season. The intent was undeniable.

He'd been certain if she would only trust Ernie and Sheriff Norwood that they could sort this out. He'd even considered waiting until she fell asleep and using her phone to call his friend but he understood now that wasn't a gamble he was willing to take.

Urging her to stay, hoping she would, wasn't the right thing. If he wanted her safe—and he did—he should do everything in his power to help her disappear.

The reality crushed against his chest, made getting a breath nearly impossible.

The hair on the back of his neck stood on end. They were really close now. He reminded himself that unless the bad guys knew about the pile of rocks, there was no reason for them to veer in this direction. The rocks were dozens of steps in the wrong direction, in fact, back toward the cabin. He hoped these bastards assumed he and Meg were heading away from it. The clouds had shifted, so moon-and starlight were minimal. They should be okay. Yet, even knowing the trouble likely wouldn't come to the rocks, it was near enough for him to understand most of the words being muttered. A new thread of tension tightened inside him.

"They couldn't have gotten far," a man said. "Not without flashlights. It's dark as hell out here."

A crash followed by a "son of a bitch" had Griff biting back a laugh. Someone had obviously run into a tree. The idea made him inordinately happy.

"I hate the damned woods." Female voice.

Not the Darlene woman. She was likely still in custody. Someone else.

"We should go back." Man's voice. Not the first guy who had spoken. Someone else.

Meg's body tensed noticeably. Griff's did the same. She recognized this voice, he suspected.

"If they had gone back to the cabin," the second man said, "we would've heard gunshots. Grayson has orders to shoot on sight. Trying to find them in the dark like this is an exercise in futility. We'll wait them out. They'll have to show up someplace, somewhere they feel safe, maybe with someone they can trust."

"I'm with you," the woman said.

"We'll get them," the first guy commented. "You can't cover much ground on foot in the dark in terrain like this."

Unless, Griff thought, *you know your way around*.

Their noisy departure faded as the group moved farther and farther away. Meg turned her face toward Griff's and held her finger to his lips.

He was just guessing here, but she apparently suspected the overheard conversation might be a ruse. She didn't move. He did the same. The natural night sounds enveloped the darkness once more. Now that the danger appeared to have passed—possibly—Griff wrestled with his body's reaction to her butt being pressed into his lap. He thought about the animals back at his place. He thought about the video he'd watched of her slicing that guy's throat. None of it alleviated the situation. His body just kept hardening.

He was on the verge of going over the edge, and if she moved, that would be the end of his control for sure.

Rustling grass snapped his thoughts away from the tension building between them.

The beam of a flashlight flickered in the trees.

Griff held his breath.

She had been right to wait. At least one of them was still out there.

The light danced over the rocks.

Holy hell.

The threat moved closer. Grass crushed under footfalls. Fabric rustled against fabric. The beam of light skipped over their location, thankfully not pausing long enough to reveal the crevice in which they remained packed like sardines.

He or she—probably *he*, judging by the sound of the footfalls—made their way around the small mountain of large rocks, pausing here and there and shining the light into gaps. Slowly, the person reached all the way around to where they'd begun. The light bounced over their location again.

Griff's breath stalled in his lungs.

The light shifted back, landed right next to his shoulder, then after five frantic thumps in his chest, it moved on.

Footfalls faded as the person walked away.

Griff managed a breath. The bastard had missed them.

The minutes ticked past, and still Meg made no move to emerge from their hiding place. He was in no hurry either. At this point, he would be a fool not to trust her instincts. She clearly knew her way around this sort of situation.

Finally, she leaned forward and poked her upper body between the rocks. Then she eased all the way out.

Griff's legs had gone numb, and other parts of him remained stiff and at full attention. It took a minute, but he managed to get up and thread his body through the opening as well. Not nearly as gracefully as she had, but he got out all the same.

She moved in close to him again, whispered against

his ear, making his body tingle despite the gravity of the situation. *Damn.* He had to get a hold of himself.

She said, "We need to go back to the road, around the cabin where we can see but they can't. Can you find the way?"

He nodded.

She tugged her backpack on her shoulder once more, tucked her weapon into her waistband at the front this time and reached for his hand.

He closed his around hers, and his heart clutched. He wanted desperately to keep her safe, but she sure as hell appeared better at this than he would be. He'd have to follow her lead on that part. But he knew the woods, and that would be his contribution to saving their lives.

MEG HELD TIGHTLY to Griff's hand as he started the slow, laborious process of moving soundlessly through the woods. She followed his steps precisely to avoid bigger clumps of wild grass and underbrush. Not to mention trees. It was so dark. Even though her eyes had adjusted well enough, it was still like walking blindfolded. The clouds had moved in, blocking the meager moon-and starlight. Probably had saved their lives back there. She sure as hell wasn't going to complain now.

The air was crisp at this hour. She couldn't be certain what time it was, but she estimated around midnight.

She struggled to stay focused on getting out of here. The struggle lay in the voice she had heard back there while tucked into that rock crevice.

His.

She would know that voice anywhere, anytime.

Kase Ridley. They had worked together off and on over

the years. Had been on-again-off-again lovers. Friends. Or at least she'd thought so. Then he'd disappeared on an operation, and she'd been sent in to find him—dead or alive. But she hadn't found him. All she'd found was serious trouble, trouble that almost got her killed, and then she'd had no choice but to disappear.

Now she understood. He was alive. And he was working for the other side.

Fury roared inside her, but she had to push it down. Getting the hell out of here alive was all that mattered just now. She would deal with the Ridley issue later.

The progress was slow on the route Griff had chosen since the trees were thicker, which meant the undergrowth was as well. Occasionally she caught a glimpse of the cabin light, so they weren't far from their destination. She was immensely grateful for Griff's ability to navigate these woods.

They moved beyond the cabin close enough to hear the sound of voices. The four remained gathered there. Likely looking for any clues that might suggest where she and Griff had headed next. One of the scumbags was going through Griff's truck. Another stood by and watched the search or kept a lookout. The other two were inside ransacking the cabin by the sound of it.

Griff moved faster now and she was glad. They needed a certain level of a head start when they reached the vehicles the thugs had left at the road. It would be fairly easy to call one of Griff's friends to pick them up, but that would only draw someone else into this mess. Calling an Uber or other hired car would waste too much valuable time and put those drivers at risk too.

When they cleared the tree line and started toward the

road, Meg broke away from him and ran. There were two sedans. Both black of course. Hopefully at least one was unlocked.

Not the first one. *Damn it.* She dug her knife from her backpack and passed it to Griff. "Take care of the tires," she murmured.

He gave a nod and set to work on her request.

The driver side door on the second one opened. Meg smiled. The fob lay in a cupholder. "Sloppy," she murmured as she slid in.

Griff rushed around the trunk of the second vehicle and dropped into the passenger seat. Ensuring the exterior lights were off, she started the engine and eased backward along the narrow gravel drive until she was on the pavement, then she cut the wheel and drifted out onto the road. Once she was on the road, she gave it some gas. Not enough to squeal tires but enough to get moving in a hurry.

She drove a mile or so before turning on the headlights.

"What now?" he asked.

"I have a backup vehicle in a storage unit. We pick it up and dump this car."

"Sounds like you thought of everything."

Not everything, or she wouldn't have been caught off guard by the voice she'd heard in those woods. Not all that she should have, considering Griff was with her. She glanced at him; his profile was set in stone, his beard-shadowed jaw tense. She could just imagine the thoughts going through his head. None of which would be good.

Just drive.

She focused forward and drove as fast as she dared

until she hit the main road, and even then she was careful. Getting pulled over would not be a good thing by
any stretch of the imagination. She couldn't afford the
wasted time or the potential that Ernie had put out a
BOLO for them. The one thing that would keep them
alive with any certainty was staying a step ahead of the
thugs Lorenzo had sent.

She blinked at the idea that Ridley was one of them.

Was it possible he was undercover? That he really
wasn't one of *them*?

No. He'd said they had orders to shoot on sight.

Would he have shot her? Killed her?

She shuddered inside. Every instinct she possessed
warned he would have.

Taking the back roads to her destination, she surveyed
the dark houses. The world was sleeping. They had no
idea that killers were so close, that there were people—
like her and Griff—who were running for their lives.
Running right past the homes where they slept. Wouldn't
it be nice to enjoy the sleep of ignorant bliss? Sure, the
news could be scary, but the news never told the whole
story. The stories about those who sacrificed their lives
to find the whole truth, to bring down the worst of the
worst. The stories that no one ever heard.

The stories of those who could never be honored for
their heroism. Never be publicly thanked for what they
had sacrificed.

Didn't matter, people like her didn't do it for the shiny
awards or the kudos. They did it to see the bad guys pay
for their evil deeds. To see that justice was served—no
matter the cost required to make that happen.

"You okay?"

The sound of Griff's voice startled her from the unfortunate musings. "Yeah. You?"

"I'm good."

She smiled as she thought of the way his body had responded to hers while they were stuffed between those rocks. She had longed to shift around to face him, straddling him in a way that pressed her more intimately to him. Part of her wished now that she'd acted on the attraction that had sparked between them from the very beginning. But she had known that getting so close wouldn't be a good idea. Wasn't one now. Still, she was only human. She had needs. Needs that had been ignored for about two years now.

They drove the rest of the way to the destination in silence. She wasn't looking forward to any questions he might have, and the more they talked, the more likely he was to ask things she didn't want to answer.

The storage facility office was closed, but there was twenty-four-hour access to the units. She pulled up the gate, entered the code and it opened. She drove through and worked her way along the maze of units until she reached the one that was hers. The units for storing vehicles were at the back and were set a broader distance apart from the others to facilitate pulling in and out. She parked the car to the left side of the door and grabbed the fob as she emerged. Not that she didn't trust Griff, but on some level, he had to be afraid of what would happen next. Fear made people do desperate, generally unwise things. She didn't want him making a mistake.

She entered the code for the unit and raised the door. The small SUV waited, full of gas and with a trickle charger to keep the battery fully operational. She removed the charger, closed the hood and climbed in. The car started without hesitation. She eased it from the unit and parked it to the far right of the door.

She backed up the stolen car and then pulled it into the unit. She then closed the door and set the locking system. Good to go.

Griff followed her to the SUV she'd had stored and climbed into the passenger seat.

When she'd driven out of the facility, he asked, "What now?"

"We find a place to lay low and figure that out."

She eased along the dark street. Breathing unhindered for the first time in hours.

"You recognized one of those guys."

It wasn't a question. He'd likely felt the tension in her body. The unexpected shock had disabled her ability to hide her response to the voice she hadn't heard in two years.

"I did."

"Was it someone you worked with before, when you were Angela Hamilton?"

"Yes."

"Is he the reason you're on the run?"

Meg drove for a bit before figuring out the best way to answer without revealing too much. "In part."

"Was he more than a colleague?"

The change in his tone told her he hadn't wanted to ask that question but hadn't been able to stop himself. She should be flattered that he was jealous, obviously. But what she felt was fear. Jealousy was the kind of emotion that got a person into trouble faster than most others.

"Sometimes."

Griff stared out the window at the closed shops of downtown Chattanooga.

"Sometimes," she went on, deciding it would be better to assuage whatever he was feeling than to allow it to smolder, "when you're deep into an operation and everyone around you is the enemy, you grab onto the only one who is in the same boat as you."

"He's one of the good guys?" He didn't attempt to conceal his doubt.

"When I knew him, he was." Obviously, that had changed.

"If you can no longer trust him, is there anyone in your old life you can trust?"

That was the problem. She couldn't be sure.

"I wish I knew the answer. But I don't. I'm on my own here, and I'll just have to wing it until I see some other way."

"You've still got me."

The words were spoken in such a heartfelt manner she could hardly breathe. Griff really meant what he said. But it was the biggest mistake of all. If only she could make him see that.

"I appreciate that you still want to help after all that's happened," she said carefully. "But helping me has already put you in grave danger. Has caused you serious trouble. They now recognize that you're with me because you want to be and not because I'm forcing you. That's a dangerous place to put yourself in all this."

He stared straight ahead into the night, his jaw working with mounting tension. "I'll take my chances."

"Everyone loves a hero, Griff." Meg drew in a breath.

"Except the family and friends he leaves behind to grieve the loss."

"But what would the world do without heroes?"

He stared at her profile. He wanted an answer. Wanted her to look him in the eyes. She wasn't sure he was going to like the answer she had to give.

She braked for a red traffic light and turned to him, looked directly into his eyes. "Don't be a hero for me, Griff. Save it for someone who actually deserves it."

Chapter Twelve

Givens Road
Chattanooga, Tennessee
Tuesday, May 7, 1:18 a.m.

It was late—or early depending on the way you looked at it—when Meg reached the address she'd found on Zillow. The house had been on the market for several months, and it was empty. More importantly, the neighbors weren't terribly close, and the acre and a half lot was thickly treed, providing lots of privacy.

She drove around behind the house and parked, shut off the engine and reached for the door handle.

"You're really going to break into this house?" He stared at her in the darkness.

He'd watched her kill another human being, twice, and shoot yet another. Not to mention the ass-kicking she'd given the two hooligans who'd showed up at her shop. And he was worried about her breaking into a house?

"I'm borrowing it for the night. If anyone stops by, we're giving it a test run to see if we like it."

He exhaled a big breath. "Okay."

Yeah. Okay. She got out, grabbed her backpack and

the bag of stuff she kept in her backup vehicle. Toiletries, a couple changes of clothes. Snacks, bottled water. Preparation was key to most all aspects of survival. Her former boss had drilled that concept into her head. *Never get caught without a backup plan. Never get weighed down by extra baggage.*

Her gaze settled on Griff. She surely botched that last one.

He took the extra bag from her, made a face at the weight of it. "What've you got in here? Ammunition?"

"Stuff we'll need," she said as she considered the best way to enter the house.

First, she walked around with a flashlight (a handy tool also stored in the backup vehicle) and checked for a security system. The media cable was shut off. No sign of a landline. No other wires that shouted security system. So unless there was a wireless one, they were good to go on getting in without any trouble.

The back door had a dead bolt, but it wasn't engaged, so picking the lock was a piece of cake. The door led directly into the kitchen area. Griff shook his head at this new skill of hers as well. She didn't see how that could lower his opinion of her any farther than it was already.

First thing, she did a walk through and scanned for wireless security products. Nothing.

"We're good," she said, coming back to where he waited by the back door. She locked the door and engaged the dead bolt as the last real estate agent who'd visited should have.

Griff placed the bag he'd been holding on the counter. Meg turned on the light above the kitchen sink since it was at the back of the house and less likely to be noticed.

Not that she believed anyone could see the house from the street. It was well concealed.

She shifted her attention to her not completely reluctant hostage. "You want to shower first? I have a phone call I need to make."

He shrugged. "Sure." He tugged at his shirt. "I don't have any other clothes, but a shower will definitely help."

She picked through the bag on the counter and handed him shampoo and body wash, along with a towel. "That's the only towel, so hang it up when you're done. I'll be using it too."

He hesitated before going in search of the one bathroom the house had according to the real estate listing. "Who are you calling? Ernie?"

"The less Ernie knows, the safer we are. So, no, I'm not calling Ernie. I'm calling my former boss." She hadn't spoken to him since the day she disappeared. She wasn't so sure that talking to him now was the right move, but it was the only one she had left under the circumstances. She hoped something else came to mind soon, but not so far.

That wasn't entirely true. She shouldn't lie to herself that way. There were others she could call, but she needed to give this man the benefit of the doubt. He'd taught her everything she knew. Treated her like a daughter after her own father passed away. He'd been her rock before everything fell apart.

But something was off and she couldn't fit the pieces together. Nothing new really. She'd known there was a glitch somewhere fifteen months ago which was why she'd chosen to take herself out of the scenario rather than allowing someone else to reset her.

Now, more than a year later, it was looking like she had made the right decision.

"Can he—your former boss," Griff asked, "help you out of this situation?"

The simple answer was yes. He could extract her. Direct her to a safe house until she could be debriefed. But there had to be trust involved to allow someone that sort of power. She'd lost trust fifteen months ago. Had she been premature in her decision back then? Maybe. But at least she was alive. That was a hell of a lot better than the alternative.

"I'm not sure." She met his expectant gaze and decided to tell him the truth. "I always trusted him before, but something happened that shook my confidence in the whole system. It's possible he wasn't part of the problem. That possibility is the reason I'm going to call him."

Griff nodded as if he got it. "You're giving him an opportunity to prove himself."

"I am."

"And if he doesn't come through?"

"Then I'll know I made the right decision fifteen months ago, and I'll understand that I'm on my own now."

He held her gaze for a long moment, searching, assessing. Maybe looking for something to give him the answer he needed. Finally, he said, "I'm sorry you were let down before. I hope he doesn't let you down this time."

With that, he slung the one towel over his shoulder and went in search of the bathroom. It hadn't crossed her mind that she might need two towels. She hadn't expected to ever trust anyone again. What was it about this man that made her want to trust him? To lean into him? To be with him?

Didn't matter. Her needs could get him killed and she couldn't live with that.

When she heard the water running, she steeled herself and pulled out her cell. She entered the number she knew by heart, waited through three rings.

"Who is this and how did you get this number?"

The voice—the one that had always had the power to steady her—shook her now. She hesitated. Focused on calming the pounding in her chest. She wrestled the emotions aside. "Agent 16578 reporting in"

"Eleanor?"

"No one else has that number," she pointed out. "And I'm reasonably confident not too many people have your private cell number."

"Where the hell are you? We thought you were dead."

"It doesn't matter where I am right now." She watched the time. "What matters is that we have a situation. Our comrade Kase Ridley is working for the other side."

"What? That's impossible. Eleanor, you need to come in. We've ironed out the issues from that day. You have been exonerated completely. There is nothing to fear."

She refused to be swayed by the words that a year ago she would have given her right arm to hear. "I don't have a lot of time. You need to call Ridley back in. He's working for Lorenzo."

"Just tell me where you are, Eleanor. Let me help you."

His continued evasion of her statement set her further on edge.

"Don't ignore my warning," she reiterated. Then she

ended the call. She struggled to slow her pounding heart. Forced her respiration to steady.

Then, for a bit, she replayed the brief conversation. The surprise in his voice had been real enough. He hadn't expected to hear from her. He really had thought she was dead. And he insisted it was impossible that Ridley had gone to the dark side.

This was not good, she decided. On second thought, she decided the surprise wasn't real in terms of her being alive; it was about her calling him. She had been trained far too well, had never failed in an assignment. She wouldn't be taken down so easily. So the surprise was that he hadn't expected her to call him. Which might mean that he was aware of what Ridley was doing. Was that an indication that Ridley was acting with the sanction of the chain of command?

Her gut said yes.

Deputy Director Arthur Wisting would know if he'd lost an operative to the other side. He was far too astute to be caught off guard so easily.

Which meant she was screwed.

If she couldn't trust her old boss—certainly couldn't trust Ridley—then who could she trust? How far up the chain did this go?

Worse—sadly, it did get worse—this meant that she could not be allowed to survive under any circumstances.

She started to pace. This was why Ridley was involved. He knew her better than anyone. He would be the best option for eliminating her.

If Wisting had known she was alive all this time and didn't actively attempt to find her, then maybe he'd been willing to let her go, but now that had changed. She knew their secret. Ridley, perhaps with Wisting's blessing, was no longer on the right side.

Okay, all she had to do was disappear before they found her. No problem. She'd done it before, she could do it again. Though it was true that Ridley knew her better than anyone else save perhaps Wisting himself, she also knew Ridley. He was as vulnerable as she was.

Determination filled her. She wasn't going down easy.

The water in the shower stopped. She glanced in the direction of the bathroom. The one glitch in her plan was Griff. How did she protect him? Ridley would use Griff against her to manipulate her. It was Undercover 101. Learn the enemy's weaknesses and use them against him.

At this very moment, Ernie, Jodie and Dottie were in danger as well. But Griff would be the one Ridley zeroed in on. Meg knew how he thought. Going after Griff was the step she would take, if the circumstances were reversed. Ridley would quickly determine which of those people around her were the highest-value target. The fact that Griff was on the run with her would elevate his worth many times over.

A good friend would listen to your sob story, your issues, your mistakes, but a best friend—the closest friend—would show up with a shovel to help bury the problem.

She had to find a way to take Griff out of the line of fire.

GRIFF RUBBED THE towel over his skin. He hadn't heard much of Meg's conversation, but what little he had didn't sound good. She was in real trouble. He desperately wished he could make her understand that she had friends here. The past didn't matter. Ernie would help. Sheriff Norwood would go with whatever Ernie suggested. Loads of other people would be more than glad to throw in their support.

But Meg wouldn't take the risk.

It wasn't for her own safety that she ignored this option. She was doing it to protect him and the people she considered friends.

How did he convince her that she was looking at this all wrong?

He swiped his palm over the foggy mirror and then finger-combed his hair. Rubbing a hand over his jaw, he realized he needed a shave far more badly than he'd realized. But grooming had been the furthest thing from his mind for the past twenty-four or so hours. Staying alive and making sure Meg stayed that way too was priority one.

Not that she wasn't damned good at taking care of herself. Her skill with a weapon—hell, in hand-to-hand combat even—was stellar. Like nothing he'd ever seen in real life. In the movies, yeah, but not in what he'd thought to be an everyday person. The real problem was, in his opinion, if she was so busy keeping everyone else safe, she might fall down on the job of protecting herself. He intended to ensure that didn't happen.

He hung the towel over the shower curtain rod and pulled on his already worn clothes. By daylight, it would be necessary for them to move, so he had until then to convince her that she should accept help from him and the people who cared about her. As smart as she was, she would see through his attempts if he pushed too hard.

Griff opened the bathroom door and walked out, determined to do whatever was necessary to convince her to trust him, to work with him before going out on her own. She stood in the kitchen near the sink eating a protein bar. He smiled, couldn't help himself. She looked so young and vulnerable in that dim light.

He almost laughed at the thought. Young, she was. Vulnerable, not so much.

"The shower's all yours," he announced. As tired as he was, he felt a little better after his. All things considered, he supposed part of it was simply being thankful that they were both still alive.

She finished off the bar, tossed the wrapper on the counter. "Turn off this light and keep a watch out the windows while I'm in there, will you?"

He nodded. "You worried they've found us already?"

"Nope. Just want to make sure none of the neighbors who might be out for a nightly walk notice activity in here and nose around."

"I can do that." He reached out and flipped off the light, leaving them in total darkness.

She took a slug of water. "Thanks."

"What about your phone?" he asked. "You threw mine away—I'm assuming so it couldn't be traced. What about yours?"

"There are ways to prevent a cell phone from being traced. I've made a point of knowing them all."

With that she walked away. The sound of her bare feet padding across the wood floor had him following the vague outline of her body in the darkness. He loved the shape of her, the smell of her—even after huddling in a pile of rocks for what felt like hours and plowing through the woods for endless minutes. There was a sweetness about her skin. She tasted so good. Not to mention she was seriously hot to look at.

How many times had he covertly analyzed her long toned legs and licked his lips while tracing her hips or her breasts with his gaze. It was a miracle she hadn't caught him eyeing her like that. Several of his friends had mentioned how gorgeous she was. The best part about it was that she didn't seem to even notice how good she looked. All she had to do was glance in the mirror, but apparently she didn't see herself that way. She was just who she was. Good-natured. Kind. Sweet.

He shook his head. Sweet? Actually, what she was, was badass. He grinned. Seriously badass.

When the water started to run, he decided to do something she wouldn't appreciate if she caught him. He opened her backpack and had a look inside. He found two passports. One under the name Eleanor Holt. In the picture, her hair was darker and she looked younger. The next passport was under the name Elle Longwood. The photo in this one was Meg with her usual dark hair but lighter than in the other photo.

There was a wad of cash. Drivers licenses under the same names as the passports. Keys to what looked like lockboxes and maybe houses. Another smaller handgun. Snacks, bottles of water.

Who was Eleanor Holt? Was Holt actually her last name? What kind of operation had she been working on when things went south and she had to disappear? Who was this guy whose voice she recognized? Had he been a partner? Colleague? Lover? She'd indicated yes to all three, but was she telling Griff what he expected to hear? He had learned that about her. Maybe it was some kind of psychology move. Tell a person what they want to hear and they stop asking questions.

The water shut off, and he remembered she'd asked him to keep watch on the windows.

Feeling like as ass, he moved from window to window and surveyed the dark yard and trees. No movement. No sound. He confirmed that both the front and back doors were locked. Then he went back to the kitchen and grabbed a protein bar. He had no idea what time it was. The digital clocks on the stove and the microwave flashed midnight as if there had been a power outage at some point and no one had bothered to set them. The last time he'd looked at the clock in the SUV, it had been after midnight, so it had to be one or well past that by now.

If any of the events had hit the news, Griff's mom and sister would be beside themselves. He should call his mom and let her know he was okay. Maybe Meg would let him call since her cell was untraceable.

Considering how tough Meg was, she might not see him wanting to call his mother as very manly or strong.

But he had the perfect excuse. He loved his mother and he didn't want her to worry. He thought he knew Meg well enough to believe she would feel the same way if her parents were still alive. Had all the talk about her parents been lies? She had said it was all true...

The bathroom door opened, and he turned in that direction, pondering the fact that she was all alone in this world and that circumstance had perhaps nudged her toward such a risky career. Except she had him and the other people in Piney Woods who adored her. She didn't have to do that anymore. Would driving that detail home help her to see that she didn't need to run? They could fight this battle together.

She rubbed her hair with the towel to dry it since there was no hair dryer. "All clear?"

"All clear." His eyes had adjusted to the darkness so that he could just make out her form and a little of her face.

"We should get some sleep," she said. "There's a rug in the living room but not much elsewhere except the hardwood floor."

"Works for me."

She picked up her backpack and walked in that direction. He followed. She dropped her bag on the rug and sat down next to it, still working on her hair. He settled on the rug on the opposite side. He searched his brain for a way to kick off the conversation they needed to have, but nothing readily bobbed to the surface. Maybe he was just too tired to sort this out.

"I've been thinking," she said, her voice softer than usual.

Since they weren't worried about anyone overhearing them, her quiet tone had him coming to fuller attention. "Me too," he confessed.

She said nothing for a few seconds, then, "You go first."

Frustration thumped him. He shouldn't have said anything. He should have just let her go on. There was no taking it back now. He drew in a big breath. *Just say it.* "I think you underestimate how many friends you have in Piney Woods. We'll band together and help you if you'll only let us."

She laughed softly. Sighed. The laugh part worried him.

"I'm going to tell you everything," she said. "I think it will help you see how what you're suggesting won't work."

When he would have argued, she added, "Not that I don't appreciate the offer, and I do know that I have many friends in Piney Woods. I am very grateful for all of you."

"Then let us help you." The sound of her voice in the darkness had his body reacting. *Come on, Griff, get your head in the right place.*

"First," she said as she tossed the towel and stretched out on her side to face him, "let me tell you what I'm up against."

He opted not to correct her, but it was what *they* were up against. He lay down on the rug facing her, a safe distance between them. *No pushing*, he reminded himself.

"I joined the LAPD right out of USC—the University of Southern California. I went to the academy and rose to detective in record time. Then four years ago, I was approached by a man who was putting together a special team of operatives composed of police detectives, DEA and FBI agents. It was to be the first of its kind. He selected members of law enforcement who had excelled in their fields. He vetted hundreds of people. When he selected his group, the team's first mission was to go after the biggest drug lord on the West Coast, Salvadori Lorenzo."

"I don't know the name." Griff hated admitting this, but it was true. No point pretending. If she wanted to tell him the story, he wanted the whole story. He needed it.

"I'm not surprised. He isn't exactly a household name. The average Californian thinks he's just another billionaire who lives in Beverly Hills and donates to all the right causes and parties. But people in the higher echelons of law enforcement on the West Coast know who he is. He is the primary connection in this country to one of Mexico's most notorious drug cartels. When he says jump, even the top member of that cartel asks how high on the way up. He is untouchable."

"Your job was to infiltrate his business," he surmised. Griff knew it. She wasn't a killer. She was a cop. An undercover cop. A smile tugged at his mouth, and he wanted to reach over and hug her hard.

"Not in the beginning. I had other operations. It wasn't until things went sour with the operative we had inside Lorenzo's clique."

"Let me guess," Griff offered, "the man whose voice you heard in the woods back there."

"The one and only. Kase Ridley."

"This drew you into Lorenzo's world." Griff got it now.

"It did. My boss, Arthur Wisting, set up my profile, Angela Hamilton, assassin for hire. My first step toward breaking into his tight little group was going after one of his men who'd stepped over a certain line. Lorenzo was so impressed by my courage that he hired me on the spot. It all went down exactly as Wisting had hoped."

She really was fearless. *Damn.* "You actually went after one of his men?"

"I did. It was do or die. I tap-danced my way into his good graces, and he became quite fond of me during the months that followed."

Griff wanted to ask if she'd had to kill anyone to prove herself, but he wanted her to keep talking, and that question might just shut this moment down.

"Things were rocking along exactly as planned until

Ridley got himself into a no-win situation, and I was ordered to extract him."

He waited for her to go on, the urge to reach out and give her arm a squeeze of reassurance nearly overwhelming, but again, he didn't want to stop the momentum.

"During the attempted extraction, Lorenzo's one and only son was killed. He believes I killed him."

Damn. "How old was this son?" He felt confident they weren't talking about a child.

"Twenty-nine-year-old piece of garbage who got off on watching people die. Do I feel guilty that he's dead?" She laughed. "No way. The world is a better place without him."

"Wait," Griff said, replaying what she'd said, "Lorenzo believes you killed his son. Did you?"

"It doesn't matter. He's dead and Lorenzo wants me dead."

Griff had a feeling there was more to it. "The Ridley guy just let you take the fall either way."

"He was in deeper. It was better that I took the fall. Except then he disappeared, was presumed dead—until now."

"Wait." Griff held up his hands. "Didn't they offer to protect you?"

"Sure." She made a sound, a scoff. "Do you know how many cops survive in witness protection? I wouldn't have stood a chance against Lorenzo's reach. Case in point, Ernie runs my prints and less than twenty-four hours later Lorenzo has people right here in Piney Woods. He has ears everywhere. I knew my only choice was to disappear completely without any help from anyone."

Griff finally understood. Meg had been right. She

would never be safe unless she disappeared, leaving no trace and no one who knew.

"I'm sorry I didn't understand." She had the weight of all this on her shoulders, and she'd been carrying it alone all this time.

She sighed. "I guess you kind of had to be there."

He reached over, took her hand. He held it gently. Wishing there was more he could do. More he could say.

Her mouth was suddenly on his. She kissed him with such urgency, such need. He didn't resist. He understood. She needed him in the only way he could help right now.

And he intended to give her everything she wanted.

Chapter Thirteen

Meg watched Griff sleep. As much as she understood this thing with him had been a mistake, she couldn't really see it that way. She had never been in love. Ever. She had dearly loved her parents. She'd cared very much for friends and even some work colleagues. But she had never been the textbook definition of "in love."

Despite her lack of experience in the area, she felt confident this feeling that sizzled between her and Griff was exactly that—being in love. She wanted desperately to spend time with him, to simply be with him. She had never been a social butterfly. She'd had no long or impressive list of boyfriends or lovers. She had always been more focused on education and then work. Filling her social calendar or satisfying her physical needs had never been at the top of her agenda. Never a high priority. There were far too many other things that took precedence.

She and Griff had enjoyed each other's bodies until exhaustion had overtaken them just before sunrise. He'd fallen asleep while she showered again, and she was glad. She'd wanted to just sit and look at him. To watch him breathe. To study his face and his naked body in the morning light.

He was the nicest and kindest man she had ever met. Before Griff, her father had held that standing. He had been her idol. Her father had known how to treat a woman. He had respected and supported her mother. Always backed her up. Always stood at her side. Even as a little girl, she had known this was the kind of man she wanted to fall in love with one day.

And here he was, but the timing could not be worse.

How was she supposed to follow her heart? To pursue this love she had found? She couldn't if she wanted to protect him from the trouble that had descended upon this new life she had created.

She was out of options. The smart thing to do would be to leave now before he woke. She could write to him later and explain how difficult the decision had been. He wouldn't understand, but at least he would be alive.

Except the only way that worked was if she turned herself over to Lorenzo. They had connected Griff to her, and they would use him against her. If hers and Ridley's positions were reversed, she would do the same. To win, being heartless was by far the better position of strength.

She stood, rounded up her backpack. She had already dressed in the one change of clothes she'd had. Creeping through the house, headed for the front door, she forced herself to keep staring forward.

Don't look back.

"Are you leaving?"

Without me, he didn't bother to add. The answer was obvious.

She stalled at the front door, squeezed her eyes shut for a moment. Deep breath. She braced herself and turned to face him. That he stood there dragging on his jeans did nothing to make this any easier. From his sleep-tousled hair to his bare feet, he was as sexy as hell. The way he looked at her, disappointed and at once hopeful made her feel a level of regret she couldn't pretend away.

"Leaving is the one step I can take that will protect you and everyone else here who I mistakenly allowed to get close to me. I just can't risk what might happen to one or all of you by staying."

Griff braced his hands on his lean hips. That he had left his jeans unfastened made her want to sigh. Made her hungry for more of what they'd shared in the wee hours of the morning.

"What you're saying," he suggested, "is that if you leave—run away—we'll all be safe because you're gone. These thugs will just leave, probably in an effort to pick up your trail."

He knew she wasn't saying that. "They will leave when I leave because I will give them my location."

His lips tightened. She watched, vividly remembering the feel of those lips on her skin, on every part of her.

"You're going to sacrifice yourself to protect me and the others." He shook his head. "Doesn't sound all that smart to me. Based on your actions so far, I was expecting a far more ingenious plan. This one sounds a little like the easy way out."

"Less complicated," she agreed. "Not so much easier."

She would not sacrifice him or anyone else who'd had the misfortune of landing in her path to save herself. No way.

He stepped closer. She had trouble drawing a breath.

"All right then. If you have to go, then I'm going with you."

Damn it. What part of this did he not understand? "You can't do that."

"Why not?" His chin went up in defiance.

"Think about your family. Your mother. Your sister and her family. The animals. All those dogs, cats, horses…chickens." She shrugged. "They're all depending on you. You can't just walk away."

"Lonnie will see that the animals are taken care of," he argued. "I'll find a way to see my family when I can."

He was serious.

"Griff." She exhaled a weary breath, felt suddenly exhausted all over again. "This is on me. I have to handle it. I promise you that if I can find a way to come back, I will. But you cannot be involved in what happens today."

"If," he echoed, "you know they'll kill you, then there's no coming back."

The tremor in his voice as he said the words ripped her apart inside. "They've tried before." She forced an exaggerated smile and a lackluster shrug. "Killing me isn't as easy as they'd like it to be."

"If I can't talk you into staying," he said, "then at least let me help you."

How could he be that sweet, that willing to sacrifice himself to help her? He could not be that dense. He surely understood that to go with her was pure suicide.

"I'm willing to listen to what you believe you can do

to help." It was the least she could do. He deserved her respect even if she would never agree to whatever he suggested.

Her tone no doubt conveyed the lack of confidence she had in the possibility that he or anyone could help her.

"We set a trap," he offered, "lure them in using the two of us as bait."

"We could do that," she agreed. "If we're lucky, we could take down Ridley and his crew."

"Then why aren't we planning that move right now?" He turned his hands up in question. "It makes sense."

It did. To a point. Good men like Griff believed in standing on the side of right. Of fighting for truth and fairness. He couldn't fathom the depths of depravity to which someone like Lorenzo would go. "Here's the sticking point in your plan. Lorenzo will send someone else and then someone after that. He will keep sending hired killers to take me and anyone close to me out until the job is done."

Griff turned his hands up, clearly out of suggestions. "Then we go after him."

That wasn't a suggestion; that was a death sentence.

"Many have tried," she said with a genuine note of sadness. "All have failed. They either end up dead or working for him."

He looked away. "I guess that's a good enough reason to simply give up and let him win."

Now he was just trying to anger her. "There are some wars that can't be won." She couldn't keep doing this. "Goodbye, Griff."

She turned back to the door.

Her cell vibrated. She started to ignore it. To wait

until she was in the SUV and driving away to check the screen, but some deeply honed instinct warned that she shouldn't miss this call.

She pulled it from her back pocket and checked the screen. Not a number she recognized. She hit Accept and pressed the device to her ear. "Yeah."

"Long time no see."

Ridley.

"Not long enough." Why sugarcoat it? He was one of them now.

He chuckled; the sound held no amusement. "Look, I'll cut to the chase."

"Please do, I have places to go." Except she had a feeling her travel itinerary was about to change dramatically. "You know, I talked to the boss about you. He was surprised to hear you were working for the other side now."

"You see, Elle, that's what happens when you stay out of the loop for too long. Things change. Maybe the boss didn't mention it, but he works on this side too. He doesn't like to talk about how the government has left him needing to plump up his personal retirement plan. You just can't rely on anything anymore."

Why wasn't she surprised? "You can't trust anyone either."

"No," he agreed, "you cannot. Speaking of which, several of your friends and I are having breakfast at the diner in this quaint little town you've been holed up in. We'd like you to join us, oh say, no later than eight thirty."

Equal measures of fear and fury roared through her veins. "You know me, Rid," she shot back, keeping all that fear and fury out of her voice, "I don't have any friends."

"Let's see," he mused, "we have Jodie."

A squeal told Meg he'd nudged Jodie with his weapon or made some other thuggish move. Meg gritted her teeth to hold back a reaction.

"Dottie."

Another yelp.

Meg flinched.

"There are half a dozen others sitting around waiting for breakfast. Including Deputy Battles and one of his little minions. I'd hate to see anyone get hurt, but you know how the boys I hang with can be sometimes. Oh wait, I should mention that the two deputies are a little worse for wear, but not to worry. It's nothing a good ER doc can't fix. Assuming they arrive in a timely fashion."

Her rage mounted, searing away the fear. There were things she wanted to say to him. No, actually she wanted to shove her weapon into his mouth and blow his head off. That would make her immensely happy. But chances were, she would never get the opportunity. Not now.

She smiled sadly. This was the life she'd chosen. The one that had made her feel as if she were making a difference. Too late to regret those decisions now.

She glanced at Griff. Too late for a lot of things.

"I'll be there," she assured him. "By eight thirty."

She ended the call. Stared at the screen for a long moment.

"Wherever you're going," Griff said as he tugged on a shoe, "I'm going too."

He'd already pulled on his shirt. As she watched, her ability to relay the gist of the conversation suddenly unavailable, he slipped on the other shoe, then stuffed the tail of his shirt into the waistband of his jeans.

"Where are we going?" he asked, moving closer.

She cleared her throat, somehow found her voice. "That was Ridley. He has Jodie and Dottie and Ernie. Some others too. At the diner. He and his pals are holding them hostage until I show up."

The look on Griff's face lanced her heart. He understood just how bad this was.

"I'm calling Sheriff Norwood."

Meg wanted to tell him it wouldn't matter, but why bother? The debate would only waste time.

Griff held out his hand and she placed her cell phone there. He made the call and talked to the sheriff, giving her a quick overview of their state of affairs.

Meg listened to the way he framed the situation, to the things he said about her. The way he described Meg as a hero in need of backup. Her throat tightened; her heart expanded, making it impossible to breathe.

His words reminded her of something she'd almost allowed herself to forget: you could be down or you could be beaten. As long as you were still breathing, the choice was your own.

She smiled. She was down for sure, but she damned well was not beaten.

She had one potential ace up her sleeve. Making that call was a risk. A damned huge risk, but it was better than going down without a fighting chance. She knew the whole truth now. Maybe it was time someone else did as well.

Maybe it would help, maybe it wouldn't. Either way, distraction always provided opportunity. Whether it kept them alive or not was yet to be seen.

Chapter Fourteen

Pampered Paws
Pine Boulevard
Piney Woods, Tennessee
8:05 a.m.

"I don't like the idea of you going in there alone," Sheriff Norwood said.

Griff didn't like it either. "They know I'm with you," he tossed in. "Why wouldn't they expect me to be with you?"

"At this point," Meg argued, "any and all things beyond my walking into that diner are irrelevant."

Griff refused to believe there was nothing else that could be done. The sheriff had put in place a roadblock at each end of the boulevard. She'd set up a sort of command post at Pampered Paws. The view of the diner from Meg's upstairs apartment provided a good vantage point. Having all involved come in through the back had provided decent cover as well.

Norwood continued to argue with Meg's conclusion about what happened next.

Like him, the sheriff believed they needed a damned better plan for going in.

"Either way," Griff tossed in once more, "I'm going in with you."

Meg looked from Griff to Norwood. "If he goes with me, that's just another casualty to have to deal with, because this will not happen without casualties. The fewer bodies in their path, the fewer lives lost."

Her insistence that Griff couldn't help in any capacity infuriated him. "I'll take that risk," he growled.

Norwood held up a hand for him to settle down. The other four deputies in the room stood back, waiting for orders.

"I've got Deputy Phillips on the second floor of the urgent care. He's got a direct view into the diner. We know this Ridley character has three others with him. Two males, one female. Phillips can take them out if he catches one or more in his crosshairs. He was a sharpshooter in the military. He won't miss."

Meg shook her head. "Ridley will never be that careless, and if one of the others is taken out, there will be retaliation. People will die."

Meg had insisted they call in a bomb squad. Just in case. The one Chattanooga had wouldn't be here for another ten minutes.

"Sheriff."

The word rattled across Norwood's radio. "What've you got, Phillips?"

"Ma'am, look closely at the diner window. Something's happening."

Norwood, Meg and Griff rushed to the window. Norwood had binoculars. Meg had the ones they had found in the cabin. Both peered for a long moment toward the diner. Meg drew back first and passed the pair she'd used to Griff.

He moved closer to the window and set the binoculars in place. Next to him, Norwood swore.

"He's lining them up to provide cover." She swore again.

Jodie, Dottie, Ernie and all the other Piney Woods residents in the diner, including Katie, the owner, now stood in a line along the plate glass window. There would be no sniper shots getting to one of the bad guys. No flash bangs or smoke bombs would be thrown in through the window. Griff drew back. His attention landed on Meg once more.

"I told you he wouldn't take any chances." Meg turned to Norwood. "I'm guessing your man Phillips doesn't have sights on Ridley or any of his people now."

Norwood spoke into the radio. "Phillips, can you get any of the targets in your crosshairs now if they step away from the counter?"

So far, all four had stayed just beyond the sniper's line of vision into the diner.

"Negative," Phillips confirmed.

"It's time," Meg said. "I have to go."

Griff stepped toward her. "I'm going with you." When she would have argued, he said, "Unless Norwood takes me into custody or you kill me, I'm going. Either with you, or I'll run down the middle of the street behind you."

THE MAN WAS the most hardheaded—

Meg drew in a big breath. She was wasting time. "Fine. You can go with me and get yourself killed too."

That was exactly what would happen. They would walk in and they would both be killed. Ridley would likely kill Griff first just to torture her. The endgame was shutting her up. She had nothing else to offer. Nothing to use in trade. The only potential distraction she dared to hope might give her a fighting chance might not come through. At least she had tried.

Norwood pressed her lips together and shook her head in something that resembled defeat. "We've got people in the woods behind the diner. Deputy Porch is working on getting into the diner's attic from the one in the bookshop. If he's successful, he might be able to help. We've got Phillips directly across the street watching through his scope, ready to take one or more out. Roadblocks. Whatever happens, they are not getting away."

Meg decided it was pointless to tell the sheriff that she had no idea who she was dealing with. Ridley would find a way. It wouldn't matter if no one else survived. He would take care of himself above all else. He would vanish like fog rising off a lake in the sunshine.

It was the way they were trained. Meg had her knife in her sock. Her gun at the small of her back. And her one secret weapon that may or may not prove useful.

If she was really, really lucky, it would work, but she'd have to get that extra luck to even hope.

"There's just one more thing," Meg said to Norwood.

"Whatever we can do," the sheriff insisted.

"Get your guy Phillips on the radio."

Norwood did as she asked. "All right."

"Phillips, if you get Ridley in your sights—"

"How will I know which one is Ridley?"

Meg purposely kept her gaze from Griff as she responded, "Because I'll be with him."

Griff's forehead creased in question, but he said nothing.

"Noted," Phillips said.

"If you get Ridley in your sights," Meg went on, "take him out. I don't care if you have to take me out with him. Just take him out."

Meg didn't give Norwood or anyone else time to argue, she walked away. Griff followed. They hurried down the backstairs and out the rear exit of her shop. Griff said nothing, just followed until she had loaded into the SUV.

He stood at the open passenger side door, but he made no move to get inside.

She glared at him. "I have to go."

He nodded. "I know. But don't go to the diner. Drive away. Get as far from here as possible. I'll go take care of this for you."

What the...?

He slammed the door and hurried away. She got out and shouted across the hood. "Griff, we have to go now. Get in the damned vehicle."

He kept going, moving faster. Then he vanished around the corner of the building.

She jumped back into the driver's seat and started the engine. By the time she had backed out and driven around to the street, he was in a dead run and nearly to the diner.

"Son of a..." She rammed the accelerator, barely overtaking him before he reached the diner. She made a hard right and stood on the brake to skid to a stop directly in front of him.

She jumped out and met him at the hood before he could get past her. "Don't even think about it," she warned, the air sawing in and out of her lungs, her heart thundering. She should kick his ass right now.

"You should have kept going," he said, breathless, his voice loaded with something like regret.

The worry, the fear and the hurt in his eyes was like a knife ripping her open. "Just remember one thing for me."

He blinked. "What?"

"If I have to take a call, the moment I say hello, drop like a rock and roll under a table."

"What?"

"Just remember that."

She turned her back on him and walked the remaining few yards to the diner. The terrified faces of her friends and neighbors, as well as Ernie and another deputy, stared out at her as she approached. The fearful gazes sent cracks running clean through her heart. This was her fault.

The one thing that kept her putting one foot in front of the other and not falling to her knees and weeping like a child was the possibility that she would be able to put a bullet in that bastard Ridley's head.

She pushed the door open and walked into the diner. Griff moved up behind her. The bell over the door jangled as it closed.

Besides the people lined up in the window standing on the wide ledge, much like the one in her apartment, there was only Ridley and the female he'd brought with him behind the counter. Meg didn't dare take her eyes off the two to look for the others. They would be here somewhere.

"Only thirty seconds late," Ridley said.

He hadn't changed much. Still wore his jet-black hair military short. Still sported that fashionable stubbled jaw. Tall, handsome, smart. And evil. Her finger itched to wrap around a trigger and put one deep into his skull.

"I'm here, aren't I?" Meg said with a careless shrug.

"Yes, you are."

One of the other two minions appeared from the kitchen. She got it now. They were keeping watch on the rear entrance. It was the only other access to the diner. The third member of this little party patted Griff down, then did the same to Meg. She kept her eyes on Ridley the whole time. He was the one she had to watch. He was the most unpredictable. The one—she knew with complete certainty—who had the most to lose.

Number three took Meg's gun and her knife. She'd known that would happen. Then he took her cell phone. He was new to her. Younger. Blond. Gray eyes. Too bad he'd chosen the wrong side.

He placed all three items on the counter and stepped back, blending into the background near the jukebox to wait for further instructions.

Ridley took aim at Griff. Meg held her breath. "Hope she was worth it, buddy."

Her cell phone rang.

Thank God.

Ridley stared at the phone, then at Meg. "Why is someone calling you?"

Incredibly grateful that his eyes were now on her and not on Griff made her weak in the knees with relief.

"No clue," she lied.

"Answer it," Ridley said to his female cohort. "I know that area code."

The woman stepped forward, picked up the phone and accepted the call. "What?" she barked. Two seconds later, her face paled. Three seconds after that, "Yes, sir," she uttered meekly. She turned to Ridley and extended the phone toward him. "It's for you."

He made a face. "Who the hell is it?"

The woman, her eyes wide, shook her head.

Meg barely restrained a smile. Maybe luck was on her side after all.

Ridley accepted the phone with his left hand and pressed it to his ear. "Who the hell is this?" he demanded with his usual arrogance.

His own eyes flared wide for an instant, then his gaze landed on Meg. She stared right back at him as he listened to the person on the other end of the line.

"She's lying." The weapon in his other hand swung in her direction. "She's freaking lying. You know who is loyal to you."

Fury contorted the features of his face. "One second, sir." He pressed the phone to his shoulder. "Get over here, you damned bitch."

That was her cue. Meg kept her gaze on his as she walked to the other end of the counter and moved behind it. He glared right back at her as she approached him. Gun in his right hand. Phone in his left. She fixed that image in her mind.

He grabbed her around the upper chest with his left arm and jerked her against him. Then he pressed the barrel of his weapon into her temple. She settled her gaze on Griff and urged him with her eyes to stay calm. He looked frantic, terrified. She gave him a wink as if to say, *I've got this*, and his features instantly relaxed.

"Take the goddamned phone and tell him you lied," Ridley roared.

Meg looked up at her former partner, her former colleague, her former lover. The muzzle pressed into her cheekbone. "Who is it?" she asked innocently.

"You know who it is," he snarled. "He suddenly believes I killed his son."

Oh, how she was loving this. The fear and outrage on his face. It was almost worth dying for. But not quite.

"Tell him," he sneered, the muzzle burrowing deeper into her face, "that you lied."

She took the phone from him, pressed it to her ear, her gaze back on Griff. "Hello."

Griff dropped.

The woman stepped forward to peer over the counter. The man at the jukebox moved forward.

Salvadori Lorenzo's voice echoed in her ear. "If you doctored that video somehow," he warned.

Meg braced herself. "I lied…"

The muzzle dug deeper into her temple.

"…it was Ridley—"

She shoved upward on the hand holding the gun.

The weapon fired, barely missing the top of her head.

The phone hit the floor.

Ridley ranted at her, attempting to get a hold on her once more.

The woman drew back from the counter and whirled toward Meg.

In the background, above the screams, she heard Griff shouting for everyone to get down on the floor.

Meg twisted, pulling Ridley with her even as he pulled off another round, this one going over her shoulder, damned close to her ear. Meg twisted again, shoved him backward, but his grip on her was too strong to fall free.

The woman's weapon discharged. The bullet plowed into the side of Ridley's skull. Meg charged the woman, using his suddenly limp body as a barrier between them. She shoved him harder, knocking the woman down. Her weapon discharged again, hitting the wall behind Meg.

Meg dove for the handgun Ridley had dropped. She grabbed it and turned just in time to pull the trigger, sending a bullet between the eyes of the jukebox man who'd jumped over the counter to help his friends.

The sound of the woman scrambling to get out from under Ridley's body had Meg rolling to her left. She pulled off another, hitting the woman in the center of her forehead.

Meg launched to her feet, glancing around. Where was the other guy? Some people were still screaming but all were on face down on the floor. Except…

Where was Griff?

"Drop it."

The warning came from the end of the counter nearest the kitchen door.

Meg turned to the final man, her weapon leveled on him, his leveled on her. "You still have time to run," she suggested.

"No way," he snarled.

She pulled the trigger and sidestepped because she knew he would do the same. The impact of his shot jerked her shoulder.

Another shot blasted in the air.

The man stared down at his chest where blood had

started to bloom. Meg looked to her left. Griff stood at the counter, her gun locked in his hands.

The man crumpled to the floor.

Griff had shot him. She apparently missed.

Meg ignored the pain that radiated down her arm as she retrieved the woman's weapon and then the two belonging to the men. That was when she spotted the path a bullet had grazed along the side of the third man's head. So she hadn't missed entirely.

She suddenly became aware of all the crying and shouting around her. Deputy Battles was suddenly at the counter. The other deputy was ushering the people outside.

Griff appeared at her side, ushering her away from the bodies. "An ambulance is on the way. You should sit down."

She glanced at her left shoulder. *Damn.* She'd been hit. On some level she had known it.

Damn.

She looked at Griff then. "You saved my life."

She hadn't even known he could use a handgun, and he'd saved her life.

"Come on," he ushered her from behind the counter and toward a chair.

She glanced around. The place had cleared out in record time. A table to her left had been overturned. An obvious bullet hole marred its shiny red surface.

Her gaze went to Griff. "Are you hit?"

He shook his head as he settled into the seat next to her. "When I hit the floor and rolled under that table, I pulled it down for cover. The only shot the guy got off missed me."

Worry swam through her head, which was also swimming. "You could have been killed."

He grinned. "But I wasn't and neither were you."

She blinked, her eyes stinging. Griff had saved her life.

Chapter Fifteen

Pampered Paws
Pine Boulevard
Friday, May 10, 9:00 a.m.

"You're sure about this?" Jodie said.

Dottie stood next to her, both eyeing Elle with mounting worry.

She smiled. "I am positive."

Jodie turned to Dottie. "Don't get any ideas about taking one of those cruises anytime soon. I can't do this alone."

Elle laughed. She'd turned the shop over to Jodie and given Dottie that bonus she so richly deserved. Both were thrilled. Elle had also turned over her former cover as Megan Lewis to the past. She was back to being her true self, Eleanor Holt, aka Elle. No more being a detective or an undercover agent or a spy. She was just Elle from Piney Woods, Tennessee, who wasn't sure what she intended to do next in terms of a career.

"Meg." Dottie shook her head. "Sorry. Elle, we don't know what to say."

"Don't say anything," she assured her dear friends, "just enjoy."

"You better come see us," Jodie said, her face pinched as if she might cry.

"Don't worry," Elle promised, "I will."

She waved to the two as she walked out the front entrance. She took a deep breath and felt truly free for the first time in years.

In a stunningly brazen move, Salvadori Lorenzo had arrived in Chattanooga early Wednesday morning at the crack of dawn in his private jet. Two of his thugs had shown up at the farm and forced her and Griff into a car. Elle had felt certain that their lives were over. Lorenzo's thugs had taken them to the airfield, where to her shock, Elle had spoken privately with Lorenzo. No matter that the man hadn't deserved her explanation, she told him the truth. She'd spent nearly two years protecting Ridley, and it was time the world knew that she was innocent. Lorenzo's son had discovered that Ridley had been playing both sides of the game—which she had not known at the time—and Ridley had killed him to protect his secret. All this time, Elle had thought she was protecting a fellow agent when Ridley and Wisting had been using both her and Lorenzo for their own selfish gain.

Again, she felt no sympathy whatsoever for Lorenzo. He got as good as he gave. There was an endless list of the people he had betrayed and murdered.

During the brief visit on his personal aircraft, Lorenzo had apologized for sending people to kill Elle and assured her that he would never bother her again. He claimed that though he was a ruthless man, he never ended the life of anyone who didn't deserve to die. With that, he'd left.

At the time, Elle had wondered how he would feel when he discovered that in light of what she'd learned from Ridley, her former boss, former Deputy Director Arthur Wisting, had turned State's evidence against Lorenzo. A new multi-agency task force was determined to finally take him down. Hadn't proven relevant in the end, since that very next day after he'd visited Chattanooga, Elle was told that Lorenzo had vanished. With his resources, he could be anywhere in the world.

Nothing Elle could do about that. She had done her part. Her gaze landed on the man waiting for her. She smiled. Griff leaned against the passenger side of his truck.

"You ready?" he called out.

Elle took the two steps down to meet him. "You sure you want to spend an entire week away from the farm?"

"Two of Lonnie's new apprentices have it covered," Griff assured her. "He'll be keeping a close eye on things to ensure all runs smoothly." He opened the truck door. "We are taking a nice, quiet vacation in the middle of nowhere in the vicinity of Gatlinburg. No one," he said pointedly, "knows where we'll be, and I intend to keep it that way."

His mother and sister and numerous neighbors and friends had called and shown up at his door over the past few days. Several ladies with casseroles. Elle had barely kept her laughter to herself when the casseroles arrived. Basically, his home had been a regular madhouse the past few days. They had decided that a week away was necessary. It would give the story time to drop lower in the news feed and neighbors time to move on to something new to obsess about.

She chewed at her lower lip. "Raymond is going to miss me terribly."

"We'll video-chat with him every day." Griff opened the door for her to get into the truck.

Instead, she moved in next to him. "I'm not sure how much fun I'll be, injured as I am." She glanced at her bandaged shoulder. The bullet had actually missed anything important. Just a flesh wound mostly. Hurt like hell, but she was tougher than she looked.

He leaned down, brushed his lips across hers. "I have every intention of taking very, very good care of you, and then I'm going to bring you back here and show you just how good life can be."

Elle couldn't wait. This man and the life they were going to share on the farm were a dream come true.

She smiled up at him. "What're we waiting for?"

Griff helped her into the truck, and they were off.

* * * * *

MILLS & BOON MODERN IS
HAVING A MAKEOVER!

The same great stories you love,
a stylish new look!

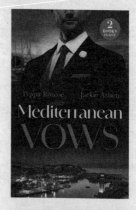

Look out for our brand new look
COMING JUNE 2024

MILLS & BOON

COMING SOON!

We really hope you enjoyed reading this book.
If you're looking for more romance
be sure to head to the shops when
new books are available on

Thursday 9th May

To see which titles are coming soon, please visit
millsandboon.co.uk/nextmonth

MILLS & BOON

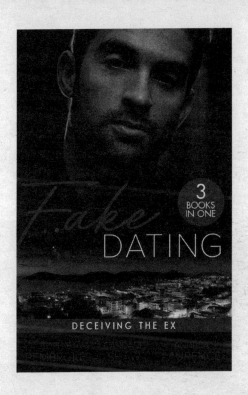